Ram turned to say something to her, and Docia was there, so suddenly, beneath his chin, bumping against his body. He instinctively reached out a hand to steady her, drawing her close, though by accident or on purpose, he wasn't certain. Her hair brushed beneath his nose and he could smell her, a sandy sweetness of musky incense from the meditation room. She was overly warm, his hands burning once more as they slid over her back. He knew the sensation would last for hours after he let her go, just as it had before, but he couldn't make himself lift his hands away from her. He couldn't seem to force himself to step back. Couldn't make himself understand that she was destined for another man and forbidden to him.

BY JACQUELYN FRANK

The World of Nightwalkers
Forbidden

Three Worlds
Seduce Me in Dreams
Seduce Me in Flames

Nightwalkers
Jacob
Gideon
Elijah
Damien
Noah
Adam

Shadowdwellers
Ecstasy
Rapture
Pleasure

The Gatherers
Hunting Julian
Stealing Kathryn

Other Novels
Drink of Me

Anthologies
Nocturnal
Supernatural

FORBIDDEN

The World *of* Nightwalkers

JACQUELYN FRANK

BALLANTINE BOOKS • NEW YORK

Forbidden is a work of fiction. Names, characters, places, and incidents are the products of the author's imagination or are used fictitiously. Any resemblance to actual events, locales, or persons, living or dead, is entirely coincidental.

A Ballantine Books Mass Market Original

Published in the United States by Ballantine Books, an imprint of The Random House Publishing Group, a division of Random House, Inc., New York.

This book contains an excerpt from the forthcoming novel *Forever* by Jacquelyn Frank. This excerpt has been set for this edition only and may not reflect the final content of the published book.

BALLANTINE and colophon are trademarks of Random House, Inc.

ISBN 978-0-345-51769-2
eBook ISBN 978-0-345-51772-2

Cover illustration: Craig White

Printed in the United States of America

www.ballantinebooks.com

10 9 8 7 6 5 4 3 2 1

Ballantine Books mass market edition: November 2012

To Natalie and Melena
Don't ever think I don't appreciate
what you have done for me,
putting up with my drama queen moments.
Melena, you are a dedicated spirit and
you have helped make my characters come to life.
I will never forget that.

And to Susan . . .
grandmother to two beautiful Down Syndrome boys.
Thanks for grasping my point and
telling me to go for it.

ACKNOWLEDGMENTS

To Saugerties, N.Y., the beautiful village
where I once lived for many years,
forgive me for taking a little poetic license
with your bridge and your police department. ;)

GLOSSARY AND PRONUNCIATION TABLE

Asikri: (Ah-SEE-cree)
Chatha: (Chath-UH)
Docia: (Dō-shuh)
Hatshepsut: (hat-SHEP-soot)
Ka: (kah) Egyptian soul
Kamenwati: (Kah-men-WAH-ti)
Kasimir: (KAS-eh-meer)
Menes: (MEN-es)
Ouroboros: (You-row-BORE-us) a snake or dragon devouring its own tail, a sign of infinity or perpetual life.
Pharaoh: (FEY-roh) Egyptian king or queen. This is used in reference to both male and female rulers.
Quolls: (kwalls) small mammals with violent mating instincts.
Tameri: (Tah-MARE-e)
Uraeus: (*yoo*-REE-uhs) crown of the rearing cobra worn by Egyptian pharaohs

PROLOGUE

Present Day
England

"Ow. Ow. Ow. And did I mention *ow*?"

Kestra chuckled as she hurried to help the enormously pregnant woman trying to squeeze herself and half a dozen books and scrolls out of the Demon archives situated in the basement of the Demon King's castle. Said Demon King, Noah, being Kestra's mate and said castle being their home.

"You would think," groused Isabella, a Druid/human hybrid, "that becoming half Nightwalker, a powerful, supremely gifted, fast-healing species, would allow me to avoid things like an aching back and swollen ankles. But noooooo. . . ."

Kestra was used to this complaining and took it as good-naturedly as it was meant. And Kestra forgave Bella for whatever parts of it were not lightly meant. She could understand. Bella, like her Demon husband, Jacob, was an Enforcer. Normally it was her calling to go out and kick ass, take some names, and keep errant Demons from breaking Demon law. But because of her present enceinte state, she was relegated to staying home and playing with her daughter or hanging out in Noah's library and playing with ancient scrolls and manuscripts. Bella's overprotective Demon husband, in his usual high-handed way, wouldn't hear of her stepping one foot outside the Demon King's protection while he was away doing his job.

Jacob, Bella, and their daughter, Leah, had permanently moved into Noah's enormous castle a few months back when Bella had suffered horribly debilitating side effects fighting the poisonous magic of Necromancers, the beginning of a great battle culminating in the final capture of the traitor Demon Ruth, who had long been a thorn in their sides. Now Ruth was imprisoned for all time in a crystal ball, which was no doubt adorning Jasmine the Vampire's dressing table that very moment, and Bella was recovering . . . but in the interim, it had been decided the family would continue to remain there as Bella moved from the vulnerability of recovery into the vulnerability of late pregnancy.

Bella was not always as upset about it as she pretended to be. After all, she had the enormous Demon archives and library at her fingertips. Which was basically heaven for a woman who had, seemingly a lifetime ago, been a librarian. Also, one of her Druid abilities was to read almost any language once exposed to it long enough.

"You shouldn't be carrying the heavy ones. I told you, Jaleal could help you with that."

"It's not all that heavy." Bella dropped a book on the table, the weighty smack of its landing echoing into the rafters and sending a plume of dust eddying in all directions. "Anyway, I wanted to show you this weird little scroll I found."

She tried to belly up to the table, exhaled in exasperation, and thrust the scroll at Kestra instead. Kestra helped her out, spreading open the scroll and using objects from the table to gingerly hold it open. It was extremely old and had not weathered time very well. She suspected it was from what had once been the poorly protected Nightwalker Library, a damp cavern trove newly rediscovered only a few years earlier. It was destroyed now, thanks to Ruth, but whatever had remained had been relocated into the Demon library archives, where it would be safer . . . better protected from both the ravages of time and . . . *others.* Had it been one of Noah's historical Demon scrolls from the archives, it would have been much better cared for.

"These are . . . what is this? Egyptian hieroglyphs?"

"Yup," Bella said, as though reading hieroglyphs were an everyday event for anybody. She leaned forward. "Okay, let me read."

"Please do," Kestra said dryly. Though she too was a Druid, her gifts were very different from Bella's. If someone needed to blow something up, she was your girl, but this was way out of her league.

The Lost Scroll of Kindred . . . And so it will come to pass in the forward times that the nations of the Nightwalkers will be shattered, driven apart, and become strangers to one another. Hidden by misfortune and by purpose, these twelve nations will come to cross-purposes and fade from one another's existence. In the forward times these nations will face toil and struggle unlike any time before, and only by coming together once more can they hope to face the evil that will set upon them. But they are lost to one another and will remain lost until a great enemy is defeated . . . and a new one resurrects itself. . . .

"What do you think it means?" Kestra asked carefully.

"Hell if I know. I mean, it sounds like a huge war between all the Nightwalkers or something. Scary thought, considering. But I'm not interested in playing guessing games. The part I found interesting was 'twelve nations.'"

"But there's only six. Demons, Lycanthropes, Druids, Vampires, Shadowdwellers, and Mistrals."

"Are natural witches a nation? That would make seven. And what if, like originally with natural witches, we just don't know about others?"

They looked at each other, then both snorted out laughs over the unlikelihood.

"More likely these others are now extinct," Kestra said.

"Other nations would explain all those books in quite a few unfamiliar languages that we found in the Nightwalker Library," Bella posited. "And surely if they were still around, whoever they are, we would have had some sign of them by now."

"Other than the books? Yeah."

"How sad," Bella said, her violet eyes filling with immediate tears.

"There, there," Kestra comforted her hormonal friend, pulling her as close as she could and laying Bella's cheek on a shoulder covered in Kestra's sugar-white hair. "It all happened a long, long time ago. None of it has anything to do with us now."

"No," Bella agreed. "None of it has anything to do with us now."

CHAPTER ONE

Saugerties, N.Y.

Docia huffed out a frustrated sound as she just missed spilling coffee on the tops of her shoes, jumping out of the way of the car that careened close to the curb she had been about to step off of. It was a miracle she didn't get killed, kept most of her coffee in her cup, *and* managed to keep her cellphone from hitting the pavement.

"Hello? Jackson?" she said quickly. "I didn't hear that last part."

"Nothing important, Sissy. Just bitching about Landon. I think I'm going to jail for murder soon."

"Nah, you can't do that," she countered. "You know what they do to cops in prison?"

"Ah, crap. You're right. I'm totally fucked."

Docia bit her lips, trying not to laugh. Despite his play at humor, she could tell her brother was seriously put out. Seriously off his game, too. He had been ever since his partner, Chico, had taken a bullet to the brain six months ago. Jackson was grieving in his own way, and that way seemed to be one of a lot less patience for a micromanaging boss than he would usually have. Unfortunately, Landon wasn't a touchy-feely type who would understand Jackson popping off and punching him in the head. It was crucial she help her brother refocus a little.

"So, how's Sargent doing?"

Jackson paused. "He's undisciplined and a pain in my ass. He keeps running away."

"Yikes." That wasn't good. If Jackson couldn't control Sargent, that could mean a lot more trouble down the line. But her brother had a special touch with these K-9 pups. No dog would ever be able to replace Chico in Jackson's heart, but Docia believed there was room for him to move over and share. The trouble was, Jackson might not be ready to think the same way. It was probably too soon for him to have the new dog. He should have waited. Given it more time. But as one of only two K-9 officers in the Saugerties Police Department, he didn't have the luxury of waiting too long to replace a downed officer. Especially considering how much time, money, and effort went into training a dog. The department needed the dog badly, and they needed him to be well trained. They also knew that Jackson was the best man to do it. "Well, you'll get him under control," she said, not a hint of doubt in her mind. "He's only a year old."

"Yeah, well, at a year I had Chico heeling with a snap."

"Yes," she said, stepping off the curb once more, "but he's not Chico, honey. It's not fair to him to expect him to be. You've only had him for a short time."

Again there were those beats of silence. Docia could almost see him nodding firmly to himself in agreement. Jackson was logical, dedicated, and very ambitious. It wasn't in him to accept defeat. He just had to get his heart in the game.

"I know," Jackson said simply, but making it clear by his tone that he had heard his sister's wisdom. "So where are you?"

Docia smiled at the turn of topic. He needed a little space now, and she would give it to him. She was just happy that he was talking it out with her. He'd been in a very dark place when Chico died. Some people huffed and called him "just a dog," but Chico was every inch the partner a human might have been for Jackson. Almost none of those scoffers were his fellow cops. They all respected Chico for the officer he had been. Even the irritating chief Avery Landon.

"Well, I just passed Kiss My Feet not too long ago, which reminds me that it's been far too long since I had a pedicure. Or a waxing."

"Okay, that's a need to know, Sissy. And I *didn't* need to know."

"Pfft," she huffed. "Like you don't like a girl with all her"—she used her coffee-filled hand to gesture in a circle over the front of her body as if he could see her—"landscaping trimmed."

"I'm not talking about my sister's landscaping!" he choked out.

"Wuss."

"Brat!"

She punched a button, chuckling as she hung up on him. She loved leaving him flustered like that. It amused the bejeezus out of her. Well, he'd wanted the change of topic. So he had gotten exactly that. She stuffed her phone in her bag, a cute little pink-and-gray pouch she'd seen at a local resurrection boutique. That was what she liked to call thrift and secondhand stores. Only in her dreams could she own a brand-new designer bag. No one noticed the slightly worn edge on the bottom, and it looked darling with her winter jacket and its faux fur–lined hood. She would wear the set the entire winter because she couldn't afford to change it up, but she was perfectly content with what she had and didn't waste time and worries on what she didn't have. Although she didn't have much time to worry about anything at all lately.

She studiously kept her eyes forward as she walked past Krause's Candy. The red-and-white-striped decorations on the columns were just screaming at her, begging her to press her nose against the glass and pretend she could smell all those pounds of delicious chocolate. But she persevered. She was late enough as it was. She had a tiny little office to get to and a grouchy boss of her own to deal with if she showed up late.

After a few minutes she was stepping onto the green steel bridge, its concrete retaining walls set about waist level, safe enough but also low enough to allow her to see the water of the Esopus River as it rushed to empty and join with the larger and more majestic Hudson River. The current was stronger than usual for this time of year because they were having such unseasonably warm weather for winter . . . if you could call forty-three degrees warm. But it wasn't freezing, so the Hudson on her left didn't have so much as a single ice patch, and the river beneath her feet wasn't slowed down in the least as it journeyed a short distance before smashing down over deceptively warm-looking tan–and-gray boulders. It was nothing compared with what it would be in the summer, though. The rushing rampage of water would spit out at a violent velocity that would have much more in common with a volcano venting in an angry upheaval.

She was romanticizing and daydreaming, she realized, picking up her pace over the bridge. The bridge itself was a throwback from a time when automobiles rushing around the curve that led onto it weren't capable of great speed and drivers wouldn't disrespect signs and logic and take the turn and narrow bridge a bit too dangerously. That equation hardly left room for even a pedestrian to make it safely across. However, it was the only way for her to get to work, seeing as how her clunky little Volvo had choked to a halt last week and refused to budge without a new alternator. That was a hearty two hundred and fifty bucks she wouldn't have until her paycheck made its appearance on Friday. Happily, that was only a day away.

"Bad Boys," the theme to the TV show *Cops,* burst to musical life in her purse just a few steps shy of the bridge's midpoint. Docia expertly snatched the cell from the depths of the little bag and put it to her ear.

"I thought I skeeved you out talking about my landscaping," she said, stifling a giggle when the reminder made Jackson stutter over his next words.

"You—you did. Just don't talk about it anymore. Not this early in the damn day. Actually, scratch that. Not ever in the damn day."

"Did you just call me back to order me around or is there a point to this call?"

"I'm serious, Sissy! Promise me you won't mention it again."

"I'm hanging up on you," she threatened.

"You're being a *child,*" he groused.

Docia snickered through her nose and had a perfect comeback for that. She really did. But as she caught sight of the huge SUV barreling toward her on her side of the bridge, a shower of sparks pluming up as it laved the wall like a lover running his tongue up his partner's neck, the juicy retort froze in her throat.

She dropped everything. Cup of coffee. Phone. Cute pink-and-gray bag. And somehow she managed to scramble up onto the wall and avoid becoming human hamburger as the SUV ground past her, close enough to catch her skirt and rip it.

Close enough for the passenger to lean his bulk out the window, reach out, and shove her hard off the bridge.

For a moment there was nothing but air. An instant where she sucked in her breath, a flash of existence where she seemed to float without gravity. That indrawn breath seemed so loud to her own ears and the scream that followed not loud enough. And just before she hit the maw of rocks and water beneath her because the laws of gravity had not been suspended after all, all she could think of was that she hoped the current was running fast enough to sweep her body out of Jackson's jurisdiction.

It was all she had time for before rocks crashed into her head and her back and a rushing swirl of icy water swept her up and slammed her into another set of rocks as though someone had tossed her into some kind of sick demonic machine in the Laundromat, filled with stones and the ultimate cold-water cycle. The pressured water slammed up her nose and clawed across her face, forcing itself into her open, screaming mouth and down her throat. It punched its way into lungs fighting instinctively to resist its invasion. She had never thought inhaling water would hurt so much. And her first instinct, the instinct to scream with the pain, was robbed from her because her lungs were paralyzed with frozen water.

Docia disappeared from the world as she knew it very shortly after that.

"Hello? . . . Helloooo? . . . Sis?" Jackson frowned at the phone, then hung it up with the push of a button. His sister's cellphone was a piece of crap. He knew it was all she could afford on her salary, but it bugged him that she dropped calls all the time and had a hard time getting a good signal. One of these days she was going to need help or something and that crappy little phone wasn't going to do her any good.

He made a mental note to get her a better one for Christmas.

* * *

You are much too young to die, a beautiful voice breathed across Docia's mind.

She agreed wholeheartedly. But she didn't see how she had much choice in the matter. Who really did? When your ticket was punched, your ticket was punched. There wasn't much that could be done about it.

So easily you give up. I have no compatibility with such a weakness.

Oh, bite me, she thought back heatedly to whatever afterlife spirit had suddenly decided to harass her at the shittiest moment of her impending death. *Since this is my first death, you'll have to excuse the hell out of me if I don't know what's expected of me!* she railed at the voice twisting around her spirit. Where the hell was the warm, fuzzy light and the peace everyone said she was supposed to be feeling? No one ever mentioned a nagging, judgmental bitch with an exotic accent picking on her flaws.

Then Docia found herself on her feet in a soft environment. She could smell the thick presence of incense in the air, pungent and sweet, yet musky and as erotic as it was exotic. She was surrounded by a swirling grayness with ever-moving clouds of fog tumbling past her as though they were commanded by a current as restless as the one she had fallen into.

Been shoved into.

Hey, what the fuck was with that, anyway? she wanted to know. If she was going to be all dead, shouldn't she be able to look down onto the world or something and find out all the answers she hadn't been able to see when she'd been alive? Oh . . . hell . . . could she be an angel if she thought the word *fuck* a lot? *Oh fuck!* What if she *said* it all the time? That was bad, right? She really wanted to be an angel. Not that hell scared her so much—no, wait, it did—but more because she wanted to be able to watch Jackson. To make sure he made it okay. Angels got to watch their loved ones, didn't they? Maybe protect them?

You will be useless to them dead, that annoying bitch in her head said depressingly. But she was less in her head now and more in front of her. She materialized before Docia, a small, petite creature dressed all in gold and rough-cut gems that seemed to catch the sudden growing sunlight that poured in around and over them both. Now here was the amazing warmth she had been expecting, but she had not expected it to feel like lying in the sun on the beach . . . that baking heat that singed her nostrils. The clearer the unseen spirit became to Docia's eyes, the more beautiful she seemed. Crisply banged black hair smoothed to straight perfection beneath a gleaming gold headdress, its crest looking like a serpent in a very Egyptian fashion on her forehead. She had skin the color of a dark nut, but her eyes were the most vibrant black and brown she'd ever seen in her life. She'd always thought brown eyes, such as her own, were dull and plain, but there was nothing dull or boring about these eyes that ran over her from head to toe. In fact, she seemed to be sharp and assessing, alive and regal in ways that Docia had envied in powerful women she had seen in the media. She had envied them their braveness and their seemingly unstoppable will. Traits she felt eddying off the woman in front of her.

"Welcome to the Ether," she greeted Docia crisply. Not that she didn't sound very welcoming, just that she sounded impatient, as though she resented the time she had to waste on the formality. She confirmed that with her next words. "We haven't much time. You show some promise, I must say. You have more strength than you know."

"Good to know," Docia said dryly, her eyes rolling.

The woman tsked. "She's impatient."

"She's in need of molding, love." A disembodied male

voice burst to life, its depth and richness seeming to come from all around her, pressing in from all sides with power and strength. "You will lend her all she needs."

The queenly figure tilted her crowned head and narrowed her kohl-lined eyes on Docia. The heavy black-and-gold accent should have made her look like an overmade piece of trailer trash, but somehow it did not. It made her even more beautiful, even more imposing, made those brilliant brown eyes all the more exotic.

"She has heart," she said after a long moment.

"The rest will come," assured that resonating, bodiless male voice.

Docia opened her mouth to say something, feeling a bit irritable, seeing as how she'd just died and all, and the woman raised a hand to forestall her.

"No," she corrected. "Not dead yet. But on the cusp. That is the only reason you are able to come to the Ether and see me," she said strongly. "You have a choice to make. To live or to die. Only now, on the brink of death, as you open enough to allow me in . . . only now do you have an opportunity like no other. I cannot promise it will always be everything that is good and wondrous, but if you let me in, it could help us both to evolve into the beings we wish to be."

"I'm supposed to decide between life and death? Well, duh. That's a no-brainer," Docia said dryly.

"But you will not be Docia any longer," the regal beauty warned her. "You will share everything about yourself with me from this moment forward. In some ways you will supersede your mortal flesh. Nothing will ever be the same for you again."

"Nothing? You mean, I won't see my brother?"

The Egyptian beauty hesitated, then looked over her shoulder as if at someone else. The owner of that disembodied male voice, no doubt.

"You will see him. But . . . all your relationships will change. This cannot be helped. Often, humans cannot accept change. And there will be much change. Now decide quickly. Time runs very short for you. Your hold on the Ether is weakening."

Life or death. Herself but different. Leave Jackson and make him suffer another difficult loss, or stay and—

"Leave or stay for yourself only, Docia," the stranger urged her. "Your love for your sibling is admirable, but he cannot be your reason for staying. You must make this choice for yourself and yourself alone. No other reason."

No other reason. No other reason except that she was too young to die. Hell, she'd barely even had a chance to live. She'd never traveled outside of New York. She'd never fallen in love or had mind-blowing sex. Sex, yes, but her mind had remained decidedly unblown. She'd wanted to go white-water rafting . . . Oh. Wait. Scratch that. She might have been missing a raft, but that definitely had just been a white-water classification.

And she wanted to find out just who the hell had pushed her over the wall. The jerk. Was that some kind of joke? Not to her! There was no way in hell she was going to let someone get away with killing her!

"I want to live," she said quickly, before the ethereal queen could tell her vengeance was an unacceptable reason for living. It was only one of them. And it wasn't vengeance so much as a powerful desire for justice.

"Justice is one of the best reasons to fight for survival," the other woman countered as she reached out to touch Docia's face. But just before she made contact, she stopped. Docia realized the Egyptian beauty was breathing hard, her hand shaking as it hesitated in the air. That was when Docia realized the grand and composed woman was more than a little afraid. She glanced over her shoulder once again, and there was another wash of warmth, again like sun radiating off well-baked sand.

"Go. It is well past your time, love. You will be very needed," the male encouraged her in a warm whisper of strength that seemed to emanate all throughout.

"I will see you again," the beauty whispered to him just before she touched Docia's cheek, leaned in, and kissed her full on the lips. It was a kiss of warmheartedness, almost tender at first, but it quickly grew stronger and more passionate. Docia was shocked by the aggressive sensation of a tongue parting her lips, reaching to touch her own. She wanted to balk . . . she would have balked . . . but the moment that tongue touched hers, a searing golden light began to pour into her from every orifice, starting with her hot, burning mouth.

She breathed in, a reflexive reaction, and just like breathing in ice-cold water, the act of breathing in the fiery heat of this burning light was excruciatingly painful. She felt as though her body and soul were bursting apart, devolving into a molecular state where all the tiny bits of atoms that made up Docia came apart, unraveled, and hung suspended in that hot, golden light. Then the molecules slowly drew together again . . . only this time when they connected, there were newer little atoms weaving their way into her makeup.

By the time she was whole again, she had collapsed into unconsciousness and let the comfort of darkness take hold of her.

Of them.

CHAPTER TWO

"Jackson!"

Jackson Waverly felt the back of his neck cringe a little at the familiar bark of displeasure his boss managed to make of his name. Then again, everything his boss said came out as a bark of displeasure. It just got on his nerves some times more than others. And this was one of those times. One of those days. So far, he'd accidentally let Sargent, his dog, get past him, allowing him to run loose in the neighborhood for a full hour before the untrained and defiant SOB had finally tuckered out and come to his call, tongue wagging in a full-on doggy pant while he looked at him with eyes that said very clearly, "That was fun! Can we do it again tomorrow?"

Mmm. No.

But no doubt about it, Sargent would do his damnedest to get his way. However, that was the least of his worries at the moment. His main concern was his boss, who was headed for him in ground-devouring strides. Jackson thought he could actually see steam coming out of Landon's ears. Not that any of this was unexpected or surprising, seeing as how he'd shown up almost a full hour late for work and as a result had missed the morning briefing.

"Where the hell were you this morning?" Landon demanded instantly.

Chasing a multi-thousand-dollar police department investment across a four-lane highway.

Mmm. No.

"Car trouble," Jackson lied smoothly. "Couldn't be helped. Say, when are we starting group basic with Sargent?" He was convinced that Sargent was one of those dogs that would absorb training better and faster in a group setting.

Landon opened his mouth, but the seemingly strange change of gears threw him off his game. Little did Landon know they were still talking about the same thing.

"I think you're on the new schedule. Provided you can manage to show up on time."

"Eleven years on the force and I think I've been late maybe three times. Are we really going to smash heads over this, Landon? Do I need a union rep or something? Gonna formally write me up? Or should I just hang my head in shame? What'll get you off my back?"

Jackson had no idea what propelled the sudden release of ichor, but something inside him snapped loose and he lost patience with his boss, his dog, and the world in general. Right there. That very second.

It was clear to him how out of character the jolt of temper was . . . and how out of line it might actually be . . . as the entire room fell silent. Well, shit. If Landon can be an asshole, so could he. Right? And he was far more justified in his show of temper than Landon was with his constant griping and his seemingly dogged way of finding flaws in his staff where they didn't exist. This was a good team of cops. In a small-town police department that couldn't afford specialized forces full-time, each man and woman cross-trained to fill whatever shoes were needed at any given moment. Jackson was not only one of two K-9 cop teams, he was also a bomb disposal tech and a SWAT team member. Hell, he'd be on the hostage negotiation and retrieval team, too, if he could, but SWAT, bomb squad, and HNART sometimes had counterpurposes, and even he couldn't be split into thirds.

Jackson ran a hand through the haphazard curls of his hair, the length one of many signs of neglect that made up his life of late. And now Landon was giving him one of those dark appraisals that inevitably was followed by . . .

"Jackson, do I need to send you to Psych?"

And there it was. As if sitting across from some tenderhearted touchy-feely shrink clutching a pen in one hand and a tape recorder in the other would be like waving some kind of magic fucking wand and make things all better all at once. Well, until that magic wand could bring Chico back from the dead . . . thanks, but no thanks.

"Nope. No need. I did my time. I got my happy stamp of approval. Didn't you get the memo? They even gave me a new dog and everything. I just want to train the little bastard and get him on track for duty." Jackson gave his boss the fakest, brightest smile he could muster. He did everything but hug the prick. "It's just been a crappy morning and I'm itching to get back to work, boss."

Landon frowned and eyeballed him as if he were a brick of C4 jammed full of blasting caps. Jackson gritted his teeth, counted the seconds while he waited for Landon to figure out he was wasting his time. Finally Landon nodded, his perfect buzz cut accentuating his squared-off head and making him look a lot like the typical jarhead he had once been.

Jackson sat back with an exhalation of relief as Landon retreated to his office. It wasn't that the man didn't deserve his job. In truth, he was a strong captain at what Jackson imagined was a stressful helm to manage. He did respect Landon, it was just that they were both men of very strong opinions, and often those opinions clashed. And Jackson didn't much appreciate the fact that Landon didn't seem to trust him enough to let him have a little autonomy. Jackson didn't take it personally, because Landon was a control freak and treated everyone the same way. It was kind of a craptastic quality in a leader of strong individuals, and Jackson had to wonder who the hell had thought it was a good idea to put Landon in a leadership position. Then again, he doubted Landon had ever been introduced to a rule book that he didn't enjoy following to the letter. In a bureaucratic environment like the upper echelons of the SPD, that was no doubt an excellent quality to have. An attractive one, too, to those who were looking for a police lieutenant they could be assured wouldn't go maverick on them.

Jackson decided to take his sister's lead and switch his attention away from his boss's more irritating qualities. Touching his laptop's mouse, he woke up the screen. He went straight for the schedule, and sure enough, he was off the streets for the next three weeks. It was an immersion schedule, where there would be nothing but him, Sargent, and an entire class of K-9 pups from the Catskill region with nothing to do but learn how to listen to their partners and start learning what it meant to be a cop.

It wasn't that Sargent didn't have the goods. Anyone who knew what to look for could see everything he needed right there in his personality. He was strong, fearless, and determined almost to a fault. But his willfulness needed to be worked with. Not broken per se, because that strength would serve him well once properly molded.

The truth was, Jackson hadn't been molding him. Every time he looked at the goofy little booger, he felt . . . cheated. Angry.

Crap.

Jackson glanced across the bullpen and down the hall, the blue-rimmed glass in the door of Dr. Marissa Anderson's office jumping out from all the others. But that was a whole other can of worms, he thought as her door opened suddenly and she stepped into the hall, taking a moment to adjust to the bustle of the corridor. As if she were trying to blend into her surroundings and become a part of them.

The very idea made him exhale a short, hard, and soundless chuckle. It was utterly laughable, the idea of the tall, flawless woman, wrapped up tight in a snug gray business skirt and a plain white oxford-style blouse, being able to blend unnoticed in the sea of blue unis and unkempt older detectives with their doughnut bellies. As she turned and walked toward the bullpen, every step she took in her high heels sending an impact of bouncy shimmers through her breasts and the long curling ends of her red-penny bronze hair, he recalled exactly why he couldn't wait to get her to sign him back on to duty and put an end to their required sessions together. She was entirely too hot to be some egghead doctor he was supposed to shed all machismo in front of as he plumbed the depths of his grief over the loss of his partner. He'd almost taken the option of seeing an off-site doctor, but damn it, he wasn't about to run away from her just because every time he looked at her his mouth went dry and his penis grew hard. Rather like what was happening right that minute as she hurried through the bullpen and headed for Landon's office.

But just before she entered his lieutenant's office, she glanced in his direction, her pretty blue-green eyes beneath a wrinkled brow of concern settling on him just long enough to kick him out of his shallow objectification of her and provoke a frisson of concern down the back of his neck.

Jackson sat up straighter in his chair and watched through the glass as she exchanged succinct words with Landon, which then made Landon look in his direction in exactly the same manner. Landon barked at Marissa and swept up the phone. The call lasted about thirty seconds, if that. Then Landon looked back up and saw him still looking on with interest. His boss immediately rose to his feet, lifted two fingers, and beckoned to Jackson.

He couldn't help it. Jackson looked behind himself, just to make sure that call forward wasn't meant for someone else.

No such luck.

The thoughts that raced through his mind as he stood up and made his way to Landon's office were tremendous and varied. In the end, it boiled down to some kind of paranoid conspiracy they must have cooked up between them to pull him back off of active duty. And if that was the case, it was absolutely insane! He'd done everything he was supposed to do, and neither of them could say otherwise. She couldn't suddenly change her mind about approving him for duty, could she? He wondered, as he opened the door, if he had his union rep's number handy, his free hand touching his pocket where he kept his wallet and an assortment of crucial cards whose names and numbers he'd never found the time to enter into his cellphone. He shut the door, the tension in the room telling him he wanted to be free to let his temper rise in relative privacy. Not that the glass provided much of that. Luckily, most of the bullpen was empty; everyone else had already begun their shift on patrol or working cases.

Jackson felt his gut burn when Marissa moved to close the blinds over the glass in quick, practiced movements. He could smell her warm, delicious perfume as she moved past him, but it only put him more on edge as the response it created in his blood warred with the anxiety ratcheting up his adrenaline.

"Have a seat, Sergeant Waverly," Landon offered, tension making a muscle in his jaw twitch, betraying the way he must be clenching his teeth.

"I'd rather stand. What is it?" Jackson asked, trying to temper the defensiveness he was feeling so it wouldn't echo in his voice. He wanted to play this as cool as possible. Manage his emotions. Prove to them just how in control he was.

"Sergeant, you really should sit," Marissa repeated, those warm eyes as clear as the Caribbean Sea they emulated, but far more turbulent than gentle waves against a beach in Aruba ought to be. It was as irritating as nails on a chalkboard, and he was ready to snap.

"Jackson," Landon overrode Jackson's hostile refusal with a brusque, no-nonsense tone, "they just pulled your sister's body out of the Hudson River."

His eyes jerked to his boss. The words seemed to bounce off him like icy hail, stinging cold and hard in tiny bits over all the exposed parts of his skin. Then, as if someone had plucked his spine out of his back, leaving him with no way of supporting himself, his knees gave way. Landon wasn't close enough, but a surprisingly strong feminine body was under his arm and plastered to his side like a warm, exotic-smelling crutch. But she had no hope of holding up a man who towered over her by nearly a foot and had nothing but muscle strapped to his 215-pound body. And all that machismo he'd held on to so diligently in front of her for three months of sessions mockingly abandoned him in the face of the one thing . . . the absolute single most thing . . . that could take him out like that bullet to Chico's brain that had stopped his partner dead in his tracks.

Landon was around his desk by then, keeping him from hitting the ground, helping Marissa move him into the twice offered chair.

Jackson drew in a breath. Then logic seemed to race over him and he laughed.

"That's ridiculous," he said. He felt suddenly stronger as he pushed away hands that abruptly felt obnoxious. "That's bullshit! I was just on the phone with her not twenty minutes ago! On my way to work!" He fumbled for his watch. Checking his time. God, more time had gone by than that. "Thirty minutes, then. Still, not enough time to fish out anything, never mind identify it, *if* it were my sister. What the fuck is wrong with you people? Don't you fucking check your facts before saying something like that to someone?" He was shouting at them, his hands shaking with a sickly combination of fear and fury.

"She went off the bridge at the tributary outlet right after . . ." Landon paused to look at a hastily scribbled note.

"Kiss My Feet," Jackson said in a croak.

. . . I just passed Kiss My Feet . . .

"Someone took the turn like a demon. That turn into the bridge is notorious . . . ," Landon said, his words fading as he ran out of things to say about it. Every cop in Saugerties knew about that turn. Having been raised there, Jackson knew what was under the bridge as well.

They'd fished her out of the Hudson. That meant she'd gone over into the water. The rocks. She would have been screaming the whole way down.

Jackson's phone went off in his gun belt. Numbly, he silenced it.

"Where is she?" he asked hoarsely.

"Kingston Hospital. The officer on scene called me and said she was . . ." Marissa seemed to lose hold of her professionalism, seemed unable to say the word. "The hospital is just a formality, as you know."

Jackson's phone went off again.

And that, more than anything, made what he was hearing real. Friends in the force and in the hospital were trying to reach him, he realized. They were breaking confidentiality and protocol to be the first to warn him.

Jackson lurched to his feet and stumbled for the door, but Marissa threw herself in the way, her warm, soft body once again providing strength and comfort. So unexpected. So grating and consoling all at once.

He looked down into her face, his entire body rippling with cinders of fury that were rapidly turning into a conflagration of flames. He danced, in turns, with numbness and a rage unlike anything he'd ever felt. Not even when he'd watched that meth-head prick shoot his dog down as if he were nothing. Tearing him up and throwing him away like frail paper. Not even then had he felt such an all-consuming, virulent wrath.

"Breathe," she whispered to him, her hands coming up to cup his face, forcing his eyes to look into hers. "Take a breath in, then slowly let it out."

Did she have any idea how infuriating and ridiculous such moronic psychobabble techniques were in a moment like this?

"Breathe, Jackson," she said more firmly, giving him a shake and forcing him to be present in a moment he didn't want to be present in.

He was floundering, trying to find the strength he'd always had to look the worst in the eye and just move along; but for some reason, when he needed it most, it had abandoned him. And now all he was left with was this infuriating female acting as though all he needed were a crash course in Lamaze and he'd somehow be able to give birth to the control and focus he needed.

"Jackson!"

She hit him. Not so Landon could see, but a covert knee just shy of his crotch, forcing aeons of male instinct to jerk back protectively and suck in a much-needed breath.

The wash of oxygen flooded his blood and his brain, even as he grabbed hold of Marissa and crashed her back into the door, the tinny sound of blinds crackling giving away just how old this place was that it still had aluminum blinds. That small detail crystallizing in a maelstrom of grief seemed to anchor him. Not permanently. Not even strongly. Just enough to keep him from throttling a gorgeous redheaded doctor who always smelled too delicious for her own damn good and always seemed one step smarter than he was at any given moment. Jackson let go of her long before Landon could swoop in and play jarhead protector. He took another breath as he stared at her composed features, resenting her for how much more centered each draw for oxygen was making him feel.

"Low blow, Doc," he said in a dark voice paced to keep his emotions in check. "I doubt they taught you that in touchy-feely doctor school." He leaned in just a touch, the muscle at his jaw twitching as he gritted his teeth. "How about you take me to identify my sister's body and we'll call it even?"

CHAPTER THREE

Docia would've woken up with a gasp, but the tube jammed down her windpipe had other ideas. She gagged, wanted to vomit, flailed about weakly, looking for a way to grab for breath. She also had an overwhelming need to pee.

"Docia!"

There was the sound of something wet splashing on the floor and then suddenly she was looking into Jackson's face, his pallor far too pale and the stress on his features instantly apparent. She couldn't focus on those details too much, however, because she was suffocating to death.

There was a quick swarm of people over her, nurses and a doctor by the look of their clothes, the reassuring things they said, and the hurried explanations meant to calm her. But the only thing she could find of comfort in the room was Jackson's familiar face. They had tried to shove him into the corridor, but he had fought to remain, and apparently he was the least of their worries, so they ignored him in order to focus on her.

Finally that horrific tube was yanked out of her throat, leaving her to gag and gasp for breath, the act of coughing sending furious fire burning through her sorely abused lungs. Some moron kept telling her to breathe, as if that were some kind of option. As if the idea had never occurred to her.

She heard Jackson laugh in a burst of incredulity and then realized she'd managed to choke out something like "Go fuck yourself" to the nurse or whoever kept yammering at her.

Though it was surprisingly satisfying, she shocked herself, saying it aloud like that instead of keeping it in her head as she usually did. If not for the need for air, she might have slapped a hand over her mouth in dire feminine despair. But Jackson's amusement and the desired result of shutting the nurse up stayed her from having too much of a guilty conscience.

Finally she was breathing rather than gagging for every breath. Apparently satisfactorily enough to allow the medical personnel to back off. Then Jackson was on her like white on rice, hugging her as gingerly and as tightly as he could all at once.

"Oh, my God, Sissy, you just about aged me fifty years," he rasped against her ear as if he were sharing the most horrible of secrets. His desperation was clear and cold, his relief warm and touching. If she'd had any doubt about her brother's love for her, it was forever erased in that single instant of touch and tragedy. "They told me you were dead. For three hours and twenty-seven minutes I thought you were dead and it was the worst three and a half hours of my life."

Tears lifted into Docia's eyes as she felt her brother's agony, remembered dropping into the water and thinking about him. Hoping he wouldn't find her body on one of the shores of his patrols. A strange knowing told her he'd been spared that. But still, he'd suffered the loss of her in spite of her having somehow survived the seemingly unsurvivable.

"I'm here," she whispered to him, unsure if her abused

lungs and throat could work but determined to give him the reassurance nonetheless.

"Goddamn right you are," he said gruffly, pulling back to hold her face in his hands, giving her a little shake. "We Waverlys are made of stern stuff. You kicked that river's ass."

"It kicked mine first," she croaked.

"Details," he said with a smirk and a shrug. "You can kick a Waverly down, but we'll always get back up again."

She nodded in agreement. "But right now, this Waverly has to pee really bad. And can you shut the curtains? That sunlight hurts my head like crazy."

Jackson glanced down at the side of the bed as he stood up to do her bidding. "You have a catheter," he told her, moving so she could see the bag partially full of urine and pulling the drapes to seal out the sunlight.

"Eww! Tell them to take it out!"

"That knock on the head has made you very bossy," he observed dryly.

"I've always been bossy," she argued.

"Have not."

"Have, too! Now go get the nurse!"

Jackson grinned and moved away from her, although very slowly, as if afraid to let her out of his sight. He inched out the door but finally committed to it and left to do as she asked. That was when Docia realized there was a cop in full uniform standing outside her door. Jackson had been in plain clothes, making her wonder how long she'd been out and what exactly had been going on.

Then she remembered powerful hands slamming into her, shoving her off the rail of the bridge. She remembered with chilling clarity sparks flying as the truck had tried to grind her against the stone.

"What the hell is happening?" she demanded of her

brother the instant he returned. "What happened? Why?"

"All good questions," he said grimly, knowing immediately what she was referring to, it seemed. "What do you remember?"

She told him, surprised at all the details she could recall. At least, she told him about everything before hitting the water. The crazy near death experience she'd had she kept to herself. It was all probably some brain-damage-induced hallucination anyway. Besides, the nurse came in to give her back control of her bladder and she shooed Jackson out. Under normal circumstances, she would have jumped on the opportunity to needle her brother's squeamish side when it came to the brother/sister wall of privacy he insisted on . . . such as what bits of her landscaping she liked to keep trimmed or waxed. But they'd both been through a little too much to fall back on old routines so quickly.

Kicked out of the room and left to cool his heels in the hallway, Jackson was dwelling far less on the medical needs of his sister's body. He wouldn't care if he had to wipe her butt himself while she was healing. He'd do anything required, as long as it meant she was alive and getting well.

But his focus was on the sicko who had made sport of her, getting a thrill out of running her off the road and then, when it wasn't enough, pushing her off the bridge. While traffic cams had shown a complete lack of both license plates, the detectives had assured him a truck with that kind of side damage would be easy to find. Now that Docia was awake and firmly on the road to recovery, he was going to make damn sure no one tried to push her off that road again.

"Tolly."

"Mmm?" The uniformed cop had been assigned to watch over Docia, since technically this had been an attempted murder. The detectives thought it was some kind of sick prank, but just in case it was otherwise, and because Docia was like a sister to half the SPD, they were keeping a careful eye on her.

"I'm going to leave in a few," Jackson said.

"Don't worry. She'll never leave my sight."

"You better take a whiz now if you need to," Jackson said sternly, eyeing the coffee in the man's hand.

Tolly gave him a patient smile, but he put his cup down and headed for the bathroom.

Docia took a breath of the cold, crisp air. A winter storm was moving in, and she could feel it all around her. It had been only three days since she'd awoken in intensive care; Jackson had barely let her out of his sight for all three days, and when he had, he'd sicced Officer Tolliver on her ass like some kind of rabid pit bull. The man would sit in the hallway and she could swear he never blinked. He didn't so much as flip through a magazine to pass the time. He'd just sit there on high alert, eyeballing everyone who came down the hallway.

It was a little creepy.

Yet comforting.

Earlier today, much to everyone's surprise, she was discharged and Jackson had brought her home. Tolliver was back at his regular beat and Jackson was trying his best to babysit her. But she didn't want sitting. It had taken a thirty-minute argument to get him to leave her long enough to get some groceries for her neglected fridge. She welcomed the time alone, seeking normalcy. And fresh air. And walking. Even though her car sat happily repaired in the driveway, she wanted to walk. Even though it was nighttime and the storm was obscuring the clean black sky and all of its sparkly little stars, she wanted to be out in the midst of it. She stood on the sidewalk, staring back at her porch . . . her safer porch . . . and made a good show of turning up her nose at it. Safer schmafer. She wasn't going to let a couple of deviant sadists destroy her love of the town she had grown up in.

But she couldn't make her feet move away from the front of her tiny little cottage house and that very safe little porch only a driveway's distance away.

Enough of this! You are strong. You are capable! Enough!

Ever since the accident, she'd found herself lecturing herself in this strident, confident voice. It was more confident and willful than she thought she was, but she appreciated its energetic stubbornness. It gave her a steadiness to her backbone just when she needed it most.

It allowed her to put one foot ahead of the other, to begin a walk along the familiar sidewalks of her block. She kept turning her face up to the sky, as though the sun might be there and she could drink in the heat and light. Except there was no sun. It was a beautiful darkness and a crispy coldness, and she was waiting for those deep black-and-gray clouds to start spitting cold flakes at her. Docia took an extraordinary amount of pleasure in the walk, each and every step, and she realized it was because, for all intents and purposes, she shouldn't even be there. Every doctor, every nurse . . . every person who had come into contact with her couldn't understand how she had survived. They couldn't help being amazed at the way she'd healed from an inch or two past death to this . . . this walking, breathing person with another chance at life. Knowing that made every nuance of her walk touch her in sharp, beautiful ways. The rasp of cement beneath her sneakers, the distant barking of someone's dog and the way it sounded more goofy than threatening . . . the rustle of her puffy winter coat, which was such a poor replacement for the one she'd rediscovered at the beginning of the season, which she'd been told had been cut away, destroyed, and discarded by EMTs with no interest in preserving her hard-won fashions. They'd preferred to attempt to preserve her hard-won life, and she was okay with that.

Docia could almost feel the frost as it grew on every blade of grass around her. The cold made her recently abused body ache, but again she accepted it as happy signs that she was alive. She had no argument against it. Not today, anyway. Perhaps, over time, she would once again take all these nuances of life for granted, she would fall away into complaints and grumbling about cold or wet days; but then again, perhaps she wouldn't. Or at least, she hoped not. She hoped she would never take even the simple ability to breathe in for granted ever again.

And perhaps this new attentiveness to everything around her was what enabled her to sense that someone was shadowing her. At first she shrugged it off when the smattering of streetlamps showed nothing to support her paranoia, but only minutes later she felt overwhelmed by the sensation that prickled up and down the back of her neck, forcing her to pay attention to her instincts.

She supposed she ought to have been less obvious about it, been smoother and slick, like some gorgeous heroine in a spy movie who always managed to look perfectly coiffed and stylishly dressed as she made a mysterious drop to an equally mysterious and stylish hero. But she was still battered and bruised and, as earlier noted, had been forced to wear a puffy jacket that had gone out of fashion two years earlier, so suave and cool really were a waste of her time. She craned her neck around, searching for whatever or whoever was giving her this sense of hyperawareness. Maybe there was no one. Maybe her paranoid brother was rubbing off on her. Or maybe those random assholes who thought shoving innocent girls off bridges made for good fun had come to find her and wanted to drag her to the nearest bridge and try again.

By the time she had the last thought, she was breathing hard, feeling a little panicky and a lot alone in the cold darkness of the night. Everything that had been so comforting a moment ago seemed reckless and vastly dangerous, and she began to regret walking away from the safety of her home. Her heart was throbbing in her chest, clamoring near her still-bruised lungs. Everything, every nuance of it, reminded her of how weak she still was, of how vulnerable she was . . . now and even before all of this. The difference was, she had been highly ignorant of it before. She'd had all of that ignorance unceremoniously removed from her.

She turned back. Her casual stroll had taken her only a block and a half away. Too far. What if . . . ?

Docia barely made it two steps before she saw the stranger on the street. Or maybe he was one of her familiar neighbors and her state of panic was making him look ominous. It didn't matter. She had no interest in finding out either way. She was breathing hard, her breath curling out of her in long, frosty plumes, and she put energy into her steps, holding on to the belief that if she acted as though she knew what she was doing, knew how to take care of herself, it would somehow protect her from any dangers, real or imagined, on her quiet suburban and historical street.

Still, she glanced his way too frequently. She could barely make him out as he moved around the edges of the light, his slower, longer stride making him look too much like a stalking beast for her imagination's peace of mind. Why didn't he cross through the light? Why move purposefully around it? The only reason she could conceive of was that he didn't want to be seen or identified, and that understanding made sickness swirl in Docia's stomach. She hurried toward home, but even if she made it to her tiny house, there was no Jackson there to protect her. She had sent him out, sent him away.

She was clearly a moron.

You should have at least kept the guy with the gun close by for a few more days, her inner voice said dryly. This wasn't the new voice, this was the familiar voice of sarcasm she'd always used against herself throughout her life. Honestly, she could use a bit of her new voice right then, that voice that seemed to give her strength. Where the hell was it when she needed it most?

Keep calm. Panic will never serve you well. Always remain calm.

And there it was. Filtering through her with confidence and focus, her new voice settled her crazed breath and pulses as if it had cast a spell on her. The necessitated calm drifted over her, and suddenly she did feel like that movie heroine spy out to make a smooth exchange of information, keeping her cool in the most dangerous of situations.

And then the shadow crossed the street toward her and she stopped, squeezing her knees together to quell the sudden urge she had to pee her pants.

So much for smooth and cool.

The shadow was on her from one breath to the next, a blitz of movement and sudden streaking through the edge of the light. It glanced off his dark jacket and ominous ski mask, but more important it glanced off the expanse of metal he was slamming in the direction of her belly.

The sudden stop startled Docia, kept her from screaming like a crazed banshee hopped up on meth at a grunge metal concert. She stared down at the hand that had appeared out of nowhere, large and masculine and strangely bare of any gloves considering it was really cold, allowing her to see that the very large knife had punctured the palm and run straight through the back of it. As the seconds ground down to infinitesimal ticking instants, Docia comprehended several things. One, the shadow man had indeed meant her ill. For some reason, he had just tried to gut her. Two, a second man she hadn't even noticed had appeared out of nowhere and thrust himself between her and the knife.

Then, as if the agony of being run through meant nothing to him, the rescuer grabbed the attacker by the back of his head and yanked him down to meet the upward thrust of his knee. There was the resounding crack of bone smacking into bone, and the attacker fell dazedly to the ground.

This, she thought inanely, *is the part where I am supposed to run. Oh, and that screaming thing would really come in handy, too.*

Yet she was rooted silently to the spot, watching with fascination as the rescuer, a lean man about half a foot taller than the other guy, stood over his apparently unconscious victim, reached out with long, bare fingers to grip the handle of the wicked-looking blade run through his flesh, and slowly pulled it free of his punctured hand. He made only the smallest of sounds, like a deep sort of grunt, which sounded far more like aggravation than a pained reaction. The sound of the knife itself, that strange suctiony kiss as metal withdrew from flesh: *That* was a sound she feared would echo in her memory at odd moments in the future. She watched with peculiar fascination as he shook his own blood from the blade and onto the unconscious man, then spat something out at him, some kind of foreign invective that she suspected put a curse on him and all his offspring to come.

Docia felt herself shaking in her own skin as she looked up into what she could only describe as golden beauty. He was gold of hair, a dark and white, uneven blond that rested in ghosts of curls around his head, just light enough at the tips to give him a nimbus effect, like a living savior stepped free of a fresco painting. His eyes were mesmerizing in the way they matched his hair almost perfectly, that rich gold with a halo of lighter gold around the rims of his irises. It was a compelling color, a fascinating one that was framed by long, gilded lashes teasing on the cusp of being too pretty . . . if not for the hardness and depth of life she could see beyond those superficial accents. The hardness with which he was looking at her now. He was assessing her, just as she was assessing him. But all he was seeing was a puffy coat two seasons too old, almost a size too small, and a rather frumpy girl stuffed into it who looked as though someone had beat the living Christ out of her.

Well, how convenient, then, that he should look and act so much like a savior come to rescue her. Warm-skinned, tall enough to hurt her damaged neck as she looked up into his face, and broad enough in his shoulders to block out the gray of the sky behind him from her sight. He was dressed inappropriately for such cold, and she thought she might attribute some of the sternness in his face to that.

"My queen?"

He was addressing her, she realized, stifling a bit of a giggle. Yet there was something thrilling and empowering to hear one so beautiful and so obviously powerful address her as though she were somehow greater than he, as if he were possibly subservient to her.

She opened her mouth, but she honestly didn't know how to respond—not only to such an address, but to the way he had come to her assistance overall. And then there was a moment, standing there in the golden aura of strength and hardness that was emanating from him, when she wondered if her attacker had been the frying pan and her savior was, actually, the fire. It kind of felt that way. Just a little. Seeing as how he now stood over her with a bloody knife in his hand.

He watched as her eyes tracked to the knife he held clutched in his hand, and suddenly he seemed to recall it was there, as if he'd forgotten he'd been stabbed and stood armed in the aftermath. He moved immediately to tuck the blade in at his belt, as though six inches of bloody metal would suddenly seem less menacing at his strong, long waist. The handle of the knife settled in relief against a tucked-in polo shirt that clung to at least a six-pack of well-heeled abs. To say nothing of the powerful pectorals and biceps. *He must live in the gym,* she observed. If so, she really needed to know which gym. She'd *really* like to go hang out there. Watching him push weights around as though he owned them would be one of the high points of her existence.

"Docia," she managed to say at last, sounding all squeaky and fragile when she was going for cool and confident. Crap. Oh, well. He'd have to make allowances for the situation. Maybe if she played it off right, she could come across all genteel and flirty like Scarlett O'Hara. "I . . . you . . . thank you," she ended meekly, acknowledging that she also sucked at genteel and flirty. This lack of confidence was why she was still stuck at a desk as an office manager . . . with her being the only person to be managed.

"I am ever at your service," he said, his rich, rumbly voice falling all over her. And then he bowed. It was a slight forward tipping of his body, the most perfect debonair act she'd ever witnessed in her life. And despite his lean, athletic power, it looked comfortable and genuine on him in a way she couldn't describe.

Wow. For real? Docia resisted the urge to pinch herself, though she highly suspected she was asleep . . . or maybe still in a coma in the hospital and she'd just been dreaming these past few days.

"Well, as nice as that would be," she murmured a bit dryly, "we need to get you to a hospital. And the cops. Cops would be good here," she noted as she observed the immediate area around her and its sense of carefully controlled chaos. An unconscious man, blood dripping into the snow from big fingertips, and battered, vulnerable little her standing toe-to-toe with a rather dangerous-feeling stranger. "I have to call my brother."

It was a pretty lame thing to say, considering her phone had probably ended up in the drink along with her pretty new old purse. Not to mention a far more flattering winter coat.

Docia rolled her eyes at herself. Granted, she liked her precious pearls of fashion reacquisition well enough, but she was beginning to sound obsessive about it in her own head. Maybe it was because she hadn't seen so much as a single reflective surface since the morning of the accident. Jackson had gone out of his way to deny them to her in a Nazi-like fashion, presumably because she looked like a hot mess that had been dashed up against about thirty unforgiving rocks on her travels into the Hudson River.

The sudden understanding had her feeling self-conscious over what she must look like to this gorgeous hunk of rescuer. She hadn't exactly led the search for a mirror with a full battle charge. She didn't need a mirror to feel hanks of hair shaved away and inroads of stitches crisscrossing her scalp. She'd rather suspect she looked like hell than see proof of it.

She gave the blond god a sour look, as if his extraordinary good looks were proportionately to blame for the wreck she'd made of hers.

"I'll go call my brother," she grumbled at him, taking

a step toward her house. He reached out to grab her arm, drawing her to a halt. She squealed . . . no, wait . . . she screeched, a shrill, obnoxious sound leaping out of her like that alien thing bursting out of people's chests in the movies. "You idiot! You've gotten blood all over my coat!"

They both seemed to freeze for a moment, the air hanging between them more than cold enough to do it and the caustic words dangling like ice crystals, frozen for all to see as the outright thankless, bitchy things they were. That *she* was.

Docia slapped both hands over her mouth, her eyes rounding with horror. Then they burned, liquid rimming and filling them.

"Hush," the stranger said to her as he stepped closer, the word not reproachful at all, but soft and gentling. The tack was rather like that of a cowboy to a wild horse, but she was not so upset that she didn't see him brushing his attentive eyes all around them. She'd seen that before. Hypervigilance. As an adopted sister of the SPD, she'd seen it in cops who suffered from PTSD. It was one of those symptoms that jumped out at you. However, he didn't wear it as if it were out of control or even out of context. Given what had just happened, it wasn't out of context for him to be worried about the area. "The Blending takes time. It draws on all the best and worst of what we are and what we have been, whether openly or just in our thoughts. I won't hold it against you. Not just now, anyway," he said, taking a moment to tilt half a smile at her. And somehow that half smile was more delightful than most men's whole smiles. It gave immediate comfort; it flashed a deep dimple and added a ripple of golden light in an almost lightless night to the brushes of gold limning the coronas of his eyes. She barely comprehended what he was saying, who he was, but that one brief expression settled more warmth and well-being over her soul than she had felt in all these past days. Not even waking to Jackson's familiar face or knowing he had seen to it that she was flawlessly protected had made her feel that she had both feet firmly back on the ground instead of tumbling over the side of a bridge.

"I'm so sorry," she felt compelled to say to him, in spite of his ready forgiveness.

"Think no more of it," he insisted, pulling her back in the direction of her house with sure and knowing steps, with those bright eyes that settled on her home in the distance and none of the others. That detail jumped out at her instantly, and this time she was the one looking all around herself in concern for what next danger would be coming out at her. In the end, he was the only one to settle her attention on, seeing as how they'd left the only obvious threat in a dark heap on the sidewalk behind them.

"Who are you?" she needed to know. Years of Jackson telling her what to do if she found herself in danger worked up to the surface, and she drew a sharp breath.

"Ram. I am your guide, my queen. Your protector during this vulnerable transition period."

Docia laughed. Actually, she kind of snorted through both nostrils at once. Very attractive.

"You know, I am having a sudden appreciation for how Alice must have felt after dashing down that rabbit hole."

"Alice, however, never appreciated the danger she was in at any given moment during most of her travels, allowing her to adapt to each situation with that child-like openness and skill only the young possess. You are not as fortunate."

Was he trying to tell her that she was in danger? Well, that had to be one of those things that were stupidly obvious. Right? If the past events of her life had proven anything to her, that most certainly had to be the ringing truth of it.

"I don't understand it," she found herself confessing to this stranger in a way she hadn't been able to admit to her law enforcement sibling. "What did I do? I'm no one special. Why would . . . ?" She tried to look back over her shoulder again, but this time he held tightly to her arm and encouraged her to remain facing forward.

"Your specialness is not a matter up for question," he said, the tone he used almost scolding. "Every breath you presently draw is proof enough of that. That and, I do not doubt, all the rest will become clearer to you over time. For the present we must move from under the watchful eye of the night sky."

Before she could even think to form an argument, she was being swept into her own home and he was crossing her threshold and closing the door behind them. He took a moment to pull aside the beads she had acting as a sidelight curtain, that attentiveness sweeping the street once again. He was beginning to make her paranoid. Or perhaps he was just making her aware of how paranoid she ought to have been all along, considering the evidence to date.

But now he was in her home. In her safe space. By virtue of taking his strange, strong golden self over her threshold, he had somehow taken the dangers of *out there* and brought the awareness of them *in here*.

"Who the hell are you?" she demanded, resenting that she was letting herself be swept so passively into this situation. She backed into her living room, feeling suddenly nauseated as she stumbled toward the receiver for the landline. The only way to fix this, she knew, was to call Jackson and get him here ASAP. But just when she turned to pounce on the phone, a powerful brown hand was covering it, pulling it out of her reach.

Choking on a screech, Docia looked up . . . and up . . . and up . . . the length of a male body seemingly twice as huge as the already impressive man behind her. The breadth of his shoulders loomed over her, making her feel like an ant scrambling over a picnic blanket that was suddenly spied by an enormous human who hovered over it, blocking out the sun and most of the world.

"Don't be afraid," the warmer, safer of the two evils said to her from behind, a hand of what she could only assume was comfort resting at the side of her neck. Either that or he was getting ready to snap her head off. "Asikri looks imposing, but he is harmless."

"Fuck you, Ram," the giant man spat at the other, clearly taking offense at being labeled "harmless." He needn't have worried. Docia didn't believe it for a second. Size and bulk aside—*could those things ever really be an aside?* she wondered—the blackness of his eyes, seemingly larger than was appropriate for the white space of the sclera surrounding them, and the blue-black sheen of straight, flat hair pulled back tautly in a high-set braid were more than enough to countermand the ridiculous claim. Even the soft tip of this brute's baby finger couldn't be considered harmless. The deep burst of his voice as he spoke profanely to his companion confirmed all conclusions that this man was very, very dangerous.

"Asikri! Respect for your queen," Ram demanded, his tone brooking no argument.

Asikri looked Docia over coldly and ruthlessly. "There's no way in the great night that *this* is my queen."

The level of insult and contempt must have been the final straw somewhere in the damaged parts of her bruised brain, because it was the only way Docia could explain what she did next. She reached out and grabbed the beast by his middle finger where it lay over her phone and wrenched the digit back as far and as hard as she was able, the knuckle cracking loudly in her tiny living room.

The giant roared and fell to his knees as Docia twisted and twisted, forcing agony onto a creature she was sure could snap her in two with just a thought.

"Whatever I am, queen or no, you will show me respect, you oaf!"

Oaf? What the . . . ? Since when did she use a word like "oaf"?

"My apologies, mistress," Asikri grunted out, making his kneeling position mean something as he bowed his head to her in acquiescence. Even when he was kneeling, his head came to nearly her shoulder line.

Impressive indeed.

Docia realized she was still holding his finger, and as if awakening from a half-numbed sleep, she comprehended she'd just committed an act of violence. She let go and jumped back, appalled, only to slam into the hard body of the other strange man in her house. Hands, large and strong, lean fingers cupping her rib cage on either side, steadied her. She felt his breath against her ear as he made a long, sibilant sound of comfort against the back of her half-shaved skull.

"Peace, my queen," he said with that tone again, the one that made her feel like an easily spooked filly under the masterful touch of a man who could break her to his will with just the right amount of time and patience. "You know Asikri."

No. She didn't know Asikri. He knew that. She'd never met either of them, yet he spoke as if she should be long familiar with him. As though Ram were already a close and trusted friend.

"No, I don't know him! Or you! Why are you here? Who are you?" she demanded, trying to turn but finding herself unable to with the way she was tucked into his body and held by his hands.

"You do," he insisted softly. "And soon you will remember that. You will begin to remember who you are. But for now you must come with us. It is our duty to protect you, and we will do so at all costs."

Docia watched the bigger man climb to his feet, those overlarge black eyes looking at her with a disgruntlement that was palpable. But she saw . . . she felt . . . there was a new edge of respect in his regard of her. Still, Jackson's years of warnings welled up in her head.

"No way. If you're going to kill me or something, you do it now. Here! I know what moving to a second location means for a female victim. I'll be damned if I'm going to survive what I just did only to have you all rape and murder me in a cold ditch somewhere." Well, that, and if she kept them long enough, Jackson might walk in on them. She had hope if she stayed right where she was. If she left . . . if she let them take her . . .

"We're not here to hurt you," Ram reassured her. "Look at him," he urged her, making her look at the other stranger. "Do you think you would even be conscious right now if we meant harm?"

Her eyes climbed the massive wall of testosterone in front of her. The big bastard had the temerity to smirk at her, as if the idea of clocking her into unconsciousness had a great deal of merit in his book. He reached to pull his center finger back into place with a snap. The look in his dark eyes said she'd gotten the best of him only because he'd underestimated her and she'd taken him by surprise. He wouldn't let it happen again. Not with her and, she had no doubt, never again with anyone else.

She swallowed loudly.

Great, Docia. Way to piss off the psychopathic killers. Now Jackson would be walking in the door at any minute and would be taken by surprise just like that. And although they were not hurting her at the present moment and didn't seem intent on doing so . . . she couldn't have the slightest bit of hope that they would be as gentle with a trained SWAT officer. Did Jackson even have his gun? She tried to remember if she'd seen it on his belt under his jacket before he'd gone off to the store. She knew there was a stun gun in the table by the door, as well as one in her bedside table, both gifts from her paranoid brother. Well . . .

Okay, sorry, Jackson. Maybe you weren't being paranoid after all, she thought with a wince.

"I'll go with you," she said at last, the words falling from her in a resigned sigh. "But we better make it quick. My brother will be back soon. I don't want anyone else hurt."

"I appreciate your candor," Ram said, slowly turning her to face him. He reached for her jacket and unzipped her out of it. He dropped it back off her shoulders, letting it fall to the floor. There was a peculiar sense of intimacy to the action, as if he were undressing her of something far closer to her body than just a jacket. The feel of his fingers and the way he stood with such strong surety before her made a knot clutch at the middle of her throat and made unsure heat burn over her skin. It was a painful idea, the thought that something that looked so gorgeous could possibly hurt her in the worst of ways. She had to put her faith, she realized, in the fact that he had saved her from one danger and did not mean to become yet another.

Then, as he pulled her toward the rear door of the house, she looked back at the old puffy coat and realized that it was streaked brightly with his blood and that he had most likely removed it so as not to draw any attention to them as they went out in public.

CHAPTER FOUR

Jackson plucked up a loaf of bread and a bag of powdered doughnuts, his sister's favorites—the doughnuts, not the bread—and tore around the corner and into the next aisle. He had not liked leaving Docia alone. It went against his grain, and the more he thought about it, the more he wanted to get back to her fast. But it would be fifteen minutes until the Chinese food he had ordered would be ready, and she was completely out of food back at the house. Since she'd been hospitalized only a short while, that meant her fridge had already been in the sad state he had found it in, not to mention her pantry. He grumbled to himself under his breath at the complete lack of nutrition in her habits . . . and wondered if he should be promoting a continuation of that with the stupid doughnuts. But . . . she was all sad and fragile looking, and he simply did not have the heart to show up without the powdery confection that always seemed to make her smile, crackles of white sugar on her lips.

"Jack!"

Jackson tripped, mainly because someone stuck a foot in the path of his determined feet, almost nailing his chin on the bar of the shopping cart. He recovered and came to a stop so he could punch out the jackass on the other end of that foot.

"Whoa!" Leo Alvarez shot up a strong hand and caught Jackson's fist just millimeters from his left cheekbone.

"What the hell is wrong with you?" Jackson demanded, reaching with his opposite hand and shoving at Leo's shoulder. They both knew Jackson would not have punched him. He was far too coolheaded for that. Well, usually, anyway.

"Just keeping you on your toes." Leo smirked at him, dodging a second shove by moving out of Jackson's immediate reach. "What are you doing? You look like you're shopping on speed." Leo picked up a box of cereal from the nearby shelf, examined it briefly as he spoke. "I haven't heard a peep out of you for nearly a week. If I was the sensitive type, my feelings would be hurt." Leo put the kid's cereal full of colorful marshmallows in Jackson's cart as Jackson pushed forward and tried to continue his shopping. He frowned at Leo, a wash of annoyance warring inside him with a nagging sensation of guilt.

"Docia was hurt," Jackson said a bit sheepishly, knowing that of all the people in the world outside of his blood family and police friends and colleagues he *should* have called and told about the horrible incident, Leo ought to have been first on the list. That understanding crystallized as Leo suddenly stilled in the act of putting a box of granola bars in the cart. He was a good-sized man, easily beating out Jackson's shoulder breadth and general height by several inches, and was built as though he spent a good deal of time in the gym. Jackson ought to know . . . they usually spent that time in the gym together. So when Leo went still like that, it tended to look ominous. Very . . . *scary.*

He and Leo were a little like oil and vinegar. They

were good together for the most part, but all you had to do was look at them to see they were very different from each other. And not just because Leo was a font of dark, Latino good looks and Jackson was made from a sharper cut of all-American cream cheese. Leo's scruffy tendencies, with his medium-length black hair, semi-kempt goatee, and well-worn jeans and leather boots, were vastly different from the usually clean, almost military cut of Jackson's hair and neatly shaven face. But now Leo was narrowing nearly black eyes on his friend in that way he had that made even big, powerful men take a few courteous steps back out of Leo's way. He knew Leo was assessing him, registering the fact that he hadn't shaved in several days, that he wasn't turned out the way he usually was when he left the house, having opted for old jeans and a T-shirt because they had been fast and easy and he'd wanted to get back to Docia as quickly as possible. He supposed by this point, with her recovering so remarkably well, he should have relaxed a little. He should have gone back to work. But he couldn't shake the memory of them telling him that his sister was dead, and damn them, they were just going to have to deal with it if he needed a few extra days to calm the fuck down and see to it she was well taken care of. They owed him at least that much. They owed it to themselves as well because he still wasn't sure he wasn't going to smack them around on sight.

But not telling Leo about it . . . that was a whole different can of worms. Funny, though, since Docia had been all over the news, lauded as some kind of miracle right there in their own hometown. How could Leo have missed that?

"What. Happened." Leo dropped each word individually, his tone cold and brooking no other options other than to tell him exactly what he wanted to know.

Jackson gave him a quick rundown of events. He was

succinct but detailed . . . at least, as detailed as he could be. Docia had not had very much to offer by way of information, and their investigations thus far had turned up next to nothing. All they really had was one very discombobulated witness, the make and model and color of one of the most popular purchases in the area, and scrapings of metal and paint on a patch of stone that had seen its share of scrapings and paint.

Jackson pushed on with his shopping, the urgency to get back to Docia still ticking hard in the back of his head. Leo fell into step, every so often grabbing something off a shelf and sticking it in Jackson's cart. It shouldn't have been funny, but Jackson had to suppress a smile. Even when his mind was busy digesting other disturbing details of life, there was a part of Leo that couldn't stop being a wiseass, and loading up the cart with things *he* liked or that were so completely disgusting they ought not to be on a shelf for human consumption was as wise as it got. Jackson took a jar of pickled pig's feet out of the cart and put it back on the shelf.

"I was out of town," Leo said gruffly after a few minutes.

Ah. That explained it. Jackson also realized it was Leo's version of an apology. He had nothing to apologize for. If anything, Jackson should be apologizing to him for leaving him out of the loop. Leo cared a great deal for Docia. "I should have called you," Jackson said, letting his friend off the hook.

"Yes. You should have," he barked at him suddenly. He turned a dark-eyed glare at him. "What the fuck, Jacks?"

"Sorry," Jackson muttered, instantly contrite. "I was a little . . ." He shrugged and concentrated on pushing the cart a little faster. "They told me she was dead."

Leo's right brow lifted, such a familiar expression of surprise and sudden comprehension dawning that it soothed Jackson a little for having to say it out loud. It was the first time he'd spoken of it in nearly a week, of how they'd taken her away from him . . . and erroneously so. Though, to be fair, everyone said Docia had died. If not for the freezing cold temperature of the water . . . What was it the doctor had said? "You're not dead until you're warm and dead."

And when he had seen Docia in the trauma bay, even he had believed there was no way she could survive what he was looking at. He too had lost faith in his sister and had thankfully been proven wrong. He would never make that mistake again. He would never give up on her again.

Leo gripped the rear of the cart, his knuckles turning white with the strength of it, a reflection of the icy hardness entering what should have been very warm, very dark eyes. In fact, Jackson had seen him shut off this hardness quite easily when he was doing the second thing he liked best . . . charming women.

The thing he did best was hurting humans that he felt, according to his personal code and morals, deserved it. Oil and vinegar. The cop and the mercenary. Well, *Leo* called himself "private security," a problem solver. But if it walked like a badass and quacked like a badass, it was Leo.

"You want me to talk to some people?" Leo asked him.

The statement was fraught with danger. Leo's version of talking to people was very different from Jackson's acceptable ideas of talking to people. He liked Leo, and as long as they didn't cross paths professionally, he was willing to live and let live and not ask too many questions. Not that he ever shut off being a cop. If Leo confessed to an inexcusable crime, they both knew Jackson would be on him like white on rice. So . . . they enjoyed a strange friendship that always walked the line of knowing each other better than anyone else did and yet . . . not.

"Information is always welcome," Jackson said carefully. "But—"

"Relax, boy scout," Leo scoffed, reaching out to cuff him hard on the side of the head. "I'll try not to kill anyone in the process."

"Leo," Jackson said warningly.

Leo simply grinned at him, giving him a bright "What?" expression as he dropped a can of sardines in the cart.

"Sounds to me like the SPD hasn't got shit," Leo pointed out. "I know people who know people who are going to know more than that and they are going to want to talk to me far more than they will the rest of you boy scouts."

"Probably because you scare the piss out of them," Jackson muttered.

"Hey, you don't wear a gun on one hip and a Taser on the other because you want people to think you're not serious," he pointed out.

Of course, Jackson had seen Leo use both a Taser and a gun on various occasions. The difference between them was that Leo was less apt to remember there were rules governing his behavior with either of those weapons. Still, Leo had a point. He always did. If he'd been a mindless thug, Jackson would have found it easy to section him off in his mind as a criminal and be done with him, but damn him, Leo was too clever for his own good. But when it came down to it, they both had jobs that threatened them with reasonably short expiration dates if they weren't careful.

And when faced with Docia's safety both imminently and in the past, he felt his usually staunch principles start to waver.

"Not one word," Jackson warned after a minute,

pointing a finger at him like some kind of kindergarten teacher. "Not so much as a peep about you breaking any laws in this information gathering of yours, Leo. I mean it."

Leo smiled, his eyes gleaming with mischief and that warm, charming *thing* that won over so many of his female conquests.

"I promise," he said, "you won't hear a single peep."

He turned and walked away, whistling brightly as he tossed a bag of candy over his shoulder, hitting the cart dead center, next to the cereal and the granola bars.

Ram didn't know what to make of this fragile little bird that held his queen captive inside her. Her wounds and injuries were to be expected. It happened to all of them in one way or another, this weakening unto death. It was the only way they could come out of the Ether. It was the only way the Blending could be initiated. The only way each new life could begin.

But each of them chose that new life with increasing discrimination. Each to his or her own parameters, of course, but still . . . this would have been the last place he would have thought to look for the grand and sophisticated queen of them all and the mate of his king. But it wasn't as though he had randomly found her out of the billions of humans in the world. It had been Cleo, their most powerful prophetess, who had guided him to Docia's hometown and the general location of Menes's future and past queen. His skills had led him the rest of the way. That and the local news media. He knew all he had to do was look for a sensational tale of survival against the odds. . . .

Ram looked down at his hand, his fingers absently rubbing together at the tips, the ghosting sensation of having been burned still lingering near his nails. It had happened when he had touched her, reminding him of the long-ago sensation of touching hot desert sands or the feel of heavy brick that had been baked beneath the sun. Each time he had come in contact with her, it had seemed to grow stronger. It convinced him that she was indeed the vessel his queen had chosen. Though he'd never felt the sensation before, he could easily imagine that containing a presence as powerful as his queen was bound to throw off strange, residual energies.

It would simply take time for his queen to find her way to the surface, and in that time she would be vulnerable and swimming in a state of confusion. It would be his and Asikri's duty to see to it that she remained safe during that process. Because as Cleo had pointed out before she had sent them to Saugerties, the only way they would be able to find their king would be to stick very close to their queen. If their king crossed from the Ether and into this world only to find that they, his loyal soldiers, had allowed his queen to slip back into the Ether for another century, there would be no consoling him.

And frankly, as loyal as he was, Ram had no desire to spend a hundred years bearing up under the wrath and pain of their king. Not after what had happened the last time they had failed him.

Ram grabbed at the steering wheel of the large SUV, trying to focus on the road. However, his attention once again drifted toward the delicate skull road-mapped with skillful stitchery and a few butterfly bandages to help reinforce the worst torn areas. They had thought little of her hair as they'd shorn it away, or the crowning glory it must have been before this tragic brush with what should have been her final death. But there were many deaths in the world to be had. The afterworld had not been ready for her, as it never was when it came to the shocking death of one too young to have a place at the table of Set. There had been a new purpose brought to her, one she was only beginning to discover.

If she survived that long.

Her cheeks were yellow with the full glory of aging bruises. Black, purple, and myriad other sickly colors also came to play across the bridge of her small nose and the flare of her forehead and jawbone. She must have hit nearly every exposed piece of her head that was possible. It was amazing, really, that she had been at all reclaimable. It was no wonder the hospital had been abuzz with tales about her.

But he and Asikri had not been able to get close to her at the hospital. Between her brother's watchful attendance and the guards outside the door and at the end of each hall, no one was going to get close to her. Ram was actually quite surprised Jackson Waverly had left her for an extended period once he'd brought her home. How could he be so careful for so long and then suddenly turn his back on her? Then again, the actions of the young originals were always a bit careless. He remembered what it had been like when he'd had only one life to live, before he'd touched the Ether the first time, before he'd learned what it meant to be an enduring copy. He too had squandered the gift of his life, had taken very little care of it.

It was the curse of mortality, he supposed. Or perhaps it was the blessing of it. If you knew you were going to live forever, would you take life much more slowly? Would you savor it? Or would you ignore the preciousness of each moment all the more?

He knew the answer to more speculations on the matter than he cared to. And even this lost little bird, would she one day come to know the true potential of one of the greatest queens ever to have lived, or would she devolve into the corruption and moral abyss that was equally available to her free will? That was the trouble with a copy, was it not? Each carbon layer became a little fuzzier than the original before it. A little bit more off center, a little bit harder to see and read. And sometimes, sometimes it was completely unreadable. Completely lost.

"Why do you keep staring at me?"

She asked him the question in a meek little voice as she sat hunched forward toward the blasting heat of the car vents. He had stripped her of all protection from the cold, but something inside him had balked at seeing her one moment longer in that ridiculous too-small thing she was using as an excuse for a jacket. Down had been leaking out of it in two places, bloodstains streaked it, and he suspected those had been coffee stains spattered across the chest of it. She was torn and tattered enough in her own skin; the jacket had only made her look twice as pathetic.

And there was nothing pathetic about her. Even that meek-voiced little question had the backbone of a tiger behind it. She could have sat there shivering, accepting her fate, but instead she challenged him. The question he had was . . . was that his queen he saw leaking outside of her edges, or was that something she had always been?

"I am concerned. You are taking a long time to regain your warmth."

"Of course I am! You took my coat off in twenty-degree weather, stole me out of the warmth and safety of my home, away from the protection of my brother . . . oh, and let's not forget the part where I just got out of the hospital after a seriously violent brush with death!"

There was a snort from the backseat. Presumably Asikri's amusement at the idea of Ram having his turn at an upbraiding by their queen.

No. This was definitely not a leak. This had already been there. The way she had taken Asikri in hand earlier, *that* had been a leak. A definitive one. And a good lesson for the other man. He had far too much contempt for the originals of the world. Although, to be fair, he had a great deal of contempt for Bodywalkers as well. It was a wonder Asikri tolerated *his* company at all. But antisocial tendencies aside, Asikri was a devoted warrior. He knew his place in the order of things, and he would rather die than fail. The Politic had been in a dark time these past decades, the ravages of civil war taking their toll. The struggle against the Templars was going badly. But there was light ready to shine on this dark night of theirs, and it was hopeful that it was going to start with her.

"I'm sorry for all of that. You will be warm and safe soon. Trust me."

"Trust you? Oh, sure. Because we go way back, you and I. A whole, what, fifteen minutes?"

"The value of a relationship can never be measured in time, but instead in the worth of what each member involved brings to the connection. I bring you trust, protection, and strength that you may use in any way you deem necessary. What have you brought to these fifteen minutes?"

She opened her mouth to retort but didn't say anything. She thought on his remarks instead, her teeth chattering as her hands fisted and flexed in turns over the heater. Ram reached over to increase the heat, then turned his hand briefly back and forth to inspect the knife wound through the center of it. It had closed and was already healing under the mess of blood that had dried over it. It was probably better that it was so obscured. If the precipitous healing had been more obvious to her inexperienced eyes, she might have flown into a full-blown panic. To be honest, he was rather amazed she hadn't done so already. For all intents and purposes, two total strangers had just kidnapped her.

"If you two don't kill me, I'm fairly certain Jackson will," she muttered at last.

"Oh, for pity's sake. Can't I knock her out or something?" Asikri spat from the backseat.

"Asikri!" Ram barked the man's name like a whip, and Asikri immediately sat back and sulked in the dark rear of the truck.

"Well, she whines a lot," he whined in defense of himself. "It's highly annoying."

"Well, why don't *you* get kidnapped by a bunch of thugs twice your size without explanation and see if *you* can win Miss Congeniality!" Docia bit back at him, those threads of strength glowing across her entire body as she faced off against the man who could snap her like a dried twig.

It made her amazingly beautiful. For that instant, as her inner determination fired into her aura and her features, she looked like a gorgeous virago risen from defeat to do battle once more. That she found the strength for it was remarkable, Blending or no. She couldn't be far enough into the process to reap the true power of it.

"You have not been kidnapped," Ram assured her. Or lied to her. It depended on whose perspective it was. "We're just bringing you somewhere far safer than where you were."

"My brother is a highly trained SWAT officer. You can't get much better protection than that," she argued icily. "So that settles that. Back we go. Go on. I have a comfy pair of jammies awaiting me."

"And where was this highly trained SWAT officer when that man was trying to gut you just before?" Ram countered.

"That's not fair! I told him I'd be okay. I convinced him to get me some food," she defended him, her voice becoming small by the end of the statement.

Ram took his eyes from the road once more and met

hers, their ermine brown so defiant and the spirit within them so protective of the brother she loved.

"I would never let you convince me of such when I know in my soul it would be a mistake. Your brother had three officers other than himself watching you every minute you were in that hospital because his instincts told him there was danger still waiting for you. He allowed himself to waver and turn his back." He made sure he held her eyes. "I will never so much as blink if I think it will give evil a chance to harm you."

Docia stared at her adversary . . . or was he an ally? She couldn't seem to decide from one moment to the next. But there were more arguments on the side of ally than there were on the side of enemy, and she was beginning to believe she might not end up dead once they got to wherever they were going. She knew they were driving north, that the car they were in, large and nondescript, was not cheap to come by and was possibly top of the line in its margin. But signs of wealth did not make for instant reasons of comfort. Besides, she was pretty sure it was a rental car. It was far too clean, and she could see the streaking path of the vacuum cleaner that had recently slurped its way across every carpeted surface. The mileage told her it wasn't a new car, and if she looked long enough, she could pick out a scuff here and a ding there on the interior. Still, it wasn't cheap, renting this type of car.

For the first time, she began to feel warmer. Thank God, because chattering teeth were not helping the headache she had blossoming between her ears. Her whole body ached, and the cold only made it worse.

"We would have waited," the blond explained quietly. "If you hadn't been in immediate danger just now, we would have waited. Given you a few days to rest, heal, and Blend."

"Blend?"

"At first I thought that man was a reporter. I expected them to show up again."

"Again?" she demanded. She was beginning to sound like a parrot.

"You're something of a local . . . miracle. They're calling you the 'Bridge Girl.' The girl who survived the odds. Your brother has kept you isolated so far, but he had to know that wouldn't last once they released you."

"Bridge Girl?" There she was again . . . *Polly want a Docia*? "Really?" She rolled her eyes and regretted it for the instant backlash of pain she received in the seat of her skull. "They couldn't come up with anything more . . . I dunno . . . miraculous?"

"It would have been better if they hadn't come up with anything at all," Ram said tightly. "The attention has allowed those who originally tossed you off that bridge to learn you survived. That makes you a witness. I highly doubt they like the idea of you potentially being able to identify them. Attempted murder is not an easy rap to beat."

"Especially not the attempted murder of the 'Bridge Girl,'" she said wryly.

"And as you saw, they had little interest in letting you run around with your memory—or anything else, for that matter—intact."

"I don't understand," she said, finally deserving the label "whining" and not caring if she did. She was frustrated, tired, and cold, and screw Ass-whatever-his-name-was if he didn't like it! "I didn't do anything! I'm not anyone special! I'm a tiny little secretary in a tiny little office for a tiny little company!" She made a tiny little box out of her hands in case they weren't getting the concept of just how tiny she meant.

"Your specialness goes without saying," Ram said, reminding her gently that for some reason he disagreed with the assessment. "And you may not realize why, but you most certainly are special to these people as well. You must have been somewhere at the wrong time. Seen something without realizing it."

"Back to your witness theory?" She sniffed. "I walk to work in the morning and walk back home. That's it. In the morning I stop for coffee and on the way home I either swing by Price Chopper for groceries or Mr. Cheung's for Chinese."

"And that's it? You never go out? Shop? Anything?"

"If I shop, it's on the weekend at my favorite resurrection stores. Oh . . ." She flushed a little. "And occasionally I stop at Krause's Candy store for a chocolate-covered pretzel. But it's sugar-free," she felt it necessary to point out.

The detail made him smile softly for some reason, a mysterious sculpting of his lips, drawing her attention to their unusual voluptuousness. Did he know he had girl lips? Well, actually, lips any girl would give her left arm for. On him, there wasn't anything the least bit feminine about them. No. The way testosterone rolled off him in confident waves, you could stuff him in a frilly polka-dot dress and he still wouldn't reflect a sense of femininity.

The thought of him in drag made her giggle a little. Then she took it a step further and thought of Asikri in drag. Now she laughed with energy, her hand going to her head in an attempt to lessen the vibrational pain of the emotion. It was worth it, though. It helped bring her anxiety down to a more manageable level.

It was another ten minutes of silence before they pulled into a gravel driveway, driving through a heavy pair of spiked gates that crossed each other for stability and withdrew into thick walls of stone that extended pretty far out on either side, walling in what promised to be an expansive property. The idea was reinforced as they continued up the drive a good distance before hitting a second wall and second pair of gates. Docia turned a little in her seat to look back at the heavily wooded region on the left side between the two walls before they passed through the second gate. She could see cameras posted at every square column that peppered the wall. Two of them, facing in each direction, resting on pivots that allowed for a complete scan in all directions. There had been the same thing on the first wall, both on the roadside and on the interior side, and she suspected that as they passed through she would see cameras on the other side of this wall as well.

This gate had a guardhouse with mirrored glass on every window. The guard who came to the car was of the same ilk as the men who held her: big, healthy, and not suffering from an excessive need to smile. Nor was he dour. Just polite as he glanced into the car from Ram's side at her.

Well, Ram hadn't been kidding when he had promised to bring her somewhere safer. As two other guards popped out of the house, one with a shepherd on a leash and another with a long stick with a mirror stuck to the end that he quickly ran beneath the car, presumably checking for explosives, she decided that she was either really safe or under more threat for heading into a property where the people within felt they needed this much security. The shepherd was well trained, not just teeth and fur to make an impression. She could tell as his handler took him around the car in precise steps and with focused commands. The dog then sat and looked up at the guard with that undeniable devotion she had seen Chico use toward her brother, his big pink tongue lolling out happily as he waited for his next rewarding task. The dog loved his job because he loved his trainer. The trainer was slim and dark, the dark suit he wore was tailored well and very sophisticated, but his shoes were rubber soled and laced up. He was ready to run if needed. They all were.

All this and the house had yet to come into sight.

It forced her to wonder just what they were protecting in the house. Or whom.

For the moment, it appeared it was her.

CHAPTER FIVE

"Mmm. There's no denying Ram's special touch," Kamen said dryly as he crouched down to survey the damage that had been done to the original left lying in the snow. Ram, Kamenwati noted, was very particular about whom he chose to kill. All of Menes's Bodywalkers had a special appreciation for life and took particular care in which original lives they chose to end. After all, the art of spiritual preservation was long lost in these modern cultures. Not that this spirit was worthy of any kind of preservation. It was a criminal. A thug. Small-minded and inferior in its thinking and goals. It had wanted to kill the incarnation of what was obviously a precious soul for such petty reasons. Over such petty fears.

Kamen wanted to kill her for much more complex reasons. Much worthier ones. He had been watching Ram's and Asikri's activities very closely, knowing just as they did that the time for the Bodywalker Politic's so-called king's resurrection was at hand. He knew they were looking for their queen in anticipation of their king's arrival. He also knew that his best advantage was during these first weeks of the Blending, when queen and, eventually, king would be at their weakest.

"Tick tock. Tick tock. What to do, what to do," he mused.

"Kill it?" Chatha suggested.

"If you must," Kamen replied with a put-upon sigh. "But why waste your energy on these little mortal things? There are more important immortals we must worry about."

"Need skills," Chatha said, his mongoloid features lighting up so brilliantly as his smile took up half his face. It was just like Chatha to find a perverse sort of humor in the incarnation he had chosen this time around. He seemed to be dwelling happily in the juxtaposition of its apparent harmlessness and its immediate innocence in the eyes of all the mortals he came into contact with. All he had to do was lapse into the simpleton behaviors the mortals expected from a Down syndrome adult and he could smile and bounce his way through any door . . . under any guard. It was a stroke of genius, actually. Chatha had found the perfect sheep's wool in which to hide the exquisiteness of the wolf that he was. But Chatha would never rise above his position in the universe because he was pretty much a psychopath. He had been as an original and he continued to be more so with every copy.

As Kamen turned his back on Chatha's murderous little frenzy to follow, he made his way to the warmth of the SUV waiting nearby. He climbed behind the wheel, sitting silently for a long moment, watching Chatha pounce over and over again on his dying amusement.

"Somehow I find his frenzied attacks far more comforting than watching him go about his business in that more methodical way he has."

"He's had dozens of incarnations in which to perfect his mania. I consider it something of an art form," Kamen remarked in return to the woman sitting beside him. "This frenzy you see, that's the interference of his host. The host is disorganized, most likely because of its disability, and almost frantic . . . probably because it's being forced to take part in something that might usually go against its moral code. Though he has subjugated his host's soul for the most part, it still bleeds through on occasion."

She tilted her head, her clear blue eyes narrowing on the bloody tableau in front of her, the analytical mind within her contemplating so many possibilities. There were many explanations, but only one really mattered at the moment. One truth that made a difference.

"So I gather we missed her?"

"So it would appear. But—" He broke off as movement down the street caught his attention. He reached to rap a knuckle on the glass, and Chatha immediately went still. Kamen watched as a man skidded down the drive of a small house, pulling out the service weapon on his belt as he ran shouting down the street.

"Well, that's not good," his companion noted dryly.

"Watch. He's pure poetry," Kamen reassured her.

The cop ran down the sidewalk toward Chatha, who immediately plopped down in the snow on his backside beside the body he'd been manhandling moments ago.

Jackson drew a bead on the two bloody figures in the snow. One of them was still as death, the other was bawling his eyes out as if someone had stolen his puppy. He saw Jackson's gun and shied away, covering his head with both hands as if it would afford him protection.

"Don't shoot me!"

"I'm a cop," Jackson said quickly, taking in the bloody skin and clothes of the weeping adult male. His features were instantly identifiable, his innocence automatic and obvious. Now that Jackson had dismissed the Down syndrome male as a potential threat, his eyes darted up and down the street warily. "Was there a woman here?"

"They took her," he answered helpfully, his whole face lighting up in a smile. "Can I be a cop? Did I help?"

"Sure," Jackson said absently, even as panic was washing sickly through him. "Who are 'they'?"

"Two bad men. They took the nice lady after they killed this man. They were mean bad men. I couldn't help. They hurt me." The frown and tears reappeared.

Jackson's frustration knew no bounds. Something had happened to Docia, and his only witness, it appeared, was a man with what appeared to be the mental maturity of a six-year-old. But maybe he'd get lucky. A lot of Down's adults could be very high functioning and were veritable fonts of information. Maybe once he calmed down he would be a better source of clues as to where Docia had disappeared to.

"What's your name?" Jackson asked him.

"Andrew. Andy."

Jackson lowered his weapon, hoping to calm Andy down a little by coming across as less threatening.

"Andy, that lady they took was my sister. I'm really worried about her. Did you see them hurt her?"

"I tried to help. They hurt me."

Jackson sighed and reached for his phone. He tried not to let guilt and a slew of other emotions sicken him as he called the precinct. He had known better than to leave her. What the hell had he been thinking? He'd been thinking about Dr. Marissa "Hotbody" Anderson telling him that a sense of normalcy would be very important to Docia when she got home, that he wouldn't be doing her any favors being overprotective of her. So when Docia had begged him to leave her alone for the thirty minutes it would take for him to dash to the store and acquire dinner, he'd actually gone against his better judgment and agreed.

But now he'd come home to Docia's bloody jacket on the floor of the house and his sister nowhere to be seen. Mere steps away, this gruesome sight, a corpse dead and bloodied and a gentle overgrown child possibly hurt as well. If they'd had no compunctions about hurting this harmless man, what would they do to his sister, whom they clearly saw as enough of a threat to have tried killing once before? And who the hell were *they*?

Jackson fought down the surge of bile in the back of his throat. His sister was going to turn up dead, and it would be his fault. The only thing in his favor at the moment was that they had taken her away instead of killing her on the spot. But as a cop, he also knew that bringing her to a second scene was like writing a murder book. They wanted time to get cozy with her, in privacy, to do whatever it was they wanted to do with her. Extract information? Maybe. Torture?

His eyes jerked over the corpse lying in the road. He had yet to understand how the body figured into all of this. A Good Samaritan, perhaps? Had the man tried to help Docia and paid for it with his life?

"This is Sergeant Jackson Waverly, badge number 1131. I need backup at Washington and Prospect. The coroner and some detectives." He eyed his potential source of information. If he called Social Services, they'd circle the wagons and he'd never get a decent interview out of his only witness. But he couldn't exactly hide a witness from the detectives, either. Frustration burned along with rising agitation and seething panic inside of him. He'd never been in the position before of choosing between doing what would keep his family safe and upholding the law and its protocols. But he'd put his entire faith in the law and those he called his second family . . . the second family that had taken his sister in as one of their own for years now. He had to trust that they would help him do the right thing. To do everything they could to get her back.

He hung up the phone and immediately pressed a speed-dial button.

"Alvarez."

Jackson took a deep breath, but words refused to come to his tongue. They jammed in his throat for some reason, sticking together and keeping him from speaking.

"Jacks?" Leo's concern was immediate and cautious. "Man, did you just ass-dial me?"

"Leo," Jackson finally managed to say. It was all he said. All he could catch breath to say. Apparently, it was all he needed to say.

"Where are you?" Leo demanded, his longtime friend knowing instantly that something was very wrong.

"Docia . . ." Jackson took a breath, and it seemed to be helping. "Leo, they took her. She's gone."

"Three minutes. No more. You hear me? I'll be there, Jackson." There was the sound of screeching tires over the phone and the wail of an angry horn. "*¡Jodete Cabron!*" Leo shouted before hanging up his phone.

The knowledge that Leo was on his way helped Jackson to draw his wits back together. God almighty, he couldn't afford these paralyzing hits of panic. Where the hell had they come from, anyway? He wasn't some Sissy Mary always crying every time his life hit a hiccup. He'd been trained to keep a level head . . . and usually he did.

"So, Andy," Jackson said after clearing his throat. He checked the streets once more before slipping his gun back into its holster. "You want to be a cop, right?"

"Yep!"

"You know, a good cop has to remember everything they see in a split second."

"I can do that," Andy said brightly.

"You think you can describe the men who took the nice lady?"

"Yep!"

There was a long beat, and Jackson tried not to get impatient. "Do you think you could do that *now*?" he asked. Literal. Children and challenged individuals tended to be very literal, he reminded himself.

"Oh sure! One was tall and big, like a monster. The other was big, too, but yellow haired. The monster had black hair and he looked like this." Andy scrunched up his face and body as ominously as he could manage. Jackson let his eyes wander over the boy-man, trying to figure out how he had gotten covered in so much blood.

"Was she hurt? Did they make her bleed?" He spoke through gritted teeth, fighting back the resurrection of his panic. Maybe the blood on Andy's jacket was Docia's. But . . . how had her jacket gotten back in the house? And a few smears on the outside of the jacket didn't indicate signs of any great injury.

Yet.

"No, she was right as rain," Andy said helpfully.

Strange. Anyone who looked at Docia wouldn't use that sort of a descriptor for her after the hell she'd recently been through. She certainly didn't look right as rain. But this wasn't just anyone, he reminded himself once again. Andy saw things in his own way.

What he wouldn't give right then for Chico. His K-9 partner would have been able to tell him more in just a few minutes than this adult witness was going to be able to do. But Chico wasn't there, and he never would be again, so he'd have to make do. He couldn't lose focus. Couldn't waste time wishing for what he didn't have.

"Andy, which way did they go?" Jackson asked, crouching down to meet the other man eye to eye. "The lady and the monsters?"

"Away," Andy said matter-of-factly. "In a car."

"What kind of car?" Jackson asked, trying not to let a sudden surge of hopefulness fog his need to focus. This, he acknowledged at last, was why cops weren't allowed to work cases related to family members. He clearly couldn't think straight. All he could do was feel the nausea of knowing his sister was out there, helpless, and in the hands of monsters. And that he had let it happen.

"A big car."

Great.

This was going to take a while, he thought painfully.

"Amazing," the female mused. "In a matter of minutes he has a well-trained police officer disarmed, off guard, and lowered into a position of weakness and vulnerability. So why doesn't he attack?"

"That's the beauty of Chatha," Kamen explained. "He gets far more pleasure watching his prey squirm than he does in the actual attack. Whatever the cop is doing or saying is providing Chatha with more delight than killing him outright would. And as long as he continues to do so, Chatha will allow him to live."

"I've been away much too long. . . ." She sighed, smoothing delicate fingers down the side of her face as she leaned to look into the mirror off the passenger-side door. The glass magnified her stunning blue eyes, as well as the faint scar on her temple. It had been her entry point, the wound this original had suffered that had allowed her to come out of the Ether. That had been two months ago. The Blending had come and gone, and now she was the dominant inside this mind. But as with Chatha, occasionally the less controlled original would rise to the surface and its impulses would disturb her control and focus.

"Never fear, my mistress. You'll be the queen you deserve to be. This time will be very different from the last," Kamen reassured her.

"Last time we came so close." She sighed.

"There will only be success this time. I have created a plan far more complex than anything they will be suspecting."

"Simplicity has its beauties," she warned him. "Depend on no one, Kamen."

"No one but you, my divinity. You are the divine, your hands around the hearts of the gods. It is you and no one else who should rule the Bodywalkers."

"Mmm. Clearly there are those who would argue the matter with us. As they have for aeons. Sometimes I win, and sometimes I do not. I am not in the mood for failure. Time is growing short, Kamen. The god Amun is rising. I can feel it. And we must be ready to greet him when he does or all of the world will suffer for it."

"I don't imagine anyone is ever in the mood for failure," Kamen mused, amusement glittering in his eyes. She clicked her tongue at him in admonishment and gave his shoulder a shove.

"Anyway, whatever your plans, you might have to alter them a little at first," she cautioned him. "I have an idea of my own. Something equally unexpected that I wish to try first. But neither of our methods will bear fruit unless we *get hold of this girl*."

"Agreed. But no doubt she is at a safe house by now."

"No doubt. But there are ways around that, just as Chatha has proven," she said with a smile that curled in wickedly beautiful amusement.

Ram watched her face as they drove the distance from the final gate to the house itself. It was a ways farther up the mountain, the road hard paved now to provide surety and ease of plowing for the rough mountain winters they sometimes had here. Since the long drive was a dual switchback, that surety came in handy. There were huge stone pillars lining the drive, each topped with a stone-carved gargoyle of grotesquely giant proportions. Some had wingspans stretched to full glory, others grasped at the tops of their column perches in a low crouch, their faces sinister and foreboding.

The trees obscured the house in spite of their winter bareness, just a hulking impression at first glimpsed only in parts like a gothic film flashing images of the vulnerable body parts of a woman. But there was nothing vulnerable about the Catskill Sanctuary. It was one of the smaller sanctuaries they owned throughout the world, and he had not been surprised to find one so close to where they were. These things tended to happen in this way. There were some places on Earth, resonance chambers of a sort, that drew arrivals from the Ether far more frequently than other areas. Something about the nature of a place made it so much easier to cross that stubborn veil between, more so than was found in other areas, bringing the attention of those in the Ether to this plane and the people available within it. Over time, it made sense to make certain that safe havens were awaiting them within reasonable distance of these areas when they arrived. The first weeks of a Blending were the most trying, the most vulnerable, and there were plenty of factions far worse than some two-bit human thugs out there that would go to great lengths to see to it their king and queen never made it out of the Ether. They were the same factions that had without a doubt returned them there once more, just a century ago, devastating them all.

They were the same who were just as aware as Ram's people were that the waiting time was done and resurrection was at hand. They would do anything to see to it that these Blendings failed, that Ram failed in his duty to protect his king's soul mate. Ram's duty was to make certain she was here waiting for Menes when his time came to cross free of the Ether; theirs was to make certain she wasn't. They knew that to rob the great king of his beloved wife was just as effective as hollowing him out, stuffing him with nothingness, and propping him up emptily for the people to see. Ram knew that for all he was the greatest pharaoh of all time, Menes was violently connected to his queen and had, in the past, preferred to return to the Ether in order to pass time with her there than be without her. But the people needed a ruler. Now more than ever. And they did not have the luxury of letting their king waste time in the Ether.

Ram refused to give the option life by thinking about it. He would not fail. His king had but one weakness, and Ram would see that nothing exploited it.

They drew up to the house, and her reaction was clear.

"Holy Christ. Who lives here, Bill Gates?"

Asikri was out of the car and yanking her door open before Ram had opportunity to respond. The warrior stood peevishly waiting for her to alight from the vehicle, looking for all he was worth as if he were about to tap his foot with schoolmarm impatience. Ram could swear she moved slowly to her feet out of a perverse enjoyment of making Asikri cool his heels rather than a reluctance to step into the cold.

Ram came quickly around to her side, offering her the warm shelter of his body and the inside of his own coat by unzipping it and drawing her into its fold like a mother bird tucking its nestling under a wing. Ram hurried her to the front door, Asikri's heavy footsteps following tightly behind them. The door opened and Ram immediately recognized the portal keeper.

"Vincent," the Sanctuary keeper greeted him with a smile. But when he took in the tower that was Asikri at his back and the battered dove he held protectively at his side, his whole demeanor changed, his face lighting up in such a way that the elder man dropped about twenty years in heartbeat. "Vincent! Wallace! Good fortune to you both and to me! You bring the greatest of treasures with you, I see. Please, come inside. The Sanctuary is yours to use as you wish, of course."

They scuttled into the doorway, a huddling little flock for all of a second, and then Asikri broke away immediately, marching off from the so-called whining woman who had so irritated him. Then again, everything and everyone irritated him, so there was nothing of note to the moment. As he passed the portal keeper, he grumbled dangerously in his face, "Don't call me Wallace."

Of course, the keeper was aware of Asikri's hatred for the name his mortal half had been born with. Everyone in their world was aware of it. That meant the sly portal keeper had done it on purpose. There was no doubt that Asikri knew it, too.

Ram reached to take hold of the small, cold hand of his king's betrothed, drawing her quickly into the first salon with a lit fireplace. Heat emanated from it in heavy waves, and he let his own clenched body relax in the bask of it. He had lived so many lifetimes, in so many countries and in so many styles, but he had been born a man of the desert and a creature of the heat. He would never get used to these colder climes. He could tolerate and function, but he would never grow accustomed to it, nor would he willingly desire to dwell in it. He much preferred New Mexico, the seat of their government at present and his usual home. It was not the arid perfection of Egypt, but it would do for this lifetime.

He looked down on the top of Docia's head as she leaned eagerly for the warmth of the fireplace. The injuries she had suffered pained him for some reason. Maybe because she was so small, or because her half-shorn head made her look like a frail waif, but no matter how much he told himself it was only a temporary state, it still grated on him. The fact that she was out of the hospital already attested to the fact that the Blending was in full swing and that she was healing far more rapidly than she would have without the influence of his queen within her.

"I thought your name was Ram," she said after a long minute of clenching her jaw to keep her teeth from chattering.

"Ram is an old nickname. I was born Vincent." It would do for an explanation at present. He would bombard her with truths a little bit later.

"What, were you on the football team or something?" she asked, trying to theorize how they managed to get Ram from Vincent. Ram seemed to visibly do an internal check of his memory, as if he had to work at it.

"No. No football. I was . . . I was twenty-eight years old when I hit a reef outside the Cape of Good Hope in 1972 and drowned."

Docia gaped at him. It sounded exactly like what she'd just gone through.

"Wait a minute . . ." She narrowed her eyes on him, having no idea how exotic it made her look. Exotic and strong. Strong in a way others shouldn't try to defy. But Docia, while having her share of *no nonsense allowed* behaviors, would have laughed to think anyone would ever take her that seriously. "That was forty years ago! You can't be a day over thirty-five."

He was lying to her and toying with her for reasons she couldn't fathom. Was it some kind of a joke to him, to make up empathetic incidents in his life?

But really, if he was going to lie about something, he ought to have made a better effort at it. Did that make him stupid or just careless?

Ram/Vincent looked at her from under golden lashes, somehow managing the hooded expression in spite of being significantly taller than her. She wondered why she hadn't come down with a case of the screaming meemies so far. She'd just been kidnapped! Now she'd been brought into the fortress of solitude. She was his prisoner in effect and by all definitions.

And he was smiling at her.

"I'm older than I look," he said, no doubt hoping his charming smile would be enough to blow her off. Honestly, it almost was. It was a hell of a smile. Extremely pretty. She was caught up in just staring at those white teeth and full masculine lips for much longer than she ought to have been.

"Crunch the numbers all you like, pretty boy." She forgot about being cold as her temper percolated. She leaned forward and poked a finger hard into his chest. "There's no way you're sixty years old."

"Sixty-eight," he said directly, looking her dead in the eyes as if what he was saying could be believable on any level.

Docia guffawed, her hand going to her temple as the bright, hard laughter made her head ache. "And I'm your dear aunt Fanny."

He smiled again, leaning in toward her just enough to coat her in his body warmth in a manner far more effective than the emanation of the fireplace fire. He reached for her hand where it cradled her head and pulled it between his own.

"Perhaps," he said softly, "you will accept my truth a little more easily once you accept that facts don't change just because you are unwilling to accept them." He closed her palm between both of his, gently rubbing the chilled appendage until it began to warm. "When you tell people you survived an unsurvivable death, will you appreciate it when they laugh in your face and call you a liar? No, you will not. So you will learn to fudge the facts, haze them over, even lie a little, so that people will allow their narrow minds the capacity to comprehend. And when you are sixty-eight years old and even more beautiful than you are today, you will know you have to come up with other stories, other tales, to divert them from the truth of the matter. You will have to leave behind everything associated with Docia Waverly and embrace a newer version . . . a newer generation of yourself."

Docia gaped at him. She really didn't know what else to do.

"So you're telling me that when I'm sixty-eight years old I'm going to look like I'm fresh into my thirties, just like you?"

Again, that smile that was too pretty and beyond comforting blossomed over his lips. Perhaps to counterbalance the craziness that was about to spill out of his mouth, she thought. She'd gone along with things so far because she hadn't much of a choice, but she was beginning to think this guy was starkers and she had willingly walked into an insane asylum.

"I doubt that," he said, for an instant sounding relievingly sane. "Females tend to look far younger than their years as time passes."

Then, before she could snort out a new laugh, he took her chin in his hand and made certain she was looking deeply into his golden-bright eyes.

"You have left normal humanity and mortality behind today, Docia. Today you have become a Bodywalker. You came to the brink of death, weakening the protective walls of your Ka . . . your soul . . . enough to allow the Ka of another to Blend with yours. Think. You met her briefly, in that moment of death and life, where they balanced together. She asked you if you were willing to share your mortal body with her, and you agreed. You cannot feel her at present, except perhaps in bursts or hints. She is weakened by her journey out of the Ether and into this existence. But she will become stronger, as will you, and you will eventually Blend together. One of the benefits of that Blending will be that you will not age in the normal way of a mortal. Enjoy that benefit, because I promise you, there are just as many detriments that will make things very difficult for you."

"But always remember that you were given a choice and this is what you chose, blah blah blah . . ."

The strident female voice entering the parlor was full of amusement and disrespect all at once, the loudness of it immediately drawing the couple's attention. Docia was a little numb as she watched the tall, slim woman whose shimmering black hair snaked in a single long tail from a point originating high on the back of her head, a perfect sheet of healthy, rich ebony that ended in a perfectly straight cut near her hip bone on the right side. She was prettily pale-skinned and boasted brightly faceted cerulean eyes as rare as the finest of jewels. It was a beauty Docia couldn't have hoped to achieve even with the most expensive hair dyes and realistic contact lenses. The mink lash color had to be all natural. The enhancements of a thin purple eyeliner and warm reddish-pink lip gloss were the only obvious man-made fabrications to her otherwise flawless beauty.

"Honestly, Ram, must you be so serious and pedantic? You'll scare the second life out of the girl."

"Cleo . . . ," Ram said with a pained rolling of his eyes. "What are you doing here?"

"It's ski season!" she said happily, as if that explained everything. The bounce in her shoulders and pitch in her tone belonged on the ditziest blonde in creation.

Only, Docia had a hard time believing she was any more ditzy than she was blond. Cleo strode across the room toward Docia, her hand extended for a greeting shake. Docia immediately noticed everything about her. And that was really weird. Docia had always been observant about people, so it wasn't weird in that respect. It was weird in the respect that she could tell Cleo balanced her weight almost perfectly between both feet. Normal people, normal human people, always favored one side over the other. It was a whole right-brain, left-brain dominance thing. They couldn't help themselves. They always leaned toward one side or the other. It was just the way their brains were wired. Even so-called ambidextrous people had a dominant side. One side they used in preference to or with more strength than the other. But as Cleo walked toward her, Docia saw the strange evenness of her gait and weight. It lent a peculiar strength and grace to her carriage. Not a runway model walk to make her seem gangly pretty like some long-legged, tall women, but an athletic glide. As if she weren't beautiful enough, this made her unique and strangely stunning.

"Don't listen to his rhetoric," she commanded of Docia as she took her hand and promptly tucked the fingers into her inner elbow, covered them securely, and turned to draw Docia into step with her right back out of the room. "The older royals like him are so mired down in who they used to be. They forget they are dust, linen cloth, and canopic jars somewhere and that these are modern bodies in a modern world."

"Cleo," Ram said warningly, the name almost a growl of displeasure. Cleo was clearly unimpressed.

"Here's the scoop. You died, right? Almost. When you died you stepped into the Ether. Right?" Docia nodded, not knowing what else to do in response to

Cleo's questioning remarks. "There you met . . . whom did you meet, anyway? Did she say?"

Docia shook her head mutely, trying to figure out how everyone knew about what had happened during *her* near death experience.

"Was it even a her? Kahotep came back as a woman in two of his Blended incarnations just to see what the experience would be like. I thought of choosing a male myself once or twice. But really, who would want to be a man? The idea of not being able to grow a child . . . it saddens me."

"It w-was a woman. . . ."

"Of course it was! And who are you?"

"I—she didn't . . ."

"Hatshepsut." Ram spoke up from behind them, his voice falling dark and hard, the word spitting from him like a cross between a curse and a sneeze.

Cleo froze midstep, her carefree air evaporating instantly. She immediately let go of Docia's arm and dropped to her knees, bowing her beautiful head down low, her hands reaching out to touch Docia's feet as her tail of hair fanned out over the tile floor before settling into stillness.

"My queen. I apologize. I did not realize it was you," she said with breathless reverence. "Ram, I never thought you'd find her this quickly! I assumed . . ." She went silent, leaving Docia to stare down at her in shock and an absolute sense of having leapt down a rabbit hole somewhere along the way. She was struggling to figure things out, to catch up and work off the same script that they seemed to be working off.

"I'm a little confused," was all she could manage to eke out.

And that was as long as Cleo's contrition lasted. She was just as quickly back at full height and had Docia's shoulders snuggled under her arm in that very next instant.

"Never you fear. Cleo is here to help you."

"Cleo, *I* am here to help her," Ram said darkly in warning.

"Sorry, I didn't get that," Cleo lied breezily, brushing a hand of dismissal in Ram's face. "You know, this original is deaf in this ear, I think." She wiggled a finger in the suspect ear.

"Cleo!"

"I understand how you feel," she continued on in Docia's ear. "My last incarnation before this one, it took nearly six weeks for the Blending to happen. I walked around the whole time utterly confused. It didn't help that it was the Civil War and every time I turned around someone was stuffing me into a corset. Damned distracting, let me tell you. Let me finish giving you the scoop. So. Died. Ether." Cleo ticked off the steps on her finger. "Our queen chose you. She piggybacked on your soul, so to speak, to get back here to the mortal plane. Now you and she are going to Blend over the next few weeks. Downside? It's as confusing and disturbing as a game of drag queen bingo in the lobby of the Carlisle Hotel." Cleo brushed that off. "Upside? You'll heal superfast now. You'll become very strong. The aging process comes to a screeching halt. Even reverses in some cases! Yay, right?" She was obviously excited about that one. "I forget what other power Hatshepsut draws with her . . . but one step at a time. Right? You look like you went through hell. I'm amazed she was able to claim you at all."

Docia just stared at her, mouth agape.

"I guess that's . . . um . . . good?" she said when Cleo looked at her expectantly.

"Good? That's great! You're so lucky you were

claimed by the highest of all queens! You are destined to be—"

"Cleo!"

This time Ram's bark of warning was something even Cleo couldn't ignore. It rolled over them both like storm clouds, and Docia could swear she heard and felt a slam of thunder outside in time with it. *Now that was just creepy,* she thought. Rather like the scary butler in the vampire mansion who elicited a clap of thunder and lightning after opening the door and saying, "Good *eeeevening*!"

Again, Cleo wasn't in the least impressed. She huffed at Ram, but she also discontinued her sentence, much to Docia's frustration. The highest of queens? Was that who was knocking around inside of her? That is, if she was going to listen to either of these raving lunatics. Of course, it was a little compelling as far as lunacy went. Highest of queens? Destined to be something other than the manager of a dinky little office? If she had to almost die, that'd be kind of a really nice side effect of the whole nasty business.

"I think I need something to drink."

"I'll get you some water, beauteous majesty," said a quiet man she hadn't had time to notice, kneeling deeply before he rose to leave.

Beauteous majesty? Fucking *A*! What woman couldn't use a bunch of men referring to her as "beauteous majesty"? That alone almost made the dance on the rocks worthwhile.

"Liquor," she managed to choke out. After all, being a beauteous majesty was going to take some getting used to. Just resisting the urge to giggle was going to take superior training and maybe some severe lip biting. "Need liquor."

The man stopped and nodded. "As you wish."

"No," Ram barked. "The doctors said you were not to have any such spirits."

And bam. There it was. The end of her beauteousness and her majesty. Well, as far as Ram was concerned, in any event. The other man looked torn, however, hesitating between the two commands he'd been given. He shifted his weight awkwardly on the balls of his feet, his gaze darting from Ram to her.

"I think I made my wishes clear," she said firmly and reproachfully, not really knowing where the mischief came from. *Hmm.* It couldn't possibly have anything to do with a wild urge to pull rank on this man who had done nothing but move her around like a frigging chess piece as she stood there all confused on his little chessboard, could it? But if she was the queen, that meant she was the strongest piece on the board . . . and she wasn't above testing that out.

"Anthony." There was a clear and present warning in the way Ram said the other man's name. Anthony swallowed hard, even as he went terribly pale. But he didn't look at Ram, he looked at Docia. His eyes were begging her for reprieve. He certainly knew she was more human than she was his queen at present, and he was hoping she would be willing to relent based on that fact. It made her wonder just how much of a bitch this queen of theirs was. Was that the calm, strong voice that had suddenly appeared in her head? Was there going to be a major bitchy side to her as well?

"Fine. Whatever," she said, waving off the suffering man. She felt terribly guilty when she saw the wash of pure relief that went through him. She realized as he turned and the light glinted off his skin that he had broken a significant sweat. She had not meant to cause him any real discomfort. It wasn't as though he'd been in any kind of danger . . . was it?

"Cleo, if you don't mind, I would like to give Docia a

better explanation of what she can expect," Ram said, coming across the room and standing over her, making her suddenly recall just how big and tall he was in comparison with her reasonably shrimpy proportions. Truth was, outside of their respect for this queen she was purportedly lugging around inside of her, she had absolutely no bargaining chips in this situation.

Cleo opened her mouth to argue, but Vincent or Ram or whatever the hell he wanted to call himself from one minute to the next had pulled out a cellphone and snapped it open and was holding it in front of Docia's face.

"I assume you'd like to call your brother?"

Holy shitcakes!

She grabbed for the phone, panicking as she stared at the unfamiliar configuration and tried to decide which button required hitting first. What was his number? "Oh, my God, I can't remember his number! My brain is broken!"

"Or, like most humans, you've become overly dependent on your contacts list," he said dryly, coming around so that he was behind her. He reached out and cupped her flailing hands and fingers in his, holding them firmly for an instant, willing her to calm down. It worked for some reason, the strength and warmth of him surrounding her like the powerful heat of a fire that fought back a freezing chill. And just like that, the contrast in temperatures, the clash in counterproductive forces, caused a deep-rooted shiver to rattle through her, and goose bumps rippled up her arms and across her breasts.

God, he is so freaking warm! It was like lying out in the sun as a child without a stitch of shade around . . . and not a single instant of worry in your mind about the harm it could be causing you. An abandoned and beautiful warmth, one that made prickles dance on your skin if, say, a stray hair was lying the wrong way or a dust mote skipped over it. Only then, in the quiet of that baking warmth, were you still enough to notice those things.

He also smelled incredibly . . . well, the only word she could think of right then was *yummy*. It wasn't some gagging, cloying cologne manufactured by man in an attempt to lure a woman with falseness and trickery . . . a trickery that often failed because the man himself failed to consider the whole "less is more" approach to these things. It was clean, pure . . . with a dusting of something . . . not smoky, but . . . *crap*, she couldn't figure it out. And somewhere along the line she had turned her head so her nose was almost touching the long, strong column of his throat. It was also intriguing to see he had a hard, strong pulse dancing through his carotid artery. Of course, they *all* had pulses in their carotid arteries, but . . . *anyway*, despite all this weird possession mumbo jumbo she was being subjected to, it was nice to know they weren't the walking dead or anything.

She snapped her attention back to the phone. *Phone. Brother. Jackson. Must call Jackson.* Wait a minute . . .

"Just like that?" she asked as her already overloaded mind jumped focus once again. "You're just going to let me call my police officer brother?"

"Are you trying to talk me out of it?" he asked, sounding amused as he dialed Jackson's cellphone number. *Okay, well, should this worry me?* she wondered. How the hell did he know her brother's cellphone number better than she did? "Just tell him you are safe with friends, not to worry about you, only that you needed a change of pace."

"Lie to him," she said with a frown. "Okay, I don't think you understand the whole dynamic between me and Jackson. First off, I suck at lying. I mean supersuck at it. And second, Jackson knows who all my friends are and he's going to have already tried to call all of them, I'm sure."

"So, you *are* trying to talk me out of it?"

"No. I just—"

"Listen. I want you to try something. Just . . . be still a moment. Try going quiet in your head . . . as if you were trying to go to sleep."

"Right now? Like this?" *With big, hunkalicious male arms around me?* Yeah. Not so much conducive to calm, if her jittery heart were anything to go by.

"Try it. Do that for sixty seconds and then hit send. What's the worst that can happen? He realizes you've been kidnapped and he tries to hunt you down. Which is exactly what he's doing right now, I assure you. Either way, he'll hear your voice, know you're still alive, and find a small piece of comfort in the knowledge."

Docia looked at him curiously. There was such a strange thread of thoughtfulness in his dissection of the situation. She had been picking up on that repeatedly since they'd come into contact. She looked back at the phone, at his hands surrounding hers, and invariably at the wicked red line down the back of his hand that indicated where, less than a couple of hours ago, he'd allowed himself to take a knife through his hand to keep her from being stabbed instead. How had he healed so much so quickly? Was it true what Cleo had said? Would *she* heal that quickly now? Did that explain how she had gone from near death in the ICU to walking around the way she was in just a matter of days?

"Shh," he said softly, whispering the sibilant sound against her right temple. "As if you were going to sleep. No thinking."

"Well, I don't know about you, but when I go to sleep I do nothing but think. You're sitting still and it's kinda boring just lying there, so really there's nothing else to do but—"

"Docia," he said, sounding pained in that way Jackson frequently did. "Just try."

Docia huffed at him, again, in much the way she did with her brother. They both could just bite her, she thought as she closed her eyes. As far as she was concerned, there were far too many bossy males in her life already. The last thing she needed was to add to the pack.

She realized that Cleo had disappeared. Strange, that. She'd balked against everything else Ram had tried to instruct her to do so far, but suddenly she had obeyed him. Well, Docia might have just lost all respect for the other woman. Until then, she'd found Cleo pretty damn refreshing and informative. In fact, she was the only one who'd told her a single blessed thing about what was going on.

Explanations will come. Take things one moment at a time, that serene voice in her head said softly. Calmingly. It was like listening to a gentle, warmly haunting piece of music. So beautiful. Was this the queen inside of her? *Explanations and changes will come when I am stronger. The transition from the Ether has taken much of my strength. But I will be here for you, as you need me. We will be here for each other. You will protect me, and I will protect you.*

Ram hit send and set the ringing phone against her ear.

"Who the hell is this?" Jackson barked angrily into the phone.

"Hello?"

"Christ almighty, Docia! . . . Docia? Docia answer me!"

"Jackson, I will if you give me a moment to speak," she heard herself saying calmly. There was a solid beat as her tone apparently took Jackson by surprise.

"Where are you? Are you okay? Did you manage to get away?"

"Jackson, I am fine. I'm not a child, you know. I'm sorry if I worried you. I just needed to get away. These two reporters cornered me in the street and I was upset. I figured the best thing was for me to get away and go somewhere quiet and safe."

"Where are you? I'm coming to get you *right now*!"

"I'm fine, Jackson. Perfectly safe, I assure you. I'm with old friends, Jacks. And don't take this the wrong way, but I don't want you to come get me. I don't want you to swoop in and try to take over. I'm fine. It's quiet here. I just want to relax, sleep, and heal. And I'll do that much better if I know you are back at work and getting on with your life. You don't need to babysit me."

"But . . . I . . ." Jackson was flabbergasted. "There was a dead body . . . and a witness. There was blood on your coat!"

"I don't know anything about a dead body or witness. As for blood, I pulled a stitch. It's fine. Nothing a butterfly bandage didn't help."

"Jesus Christ, Docia, you scared me half to death! I was sitting here thinking the worst!"

"Jackson, listen to me. I'm fine."

She heard him exhale long and hard.

"You should have called me," he said, sounding utterly petulant.

"I'm sorry. You're right. I won't do it again. I'll call you in a few hours."

"Whose phone is this? The number is blocked. Can I at least have a number to reach you at?"

"Jacks, I'll call you later," she said firmly. "Don't you trust me? Don't you believe me?"

There was a long pause.

"Of course I do," he said, sounding contrite. "But if you're safe, then that means someone else has come across foul play . . . and right on your damn street, Docia. So just . . . just be careful. I don't believe in coincidences, and after what happened to you . . ."

"I'll call you tonight. Stop worrying. I'll be just fine. I love you."

"Love you, too."

Docia snapped the phone shut and exhaled. She swayed suddenly as a terrible and painful headache rose up around her all at once.

"Jeez!" She shook her head, as if she could shake off the pain. "What the heck was that?"

What it was was a bit scary. She had listened to the whole exchange almost as if from inside her body while someone else took it over. She had contributed things to it, things from her memory and personality that had been needed to help her be as convincing as possible to her brother, but the smooth lies and explanations that had come so quickly and believably, those had come from something else, some other person inside of her. For all intents and purposes, she'd just been hijacked.

"That was your Bodywalker, Docia," Ram said softly near her ear, "and my queen."

CHAPTER SIX

Jackson hung up the phone and stared at it as if it might grow teeth. Then he looked up at Leo and the room full of people, including two detectives, Dr. Hotbody Anderson, and Lieutenant Avery Landon, who had also heard the phone conversation when he had immediately switched to speakerphone out of instinct. The more people who heard the conversation, the more brains involved, the more opportunities there would be to take notice of details that Jackson alone might miss. They hadn't had a chance to tap his phone yet in order to tape incoming calls, so it was the best they had in a pinch.

"Well, that's a relief," the junior detective said.

"Are you serious?" Jackson and Leo bit off at the same time.

"You heard the girl. I have to agree that she sounded fine," the senior detective said. "Sounds like she just wanted some time on her own. Clearly what happened on the street was completely unrelated to your sister."

"Clearly?" Jackson snapped. "Really? You know my sister so well that it was *perfectly* clear to you?"

"Sergeant Waverly . . . ," Dr. Bitch-Who-Had-Led-Him-to-Believe-His-Sister-Was-Dead started to say.

"You shut up," he snapped, pointing a finger—and all

the rest of himself, for that matter—in her face. "Every time you have something to say to or about me, the whole world goes to shit."

She bristled, of course. Who wouldn't with that much male aggressiveness pouring out at her?

"I wasn't the one on the banks of the Hudson River taking your sister's pulse," she said in hard, punctuated words. Then she disappointed him by drawing her temper back down. She was even more attractive when she was putting him in his place, and a sadistic side of him liked to see it. "And she did not sound stressed or as though she was lying. There were no markers I heard that would immediately cause concern for worry—"

"And how long, exactly, have you known my sister?" he demanded of her.

"Well, I—"

"Not at all, right? So how the hell do you know anything about it? You are just as clueless now as you were when you walked me into that office and told me she was dead." Okay, so maybe some small part of Jackson knew he was being irrational and completely unfair, but it was a *very* small part.

"I don't know how much I can possibly apologize for that, Sergeant Waverly! I was only acting on orders and information given to me by someone else." She took a calming breath. If Jackson weren't so worried about Docia right then, he'd have been utterly turned on. Oh, hell. Maybe he was anyway. She was standing up to him as though she weren't the least bit afraid of him, standing up for herself because she was right. In the end, Jackson knew it wasn't her fault that someone down the chain of command had screwed the pooch. But she was the one who had been in front of his face that day, and she was the one in front of his face right now. He just wasn't done dealing with her or the fallout of how he had felt in those horrible, horrible minutes. Two hundred and seven of them, to be precise. And now Docia was in danger again, her life hanging in the balance, and she was going in the opposite direction, trying to make everyone else there think she was fine when she most certainly was not fine.

"Fine," he growled at her. "Did you hear it? How many times she said it? 'I'm fine.' Everything's fine. If you knew a single damn thing about Docia, you'd know how she turns phrases, and she most certainly doesn't say she is 'fine,' and even if she did, she most certainly wouldn't repeat it eight times in a single conversation. Docia is one of those quirky people who likes to say the same thing in different ways instead of sounding like a repetitious parrot."

Marissa and the rest of the room, sans Leo, looked at him as if he were in serious need of an intervention. Perhaps a vacation. A long one. On some secluded farmhouse in the mountains staffed with lots of doctors and nurses.

"Leo, help me out here," he said through his teeth.

"Right as rain," Leo said softly, his rich voice starting low and slowly growing in power. "Super-duper. A-okay. Five by five. Happy as a pig in shit. All in one piece. Okie-dokie. Running on all four cylinders. Peachy keen. It's all good. Marvelous. Splendiferous. Super-frigging-califragilisticexspialidocious! *Do you. Get. The picture?*" He was staring down Landon. "She would have said 'safe as houses,' not just 'safe.' She would have been profuse in her apologies. And Docia . . . as weird as she is . . . she uses all of what we're telling you to cover up her awkwardness. To pretend she isn't as shy as she is. She's not assertive, she just throws a storm of words at people so that they think that she is. God. You guys have all eaten in her kitchen, helped her around the house . . . Christ. Farley, you even tried to date her once, didn't you?"

The junior detective paled as though someone had

sucked all the iron out of his blood. He stuttered, looking at Jackson.

"I—I . . . n-no, I—I w-w-w-w-w . . . no, Jackson. I never—"

"Relax, Farley," Jackson said forgivingly. The detective sighed in relief. Jackson smiled. "I'll kill you later."

"I . . . w-well, they have a—a point," Farley said in a choke of words. Jackson didn't care if he was switching sides to suck up to him in hopes he wouldn't kill him for trying to date Docia. Every cop there knew he had outright promised to kill any cop who tried to date his sister. He didn't want the life of a cop's wife for her. She deserved to be happy and safe and not worrying if her husband was going to come home at night. Bad enough she worried about him.

"I'm not going to devote time and resources to finding a woman who just said she doesn't want to be found," Landon said shortly.

"And a mutilated body just happened to show up on her street the same time she disappears?" Leo scoffed. "Screw this, Jacks. I'll help you find her, and I promise you it'll be twice as fast as anything these stiffs can manage." He grabbed for the midnight-blue leather jacket he'd slung off the corner of a nearby chair and marched out of the room without so much as looking back. Jackson was overwhelmed with the desperation that was bleeding into him.

"I'm asking for you to help me do this. You're my brothers. If *you* told me this, I'd take you at your word. I'd do whatever you needed to put your mind at rest. All I want to do is find her and lay eyes on her. If she turns up *fine* and I've wasted your time . . . I'll work the equipment cage for a week."

"Make it two and you have a deal," Landon said, the smirk in his eyes telling Jackson he probably would have helped him without the offer. But his boss could never get anyone to work the cage without bitching about it or fighting him tooth and nail, and he wasn't about to lose an advantage like this.

"I'll make it three if you find her in under an hour," Jackson countered.

"Two is sufficient. You have a dog to train, Waverly. So let's do this. Want to go at your witness again?" he asked, nodding his head in the direction of the man-child who was sitting at Jackson's desk pretending to be a cop and entertaining the rest of the bullpen with his antics.

"I have a better idea. Didn't the town mount traffic cameras on 9W? If these 'friends' of hers had wanted to get out of there fast, they would have driven north on 9W and through town toward I-87."

With the Esopous River on the west side and the Hudson on the east, Saugerties was literally cut off in any other direction, save north and south, and there was only one main drag to be found.

"Agreed. The only other way out of town is south on 9W and that would be way too slow for anyone in a hurry. Either way, north or south, they still have to pass a mounted camera. Of course, if they've hit I-87, and considering the time window they've had, they can now be anywhere between here and eighty miles from here."

"Let's get the feed from those cameras. Maybe it caught the car. And even if we can't figure it out from those cameras, every single exit off of I-87 is a toll exit and you can bet they went through one of them and got their picture taken."

Landon smiled and nodded.

"Looks like I'm going to have to rework the schedule for the next two weeks."

"So, I was wondering, how long have you been around? Bodywalkers, I mean," Docia asked carefully, trying to figure out if it was okay to ask questions. They had seemed very forthcoming so far, so why not? Didn't she have a right to ask about the thing that was inside her?

Oh jeez. She suddenly had a violent fear that something was going to come bursting out of her chest and fall wriggling to the floor. She laid a hand on her chest and tried to take soft, steady breaths. Nothing of what she had learned of them had suggested the Bodywalker inside her had any desire to leave. Or that it even could. By the sound of it, her hitchhiking Bodywalker was very much dependent on her. But what was the Blending? And . . . at some point was this strong, dominant female presence inside of her going to take her over completely?

"Thousands of years. We predate Christianity. By quite a bit," Ram said, resting a hand on the small of her back and guiding her a little deeper into the house. It was clear as they went that the Bodywalkers did not lack wealth. Or taste, for that matter. Every room they passed or entered was more magnificent than the last. There was a tremendous collection of antiques throughout. Conspicuously placed in the hall in a glass and gold-etched cabinet mounted on the wall was a beautiful Egyptian crook and flail, the accoutrements of Egyptian royalty. The cobalt-blue inlay and gold that striped them looked as perfect and splendid as it no doubt had when some distant pharaoh had handled them. If it had looked a little more worn, she would have wondered why it wasn't in a museum somewhere. But its clean condition told her it was most likely a replica and not the actual item.

At least, she *thought* . . .

"Thousands of years?" she echoed as he led her to a pair of enormous doors. It was as if they were made of obsidian stone, only in hundreds of crafted pieces, each shape laid into the door like a stained-glass window, where the individual pieces might not make much sense but a true artist could shape them into something beautiful that told a story. Here the image was of a sun, raised high in the upper right-hand corner of the right door, its strong rays streaming down across both heavy doors until they touched the bottom of the left-hand door.

The raised curves and shapes of the stone begged her fingers to touch them, but Ram was already pushing through the doors, their heavy size and weight seemingly nothing to him. She could see the flex of muscle in his forearms as he grabbed the long vertical handles, also made of black stone, two bands of gold on each at top and bottom and the metal mounts equally golden. It was clear they had cost a fortune to make, and as those doors swung open she quickly came to realize that they were a minor detail in comparison with the room they guarded.

It was what she imagined walking onto the set of *The Ten Commandments* might have felt like. That the theme was ancient Egyptian would have been obvious to any idiot. The quantity of stone in the room was astounding. Walls. Floors. Ceiling. Beams and columns. And every inch of every surface was either carved or painted with bright, colorful pictures laid out in rows and rows, around and around the room, reminiscent of Egyptian hieroglyphs, only it was hieroglyphs as if they had evolved over time with modern paints and medium, modern artist flairs and training. Docia stopped, feeling breathless and overwhelmed as the enormous room surrounded her. There was a fall of water at the far end directly across from the doors, but the water was running down a channel in the far wall and was diverted through a series of other channels down to the floor, where it ran all the way around the room in a collection of canals covered in beautifully etched frosted glass.

There wasn't a single surface she could see that wasn't covered or carved in a breathtaking pictoral impression or story.

"Thousands of years," she squeaked out. "Holy shit-cakes. You're from . . ." She pointed wordlessly at the walls.

"Ancient Egypt. In those ancient times, as you may know, we practiced complex burial ceremonies." He shut the door tightly behind them. That was when she noticed the infusion of soft, smoky musk and a layer of other scents. Golden burners hung in dozens of places, and several of them were smoking in delicate curls of fragrance. "We worshipped our pantheon of gods, had our deep belief in the nature of the afterlife and how best to bring the mortal world and our possessions with us. We were very material . . . and very arrogant to believe that we as mortals could in any way dictate to death.

"The Templars—our priests and priestesses—prepared our bodies and, presumably, our souls, for the afterlife. They promised us they knew how best to deliver us to the eternity we craved." Ram moved forward to the enormous statues set on either side of the stream, sandstone carvings of a distant and majestic pharaoh, one a king and the other a queen, both holding the crook and flail, one wearing the double crown of Egypt and the other wearing the striped nemes that marked them for the important beings they were. "The methods evolved and became more complex over time," Ram continued, reaching to pick up a small, carved jar resting at the feet of one of the statues. He held it up to her. "The use of canopic jars, herbs, and wraps were all methodical steps taken to prepare us for the afterlife. But . . ." He set the jar back down, his golden lashes dropping for a moment to hide the emotion that was racing through his equally golden eyes. "We were arrogant to think we could force the hand of death. In the end all we managed to do was deny ourselves the comfort of final peace. The mummification process, instead of preserving us for the afterlife, ended up tethering us to the mortal plane. We had stumbled on a way to live forever."

There was grimness in his tone, telling her that there was a great deal of regret attached to what so many others would consider an amazing gift.

"You never die? *Forever* forever?"

He laughed under his breath, the caustic sound full of painful irony.

"Oh, we die. Believe me. Over and over again, we die. I myself have experienced eleven deaths. Each was excruciating and devastating." He met her eyes, his pain radiating clearly within them. "And I remember every second of them as clearly as I recall my own name."

"Oh, my God. That . . . how horrible for you!" she said, feeling in prickling touches over every inch of her skin the anguish emanating off of him.

"It is even worse than you can imagine, Docia. You see, when we tethered ourselves to this world, we found ourselves in the Ether. It was quite by accident that we discovered the ability to choose a new human body like our queen chose you; choose a human willing to share their mortality with us. And yes, by entering a mortal, we make them incredibly strong and significantly extend their life span. Perks, as Cleo likes to call it. But there is . . . a downside to that."

He turned away a little and she saw him shrug his shoulders, as if shrugging away a terrible cloak of negativity.

"But this relationship is not about death, Docia. It's about a second chance at life. For you, the host . . . or the original, as we like to call you . . . and the Bodywalker within you, which we sometimes call a carbon."

"That's very modern of you. But . . . I'm trying to . . . I don't mean to sound callous, but only eleven lives between ancient Egyptian times and now? That seems like . . . well, kind of a small amount for such a vast time span."

"Every time we die we return to the Ether. Whether because of the trauma of death or just some arbitrary cosmic rule, we cannot leave the Ether immediately after being ejected from our last original. Firstly, death is a very weakening experience, to say the least. It takes quite some time to overcome the trauma of it."

She could tell he was fudging. She didn't know how. How could she know anything at all about this stranger? And yet listening to him talk about the ultimate of intimate experiences, a person's relationship with death, it was like seeing into him, straight to the core of him. And the heat in his gold eyes with their nimbus-edged pupils told her he was quite aware of that fact. He had chosen to bare these parts of himself to her. She knew he could just as easily have turned her over to Cleo and let her explain all the finer details about what it meant to be host to a Bodywalker, sparing himself this emotional nakedness.

But he was glossing over certain details. Docia knew from recent experience that dying was very much a private experience, and sometimes a horrific one. And doing so multiple times . . .

"But you will live your life pretty much exactly as you would have otherwise," he went on to say. "Although you will most likely outlive the rest of your family . . . and sometimes the Blending, the combining of what makes Docia unique and the soul, or Ka, of the Bodywalker, can cause significant changes in the host's life and personality to the point where . . . the people in your life might not be able to adapt to you. You might find you lose some of the relationships you hold dear at the moment. Humans can be very limiting like that. They have a hard time expanding their understanding of things they have grown comfortable with."

Docia found herself toying with the cuff of her sweater. She reached up and scratched her shoulder, too. She had noticed this morning that some kind of weird rash was evolving under her skin. She had not said anything for fear Jackson wouldn't let her leave the hospital. But all her fidgeting couldn't help her escape the dreadfulness of what Ram was trying to explain to her. Trying to brace her for. Her life would not be the same. She could even lose her friends. What of her family? What of Jackson? She didn't want to live a life without her beloved brother in it. Even the foreknowledge of outliving him made her heart ache.

"What is the point of living a long life if you can't keep the things that are most important with you?" she murmured.

Ram chuckled softly and moved to stand in front of her, reaching to touch the pad of a single finger under her chin and guiding her gaze up to his own.

"This was the most painful lesson we learned as our existence evolved into what it is now. But, I promise you, for all the hurt you might experience, there are other beautiful souls, fantastic people that you might otherwise have missed in a shorter life span that make it very much worthwhile. But as with all things, this opportunity is only what you make of it. What you and your carbon make of it together."

"I don't know anything about her. I don't know . . . what can you tell me about her? Did you know her? I mean, *do* you know her?"

She saw hesitation in his eyes, and again she had the feeling he was guarding information from her. Only this time she suspected a deception behind it that she had not felt the previous time. Strange that she should feel that way. She wasn't known for being all that intuitive when it came to others.

"It is not my place to tell you who she is. You have to find that out for yourself. Your relationship must be built together, based on your own experiences with each other, not based on the outside opinions of who she is."

"That's very diplomatic of you," she said, rolling her eyes. "I have some ideas, though. She seems very composed. Very calm. And I think she's sophisticated. She seemed so when I met her briefly, and I get a strong sense of it when I find I would normally be inclined to run around screaming with my hair on fire."

He grinned at that, a healthy flash of bright white teeth. It was a crooked sort of smile, half of his rugged face curling up with it much more strongly than the other. It was ridiculously endearing and made him ferociously handsome. But there was nothing boyish about it. There was too much eternity in his eyes and too much power and strength in his stance. He couldn't have affected boyishness in a million years. Or even a few thousand of them.

"Of course, I get the feeling she doesn't take any shit, either," Docia observed, trying to stay focused on the situation at hand. "So . . . you have two names. Everyone does? Which is very confusing."

"We tend to choose one of the two after the Blending . . . but as you can imagine, it is the human name we must use publicly in order to function efficiently in human society and not raise any questions. Things have gotten more difficult over time and as everything became automated and computerized. It's far easier to keep track of us and our unusual age spans than it used to be. Used to be all we had to do was move from one place to another and just lie about our ages. Now, that's not as easy. Of course, we have people among us who specialize in altering IDs and hacking into computer systems. Still, hack all you like, there's always a piece of paper somewhere that could give it all away. And then there is a matter of fingerprints and crossing the law. I'm sure you can grasp the complications that could arise there. Your society is very keen on documenting everything in triplicate."

"Says the man who calls himself a carbon. You've been through life quite a few times now. Done many of the same things, I imagine, over and over again. Like, do you have a wife? Did you have one before? Do you have children? This is a new life for you, but really, you'll never experience any firsts anymore, will you?"

The thought was a very sad one. She suddenly felt a heavy, exhaustive weight on her chest. She couldn't figure out if it was just an empathetic feeling or if the woman inside her was reacting to the truth of the observation.

"The world is always changing, always renewing itself in spellbinding ways. And when we die, we are secluded from it for a hundred years and know nothing of it when we are reborn and Blended with our new original. Only their familiarity with the ways of the world make it anything resembling bearable. It's part of the reason why it will take so long for your carbon to assimilate herself with you."

Docia gave off a wicked shudder. "Let's not use the word *assimilate,* shall we? I just had flashbacks to *Star Trek* and the Borg, and even now I'm imagining tubes, machinery, and lasers popping out of all my body parts." Again, she shuddered. It wasn't such a far-off concept, she was realizing. There might not be biomechanical bits and bobs involved, but for all intents and purposes, she realized, she was being assimilated into the strange cult of Bodywalkers. Her life, as he had been trying to explain, would never be the same again.

His perplexed expression told her that the pop culture reference had been lost on him. She wondered then how old he was, how long he had been in this particular original.

"How long since the last time you had to find a new original?" she asked him. It had to be relatively recent if he was lost on a *Star Trek: The Next Generation* reference. And shouldn't his original, Vincent, be able to identify the markers even if Ram couldn't? Of course, she was assuming everyone in the world knew about . . . "Captain Jean-Luc Picard or even Seven of Nine from the later series *Voyager*? What about Neo from *The Matrix*? Luke Skywalker? *Any* of this ringing a bell with you?"

"Vincent wasn't the type to dwell on items of pop culture. He and I are very similar in that we are very serious about very specific things and very rarely drift from that focus. Vincent and I have been Blended for thirty years now."

"So . . . you really are sixty-eight," she murmured.

"A great many of us are going to be emerging in the next short while," he informed her solemnly. "There was an incident about a century ago that decimated a large portion of the Bodywalker society."

"An incident?" she repeated just as carefully as he had. "As in a war?" she said intuitively with a sudden frown, her fingers lifting nervously to the fresh map of stitches on her head. "Since you are resistant to age and disease by the sound of it, it's the only thing outside of natural disaster that usually causes massive deaths."

"Yes. A war. Several of us died in the five years leading up to the last devastating battle, but most died in the final week. Our king and queen were among them."

"Queen." Her eyes suddenly expanded in her own head. "Wait a minute. There's a king? And I'm . . . you're expecting me to rule a whole bunch of—"

"He has not returned as yet, as far as we can tell. That is a worry for later," he instructed her. "And the woman inside of you knows everything you will need to know in order to fulfill the role of a queen. Try not to panic."

"Ha! Easy for you to say. You're the carbon here. You've done this before! I've only had one life and, to be really friggin' honest about it, I've kind of been screwing it up, professionally speaking."

"I doubt that very much," he said kindly. Well, maybe not kindly. He wasn't patronizing her. He honestly didn't think she was the professional retard that she was.

"Pfft. You haven't seen me try to type a letter," she mumbled. "So, what was this war about, anyway?"

He reached out to touch her elbow and indicated a stone chair, the arms and legs of which formed a curved X, the upper cup of the X holding a soft velvet cushion of shining gold. She sat down, settling in for what promised to be a good story. The understanding made her both a little excited and a little nauseated. What the hell had she gotten herself into?

"It was a civil war," he said simply. "A war as old as our people, and as old as time in almost all civilizations. The war between those in government seat, the Politic, and those in the temples, the Templars."

"Church and state," she said grimly. "We have a version of that problem, only . . . nothing we're on the brink of war for."

"You would be, in this instance, and on many occasions in the history of the world you were. But this isn't a matter of freedom to practice religion, for we Bodywalkers all believe in the same gods. And we have also learned to accept that our original halves may not always agree with us, if they have been brought up strongly otherwise. However, the very nature of learning of our existence often challenges many belief systems. And when they know what we know, when they see the Ether . . . minds often are changed."

Docia nodded, swallowing hard as she recalled her own experience. "I can see how that would be. But if the war isn't about intolerance, then what is it about?"

"The Politic does not seek to know the hearts and minds of its people, or to rule its beliefs. Quite the opposite. However, the priests and priestesses, the Templars, they believe it is they who should be ruling the Bodywalkers in all other matters, as well as in religion. They believe they who are closest to the gods would make the truest of statesmen. They do not acknowledge the laws of ascension as was agreed upon many thousands of years ago. They do not acknowledge the body Politic or the blood and spirit of the greatest king and queen ever to rule in Egypt."

"And they are?"

"Menes, the great unifier of Egypt. In his reign he was able to bring upper and lower Egypt together by both war and diplomacy, proving himself capable of both. And then there is Hatshepsut. It was rare for a woman to rule all of Egypt in her time, and yet she did so with strength and fortitude, also unifying many nations into Egypt, expanding trade routes that made the kingdom flourish. She was pharaoh in her own right, long before Cleopatra's time."

Docia narrowed her eyes on him, suddenly rising back to her feet as she took in his powerful build and bearing.

"Ram," she said softly. "Holy hell, is that short for *Ramses*?"

"Indeed it is," he said with a brusque nod.

"Umm . . . which one? There were . . ."

"The second. Ramses the Second." He shrugged, as if he hadn't built half the statuary in Egypt, most of it bearing his likeness. His original likeness. She stared at his face, wondering what he had looked like when he had been the original. She suddenly felt breathless and light-headed. She was standing in front of *Ramses the frickin' Second!*

"Hey, wait a minute . . . weren't you the one who resisted the whole freeing of the Hebrew slaves thing?"

He grimaced. "Details of that situation have been greatly . . . misrepresented," he said, sounding put-upon and pained.

"So, no locusts?"

"Docia, I am not interested in discussing the past. It is gone from the world now. There are more important things in the immediate present we should be focused on."

"What about the fiery hail?"

"Docia," he warned.

She bit her bottom lip to keep from giggling at his expense.

"Oh, c'mon. Did the Red Sea part even just a little bit?" She held up her thumb and forefinger an inch apart.

He huffed out a sigh and rubbed a pair of fingers against his right temple as if he had a headache. But despite her teasing and her rudimentary knowledge of Charlton Heston's portrayal of the past, she did know that history looked upon Ramses II as the greatest architect and the most significant pharaoh of all time.

And yet . . . she realized then that somewhere along the way he had ceded his authority to another . . . to someone he had looked on as more powerful and more worthy than he. There was a distinct lack of arrogance in an act like that. Provided it had been a peaceful and willing surrender. . . .

War. Was the war that had killed all those Bodywalkers a century ago still ongoing? The Bodywalkers had decimated themselves . . . had they learned anything from it?

"Are you still at war?" she asked, her voice sounding very small and squeaky.

"Things have been quiet . . . but the instigators of the last altercation, as far as we know, have not yet been resurrected into new originals. They died in tandem with our king and queen, who sacrificed themselves to see to it those Templars' influence and seditious voices were dragged back to the Ether. It was their hope that a hundred years of cooling their heels would calm them down a little . . . and would keep the unsuspecting human race safe for a while longer."

"Safe?" she echoed.

"Mmm." He frowned. "Part of the Templar belief is the subjugation of what they look on as the inferior human race, not to mention the subjugation of the originals who host them."

"Oh," she said, the word coming out meekly. She didn't need a lengthy explanation. She could well imagine what that meant. Docia put a hand to her stomach, rubbing it anxiously as nerves and fear clenched. A Bodywalker had the power to subjugate the soul of its original host.

"God, what the heck have I done? What in hell is inside of me?"

Ram didn't blame her for her anxiety. There was much to be worried about. The internal squabbles of Bodywalker politics were nothing compared with the malevolence of the other Nightwalkers lurking out there, the other breeds lashed down to the night like the Bodywalkers. There were creatures out there that would tear her apart as soon as they got a whiff of the Bodywalker inside of her.

But she was overwhelmed as it was. She hardly needed more horror stories, and as long as she remained in the compound she would be safe from those other threats, so he saw no need to burden her with it all at once. He wanted to give her a little time to adjust first.

He had held off touching her all this time, even though he'd had urges to do so in order to give her comfort or the strength of support. He was unable to reconcile the way she made him react on such a strangely visceral level. But if touching her was disturbing, *not* touching her was proving to be frustrating and painful. He turned away from her, paced a couple of steps, running a hand through the thick waves of his hair in a gesture habitual of Vincent far more than of Ram, a bit of minutia she would not be aware of.

You need to relax, he heard Vincent say in a rare aside as himself rather than the Blended voice they had long spoken with in thought and deed these past years. *She's just a girl.*

Not just a girl. A queen. She may have been just a girl before, but now she was Hatshepsut, the greatest queen of all time, a dominant, strident personality . . . and the eternal mate to his king, the one and only man he could have ever stomached ceding authority to. The man who deserved it based solely on his strength and wicked intellect. For as great as Ramses had been in his time, Menes had been greater. Ramses had existed and worked off the backbone of the dynasties before him that had forged the way. Menes had been the core of that backbone. She would see that one day very soon. And, just as she had many times before, she would fall in love with Menes for it.

Ram turned to say something to her, and Docia was there, so suddenly, beneath his chin, bumping against his body. He instinctively reached out a hand to steady her, drawing her close, though by accident or on purpose, he wasn't certain. Her hair brushed beneath his nose and he could smell her, a sandy sweetness of musky incense from the meditation room. She was overly warm, his hands burning once more as they slid over her back. He knew the sensation would last for hours after he let her go, just as it had last time, but he couldn't make himself lift his hands away from her. He couldn't seem to force himself to step back. Couldn't make himself understand that she was destined for another man and forbidden to him.

He couldn't do that because electricity began to thump through his body everywhere they connected. It tingled and sparkled along all the surfaces of his skin, almost ticklish at first, but it quickly evolved into something much less innocent, something deep and sinful . . . something that made his blood burn.

And he knew she felt it, too. He could tell by the delicate little gasp that erupted from her pillowy lips, by the warm blush that flew like wings up very fair cheeks, beneath what remained of her bruises. She looked up at him then, her mink-brown eyes widening.

"Who are you in there?" he asked with sudden, breathless heat. He knew who she was. But he had worked side by side with his queen over many ages, and never had he allowed himself to feel . . . never had he truly felt anything like what he was feeling whenever *this* woman drew close to him. *They had to be wrong*, he thought a bit wildly. He would never betray Menes or her in such ways! And so the demanding question burst out of him, and he found himself giving her a small, jolting shake . . . as if he could rattle her around a bit and rush her carbon to the surface.

Still he held her. Still his hands remained on her body, keeping her close up against himself. He did not step away. Did not turn free. Did nothing to reinforce the knowledge that she was forbidden to him.

"I'm Docia," she answered back at last. "I know you say I'm someone else, too, but I don't feel that so much yet. I feel like I'm still just Docia. Nothing has changed for me. I'm just *me*."

Even as she spoke, she absently scratched at her shoulder. He pressed his lips together and reached to hook a finger into the collar of her sweater. The soft knitted material gave easily, identifying her braless state as he exposed her shoulder and took note of a lack of a strap. He forced himself to ignore the onslaught of heated speculation that tidbit of knowledge threatened to provoke in him. The area of her upper scapula came into view, and the redness of it was distinct.

"This rash," he said quietly, "is the evolution of the ouroboros. The mark of the Bodywalkers."

"Mark? What *kind* of mark?" she demanded.

He reached up with his left forearm, catching the cuff of his shirt in his teeth as a means of pulling up the sleeve of his sweater, exposing the ouroboros tattooed on his forearm. The dual sinuous, elegant snakes were deeply entwined, the head of each snake devouring the tail of the other snake; around and around they went, in perpetuity, a never-ending cycle, the perfect symbol of the symbiotic Bodywalkers, whose lives could not exist without their hosts and whose hosts could not survive without their Bodywalkers' spirits. And as he turned his wrist, the tattoo glimmered with the iridescence of black scaling, as if they were very real. And if she watched long enough, she would realize that the snakes wrapped around the Egyptian dagger were actually in motion. The tattoo was a living thing on his body, a phenomenon exclusive to the Blending.

"I'm going to have a tattoo? A *snake* tattoo?" She didn't sound horrified. There were no delicate sensibilities being offended here, he realized immediately. It was pure fascination, and her mink eyes were warm with a seemingly secretive delight. "I always wanted a tattoo. I never had the guts. The needle scared the bejeezus out of me." She reached up to fondle her bare, irritated shoulder. "It will be visible with certain clothing. Tanks and camis and such," she noted.

"Do you wish to keep it hidden?" he asked, unable to keep from following her fingers over her skin with a couple of his own. She was so very warm, and it radiated with the permanence of the tattoos she spoke of into the pads of his fingertips.

"No. I don't see why. Yours is very beautiful." She then reached with both hands to touch his forearm, her fingers running through the light, crisp hairs, tracing the winding snakes. The active sensation of her touch on his skin was like the unexpected smack of a cold hand against a hot cheek. Not that she was cold. Far from it. Only that everything about it was sharp, unexpected, and shocking to his whole body. That one simple touch. He must have gripped hold of her at her waist, because she let out a surprised gasp. Knowing how strong he was and how fragile she was as yet, he pulled away sharply. Yet everything about the action felt wrong. It was like leaping out of the warmth of the fine, beautiful desert and plunging into the brutality of an icy, dangerous mountainside.

Then of all things, she blushed. Not because of some shyness that he could perceive, but because of this sense of rejection he felt emanating from her in a wave of tangible emotion, the power of it prickling all over his skin. She didn't want to feel this way, certainly not visibly, and he could see that struggle all over the awkward turn of her body as she tried to shelter her expression. It was the first indication he had that she was just as aware of or affected by the chemistry roiling between them as he was. He had thought that somehow it was all in his own head . . . that he was losing hold of the clarity of who he was. . . .

He took a breath, slow and deep, and tried to shake off those thoughts. He would not be one of those carbons who went mad, the dissolution of the self and core of who they were so faded over time that they became utterly lost. Just shallow copies of the greatness they once were. His original, Vincent, had come with a stunning fortitude and strength that powerfully reinforced everything that made Ram who he was, who he always had been. A king in his own right, in his time. He had once been powerful enough to choose any woman he wanted. None were off-limits to him.

None.

But this one was. Because he held his friendship and his loyalty with Menes dear, he could not betray either of them by looking sideways at his queen and mate. The sands of time had flowed over and over again, and *every single time* Hatshepsut and Menes had cleaved to each other with stunning devotion and need.

So much so that Hatshepsut's death a hundred years ago at the hands of seditious Templar traitors had devastated Menes, and Menes had thrown himself into death in order to follow her to the Ether, rather than forcing himself to live without her.

But this creature was not yet Hatshepsut. The queen was all but dormant inside of her, too weak to move. Perhaps too weak to observe. . . .

Ram lifted a hand to her, touching her head where her injuries showed worst, although not nearly as bad as when he'd found her a few hours earlier. But he ignored that sign of the Blending and let his touch skim back into her hair.

"What are you . . . ?"

But she already knew the answer. It was eager in her eyes and in the step forward she took, the way her chin lifted to present him with the opportunity of her mouth. He smiled for a moment, the expression hard on his face, feeling the bittersweetness of the moment.

This is what you choose to trade away your honor for? Vincent questioned inside of him.

It was. And if Vincent did not understand what drove Ram to touch his lips against hers, he quickly learned. Ram had suspected there would be something there, that an experience like no other was awaiting him, and it immediately crystallized for the two male essences sharing their single body. It was a brief touch, barely a kiss, but it was enough to make her draw her breath in sharp surprise. The sensation was all-powerful, a whippet of heat and electricity lashing away from the contact, scoring them both. She drew back with surprise, but he was having none of that. His hands shot to her upper arms, locking around them like steel manacles, holding her and dragging her forward again, this time for a deeper touch . . . a deeper kiss.

It was like unleashing a tempest. Something he of all people should understand, and yet he did not. Where it came from, he hardly knew, but suddenly there was thunderous sensation riding through him, shocking bolts of heat coursing through his veins. It was that instantaneous and that overwhelming. Thunder and lightning crashed outside of the house, shaking it from the rafters down, making her startle. He ignored it. He crushed her delicate mouth under his, squeezed her arms so tightly it was a wonder they didn't snap. But he quickly realized he must maintain his hold on her arms for all he was worth or his hands would find other things to do, find other flesh to hold.

And they had yet to touch tongues.

A situation he rectified a moment later. The moment it happened, the moment she parted sweet, shy lips to give him his way, it felt as though her whole body went limp against him, as if in a faint, but her moan of delight was lusty and vibrant and shook him to the very seat of his pounding heart. The souls inside him lit up like tinder as he kissed her deep and well. What was Vincent and what was the great Ramses were suddenly being pulled apart, so that for the first time since their Blending each could experience the moment as himself. It was a raw, humbling sensation, and it was all the more antagonistic for it. As they came together again, it was with like purpose . . .

We must have her.

Vincent led the way this time, loosening his grip on Docia's arms and putting his hands on her in other ways. Better ways. He caught the curve of her upper back and shoulders, fondling the shape of her through the pettable softness of her sweater. Within a few moments he was contemplating getting his hands on her ass when *her* hands suddenly made an appearance. He had no idea where they had been before that moment, but right then, as they smoothed their way up over the expanse of his chest, he felt the need to growl in response to the boiling sensation in his blood. Ramses was of like mind, it seemed, because the sound came to life, rumbling out of his chest and into her mouth. It must have sounded a bit daunting because she gasped a little and pulled back, taking the moment to suck in a few needed breaths.

She licked the sugar of their shared kisses off her lips, and he was instantly hard. Before that moment he'd been too stunned with feeling her on a spiritual level; raw lust had honestly not entered the picture. But now it was there, powerful and dominant, riding him with the violence of quolls in heat. Making him want to do the very same to her.

He jerked back from her, needing to breathe and clear his head, needing to get some sort of handle on the virulent, violent desire infecting him so thoroughly that he feared he wouldn't have control over what he was going to do next.

For all the pleasure of the moment, it was a sensation he did not like. For all the burn of his arousal, his heart still ruled, and it began to speak to him firmly and seriously.

She is weak and injured and not capable of the vigor we are seeking, the vigor we will need to satisfy us.

And then, a darker version of the same voice.

She is our queen. She belongs to another man. The man we call our closest friend.

Treason. What he had done would be considered an act of treason, not to mention a stone cold deception.

"I . . . ," he stammered.

No. He would not say he was sorry. He would not apologize for listening to his entwined souls, both of which had wanted her more than he had ever wanted a female before in any of his previous incarnations. He cursed aloud. He should be ashamed, yet he refused to be.

"I will not regret touching you," he rasped.

Then he pulled away from her, his movements jerky and awkward because she had gone so limp and was suddenly left to recover her own footing and strength. Surprise and confusion were written all over her; she tried to speak, but like him, she was too overwhelmed by what she had just experienced to put many words together.

"You have much to do," he said hoarsely. "You have enough complications to figure out without me adding to them."

She had another man about to step from the Ether, and when he did she would immediately fall in love with him, as she had done time and time again over the ages.

And if she didn't do so because of something he did, he would never forgive himself . . . and neither would Menes. And Menes's jealousy knew no bounds when it was warranted.

Thousands of years of friendship or no, Menes would kill him. And Ram had no doubt that Menes would find a way to keep him dead.

Ram let go of her, no longer able to touch her as his conscience pricked him with nauseating reality. He turned sharply on his heel and left her.

This would be the end of it, he vowed to himself. He had dared to taste the forbidden. He would never do so again.

CHAPTER SEVEN

Leo had never had patience for the law and their slow-assed way of doing things. Not that all cops were useless. Take Jackson—he didn't just write a paper report and push it off, eager to make it someone else's problem and responsibility. There was a reason Jackson had a perfect record in traffic court and an equally good one in criminal court when it came to remembering the details of the arrests he made. The regulars on his beat called him "the Nightmare" because of it. They would know that when they saw that K-9 car or heard Chico barking his ass off in pursuit of them that they were going down in a bad way. It was their choice whether they'd have holes in them or not before all was said and done, whether they were caused by bullets or a dog's teeth. Jackson had been fast-tracked for detective a long time ago, but that had been before Chico and the K-9 had come into his life. Becoming a detective had been put on hold because Jackson had found his passion in the K-9 unit. Leo knew Jackson could not bear the idea of leaving the field, leaving his partnership with Chico, to sit behind a desk and muddle through the more complex side of criminology.

But now Chico was dead, and Jackson had missed court for the first time in his career to sit by his sister's side as she struggled for her life. Docia meant everything to Jacks. She was all the family he had left, and vice versa, and it had been that way since their parents had died when Jacks was just turning eighteen. He had almost lost nine-year-old Docia to the system and had sworn never to let that happen or come close to happening again. He'd pulled it off, too. Not just pulled it off, but pulled it off famously. He had kept her housed, fed, and reasonably happy, all while going to school and the Academy.

But the truth was that Leo had had a lot to do with that. While Jacks was trying to make something of himself, Leo had been his . . . well, his marital partner, in a way. Leo had been in the service at the time, living off base and stationed at West Point. His apartment had been small, but it had been big enough for two men and one little girl. They'd made it work until Leo had gone off to join the Rangers and Jackson had come out the other side of the Academy.

And that was why Docia was the next best thing to a little sister in Leo's life. And *that* was why he wasn't about to let a bunch of cops natter around with their thumbs up their asses pretending to do something. All due respect to Jacks and all that, but the cops would have to follow rules and all that annoying shit. Leo . . . not so much. He was just glad that he had been in a professional lull when all of this had gone down. A week before Docia's accident, he'd been on assignment in Fallujah assassinating some jack-hole who'd been in desperate need of assassination. The gigs of child porn they'd found on his computer alone had made him feel pretty damn good about it. It was a bit sickening to know that deviants, psychos, and serial killers knew no cultural barriers. Not to mention drug lords, corrupt officials, and arms dealers.

That list could go on ad infinitum. Ad nauseam.

But hey. Jackson could fight the bad in the world his way, and Leo would fight it his way. And in Leo's reality, laws sometimes got in the way of doing the right thing.

Still, the evolution of his disdain for the legal process had been long and hard and nothing he was in the mood to think about. For all intents and purposes, his kid sister was out there and in the hands of some serious baddies. No one knew Docia the way he and Jackson did. No one. And frankly, he wasn't going to put any stock in a bunch of jag-off cops who were rolling their eyes and going through the motions just to satisfy Jackson's belief in the brotherhood.

He was Jackson's brother. In every way that mattered, and not just because they wore the same color uniform, for fuck's sake. They'd had each other's backs since high school . . . hell, they'd raised a child together!

Leo jammed the last bullet into his clip, then rolled his thumb over it to make sure it was in properly, all second nature and nothing about it distracting him from the thoughts burning through his brain. He wasn't hurt that Jackson was putting faith in others or anything like that. They had agreed a long time ago to disagree on the way things should and could get done most effectively. Jacks was a boy scout through and through, and that wasn't going to change. He didn't expect it to. Didn't often encourage it to.

Leo smacked the clip into the butt of his Desert Eagle, clicked it in, and then checked the sight. Along the spine of the gold-plated .44, he could see the three pumpkins he'd put on the fence in the distance. Sure, it was shiny and flashy and mostly a toy for armchair shooters or collectors, but damn, it was a fine gun. He had another, a Mark XIX with the ten-inch barrel in gunmetal gray strategically hidden in his house, his preference being to keep the Mark XIX with the six-inch barrel in the holster on his hip. The six-inch pulled faster and was less awkward in a clinch.

But, yeah, the gold had its uses, too.

"Whoa! Holy shit, Alvarez, where'd you get that thing?"

Leo ignored Ray Ray and squeezed the trigger. Rapidly. Three times.

One pumpkin after the other exploded, raining bits of rind and seed everywhere, reminiscent of the way a head full of brains might act on the other end of the armor-piercing hollow points. He turned and pointed the gun at Ray Ray, trying not to smile when the scrawny little crackhead squeaked and held his hand up in defense . . . as if that would do anything.

"Jesus Christ!" he yelped, drawing his knees in together like a four-year-old trying not to pee himself while waiting for the bathroom.

"Ray Ray," Leo said smoothly in greeting, lowering the gun with a smile. "You're late."

"I—I—I—," Ray Ray stammered.

"I could swear I said time was of the essence."

"But I—"

Leo leaned in and narrowed his eyes. "You're not about to give me some lame-ass excuse, are you? You know how I hate lame-ass excuses."

Ray Ray swallowed noisily, deciding silence was the better part of valor. It was probably one of the smartest things he had ever done. Not that Ray Ray was entirely stupid. Back when he'd gone just by Ray, he'd actually had a pretty good job and a very pretty family and a pretty decent life. Then one day he'd gotten the idea in his head to try a little crack to take the edge off his stress.

Fast-forward three years and now Ray Ray lived for his next smoke. The job, the pretty house, and the pretty family were gone. He was the poster boy for what drugs could do to Joe Average. But Leo had no sympathy for him. He believed men wrote their own destinies in life. They didn't deserve all this bleeding heart bullshit from all the little saviors running around trying to rescue them. In his opinion, they were lost causes until they were ready to rescue themselves.

"Ray Ray . . . ," he said, smiling and sounding magnanimously forgiving as he threw an arm around the other man's shoulders. "I'll forgive you for keeping me waiting if you"—he tapped the man on the chest with the barrel of the Eagle—"can give me just a little bit of information."

"Well, I—I'll try . . . ," Ray Ray stammered.

"Great! Now, a few days ago someone threw a girl off a bridge."

"The Bridge Girl!"

"Yes. The Bridge Girl." Leo rolled his eyes. It really was a lame moniker. The Saugerties news team needed a more creative mind at the helm. "Can you tell me why someone would want to throw a girl off a bridge?"

"Well . . . I don't know all the particulars," he hedged.

"I'll settle for rumors," Leo said, sounding highly put-upon. "Just give me what you've got. And before you say it . . . because with the mood I'm in it'll just piss me off . . . I won't give you money for information so you can go off and buy more of that poison you like to shovel into your lungs. I'll do you one better. The next time someone is in the mood to beat your scrawny ass, I'll take care of them for you. Okay?"

Ray Ray's face lit up. Clearly someone was always in the mood to beat his scrawny ass. Leo had suspected as much. Invariably, if you danced in the world of drugs, you crossed someone the wrong way. There was always someone somewhere ready to do violence against a junkie for whatever reason. And Leo had no problem removing that someone from the equation.

"Cuz there's this guy. He wants to kill me," Ray Ray said eagerly. "I swear, I didn't do *anything*! He thinks I stole something of his and sold it for drug money. But I didn't!"

"Sure, Ray Ray. Give me some good intel and I'll straighten it all out for you."

Ray Ray hesitated. *Interesting.* He was obviously highly motivated, what with death threats hanging over his head and the smell of discharged gunpowder oozing from the Eagle just about right under his nose. So why would he hesitate?

"Ray . . . ," Leo encouraged with a warning tone, like a mother scolding a wayward child.

"It's just that . . . these guys are bad, bad news," Ray explained. "Even a guy like you ought to think twice before mixing it up with them."

"And what do you know about a guy like me?" Leo quizzed archly. "You my best friend now, Ray? You know all about me, do you?"

"I—I—I—"

Leo rolled his eyes at the stammering. He wasn't making much progress, and time was ticking for Docia.

"How about you let me worry about myself, okay? Just tell me what you know while I'm still in the mood to keep this a friendly negotiation, as opposed to me squeezing the information out of you until you pop like a nasty little zit."

Ray Ray swallowed. He was probably asking himself why he'd even showed up . . . and then reminding himself that if he hadn't, Leo would have gone after him and would have been in a very bad mood when he found him.

And he always found him.

"There's this gang on the outside of town . . ."

Leo scoffed aloud. A gang in pastoral Saugerties?

"No, really," Ray insisted. "It's a house. Over by

Lake Katrine. There's a guy in charge and he gathers all kinds of . . . you know, criminals. He feeds them, gives them a place to stay. They mostly run a lot of drugs and stuff, but I've been hearing rumors of other things. Like, they're planning some kind of big score or something. Anyway, one of the guys was in one of the . . . umm . . . places I like to hang out."

"A crack house?" Leo supplied for him dryly.

"A hangout," Ray Ray hedged. "Anyway, he was drinking and stuff and started bragging about how one of his buddies was the one who pushed the—and I quote—'nosy little bitch off the bridge.' End quote. Apparently, she'd seen some paperwork she wasn't supposed to see and was suddenly considered a lot of trouble. A big risk. Big enough that the risk of pushing her off the bridge was considered more acceptable than letting her run around alive. And they watched her. All the time. Got her routine down cold. They fucked with her car, forcing her to walk to work. Then bam! Over the edge she went."

Leo had begun to tune Ray Ray out as the junkie got a little too enthusiastic about the story he'd been told. Leo felt sick to his stomach as he thought of Docia facing down that thunderous, scraping hunk of metal, leaping to what she thought was safety, only to have someone push her to what should have been her death. Leo had already gone to the bridge in search of clues; he'd looked over the edge and down into the angrily churning white water spewing through those rocks and realized it was a miracle she was alive. Between the impact of the rocks and drowning in the frigid water . . .

Leo and Ray Ray both jumped when the Eagle barked out a bullet. Leo had clenched his fist unthinkingly, squeezing the trigger and sending a bullet into the dirt at their feet. Ray Ray yelped and scuttled back, thinking the man with the gun had just tried to shoot him in the foot.

"What! I'm telling you what I know! The guy's name is George. He comes to the hangout just about every night. If you want to know more, just . . . just . . . do what you do! Come and get him!"

"I plan to," Leo muttered. The Eagle flew up to point at Ray Ray like a scolding finger. "But I swear to God, Ray Ray, if you tip him off . . ."

"I'm not stupid!" Ray Ray insisted.

"I'd argue otherwise," Leo said. "Give me the name of this guy you're having the misunderstanding with, Ray Ray. If your tip pans out, you won't have to worry about him anymore."

Ray Ray tried to feel heartened by the idea, but he was too worried about what would happen if Leo *didn't* get his man.

Odjit was drumming her fingers impatiently on the table, an annoying little quirk her original had that, despite her total dominance over it, managed to leak through when she was irritated, deep in thought, or agitated in some way. She supposed it could be worse. Some Templars fought constantly to subjugate the other soul inside them. Frankly, she considered those Templars to be weak. Humans were completely inferior. Templar Bodywalkers had evolved so far beyond the humans they had once been, their power extraordinary and their wisdom boundless. What was more, they had the will of the gods on their side. They were the most devout of all the Bodywalkers. And one day, one day when she had finally wrested control of the body Politic from the ever-present thorn in her side known as Menes, the false pharaoh in her people's perspective, the gods would find them glorious and Ra would finally, *finally* allow them to walk in the sun once more. She believed that with all her heart. It infuriated her that Menes and his people could not see the truth of it, that they stubbornly ignored their duty to the gods and refused to give the Templars the respect and reverence they were due.

Unfortunately, she had to admit that her power, while significant, and the combined power of her followers was not enough to reach her goal. What she needed was the power of the gods.

A god.

She needed to invoke Amun, to help him rise and gain his full power once more. He would unleash a righteous wrath on Menes and the Politic, would put them in their place at long last. The clarity of this plan had come to her as she had seethed in the Ether, recovering for a century from the brutal death she had suffered at the hands of the false king. Her only consolation had been that she had managed to kill his precious queen first.

And she would do so again. It was Menes's Achilles' heel. He was so pathetically devoted to his conceited bitch that his loss of her was unbearable to him. She took satisfaction in the understanding that Menes's grief last time had been so profound that he had ended his own life. It had been some kind of disgustingly romantic display, lying down beside the body of his beloved after he had ingested the only poison that could harm them: a liquefied solution of the fruit of the orange tree. The common juice that humans drank by the gallon so easily was deadly to the transformed physiology of a Bodywalker host. Some surmised that it had something to do with the amount of time in and intensity of exposure to the sun during the growth of the thing, although that didn't explain why other citrus fruits did not have the same effect. The Templars often dipped their weapons in the orange juice, and while not enough to kill an enemy outright, it would certainly incapacitate them for a long time . . . and agonizingly so.

Odjit couldn't help the little shiver that walked her spine. She had seen a man poisoned heavily by the stuff. The agony within him had been so excruciating that she had felt as though she could feel it with him. But Menes had taken such a large amount that there had been no time for pain to take root. Death came swiftly and fiercely with such overdoses.

She saw no sense or nobility in his cowardly escape from the mortal world. But regardless, Odjit knew his weakness and she planned to exploit it to the fullest extent.

And at the same time, she would retrieve the power she needed.

She lifted her drumming fingers in the air and snapped them, the sound echoing hard in the vacant, vaulted ceilings of the old abandoned church they were using as a temporary headquarters. Immediately, a young Templar acolyte appeared in the doorway. He stayed there, his head and eyes tilted downward in respect to her. Though she had summoned him, he knew he was not to approach her until she gave him permission.

"Fetch me Kamenwati," she instructed.

"Your pardon, mistress, but . . ." When the servile creature hesitated, she knew it was because he was afraid of angering her. It made her smile a little.

Toying with the spineless little fool, she barked out, "Well? Are you going to speak or just stand there blithering all day, wasting my time? Do you consider my time so worthless that I should spend it watching you trip over your tongue?"

"No, m-mistress," he stammered, color darkening the tips of his ears. "Master Kamen has been called to the rectory to settle a small matter of—"

Before he could finish, his mistress was brushing past

him, her hand pushing at his chest to force him back a step, allowing her to move through the doorway.

Kamen was frowning darkly at the two squabbling acolytes before him. He had been called to negotiate a truce between them, and frankly, the dustup surprised him. Everyone knew that Odjit had no patience for arguing or power plays among her people. And everyone feared the reprisals if they behaved otherwise. After all, in Odjit's mind there should be no power plays. She was the most powerful, and there was an end to it. Nothing else mattered, no one else was significant. As far as he was concerned, no one should dare think they were better than anyone else, because such thoughts of grandeur, she knew, could easily lead to other speculations that might one day force her to defend herself against a problem. There was no room for graspers in the hierarchy of the Templars.

That didn't mean it didn't exist. It just meant it was normally not *seen*.

"I rose to acolyte long before this . . . this reptile," one acolyte said contemptuously as he gestured toward the other man. "He should cede to my authority! Instead he disrespects me!"

The other acolyte seemed unconcerned by the accusation. He was leaning back against a wall with an air of relaxed ease, as though none of this mattered to him. It was exactly how the first man, Sheymun, should be acting. Albeit with a touch less obvious arrogance.

"Why shouldn't I disrespect a fool?" Lashtehp queried. "I have no more patience for a fool than our divine mistress would."

"How dare you!" Sheymun spluttered.

"Gentlemen, I have yet to understand what this issue is about," Kamen said wearily, his finger pressing at a tense muscle in his neck.

"It's simple. He ordered me to fill lamps with oil, as if

I were some kind of novitiate. I have more important things to do in service to our beloved mistress," Lashtehp said.

"That you do."

Every spine in the group stiffened as the voice of that beloved mistress resonated into the room. Kamenwati turned to look over his shoulder, watching her as she glided into the room. She was elegantly clothed and coiffed, as she always was. Far from the jeans and T-shirt type, she never allowed herself to be seen by her followers if she was anything less than spectacular in appearance. It wasn't that she was vain so much as it was her style and her wisdom in knowing that if she wanted to be perceived as a precious and valuable being, she had to appear to be exactly that.

She was tall this time around. Close to six feet, he estimated. But far more stunning than her height was the fiery brilliance of her red hair and the often cold depths of her nearly colorless blue eyes. He had never seen such a fair shade of blue. Or such fair skin. It was such a departure, really, from the originals she usually chose. Often she chose strong black females or an exotic one. But in all cases she chose a sexually charged body with voluptuous curves and mouthwatering sensuality. Kamen knew she did nothing by accident, and that choice was just as specific as the rest of them. The thinking, he knew, was that love and lust often went hand in hand with her male followers. With the females it was envy and awe, and no little amount of inadequacy, she wished to engender.

Kamen felt more than a little of that lust as she walked toward them with that leisurely, swinging gait. It was almost flirtatious. Playful. But he knew her too well. He knew that what lurked in her eyes was nothing so friendly or forgiving.

"Lash, were you not asked to retrieve something very

important for me?" she asked, placing distinct emphasis on the "very."

"Yes, mistress. I apologize. Your acolyte has waylaid me from my purpose." He gestured to the other acolyte with an upward-facing palm.

"I see."

Sheymun's complexion paled as the blood drained from his face. As long as it had been the more even-tempered Kamen managing the argument, he had not been afraid to bluster and throw his weight around. But now . . . now he knew there was nothing he could do to win this argument.

Arguments among Odjit's disciples never had victors.

She turned slightly, her cold, light eyes picking Sheymun apart in a single look of disdainful assessment. When she smiled, no one was fooled by its false warmth, no matter how beautiful it made her appear to be.

"So," she said as she moved closer to Sheymun, reaching out to brush her fingers over his shoulder, as if clearing it of a speck of dust. "You feel you have seniority over Lashtehp?"

"I—I . . ." He swallowed to try to control the stammer. "I only meant to say that I have far more experience since I have been your acolyte far longer than he has. The lamps were burning low, mistress, and I know how much you crave brightness and light."

It was true. Kamen sometimes thought she was absently trying to surround herself with a sense of the sun she could not otherwise touch. She demanded light and warmth on a constant, unwavering basis. When someone failed to see to it seamlessly, heads tended to roll. Kamen had to admire the acolyte for his attempt at manipulating the situation to his advantage by making it appear he had only had her best interests at heart.

"You are so kind and thoughtful," she told him in the softest of voices right before she bestowed a gentle kiss against his temple. Sheymun relaxed under the small gesture of affection. "But would it not be kinder to see to it peace was kept in my household at all times? You know how I dislike discord among my followers. It's bad enough I have to deal with the dissension of the Politic, but now I have to face dissension under my own roof?"

The intensity of her displeasure was seeping into her voice now, and with it the return of tension in Sheymun's body and fear in his eyes.

"P-please, mistress," he said hastily. "You must consider I was only trying to see to your comfort."

"*Must* I? Now you are telling *me* what *I* must do?" Her smile disappeared altogether, and the fire of her true fury leapt into her eyes. "You seek to give me commands? Perhaps you think you are Menes, now? You think, as he does, that you have the right to force your will upon mine?"

Sheymun tried to sputter out a protest . . . or perhaps a hasty apology. But in the next instant, his voice caught in his throat, his mouth gaping like a fish as sudden color rushed to shade his skin a bright pink . . . and then a more intense red. Odjit reached out to grab him by his chin just before blisters began to bubble up on his skin.

"No one will ever tell me what I must do," she hissed at him softly.

Kamen was certain the man would have screamed if his blood weren't suddenly boiling up into his throat. Steam began to rise from his body and the stench of cooking flesh filled the room. Sheymun collapsed at Odjit's feet.

Odjit turned away without even a hint of hesitation, dusting her hands together briefly.

"There now. The argument is settled. Now, Lashtehp, please continue with the task I set for you."

"But of course, divinity. I will retrieve what you want

with all due haste." The man smiled with a devilish sort of charm and bowed to his mistress with elegance and respect, if not the blithering devotion she received from most. That was perhaps why she sought him out as an aide so frequently. His capabilities as a tracker and hunter of Templar strays was another. Lashtehp never showed her anything but a gracious sort of devotion and dared to flirt with her when others were too terrified to do so. It catered to her femininity and the heart of the woman she longed to be but rarely had opportunity for. These were also the same reasons Kamen was so loyally nearest to her.

And it was why Kamen found himself wrestling with a fierce whip of jealousy. He took control of it quickly, however.

Odjit had far too much power over him already.

And with very good reason, he thought as he looked back at the bubbling mound of cooked flesh on the rectory floor.

Docia was taking a little bit of a personal inventory by the time Cleo came into the meditation room and found her a couple of hours later. She was trying to figure out if falling into the river had been the equivalent of falling down a sort of a rabbit hole, because while things were making a strange sort of sense, it all seemed far too fantastical to be real. After all, what did she have to go on, really? A near death experience and the rare sensation that some part of her was keeping a cooler head than she usually was capable of? Oh, and the word of Mr. Tall and Intense, who also happened to kiss like the devil hopped up on a lightning bolt.

Docia couldn't stop touching her mouth, her fingers prodding her lips as if somehow that would help conjure an explanation as to how all that sensation and electricity had suddenly come to life against her plain, normal little lips. She had to be going stark, raving bonkers, she eventually concluded. Odds were she was still in a hospital somewhere, suffering from severe brain damage.

Oh dear. Maybe she was in a coma. That had to be it. All of this was just what happened to brain-damaged people in a coma. They started living these outrageous fantasy lives. . . .

Yep. That had to be it. How else to explain being kissed in such a way that she had felt as though someone had taken those defibrillating paddles and slammed them against her chest, yelling, "*Clear!*" and pumping fifty thousand gigajolts of power into her to get her heart going. And man, it had worked, because her heart had gone. Totally gone. As in leapt out of her chest, wiggled to some kind of German trance/techno music, and then somehow found its way back to its usual meek little rhythms.

What the hell? How *the hell?*

"Docia?"

Docia's skeleton nearly leapt out of her body this time. She twisted around on the bench she had seated herself on to look up at Cleo. Seriously, were all of these people forty feet tall? If so, why would this supposedly great queen of all the Bodywalkers choose a body that barely reached five feet five?

"Jesus, Cleo, you scared the crap out of me!" She glared at the beautiful woman as much as she could while sitting and looking up at an Amazon. She had changed clothing, was wearing a gorgeous gown of deep velvety red that made her cerulean eyes seem to leap to life in her pretty face. Her hair, as black as night and straight as a pin, streaked down from a perfect center part, a pair of tiny braids at each temple the only exception as they pulled back and around like a thin braided crown circling her head. Even tinier strings of opalescent seed beads had been woven into those braids somehow, and now they made the braids look like a softly glowing halo.

"My apologies, my queen. I thought you might like to dress . . . we dress formally for dinner in the house."

"Dress formally . . . ," Docia echoed. "Well, I'm sorry to break it to ya, but when Tweedle Hot and Tweedle Hotter kidnapped me, they didn't exactly let me pack a bag. And even if they had, I doubt my budget's idea of a nice dress would even come close to . . ." She lifted a hand and indicated the breathtaking gown Cleo wore so perfectly. Of course, it was probably more the breathtaking body the gown was on that made it look so good. Docia tried to keep from touching her wounded head, but there was no hope for it. She felt like an ugly duckling in the shadow of the most magnificent swan *ever.*

Cleo smiled kindly at her. Docia would have read it as pity if not for the sparkle of mischief in her eyes.

"Come," she said, reaching to scoop up Docia's hands and pulling her to her feet. "You've had enough of the boring details of what it means to be host to a Bodywalker. It's far past time you get to learn about the fun stuff."

Fun stuff? That kiss had been pretty darn fun. Yep. Definitely fun. Until it had stopped and Ramses II, great pharaoh of ancient Egyptian history, had stopped it, pushed back from her, and looked at her as if she'd just told him she was a plague carrier.

Not fun. Definitely not fun.

Not knowing what else to do, she let the other woman lead her out of the meditation room. That's what she was calling it, anyway. All that burning incense and places to sit . . . running water . . . iconic statuary. It was like meditating inside a pyramid. Or what she'd always imagined a pyramid might look like on the inside.

Cleo brought her up a grand staircase, the cool green

marble like agate covered by a pristine white velveteen runner.

"God, that must be a bitch to clean," she muttered.

"I wouldn't know." Cleo laughed. "I suppose so, now that you make me think on it."

"Tell me, Cleo," Docia asked suddenly, "who were you? Before all of this, I mean. Who were you before your Bodywalker?"

Cleo stopped on the stair above Docia, turned a little, still holding her hand, and raised a questioning brow.

"Do you really need to ask me that question?" she queried. "My original's name is Desirée. My carbon's name is . . ."

She trailed off meaningfully, an obvious prompt.

"Holy. Crap. Nuh-uh. No way!"

Docia wanted to snatch her hand back and away.

Cleopatra! Cleopatra was touching her! Cleo-*freaking*-patra!

Cleo held tight to Docia's hand. In fact, she pulled it to her chest, between a pair of warm, generous breasts, so that Docia could feel her steady, sedate heartbeat.

"I am a long way from what history thinks it knows about me," she said softly. "And far more human than I was ever given credit for. It never occurred to anyone how young I was. How frightened I was. When the Ptolemy dynasty was moving its children around like crucial pieces on a chessboard, I could only bend my head and do as I was told. But then my hand was forced and I had no choice but to grow up very fast and become something cunning and powerful.

"But that was lifetimes ago, Docia dear. And things . . . are very different for me now."

There was such haunting sadness on the edges of that statement that Docia's heart ached a little. She immediately relaxed and forgot to be cowed by who Cleo had once been and reverted to liking her for who she appeared to be right then.

"So . . . you promised me fun things," she prompted the other woman.

Cleo smiled and began to hurry her up the stairs again.

"Sweet mother of God."

The room Cleo led her into was enormous, but it had to be in order to hold the ridiculously huge bed within it. It ran the far wall, about as wide as two king-size beds set side by side, a hand-carved series of posters and a headboard built right around two large windows, soaring high and wide. The occupant of the bed could lie under an open window in springtime, sleeping under the fresh breezes of the cool nights.

"I know. It's grotesque and divine all at once, isn't it? A pure display of wealth . . . of doing something just because you can. And I am so glad they did. This is one of my favorite houses."

"Houses?" Docia echoed the plural.

"Oh yes. There are many houses. There are areas in the world, we call them nexuses, that seem to attract us from the Ether. It is far more likely that a person in the area inside these nexuses will become a host to a Bodywalker."

"So . . . there's a nexus here? In tiny town, New York?" Docia asked with no small amount of awe. "Why here?"

Cleo smiled. "We don't know why. It just is. Just as we don't really know why mummification ended up tethering us to the Ether and the mortal world. It just did. And we only figured that out over much study and understanding that there is no Bodywalker who was not mummified."

"Sort of a negative proof?"

"Yes. But that's all boring, dusty details," she said,

waving the whole thing off. "Dinner is promptly at two. Let's get you a nice bath and something to wear."

Cleo snapped her fingers so hard and loud that Docia jumped. Jeez, she had to stop doing that! But honestly, could she blame herself? She dared anyone else to try to keep calm, cool, and collected in a situation like this.

The snap called forth a small young woman who appeared instantaneously from who the hell knew where. One minute she wasn't there, the next she was bowing her dark head.

"Mistress needs me?" she asked softly.

"You gotta be shitting me," Docia said, staring first at the girl and then hard at Cleo. "For real?"

"Docia, you are queen of all the Bodywalkers," Cleo reminded her, as if that explained everything. "That comes with certain . . . perks." She dropped long black lashes in a wink. "Like Miu here. She is your . . . personal assistant. She will help you with your schedule, will help organize your life, and is in charge of your personal beautician, your fashion consultant, and anything else that is required to give you a polished and current air of sophistication."

Docia gaped at her. Okay, shock aside, she had to admit it sounded pretty cool. Like celebrities. They had *people*. An entourage that followed them around, making them . . . perfect. Did that mean they were going to make her perfect? Lord. She really didn't think she could live up to perfect. Sure, she liked to play at being pretty with her pretty resurrected things, but . . .

"Come," Cleo said, hustling her deeper into the room, Miu adhered fast behind them. "Now, don't fret about size. That can all be adjusted. Miu is quite clever with a needle in a pinch, and in the future, everything will be in your exact size, of course. At present the best we could do was maintain an estimation of what would suit our queen."

She threw open a set of double doors and lights blazed instantly to life.

"Holy guacamole," Docia gasped. "It's a store!"

More or less, it was a women's boutique. Dresses hanging on cedar racks on the right side, every length of skirt imaginable. On the right were pants, shorts, skirts, and suits. Dead ahead were shirts and blouses. There were tables, glass cases, sporting rows of things like watches, jewelry, earrings, hair bands, and combs . . . some so intricate that she immediately fell into a gasping fool.

"Oh, how pretty this one is! Oh, and this one!"

For the first time, she really *felt* the lack of hair on her head. Funny how she hadn't been self-conscious the entire time the big and beautiful Ram/Vincent was staring at her or pawing at her. Very much the opposite. But mother-of-pearl-inlaid combs, pretty bands with cameos at the crest . . . even simple sparkling ties for an elegant ponytail . . . none of which she could use until her hair grew back . . . suddenly made her feel insecure. She absently fondled the straggling length of hair that remained on the side of her head and must have been pouting because Cleo patted her on the shoulder and led her forward. Somehow a remote had appeared in her hand, very likely the work of Miss Miu, and she pointed it at the wall of shirts and blouses. There was a hum and a click, and the wall split apart and swung open.

Okay, so was it really inappropriate to think of the parting of the Red Sea? Seriously, what with the whole Egyptian theme going on, did they expect she could resist . . . ?

But if the Red Sea had parted, it would have been full of dead fish flopping on the floor, rank-smelling seaweed, and maybe a few sunken ships gone awry of

Mother Nature. But even if they had been Spanish galleons, they could never have held such treasure as this!

"Shoes! Oh!" And purses. Clutches of every color imaginable. Fabrics, beads . . . each glimmered more prettily than the last, and honestly, she thought she was going to cry. Some were encased in glass to protect their preciousness; many of the bags were as well.

"Chanel. Gucci! Holy merde, that's Louis Vuitton!" And there were so many Aisling Avery designs, easily identified by the cheeky little pink snake on the sole of a shoe or hanging off a ring on the bags. Along the farthest wall were wraps, jackets, shawls . . . and a little circular staircase in the corner led up to the next level, which had more of everything. A center cabinet had drawers full of gloves, stockings, and all the other unmentionables.

She reached out to pick up a shoe, unable to help herself in spite of her shaking hands and the feeling that she'd walked into a vault full of precious gems. She had to look inside. She couldn't help it.

"Oh . . ." She exhaled dejectedly. "It's not my size."

"Don't worry. Others will be. There is a large variety in anticipation of whatever type of original our queen might choose," Cleo assured her.

"This is by far the most orgasmic closet in the universe," Docia said.

"You ought to see the one at the main house. This is merely a selection from the stock array that is kept for any Bodywalker female that might travel this way and stay. Our safe houses are prepared for all instances."

"So there are other houses just like this all over the place?"

"Nexuses, remember?"

"How many nexuses are there?"

"Mmm . . ." Cleo tilted her head, tapping a finger to her chin as if she were doing a mental count in her head.

"I believe there's somewhere in the neighborhood of thirty."

"Like . . . where are these nexuses?"

"All forty of them?"

"Umm . . ."

"I don't think I could remember all fifty . . . ," Cleo said, trailing off.

"I'll settle for the most important ones," Docia said weakly as Cleo's number seemed to jump with every sentence. Cleo either was completely oblivious to it or was pretending to be an airhead to suit her purposes.

"Cairo is a key position. Venice. Fiji. Carnaby Street, London. There's one in San Francisco, one in the French Quarter in New Orleans. A little town just north of Montreal, Canada. Honestly, I can't list all one hundred of them off the top of my head. But the most important one for you is going to be the one in New Mexico. They call it the Land of Enchantment, did you know that? Isn't that funny? If they only knew. It's home to one of the busiest and most powerful of the nexuses. And also the seat of our government. The desert sands and their towering rock formations . . . there in their raw form feel much like home to us."

"You know, this is a bit overwhelming, but I think I'm beginning to adjust." She waved the shoe under Cleo's nose. "Apparently I can be bribed!"

Cleo chuckled. "I know, right? I have to admit, when we were first Blending, this was the first commonality Desirée and Cleopatra found with each other. Fashion. Shopping. Beauty. The pursuit of all of it. Vain, perhaps, but we find it an excellent grounding point to help us make up over arguments."

"Arguments? You . . . argue with yourself? Selves? I mean . . . ," Docia faltered, not yet sure she understood what she was talking about.

"The Blending is like . . . two voices singing in beautiful and perfect harmonization. It feels and sounds true and delightful, a single note of beauty made by two separate beings. But that harmony isn't always perfect," Cleo said with a shrug. "Desirée and I are like . . . the very best of friends. Very much of one mind on most things, if you'll pardon the pun. But occasionally we will argue when we see things differently." Again, she waved away the topic of herself as if it were a pesky fly in her face. "Enough of that. We should dress."

"Isn't it a little late for dinner?" Docia asked.

Cleo put down the beaded clutch she had been eyeballing and looked at Docia with surprise.

"Hasn't anyone explained to you . . . ?" Cleo didn't bite her lip the way Docia did when something was troubling her, but Docia could sense the tension suddenly rolling off her. Of course, that just made Docia ten different kinds of anxious. "We Bodywalkers are . . . nocturnal," Cleo supplied gently. "We live our lives in the darkness of night and sleep in the daytime."

"You . . . you mean, like a *vampire*?" Docia asked, her voice hitching a little.

"Like a Nightwalker," Cleo corrected matter-of-factly. "A species of creature that prefers the darkness over daylight . . . for many different reasons. Mainly because . . ." There she went, not biting her lip again. No doubt she was trying to figure out how to not overwhelm her. Docia could have let her off the hook by telling her it was too damn late. "Let's just say, for now, that daylight causes us significant difficulties. There are those who say it is Ra's punishment, and that we angered him by thinking we could live forever. Because of that we cannot walk in Ra's light. Suffice it to say, the effect is something you want to avoid. Right now you are not as susceptible because you are not fully Blended, but it will still affect you to some degree. More specifically, it will affect Hatshepsut."

"Will it kill her?"

"No," Cleo said sharply. "But it could drive her insane given enough time. And believe me, the last thing you want is to be host to an insane Bodywalker."

CHAPTER EIGHT

Ram was lurking in the doorway of the queen's suite, eavesdropping on everything Cleo was telling her. Not that he didn't trust the oracle. He did. Mostly. Desirée had a sound head for the most part, and so did Cleo. But they both had a streak for mischief a mile wide and loved to take any opportunity to give him, Asikri, and any other highly placed male in the government pantheon a bit of trouble now and then.

However, it seemed she was being genuinely kind to the new queen of the Bodywalkers.

When he had sent Cleo in to Docia, he had realized all of this might come more easily to Docia if it was delivered by a woman's touch.

And much easier on you.

On that, he and Vincent were in complete agreement, as they usually were about most things. Vincent had been just as floored by the feel of Docia in his arms as Ram had been. He was just as stunned and at a loss as he was. They had been rocked to their core, neither understanding why or how. Ram had been advisor to Menes for thousands of years, by his side at every incarnation. He had protected and cared for Menes's beloved queen, hunted for her, and brought her to Menes every time she was reborn. Every time he had put her hand in his and handed her up to his pharaoh, giving her away to him with ease and pride in his success.

And never once in all his many years of touching her, dancing with her, handing her up and taking her down from conveyances or beasts of burden . . . never once had he felt the rocketing sensation of heat and desire that he had come to feel every time Docia touched him.

True, every original brought something new and different to the carbon it hosted, and it was because of that that they were an ever-evolving species and every incarnation, every regeneration, made them something a little bit more . . . or even a little bit less . . . than they used to be.

But the one constant in their universe had always been thus:

Menes loved Hatshepsut. Hatshepsut loved Menes. His soul was devoted to hers, and hers was devoted to his. Theirs was a love like no other in the history of man or time. It had transcended death over and over again. It was the one thing the Bodywalkers could count on never changing. It was the one thing that gave them enduring faith in their king and their queen. It was the one thing that kept them coming out of the Ether again and again. For they all wished to have what Menes and Hatshepsut had. They all hoped to one day find what their king and queen had found. What had withstood the test of time.

So when he had kissed her earlier, things had shattered within him in ways he could not explain. He had broken faith and trust with Menes. He had accosted his queen. He felt as though he had somehow tainted that perfection between Menes and Hatshepsut. It felt as though he had just destroyed his every ideal.

And yet deep inside of him there was this powerful, insidious force that seethed with the need to feel her again. It wanted her so desperately and would not listen to his harsh internal lectures about how she was forbidden to him and any other man save Menes.

Perhaps it was because she was so much more Docia than she was Hatshepsut right then. It was not his queen, but this fragile young original that had stirred his body and his soul. But that was splitting hairs, fabricating excuses. Only death would cleave Docia from his queen . . . and that made her forever and always Menes's. Menes had all but gone mad with grief the last time he had lost his beloved queen. Ram dreaded to think what would happen if he ever learned that she had been touched intimately by another. By his most trusted friend.

You must close yourself off to her forever.

But how was he to do that when she would be there every single minute of every long day that he lived and served his pharaohs?

And that was when she screamed. Screamed as though Bodywalker and mortal were being ripped apart. As though fear itself had been born in her heart. He was in the closet and by her side in a heartbeat, preternatural strength making it an action that took all of an instant. Thunder crashed against the house in a sudden violent percussion, the black beyond the window flashing a brief bright white as lightning chased back the darkness.

He was there, reflected in the mirror she had been staring at in horror only a second before she'd kicked it over, sending it crashing into pieces on the floor. The instant she felt him she threw herself against his chest, seeking comfort from the only familiar thing she knew in a world rife with unfamiliar things. He thought nothing of wrapping her in his arms in comfort, hushing her with gentle sounds against her forehead as he cupped her head and pressed her face to his chest. Her hands were gripping him against his back, trying to lock on the broad muscles she found there, but he was holding her so tightly that they had flexed into hard planes of unyielding flesh. Eventually she just fisted her hands and pressed them against him.

"No! No! I can't do this!" she wailed, her voice muffled against him. "I can't be her! I just can't!"

He knew what had upset her. Until she Blended fully with the queen, she would see only Hatshepsut's reflection in any mirror or reflective surface. At least, the way Hatshepsut had looked in the prime of her original life. He had barely caught a glimpse of black braided, beaded hair and brightly painted eyes before the mirror had fallen. But he didn't need to see it to know how beautiful she had been in her time. He had seen that reflection time and again over many generations before she had fully Blended with her host. But it wasn't that face he wanted to see. It wasn't those eyes he yearned for.

He touched her chin and pulled her face up, fighting as she resisted him, her fear still palpable. But eventually she gave in and looked up at him, her tear-washed mink-colored eyes so painfully beautiful to him.

"Do not be afraid," he breathed over her wet face, drawing on unknown strength to keep from kissing her tears away, even though that was all he wanted to do. But Cleo was there, watching anxiously. He could not take such liberties in front of a witness. He could not take such liberties at all.

"I can't be a queen! I don't know how! I like me just the way I am!"

"Were you just the way you were, you would be dead."

It was a harsh thing to say, but he delivered it in a gentle voice. Still, she jerked back as if he had slapped her in the face. In a way, he had. It made her sobs catch in her throat, and he could tell by the look in her eyes that she wanted to hate him right then.

Perhaps that would be all for the better, he thought.

But he had not overestimated her intelligence and logic. She sniffed hard, her body hiccuping in little jerks as she held on to those little sobs.

"I—I would have," she agreed after a long minute. "I suppose you think I am very ungrateful," she said, her words still hitching on her awkward breaths.

"I think you forget that everyone in this room has gone through exactly what you are going through," he said gently. "Do you think Vincent was thrilled to take on so much baggage? He was a professional soldier, born to live and die as a navy SEAL. Then I come along and screw up a perfectly heroic, noble death, telling him I'm the right-hand man to a king. He balked a great deal at first. Almost dangerously so."

"But you changed his mind?"

"Actually . . . Vincent has a very strong grasp on concepts like duty and honor. It wasn't much of a stretch for us to find common ground in that."

"Okay. Right." She took a breath. "I made a deal, after all, didn't I? I can't renege because it's not always comfortable for me. I came back for a reason."

"And that reason was?"

"Well, for a lot of reasons. I just . . . I just wasn't finished yet," she said. "And I couldn't let my brother deal with my death on top of all the other deaths he's had to deal with. His family . . . *our* family has all died, and we're all that's left. Just me and him."

That made Ram frown.

"You're saying all your family is dead, except you and your brother?"

"Yes."

"Shit," Ram muttered.

That got her immediate attention.

"What?"

"Well, let's just say if it were me and I was a cop

whose sister was the only loved one left in my life . . . I wouldn't take a phone call as proof positive that everything was okay."

"Well, he can't find me here. He doesn't even know where here is," she said hastily, reaching to take hold of his hand. "Seriously, if I say I'm okay, Jackson will listen to me. He knows I don't lie to him."

"Jackson will think you are being coerced. Or forced. Or that it was some kind of a fake. He won't be satisfied until he lays eyes on you."

And he could tell by the way she bit her lip and the worry creasing her forehead that he was right.

"So what do we do?"

Good question. It wasn't as though he could just let her go. There were too many things out there dying to get their hands on her. If they got hold of her in this vulnerable stage, there was no telling what they might do to her.

Actually, that wasn't true. He knew exactly what they would do to her.

Marissa sat at her desk, tapping a pencil anxiously. It was very late at night and there was no logical reason for her to be sitting in her office, sneaking peeks out the glass in her door at the bullpen, where Jackson Waverly and a small contingent of cops were poring over hundreds of camera shots of cars going through the tolls at estimated time slots, looking for a black Lincoln SUV.

Marissa knew she was pretty much the designated asshole in the station. She was there reminding them all that they had *feelings*, something that most of these alpha males and type A females had no interest in being reminded of. But when bad things happened, they were forced to do the dance with her, in *their* minds kowtowing to her and kissing her ass and trying to look as normal and healed as they possibly could so she would sign off on them going back to work.

But honestly, she could care less about having her ass kissed. She could care even less than that about them treating her like an idiot and making fun of her on a regular basis. She hadn't taken this job because she wanted to be liked. She had taken it so she could be on their side. So she could help those who were out there every day trying to help everybody else. Bitch and moan as much as they wanted, they needed her. A lot. And often. It cracked her up sometimes the way they would sneak into her office as if dodging a hail of bullets, pulling the shade so they wouldn't be seen, as if they were in some kind of cloak-and-dagger detective novel. But that was all right, too. She didn't mind that they didn't want to be caught dead in her office. All that mattered to her was that they came. And over time she had developed some pretty good relationships with these guys. They'd knock her in public, tease her mercilessly to her face, and when she was a good sport about it, she won them over little by little.

And then she had to do something stupid and irresponsible like tell Jackson Waverly that his sister was stone cold dead before making sure someone triple-checked the facts. But she had taken that phone call and her stomach had sunk into her heels, the memory of his mandatory visits with her washing over her. He had felt the loss of Chico so deeply. Though he had never truly exposed himself to her emotionally, he had talked about it, about the loss and the emptiness, but always in that calm, controlled tone of voice he used. She had been fine with that. At least he was talking. She understood that Jackson's feelings for Chico had been intensely private, something he shared just with himself, his dog, and maybe his Creator.

Oh. And his sister. Marissa had known without a

doubt that he had shown everything worth showing to his sister. Marissa had been with the SPD only a year and a half, but she still remembered that the first welcoming smile and attitude she'd ever had was from Docia Waverly. She'd been in the bullpen one day, surrounded by a crowd of cops about to change shifts, all laughing riotously as they made plans for some kind of barbecue Jackson was hosting. Then Docia had looked up, caught her eye, and invited her to come, too.

She hadn't gone, but the invitation had meant a great deal. She had waited until one of the actual officers had deemed her worthy of inviting, and she had gone to that one, showing them that she was more than just an annoying rubber stamp they had to get past in order to get back on the street.

And now all those months of carefully pulling down walls between her and these officers had been flushed down the toilet. Because she had just been doing her job based on really crappy information. Now Jackson was just shy of tying her to a stake and striking a match. And she was so upset about it, for some reason, that she was actually in her office lurking. *Lurking!* Seriously? He was bound to get over it eventually, wasn't he? She would just do what she had done before. She would do her job and wait patiently for everyone to come around.

Again.

Marissa groaned, dropping her forehead onto her folded hands. She honestly didn't have it in her to walk on eggshells for another eighteen months as she tried to get these guys to respect her. To like her. She could live without the liking her part. Maybe. But the respect was important. She couldn't do her job without it. If they all treated her the way Jackson Waverly was treating her at the moment, then none of them would come to her when they needed to. And these guys really, *really* had to have somewhere to go when they needed to.

Screw it. She wasn't going to sit there crying in her cold coffee. Hiding in her office. She was going to grab this bull by the horns, aka one Jackson Waverly, and convince him to stop blaming her for what was admittedly a harsh mistake. The only way she was going to do that was by hovering over him and helping him look for Docia. Even if it pissed him off more. She had to help him somehow in the hope that it would balance the scales a little in his head and he would leave off thinking about siccing his new dog on her. She didn't need his adoration or anything. As long as he moved on to civil, she would be all right with that.

She grabbed her cup of cold coffee, dumped it into her ficus, offering a hasty apology to the poor thing, and with a quick wriggle to set her wrinkled skirt straight on her hips, she moved out into the bullpen.

Strategically, the coffeepot was right across from Jackson's desk. It allowed her to come up close to them and listen and peer at their progress as they all leaned over Jackson's computer monitor, obviously in anticipation of an immediate result. Yes! Luck was on her side. The coffeepot was empty, giving her another reason to linger as she slowly prepared the coffee and waited for it to brew.

Then she had an epiphany.

"You know, if your guys are smart, they're going to figure out that you'll be doing this," she said before considering that they'd just spent hours on this little project. When several pairs of eyes narrowed on her, and one set outright glared at her hard enough to make her hair singe, she tried to quickly finish her thought.

"They would have avoided the obvious cameras, but they didn't. They went right through the 9W camera, let you get a good look at them, and went right through the toll camera, heading south. . . . Well, what if it was on purpose? I mean, you have to assume they know you're a cop, right? I mean, if they know anything about your sister, that is."

Stares.

"Instead of being cops thinking like criminals, why not be criminals thinking like cops?"

It didn't surprise her that Jackson was the first to let light dawn. She could see it in his eyes.

"The turnabouts. They went through one of the 'Officials Only' turnabouts after getting on the south toll road and went in the other direction! We should be looking at the north booth footage as well in case they used one of the turnabouts."

"I'll get everything from here to Albany to start. I doubt they'd have time to get much farther than that if they had to go to the south turnabout first, then head back," said one of the detectives, the young one. Now that was a dynamic she found amusing. Here was this cop, detective grade, and he was eager to make an impression on Waverly, who for all intents and purposes was still just a uniform.

But it didn't surprise her that many members of the SPD saw Jackson as more than a uniform. He and Chico had had all of their backs at one point or another. When it came to hunting bad men in the pitch-black woods of the leading edge of the Catskills, a well-trained team like Waverly and his dog had meant everything to them.

The other two cops hanging around Waverly, including Avery Landon, took the opportunity to stretch their legs, leaving Jackson alone with the footage he'd been rifling through and Marissa, who was still hovering over the coffeepot.

"Little late for that, isn't it?" he said, nodding to the caffeinated brew dripping with agonizing slowness into the pot. "In fact, why are you still here?" he wanted to know, narrowing his eyes on her. It wasn't suspicious so much as the look of a man trying to solve a puzzle.

The concentrated, dogged look that had been on his face for hours now.

"Just getting some work done. Usually it's not so populated this time of night and I can catch up on my notes in peace," she lied, smooth as glass.

Well, perhaps not all that smooth, because he didn't look very convinced. But she couldn't go by the jaundiced eye he was using on her since he'd been looking at her sideways for days now.

She suddenly wished the cranky old coffeepot would quit all its spitting and gurgling and just go about the business of producing coffee already. It was one thing to deal with an angry Jackson Waverly when there was a crowd of law-abiding cops in the room and quite another to deal with the still-furious officer one to one.

"So what made you think of the turnabouts?" he asked her abruptly.

"The problem with a lot of beat cops is they spend their days coloring in the lines. Adhering to laws and seeing to it that others do the same. But undercovers have to do just the opposite in a way. Figure out how to stay law-abiding while pulling off the outside appearance of a criminal. I remembered that once a UC cop said to me that it's not the stupid criminals you have to be afraid of. That regular cops mostly deal with the stupid criminals. But the smart ones . . . those are the scary ones. Though in the end their hubris tends to get the best of them. But before that happens, a lot of damage can be done. I just thought, if these guys are smarter than the average criminal, they will figure out how to deceive you. They probably planned how they were going to take your sister long before she stepped foot outside of the hospital."

"But that doesn't wash," Jackson said, leaning forward in his chair toward her, making the fabric of his shirt pull taut across the expansive width of his shoulders. Marissa pretended not to notice and quickly turned to splash coffee into her cup. The glass pot clattered against the ceramic cup when her hand shook a little.

She was *not* noticing how well built he was. *Na-uh.* Just like she'd never noticed how fine an ass he had. Nope. Never. She must have heard about it through office gossip, otherwise how would she even know his ass was finer than fine ever could be? Yeah. That was it.

"How would a criminal smart enough to evade detection like this be stupid enough to make a spectacle of shoving a girl off a bridge? Everything about it screams cheesy, Cro-Magnon thinking."

She had considered that. "I don't know." She shrugged. "Maybe it's two different criminals?"

One of Jackson's brows lifted suddenly. He straightened in his seat. "But what are the odds that two different scumbags are after my little sister all at the same time? I mean, the worst she's ever done in her life is jaywalk."

"As far as you know, anyway," she countered. Damn. Why didn't she just keep her mouth shut? He was glaring at her again.

"My sister shares everything with me," he barked at her. "And she's as straight as a goddamn arrow."

"Everything?" she asked archly. After all, if she was in for a penny . . . "So, you know who she slept with last week? You know if she sleeps in her undies or without? Or what size her fat jeans are?"

"Fat jeans?" he echoed, coloring magnificently as she made him think about his sister in ways most brothers disliked thinking about their sisters.

"Yes. Every woman has fat jeans. The jeans we wear when we've spent too much time indulging in sweets or other bad things. They usually come out around the holidays."

"What the hell does any of this have to do with—"

"I'm just proving to you that you do not know everything about your sister. You think because you are her brother and because you raised her that you know her inside and out. I promise you that *because* you are her brother and *because* you raised her, you absolutely do not know her that intimately. You're like a father figure to her, as much as you are a brother. Not to mention you're a cop. That's why she doesn't tell you about things like other cops hitting on her in spite of the Waverly Law."

"Y-you know about—"

"Of course I do. More than one cop has come to me in a conundrum over your stupid little Waverly Law. Frankly, your sister is a grown woman and you have no say in who she dates. You ought to quit being such a control freak. Maybe if you did, you'd be in the loop enough to know why one or even two criminals might be after her."

Marissa walked away from him, keeping her spine erect, falling back on her mother's old adage that perfect posture made up for whatever inadequacies a woman might feel inside. At the moment, Marissa was wishing she could figure out when to keep her opinions to herself as far as Jackson Waverly was concerned. She did it day in and day out with everyone else, doling out advice as professionally as she should, but with Jackson . . .

She could hear him jump out of his chair, his footsteps hot behind hers.

"What cops? Who's been talking about my sister?" he demanded.

Oh. She just had to.

She smiled at him over her shoulder. "Now, you know I can't tell you that. That would break confidentiality."

She heard him literally growl at her back.

"You are the most infuriating woman I have ever

met! It's no wonder you don't have anyone to go home to this hour of the night!"

If heels could leave skid marks, the industrial floors of the station would have been burning up from hers. She came to a halt so fast that it sent him crashing into her as she was rounding on him in anger. She shoved him back off her as coffee flew everywhere.

"Ow! Damn it!" she spat out, flinging the scalding liquid off her hand. "What the hell do you know about who I do and do not have to go home to?" she demanded of him. "It's not as though anyone around here ever bothered to ask me about my personal life! So tell me, Waverly, just how do you know I don't have the most understanding husband in the world waiting for me at home?"

Jackson brushed coffee off his shirt and smirked at her, making her want to bean him with her coffee cup . . . after dumping the remainder of its contents over his head, that is.

"One, you don't wear the most understanding husband in the world's ring on your finger. Two, you are always here. Always. No Friday night dates. No disappearing for afternoon delight. None of it. And three, you've never brought him to any of the barbecues and whatnot . . . that is, when you've deigned to go slumming with the rest of us commoners." He put his face close to hers. "And four, as smoking hot as this body of yours is, your attitude could freeze the Hudson River from here. No guy I know of would let his special bits get that close to an ice queen like you."

She understood that he was just lashing out at her, a continuing remnant of his fear and fury, but that didn't make his mean-spirited assessment hurt any less. The trick was keeping him from knowing that. That would be far more damaging than the feeling itself, and she refused to give him any sort of satisfaction.

"You know, Waverly, I really wish that was true, because right now I'd pay good money to be able to freeze those tiny little *bits* of yours right off and slap them on the corner of my desk as a reminder to all the macho ignoramuses just like you not to mess with me!"

Marissa slammed her cup down on the nearest surface hard enough to crack it, then with a sharp turn she marched off to her office, hoping he would follow her just so she could have the satisfaction of slamming the door in his face.

But just before she crossed the open gap between the bullpen and the offices, the two detectives working with Jackson hurried in and crossed her path, ruining her delightfully perfect exit, damn it.

Of course, she was going to regret losing her temper later . . . but for the moment she wanted at least a few seconds to savor it.

"Jackson! We got them. Northbound on 87! Looks like they got off at the Windham exit."

"Finally!" Jackson said, moving in the opposite direction of Marissa to grab his coat. "Let's take this up there and see if we can—"

"Get in trouble for working out of your jurisdiction?" Marissa said dryly. "Sure, why don't you go do that?"

You could have heard a pin drop. Everyone was still and staring at her. Marissa threw them a smug smile, then finished walking toward her office.

"Oh, and before you go and do that, you might want to call the rental companies in town about that truck. A Lincoln Navigator like that? Probably has LoJack or a GPS in it. You know, in case it gets stolen. But hey, what do I know? I'm just that annoying bitch of an ice queen sitting in an office scheming up ways to ruin your lives, right?"

She slammed the office door on them, realizing she had had her satisfaction after all.

* * *

"Come, come . . ." Cleo fluttered at Docia with quick hands, urging her up from the seat she had been in while Miu and Cleo had fussed over her every detail, from dress to makeup to the prettily styled and perfectly natural-looking wig that lay in a balanced frame around her face in place of the choppy, lopsided mess underneath. "We have no doubt held up dinner. The household awaits."

Cleo held her elbow not only as a guide, she realized, but for support as she helped her down the grand staircase. Docia had known better than to brave a heel higher than an inch this soon out from her ordeal, and she had indulged in a skirt as long as Cleo's because it hid a world of sins, rather like makeup and wigs. Of course, she could only guess at the effectiveness of Miu's dressing skills, since she couldn't bear to look into a mirror again. Besides, she wouldn't be able to see herself anyway.

The long-sleeved creation of violet silk she wore was conservative in concealment, but less so in the cling factor. It was a bit bolder than she might have chosen for herself normally, but apparently other forces within her were not as shy as she might be.

And she kind of liked that. She kind of liked these flashes of confidence and bravery inside that caused her to dare things she would not normally dare. Life, she had come to realize, was much too short for empty fears. What if she had died that day on the bridge, having never been brave enough to indulge in such a dress? Never brave enough to indulge in her own beauty? Never confident enough to flick a significant finger at the rest of the world and say, "Screw you if you don't like it!"

And that was the confidence that was strengthening her spine, the thoughts that were in her head, as she walked side by side down the stairs in the shadow of what she considered an eclipsing beauty . . . and as a result ended up feeling not that eclipsed at all.

They entered the dining area, a vast echoing room made of stone from floor to ceiling but warmed by sumptuous fabrics on the windows, elegant artwork in the tapestries hanging on every wall, and two fireplaces set side by side on the far end. Not to mention lush velvet cushions on the chairs, just as in the meditation room. There were servants standing at the ready at either end of the table, carts with silver dome-covered plates of all sizes.

And suddenly she was hungry. She hadn't been for days, something about almost being killed having taken her lust for food right out of her. A girl was pouring wine, and smells began to make their way over her. From all directions. Cleo hurried to a seat, leaving only one with a setting in front of it at midpoint of the table between Asikri and Ram. On the opposite side sat Cleo and another man and woman she didn't recognize. But it was the man at the head of the table who drew her most immediate interest. Mainly because he spoke to her in a rich, lulling sort of voice.

"Welcome, Docia, to my house. I am domini of this house and marshal of all Bodywalkers in this area."

"Ah. The law," she said with a cheeky grin. "Now that's something I know a lot about."

"The true law is the pharaoh's law, but in his absence the house dominis act in his stead and in good faith of his wishes. An easy enough task since many of our laws have followed us for many generations."

"No need for modernization?" she found herself asking. She felt Ram stiffen a little beside her. It was hard to miss, since he was a wall of muscle and energy. And heat. He seemed to radiate heat. And if she wasn't mistaken, he almost reached out to touch her, as a parent might do when warning a child to mind itself in church.

Then he seemed to second-guess himself. Well, she was queen, after all, wasn't she? Did it really matter if she stepped in it? Still, she wasn't trying to offend anyone, leaving a mess for Hatshepsut to clean up when she became strong enough to chime in with advice and a sense of these ancient laws they followed. Not to mention etiquette.

"There is always a need for modernization in all things. Some things more than others," he added a bit grimly. Now *that* she was sure was full of weight and meaning. She hadn't been reborn just yesterday, after all.

"So give me an example of something you think needs modernizing. Maybe I can give your queen a poke and a nudge in the right direction if she ever decides to show up."

She could have heard a pin drop, if not for the sound of plates being set to rest in front of them.

"I hope you don't mind, you missed appetizers. But you'll find the entrées more than satisfying," her host said smoothly, his dark green eyes assessing her as he spoke. She supposed he was trying to take her measure. He wasn't like Asikri, built and ominous and seething with discontent, and he wasn't like Ram, solid and stoic, firmly serious about life and its tasks. This fellow seemed more relaxed than that. She had a suspicion that he had something of a sense of humor. He was also leanly built, like an athlete, and so tall that he must have been gangly and awkward as a teenager. But there was nothing awkward about him now. She wondered who he had once been before his Blending.

"I'm sorry. This is rude of me. I am Kasimir. Or Henry, as you like. I respond to both. And have you met Felicity or Dixon?"

"You prefer your . . . more current names?" she asked,

hoping it wasn't rude to separate the entities within them.

"Usually the name we are introduced by is the name we prefer," Felicity said shortly, picking up her wineglass and giving Docia the eye. "Well, she doesn't look very much like a queen now, does she?"

"Felicity!" Kasimir said sharply. "I will not tolerate rudeness at my table. And I remind you it is unwise to insult her. Her memory will remain very much intact even when Hatshepsut awakens within her."

Felicity looked duly unimpressed. "There are those who believe her time is finally at an end," she said almost snidely. "After all, how many generations can a man spend with the same boring little creature before he feels the itch to try something new on for a change?" She leaned forward and smiled. "Nothing is ever guaranteed, dear."

There was the sound of a fist hitting the table, silverware and Felicity jumping . . . and Docia admitted she did as well. Ram leaned forward, an exhale of breath leaving him, such a simple sound but somehow so dark and threatening at the same time.

"If there is ever a guarantee in this world," he said, his voice low and dark, "it is the love that Menes has and will always have for Hatshepsut. Call anything else into question if you must, but never doubt that!"

Silence ticked by. Well, almost silence. The ticking came from a large, ornate set of mantel clocks, twins, each set above the fireplace below it.

And just like that, her newfound appetite disappeared.

"Wait a minute," she said, her voice barely a rasp. "Wait . . . just wait . . ."

For the first time she heard, really heard, the one little condition to this whole being queen business that had so far been escaping her.

That there was a king out there somewhere and she was expected to . . .

"Holy spitballs, are you saying I'm going to be part of an arranged marriage?" She was instantly on her feet, because she absolutely could not remain in her seat a second longer. She didn't care what the soothing presence inside her was trying to say or make her feel, and she didn't care that Ram was equally soothing, or at least trying to be. She suddenly felt trapped between the two men who had brought her there . . . between what they wanted from her and what she had always wanted from herself. Ram was on his feet beside her, and after a visible hesitation, he reached out to capture her hands in his, bringing them to the solid strength of his chest until, when she stilled, she could feel the deep rhythm of his heart beating.

"Arranged marriages are a thing of the past, Docia. We would never insist you enter a union you do not voluntarily wish to enter. We are only speaking from experience. When Menes is reborn, he will come to find you, and you . . . it is very likely you will feel as Hatshepsut has always felt toward him. But if you don't, that will be accepted."

"If you don't, you won't be queen of anything," Felicity mused, picking up her wineglass and giving the liquid inside of it a swirl. She sniffed at it gently. "Or . . . hmm . . . we've never quite had it happen, that Hatshepsut and Menes were not simply mad about each other. So, either you are no queen, or you can resign yourself to the idea that you're about to meet your soul mate."

"Felicity, shut up," Asikri growled suddenly, the silent giant abruptly coming to life. "She's barely three days into the Blending. Are you determined to scare her into something stupid like resistance? And to what end? Do you think maybe Menes would turn his eye to you? Not just any queen will do for him. This you know, and if you read up on Bodywalker law, you would recall that Menes and Hatshepsut are co-rulers. Each of them a ruler in their own right, with or without their heartfelt connection. If they choose other mates, those mates would be consorts." He picked up his fork and stabbed at his food, the metal scraping irritably against the china underneath it. "Now can we all shut up, please, and eat our dinner?"

He added something under his breath, and she suspected it was a complaint about whining . . . or perhaps a complaint about the ways of women in general. But Docia couldn't tell. She couldn't tell if it was women that irritated him . . . or just everything.

However, his words comforted her a great deal. It was preconceived that she would fall in love with this Menes when he decided to arrive, but it was not a requirement. Still, there was something in the remaining uneasiness of Ram and even the more laid-back Kasimir that kept her from fully relaxing as she sat back down to her meal. Ram followed suit after he had helped push in her chair, and beneath the fall of the tablecloth he reached out to squeeze her hand. She didn't know exactly what he was trying to convey, other than strength and comfort, but she felt a great deal more than that. She felt that keen, sparkling warmth he seemed to exude in constant waves. She felt, as she always did, very aware of his pure presence and energy as he sat beside her.

After dinner, as they were milling about the room, she came to the conclusion that everything that had transpired was definitely the side effect of brain damage. In the next instant, she rejected the thought. If this wasn't real, then that meant Ram wasn't real.

Ram.

Docia could feel his eyes on her, like a sensual weight that made her belly feel heavy and her breasts swell with a strange readying response. Something about the way he was looking at her, the hunger burning like a low, fierce light in his eyes, made her want to curve her spine, swing out her hip in soft invitation, her shoulder rounding up as she turned her head and touched her chin to it and looked at him with a coyness she hadn't realized herself capable of.

The low light in his eyes flared wildly, and Docia caught her breath. Somehow, by pure feminine instinct, she knew it was taking a tremendous amount of willpower on his part not to cross over to her, to hold back from dragging her into his strong arms and up against his hard, capable body.

She recalled his kiss. Remembered the way his mouth had dominated her, his lungs stealing her breath away and taking it for his own. She became breathless once again just thinking about it. She knew he was thinking about it, too. There was a wild, primitive sense of satisfaction when she saw his hand curl into a solid, resistant fist. Yet another sign that he was using all he had to keep himself rooted to the spot he stood in, forcing himself to continue his conversation, though it must have been stilted because Cleo looked over, following the direction of his fierce gaze and finding Docia on the other end. The dark-haired beauty cocked her head curiously, then reached out to touch Ram, an attempt to draw his attention back to her.

It worked. He looked away and Docia felt as though she had been released from his hold. But suddenly the absence of his regard made her feel strangely empty. Her heartbeat quickened and she tried to push the feeling away or bury it deep inside herself. It smacked too much of neediness, and she wouldn't let herself fall victim to that desperate emotional crutch. She had seen it destroy too many women who had invested their all into the men they were attracted to.

Yes. She was attracted to him, she acknowledged with

an inner nod. Very much so. As though by admitting it to herself she could lessen the power of it, lessen the craving in her belly for things she wasn't even sure she understood. After all, she'd never felt anything like this before. Her love life to date had been . . . well, uninspiring, to say the least. But with one smoldering look across the room, she felt more heat and more excitement where Ram was concerned than she'd ever felt while actually in bed with others. Perhaps that was why the all-powerful and mighty orgasm had proven to be so elusive to her.

She blushed as she thought that, looking down at the floor. Regardless of the thousands of reasons why entertaining her attraction to Ram was a bad idea, that lone reason was enough to keep her shut down, and for a moment she was grateful for the cold, dousing effect of it.

But only for a moment. The relief was not worth the suddenly hollow sensation it left behind. The sensual fire might have been a stranger to her, but it had been a welcome one nonetheless. The idea that she was somehow broken sexually had haunted her all of her mature life. Of course, a few minutes of getting hot and bothered didn't mean she was exactly fixed . . . but she did feel a little less broken.

She felt suddenly overwhelmed and moved out of the dining room and into a room behind the dual fireplaces. Those fireplaces, she realized, opened completely to both sides, warming both rooms with heat and light equally. But this room was empty. Blessedly empty. Empty of unfamiliar people she did not know . . . and unfamiliar people she inexplicably kept craving to know better.

She stood in front of one of the intense fires, staring hard into the light and not bothering to move away when the heat became fierce against her skin.

Yet it was nothing compared with the wash of fiery, liquid need that flowed beneath her skin, telling her that Ram had just entered the room in search of her.

"Is everything all right?" he asked. The concern was genuine, but it was also somewhat false as he tried to make it the reason for pursuing her into a room where he must have known they would end up alone together.

"I suppose I am perfect," she mused a bit stiltedly. "Isn't that so? I'm a perfect little vessel for your perfect precious queen."

"You are more than a vessel," he countered, his voice hard and filled with such conviction that it caught her attention. "Each original brings new depth and dimension into our lives, Docia. You are a treasure, a unique and wondrous being Hatshepsut felt she would enjoy getting to know. She chose you. She chose you because of how special you were in her estimation.

"And you are special, Docia. Very, very special."

There was a wealth of admiration and a deep craving in the compliment. His words held so much heated weight that she drew a quick breath and her eyes shot up to his. She saw in every line of his body how rigidly he was trying to hold himself.

Then, as if he simply could not help himself, he stepped toward her. He hesitated, then continued forward until he was directly in front of her. She turned away, her breath rapid, her face flushing hot. She could feel him, his heat radiating against her back as he loomed over her, far outdoing the heat of the fire in front of her. His breathing was hard, though not quite labored. She felt the rush of his breath against her scalp and realized he had come just shy of nuzzling her hair.

He did not touch her, but he was so close and so vital that she could feel his struggle . . . his desire to touch her and the enormous willpower he was using not to do so. She felt his craving like a physical touch, felt him lift his hand and run it down the length of her arm, but a fraction of an inch away from touching her.

She turned her head slightly, unable to resist peeking at him. The storm of need on his features made her draw her breath sharply, made her heartbeat kick up to a higher rhythm, made her skin burn from head to toe. Just that one expression of hunger being barely leashed and she went utterly and completely wet.

His breath flowed over her as he moved his head, dropped it down nearer her ear, tickling her with the stirring of her hair. The warmth of it was like hot water soothing her body . . . only this was far too stimulating.

"I wish I could understand this," he breathed in a whispering rush. "Why do you make me feel this way? This has never happened before between us."

"Us?" she queried, shivering at the breathlessness of her own voice. "There's never been an us before."

"You know what I mean. But perhaps . . . perhaps that is the issue. Insofar as you are Hatshepsut, you are also this creature known as Docia. Beautiful, sweet-smelling, unsettling Docia. You are the wild card here. You are the source of my troubles."

She turned then, forcing him to adjust his stance to avoid touching her. But that did not change his clear desire to do otherwise, and he did not step back away from her.

"If I'm so troublesome to you, why are you standing so close?"

"I wish I could figure that out," he said, the muscle in his jaw flexing, revealing how he clenched his teeth as he paused in frustration.

"Well, maybe you shouldn't come close to me until you figure it out," she said a bit peevishly before she turned and started walking toward the dining room.

"If only it were that simple," he called to her back.

She ignored the implications of what he left unsaid. Her life was too complicated and too volatile to waste time on the unsaid.

Ugh. What a cliché, she thought as she stood anxiously by a window in the dining room many minutes later. Wanting to do the bodyguard. Still, if Whitney Houston could make it work . . .

Actually, the end of that movie hadn't been all that romantic. There hadn't been a huge happily ever after together.

Crap. Not that she was in any space or position to be thinking about happily-ever-afters . . . because what it all came down to was she was no longer speaking for just herself.

Well, this is going to suck, she thought dejectedly. She had a hard enough time finding a decent guy who suited her tastes as it was. Now she had to suit the tastes of *two* women? What about when it came to buying a pair of shoes? Or a shirt? Lord, what about the things she liked to eat? Was all of that going to change once another opinion started chiming in?

We are more similar than we are different, her new companion deemed to share with her.

"You know, you're awfully quiet in there," she muttered back at her. "You could speak up a bit more. Warn me about things like this Menes business . . . and, I dunno . . . *Blend* or whatever it is you're supposed to do!"

I would not worry about Menes. There is time enough for that and for the heart of the Blending, she assured Docia. *And my silence does not preclude our Blending.*

Docia felt suddenly heartened to realize she could hear, and was gaining a sense of, her new half. It was strange, but for the first time she realized her new other half spoke with a pretty, exotic little accent—one she recognized from their brief conversation in the Ether. Nothing so heavy that she was unintelligible, but it was very much there. It was obvious that English had not been her first language.

Nor my second. Nor my third. I learn something new every time, it seems, and that something is usually language. I confess, I hardly understand half of the things you say or think sometimes.

"Well, that makes sense because neither do I," Docia admitted with a shrug of a shoulder, her eyes continuing to track the movements of her seemingly agitated bodyguard. He looked as though he couldn't decide what to do with himself. He couldn't decide if he should remain close to her on her side of the dining room or put her at a distance by traveling across the way. It was a state of mind she was beginning to understand and even agree with. The closer he got to her . . . it was as if he were some kind of scrambling device, messing with the natural flow of her brain and her body. At the moment, she could use all the flow she could get.

But oh . . . there was something to be said for the way . . . the *feel* of being scrambled.

"Docia."

Startled, she turned to find Cleo close to her, nearly standing in her shoes. Initially she was puzzled by the crowding and then by the sudden clawing grip of Cleo's fingers as they grasped her arm and dug in. Docia's attention flew up to Cleo's face, and what she saw there made her gasp. The blue of the other woman's eyes had bled out of her irises, staining the sclera to match so it was a perfect blue landscape, with pinpoint dots of black for irises.

"Run toward Ram," she said, her breath seeming to come harder and harder. Sweat stained her forehead, a bead of it trickling down the side of Cleo's neck. Docia was so stunned that she couldn't respond until Cleo spat out at her, "Go now!"

There was such urgency in her, such terrifying presence, that Docia stumbled back, staggering in the direction she had last recalled seeing Ram. Somehow she found him in spite of the blind shock surrounding her. She barely was able to reach out and touch his solid arm, barely had time to register the way her touch made his muscles flex into hardness, before a horrific explosion rocked the room.

The room, the entire house, was made of heavily poured and sculpted stone and concrete. A fortress, actually, when she thought about it. So when it blew apart from the outside wall and ceiling, it was a rain of glass and heavy stone, everywhere at once, not to mention the percussive force of the explosion itself. She had been standing near the fireplace set closest to the windows because, let's face it, that was just the kind of luck she was having these days; but Cleo's warning had brought her out of reach of the worst of it, and Ram, quick to react, had hooked an arm around her and turned her behind the wall of his body, pulling her to his chest in a death-defying hug as he bent over her protectively, exposing his back to the lash of glass and rock projectiles. She felt something hit him, the thump of it echoing in sound as well as sickly sensation beneath the ear she had pressed to his chest. Docia thought she ought to be screaming bloody murder, she ought to be a bundle of wet fear and terror. Hell, she ought to be the walking poster child for PTSD by now.

Yet somehow she felt safe.

For a second. Wrapped in Ram's strength, protected by the force that he was, in that second she felt utterly protected.

And then the second was gone, ripped from her as a

new force of energy exploded through the room, seemingly determined to tear her away from Ram.

But Ram was no slouch at this table, not just a pretty little face and a pumped-up body that didn't know a single useful thing about protecting his charge. He let the force hit him, but somewhere along the way he had locked a hand around her arm, and the power trying to rip them apart simply could not break that hold. Her shoulder wrenched and now she screamed, but it was all about pain and nothing to do with fear. Fear would have been separating from Ram. She knew that on a visceral level she probably wouldn't be able to explain in calmer moments any more than she could explain it right then.

Ram holding on to her changed the impetus of her direction, and she flew across the room with him. He was flung into the wall, but when he should have hit it like a wet rag, his feet hit it first and he ran up the surface of the tapestry as though he were running over the floor. He ran until he was nearly head down, then flipped completely over, his feet hitting the floor with a solid smack. He had let go of her briefly, knowing he would snap her shoulder apart with the move if he didn't, but as soon as he touched down he grabbed hold of her again. Now he shoved her behind him as he turned to face the threat at hand. The threat that had come after the building stopped raining down around them.

Docia couldn't help peeping around him. Sure, instinct said to hide, duck and cover, never come out, but she apparently had a stronger instinct than self-preservation, and that one was outright curiosity. Although she liked to think it was just a matter of seeing her impending death and meeting it face-on.

Yeah. That was her story, and she was sticking to it.

What she saw was that half of the building looked as

if it had been ripped away, reduced to rubble both inside and outside on the snow-dusted grounds. *When had it started snowing?* she found herself wondering ridiculously. "Nice, Docia," she muttered, "how about some priorities, girlfriend?"

Like, how about worrying about the über-ugly winged beasties, each with skin cast like dark gray stone, each with talons that sprouted from both gnarled fingers and toes, talons long enough that they could be seen even in a tempest of wind, falling debris, and the ironically delicate drift of early snow. There were triple joints on those long wings, and at the crest of each joint was yet another talon, not to be outdone by the longest one that speared out from the very end of each wingtip. Two of the creatures lay among the rubble, as if the attack had knocked them into the room. The largest of the fiends stood up with a stagger, then swung around to look Docia dead in the eyes. Even its eyes were gray, she realized as a reactive little giggle erupted from her lips. Its warped, bumpy face was terrifying, most especially its mouth because of the fangs, one set spearing down and one set spearing up, along the outside of its mouth.

"Ram," it hissed, suddenly leaping toward them. It landed awkwardly, a tear in its wing throwing it off balance. "Take her away! My lieutenants will see you to safety!"

"What are the forces, Stohn?"

"What else?" the creature said, the cock of its head hard and grim.

"You mean it's on *your* side?" Docia squeaked, pointing incredulously at Stohn as two more of the winged beasts landed in front of them and she suddenly became aware of an explosive fight taking place outside the dining hall wall. Bursts of red light and energy were streaking through the night sky, blinding her as they struck down other winged monsters. One bolt, thrown from a dark-haired man who looked as though he could step onto a pirate ship and swash and buckle with the best of them, was so powerful that the creature it targeted exploded in a crush of gray skin, bones, and blood the color of violet night. Docia couldn't tear her eyes away as it spiraled helplessly to the ground and struck with a sickening smack, sending a castoff of violet across Felicity's orange evening dress.

Suddenly she was fighting the screaming urge to vomit.

"I won't abandon the house," Ram barked out, the need to shout very necessary given the clamor of noise and wind washing around them. A tremendous clap of thunder roared around the heads left exposed to the open air, and Docia had the strangest sensation crawling over her skin . . . like . . . well, a rapid buildup of static electricity.

"Your duty is clear, here," Stohn barked back. "This house is *ours* to protect! That is *our* duty in life. Your duty is to protect *her*!" His wing snapped as he pointed the ivory spike at the tip of it at her like a demented sort of finger. "Is that not correct?"

Ram's jaw was set angrily, but after only a moment's hesitation he nodded curtly. Then he looked out into the maelstrom of the night, watching another of the winged forces get slammed into the side of the house.

"Come," he shouted to her the next instant, lifting her toward the waiting arms of one of the monsters.

"As if!" she squealed, latching on to him and resisting touching those cold-looking taloned hands by curving her body as far from them as she could manage.

Ram gave her a shake, drawing her eyes to him. She looked into his eyes, the deep seriousness in them reaching uncounted fathoms.

"I've taken you this far," he said firmly. And it was all

he said. All he had to say. That steadiness in his eyes asked her to have faith in him yet again, to trust him to protect her in whatever manner he deemed best for her. Even if it meant climbing into the arms of a monster.

She was breathing hard, unable to catch her breath, feeling as if she were in some kind of war zone . . .

. . . and understanding that it was exactly that. A war zone. And somehow she suddenly had no doubt that *she* was the war prize.

She hesitantly moved to touch the cold gray of the creature's skin, surprised to find it was warm. But for all its appearance of skin, it was hard as marble to the touch, gleaming like smooth, cold stone, yet pliable enough to move over the jutting bones and muscles beneath it. Those bones and muscles were hard, like steel, and the wings that bent forward over her like a protective shield were made of folding sections like the exoskeleton of an armadillo, one layer folding smoothly beneath another layer, flexing back and forth as needed in any given moment but without question an impenetrable hide. It picked her up, held her close, then with a snap of two sets of wings the four of them took to the bleak, wintry night sky.

Docia knew she ought to keep still, but her heart was in her throat and she didn't trust these creatures one bit. She wrenched her head around, seeking Ram. What she got was an eyeful of a battlefield, what looked like humans on the ground throwing those balls of red flameless fire at the winged forces. Where had they all come from? she wondered. Both the human attackers and the winged defenders? With all those miles of property insulating them from the roadways, how could they have gotten past those protective walls, the mounted cameras, all without a single hint of warning?

But as they gained more sky and the property below sprawled away, they flew over the drive and all those many columns leading up to the house were now naked of their prospective Gargoyles. She saw yet others, right before her eyes, on the parapets of the building changing from crouched stone critters into large, powerful fighters of all manner and appearance. It was as though a force of demons had been called forth into life to fight for the property they were guarding.

"It is better if you do not look down, my lady," the creature holding her said with such peculiar refinement, his accent sounding aristocratic. She turned her head to look into his eyes and, for the first time, realized that this one's eyes were a warm, oceanic green, like clean equatorial waters that danced along the edges of pristine white beaches. It was so incongruous a sight, set as they were in all that dark and grisly gray.

Suddenly the beast jolted hard to the left, banking in a superiorly nauseating maneuver that just barely dodged a streak of red energy that came so close, she felt its warmth against her entire exposed side and her mouth filled with a tang equal to that of having licked a row of batteries. That wasn't exactly helping her nausea any. And normally she took great delight in the screaming scariness of the worst roller coasters the eastern seaboard could dish out, but seeing as how there was no seat belt . . . no, not much fun factor involved.

"Hup!"

That was the only warning she got before the Gargoyle's next evasive maneuver, this one circling them around the soaring tops of some bony oak trees as he tried to put some objects between them and whatever was chasing them. And it *was* a chase, she realized, because the house was a pretty good distance away by then. What she had deemed as open air had not been as far off the ground as all that after all. Well, if you could consider twenty or thirty feet not all that high. And he moved so fast, cutting corners and streaking over underbrush so that it flashed beneath her in indiscernible streams first one way and then another. His wings hit branches, shearing them off at the ends, but none of it slowing him down as he built up speed.

And then a massive ball of searing red light struck them from in front, or what would have been front had the creature holding her not jerked himself around at the last minute, snapping his wings in full extension over her so the shot hit his armored webbing more than it hit her.

But that armor burned away nonetheless, leaving a gaping hole in the monster's wing. And just like that they were falling, and she was screaming as the ground rushed to reclaim the laws of gravity. Her poorly abused body and psyche could take only so much. She passed out somewhere around the point of terminal velocity.

When Jackson and about half a dozen cops from both Saugerties PD and Windham PD pulled up to the gatehouse, they were ready for just about anything . . . except what they found. The gatehouse looked as if it had been vandalized, the windows smashed in all around it; the expensive line of monitors that had no doubt kept tabs on equally expensive cameras set around the property were bashed in, strewn across the floor; and the entire little building looked as though it had been jumped in a dark alley and had the shit beat out of it.

The sound of guns leaving holsters echoed in the night, clouds of rapidly increasing breath rising from the group in faster plumes. They could tell, just as Jackson could, that this was extremely recent damage. The smell of burned monitors still hung in the air, and there was something . . . just . . . something in a cop's gut warning him to watch himself.

"I'd say that's exigent circumstances, boys," Jackson said grimly.

"Yup," someone agreed.

Jackson found the gate release, but pressing the button did no good, since it seemed the power had been ripped away from the gatehouse as well.

It took three frustrating minutes to find the manual release and to manpower the gates open enough for them to move through. Jackson had been just shy of trying to scale the bastards the hard way, even though the design of the metal would not have been conducive to an easy climb. But putting a few minutes' faith in his colleagues paid off, and he tried to remind himself to keep a cool head. It was by sheer luck and a really good argument on his part that they had even let him come along on their fishing expedition. As it stood at the time, all they were there for was a well check. They all knew he was way too close to the situation, that it wasn't a good idea to have him close where emotions could get in the way of making legal progress in the situation. And they were probably right. He was tired and frustrated and impatient as all hell to see his sister safe and sound, but everything they were looking at was giving him that sour feeling in his gut that just the opposite was going to be true.

They moved up the long drive in force, a tense readiness in every last one of them. When the drive proved far longer than anticipated, it wore on them more and more . . . until they saw the first branch felled in the middle of the drive. It was thoroughly dusted with snow, but they could see the whitish-yellow wound on the end clear enough that bore witness to its having been ripped out of its position in life. But there had been no violent storms lately to account for it. It didn't make sense, Jackson thought as he looked up into the tall trees. Given the thickness and size of the branch, it would take a few men with chain saws to clear . . . and it was clearly a stress fracture that had ripped it free.

What, other than a storm or fierce winds, could cause damage like this? And his puzzlement only grew when he found the matching wound on the near tree up so high that one could get dizzy looking at it.

He returned his focus to the driveway. They all walked along the edges of it, out of some innate instinct, perhaps, so as not to be caught in the middle of the road in case something was planned for them. There were columns lining the road, most of which were bare on top, some of which were occupied by frozen grotesques in stone. They were a bit disconcerting, and it took a moment for him to figure out why.

They weren't covered in snow.

What the hell?

Sure, it was snowing only lightly, those thick tufted snowflakes that were taking their time to make it to the ground, dancing in wending, lollygagging patterns, but it was enough of a snow to have left that branch covered in a decent white fuzziness.

So why were the stone gargoyles bare of most of it? He tried to rationalize it, tried to reason that maybe the stone was somehow warmer than the tree branch had been. But knowing how gray and dark and dreary the day had been and how freezing cold it was at present, he couldn't trick his brain into understanding an impossibility. Nor could he come up with any other plausible explanation for it. So all he was left with was the act of tucking it aside in his brain. It was a trivial thing, he told himself. It very likely had nothing to do with what they had come there for.

By the time they made it to the last turn before the house, half of them were winded and some were exhausted, the act of jockeying a desk all day not that conducive to stamina and good health.

Jackson didn't have that problem. Sure, sitting in a patrol car eight hours a day wasn't the healthiest thing in the world, but he knew how to countermand that with time in the gym. And Chico had kept him running every minute they were out of that car.

Had. Jackson shoved aside the emotions connected with that, along with the overwhelming and crippling fear he faced that he was on the verge of losing yet another person he loved. It was everything he had felt in Landon's office as he had stared at that gorgeous redhead's face and tried to process her initiating the worst thing he had ever heard in his life.

The thought sent new steam in his stride, and he was the first to see the house clearly. It was enormous and intimidating . . . an edifice of gray stone topped with more of those disconcerting stone gargoyles. They looked like demons frozen in time, their glares downward warning all comers that they were the protectors and guardians of this place . . . or so the mythos of gargoyles went.

Well, apparently they had been doing a shit job of it, because along the right side about half the house had been ripped asunder. As though a massive wrecking ball had been taken to it. And again, it had to be recent because there was barely any snow on the rubble left behind. Jackson let his colleagues knock on the front door. He headed straight for the damage path. And it was a path. The closer he looked at the house and trees around him, the more he saw that the damage extended into the trees, both low on the trunks and high in the broken, kinked-up branches, some of which dangled downward, creaking as they hung on by a thread. It was as though a huge bomb had gone off . . . a bomb with a strange sort of progressive damage path. He reached the edge of the rubble and stepped into it, all the while holding his weapon at the ready, keeping his eyes moving constantly, eating up information whether he could make sense of it or not.

And all of what he was seeing was sickening to his stomach. However this mess was caused, if his sister had been here . . .

Of course she had been here. He could feel it in his bones. Not to mention the Lincoln Navigator that had led them there had been sitting in the large driveway, along with about a half dozen other cars of equally expensive make and model. When he thought of Docia being there against her will, in a remote location, with people who appeared to have endless resources and wealth . . . it took a tremendous feat of willpower not to jump to wild conclusions but to focus just on his immediate surroundings.

He leapt from one piece of rubble to the next, carefully dodging the wretchedly bent skeletons of rebar jutting from inside the pieces of stone. He pulled out his flashlight as he reached the cavity of the building and was greeted with almost complete darkness, save the distorted flames of what had once been a pair of gas fireplaces at the far end of the room but were now just mangled pipes of burning gas. He moved into the building, the darkness intensifying as he left the bright, direct shine of moonlight behind. The beam of his flashlight lanced over a table and the remnants of what looked to be a recent meal. Plates, food, and glasses were scattered and shattered everywhere. There was a strange dark stain splattered here and there. Not blood. It was more purple than it was red. He didn't let himself be comforted by that. There was too much else around him giving him cause to have ramped-up adrenaline.

"Jackson."

Jackson jumped out of his skin, nearly losing his footing as the fierce whisper came out of the dark from behind him. He swung his light and his gun around and found Leo's face to go with the familiarity of his voice . . . once he had another moment to recognize it.

Hard to do that when his heart was pounding in his ears.

"You know, it's not often a bad guy calls you by your first name," Leo mused with his usual snarky attitude, pushing Jackson's weapon aside. But Leo was also holding a weapon in his hand, the austere black of the Talon part of the reason he blended so well with the darkened room.

"Leo! What the hell are you doing here?" Jackson hissed at him. "And fuck you. I don't care if the jackass coming out of the darkness knows my grandmother's name. You're lucky you didn't get shot, you idiot."

"As if you'd ever get the drop on me," Leo said dryly. "Like I just did on you. Besides, I got here first." He couldn't have put more smirk in the sentence if he tried.

"All right, then, tell me what happened here," Jackson gritted through his teeth, knowing now was not the time to play smart-ass tug-of-war with Leo.

"I have no idea. I just got here about five seconds before you," Leo said with a shrug. "I heard you coming up behind me and thought you were trouble. But, clearly you're about as harmless as a butterfly. I could swear I taught you to walk more quietly than that."

"How did you find this place?" Jackson demanded.

"I told you, man, you ought to stick with me," Leo said. "Now you got a bunch of cops tramping all over the place, intent on ruining the crime scene. How long do you think they're going to stand there ringing that doorbell before they remember the electricity is out? I figure that's about as long as we have to find any clues about what happened here before they muck up the works."

Unfortunately, Jackson was on the verge of agreeing with him. For the first time in his life, he had begun to feel very restricted by the laws he had sworn to uphold. Sure, there had been frustrating moments here and there when they'd tested him, when he'd been tempted to fudge it a little, but this time, in this particular situation . . . the frustration was reaching an all-time high. But there was also a sense of satisfaction in knowing that going the legal route had gotten him there at almost the exact same time as Leo, whose methods had no doubt been far from legitimate.

But he also knew that the moment the cops took this place over, especially out-of-county cops, they were going to shut him out. They'd let him come this far because they didn't think Docia was in any kind of danger, that he was just being an overprotective older brother. But everything around Jackson was screaming otherwise, and they were finally going to agree with him that something was very, very wrong. That agreement was going to be like a gate slamming down on him.

"What do you think this is?" Jackson asked, flashing a light over the dark, purplish stain near his feet.

"No idea. But the whole place smells weird. Like . . . lilacs. Lilacs are months out of season, and it's not as though anyone's been spraying a frigging air freshener to freshen up this mess."

"Let's go deeper into the house. The only thing making me happy right now is that there's no body count. Not that I see, anyway."

"I'll lead," Leo said, moving forward before Jackson could agree or disagree.

"Leo! You're not a cop!" Jackson hissed, following him at the ready. "You can't—"

"Shh!"

"Did you just shush me?" Jackson growled, his voice low and soft.

"Gentlemen, may I be of assistance?"

Both men jerked around, their flashlights streaking over the tall, lanky man who had somehow come up behind them. They could hear the resounding banging on the front door as the cops outside tried to gain invitation.

It was odd, but the man did not react to two strangers in his home holding guns on him. Not even the twitch of an eye. It was the first thing Jackson noticed about him.

"Police! Hands where I can see them," he barked, stepping in front of Leo, blocking his friend's line of sight.

"Douche," Leo whispered at his back.

"Officers," the man said, gently exposing both his palms, "I'm not armed. I was just coming to answer the ruckus at the door."

Jackson sighed. "Leo, for Pete's sake, let them in already."

"Nope. I'm not supposed to be here, remember?"

Jackson decided then and there to kill his best friend.

Maybe even twice.

"Sir, can you tell me what has happened here?" he barked at the stranger.

"First, let me introduce myself. I am Henry Kamin. This is my home. I welcome you readily, Officers, so there is no need for your weaponry."

"Like we're going to take your word for it," Leo said dryly.

"Shh!"

"Did you just shush me?" Leo demanded of Jackson, who ignored him. Jackson reached out and pushed a hand down over Leo's, forcing him to lower his weapon. He did so himself, but only slightly.

"You'll forgive me, but this place looks like a war zone. I'm not certain it's all that safe."

"It wasn't," Kamin agreed with a nod and a grim set to his lips. "But it is now. In fact, I have a call out to the local police, which must be you. We've had an incident.

Some sort of horrible gas explosion. We were able to manage the worst of it, as you see, and have evacuated most of the house except for myself and my personal guards."

He held out a hand, and as if he'd conjured them, three very strong men appeared out of the darkness. Another oddity, Jackson stuffed into his mind, was that no one had thought to light so much as a candle or spark a flashlight. These men were walking around in the dark as if it were nothing to them.

"Stohn, Hagen . . . can you see about getting some lights?" Kamin directed, almost as though he had pulled the idea right out of Jackson's head. "Forgive me, we're still recovering and haven't had a chance to touch all our bases yet."

Jackson watched the ones called Stohn and Hagen move away, the enormous men seemingly more than capable of repelling the Axis forces single-handed. He did notice that Stohn was injured; his left arm looked terribly burned.

He should have offered ambulance services, called for more backup. But that ranked very low on his list of priorities.

"Mr. Kamin, I am looking for a girl. Her name is Docia Waverly. She was last seen in the company of the men driving that vehicle parked in front of your home."

Jackson watched his aristocratic features very carefully, looking for the slightest flinch, for a shift in his eyes as he prepared to lie to him.

"Of course. Miss Waverly was here, but when all of this happened my friends decided it was safer to take her elsewhere."

"*Where* elsewhere?" Jackson demanded. He was taken aback that the man would admit to her being there. It immediately made him complicit in any crimes that might be perpetrated against Docia. If anything happened to her, if she turned up hurt or . . . worse . . . they would come back to him and demand answers. As it was, Jackson wanted some of those answers now.

"What was she doing here? Where have they taken her? I want the names of these friends and the address of where she has gone."

Kamin absorbed the demands for a moment and then drew a breath, still as calm and even-voiced as before.

"You must be Jackson," he said. "Docia told us all about you. I thought she called you and told you she was safe with friends?"

"Seriously? Does this look safe to you, pal?" Leo barked, indicating the devastated dining room.

"Indeed. An unfortunate event of timing, I promise you. And she is safe. She is with my longtime friend Vincent Marzak. And believe me, as long as Vincent is with her, she is very, very safe."

CHAPTER NINE

Docia opened her eyes slowly, the grit under her lids scraping at her eyeballs like sand in private places after playing in a powerful surf. She opened them and focused on whatever she could. It turned out to be a floor tile, something Spanish looking, if the bright primary reds and blues were anything to go by . . . and chipped all to hell. The whole floor had definitely seen better days.

"Are you kidding me? I'm *still* not dead?" she said aloud, her voice rasping just like her eyes. Honestly, she didn't know what else to say. What else to think. The last thing she remembered was heading for the ground at breakneck speed, a surprisingly fallible armored creature hurtling to his death right along with her.

She tried to look up but realized she already was . . . well, in accordance with her body, anyway. It was just that her body wasn't upright. Not in any normal sense of the word. She was suspended over the floor by her torso, her wrists lashed wide apart like a wingspan of her own, her legs bound tightly together. Looking ahead once again, she noticed there were little drops of blood dripping slowly with a pat-pat-pat sound, right about level with her nose. Now that she was aware of it, if she crossed her eyes a little, she could see the droplets originating off the tip of her nose.

So she was apparently hanging parallel above those worn-out tiles. All she needed was a hang glider to help it make some kind of sense. Bound as she was, she really wasn't getting a good feeling about it, and the bloody nose wasn't adding anything to the contrary. On the dubious plus side, she'd lost her pretty new wig along the way, so only half of her side vision was obscured by her hair.

"Hello?" She cleared the crackly crud from her throat and tried again. "Hello? I'm kinda hanging here! I mean, I appreciate not being left on what looks like a really cold and somewhat dirty floor, but . . . I sorta can't breathe through my nose. And you have some kind of rope or something over one of my . . . um . . . *girls* . . . and she's not very comfortable. . . . Hello?"

"Docia, hush."

Well, she didn't have to see the owner of that voice to recognize him . . . though he did sound a little off to her for some reason. She tried to twist to see Ram, but he was somewhere past the bottoms of her feet, and when she looked beyond her toes she saw absolutely nothing of him.

"Ram, did you do this to me? I'm really starting to not like you, mister. Ever since you showed up, things have just been going to hell in a handbasket for me!"

"Hmm," was the dry reply.

"Hmm? What hmm?" she demanded. "What's that supposed to mean, 'hmm'? It's true!"

"I don't recall being anywhere near New York when you got yourself shoved off a bridge," he said.

She opened her mouth to snap at him but shut it again almost instantly. He kind of had a point there.

"And I wasn't there when you entered the Ether."

Silence seemed the best course of action.

"And *I* had nothing to do with that nice gentleman trying to gut you with a knife."

"Vincent . . ." She sighed. "You must be Vincent." Because Ram had never spoken with such sarcasm and irritability before, so it was the only conclusion she could come to. This was Ram's other half . . . but somehow it was undiluted by the Blending. She hadn't realized that was possible. She had assumed that the Ram/Vincent persona, once Blended, was just that. Blended. So how was it that she could clearly hear another man, another personality, using this familiar voice?

"Damn, skippy, I'm Vincent. And because of you our boy Ramses here has us in a hell of a lot of hot water."

"Look, I never asked him to show up and be all . . . all everywhere in my life all of a sudden!"

"You're his queen. That apparently means something to him. So, like it or not, he and I are here to stay. Provided we make it out of this mess alive."

Definitely not Ram. She preferred Ram. He was far more comforting. But on the other hand, since she had nothing but time to kill, it seemed, she was overrun with curiosity about more than one thing. But for the time being, she'd start with just one.

"Vincent," she said after actually taking the time to think about how to word something for the first time in her life, "why did you agree to share your body with a Bodywalker?"

There were several strong ticks of silence.

"Same reason you did. I didn't want to die. I wasn't done yet."

"Oh."

"And I wanted to kill my fucktard ex-brother-in-law very precisely and very, very slowly. I couldn't exactly do that flying around in heaven. Or carousing with demons. Whichever way it was going to go."

"Oh. Is that why you almost died? Your fucktard ex-brother-in-law?"

More of those intense moments of silence passed. She couldn't tell if he was trying to think about what to say to her or keep himself from getting really pissed off.

"Let's just say he was of a mind that his son, my sister's son, was *his* son, and when my sister finally found the courage to divorce him and won full custody of their son . . . well, it became a case of if he couldn't have *his* son, he'd see to it no one else could. Same went for my sister, I guess. As far as he was concerned, she belonged to him. Forever. And nothing was ever going to be allowed to change that." He sighed. "But that was a long time ago."

"And . . . did you? Kill your fucktard ex-brother-in-law, I mean."

She could feel him smile all the way across the room.

"Yeah." But the satisfaction in his voice faded instantly. "But it didn't bring back my sister or my nephew, so . . ." She imagined him shrugging. She also appreciated his forthrightness. Candor, it seemed, was something he shared with Ram. Among the obvious other things.

"So you got your revenge. And now you just . . . do what Ram wants to do?"

"I'm not his bitch, if that's what you mean." He chuckled. "Seems to me like that's your calling."

"Hey!"

"Well, if you haven't noticed, the boy's got it bad for you."

"He does not!" she cried, her face flaming with heat, a cross between embarrassment and sudden feminine sexual awareness. In the end, her ego got the best of her. "A-are you saying that you don't feel the same way? That he can like a woman, but you can . . . not?"

"Not really," he admitted. "You're trying to separate

us, but we're inseparable, for the most part. One of us feels stronger about volatile things than the other does from time to time, but normally, there's no separation of one from the other."

"So . . . why are you . . . ?"

"I honestly have no idea why I'm here alone," he confessed. "And to be even more honest with you, after all this time being Blended with Ram, it's a little effing scary."

"I can just imagine," she said softly, trying for a moment to poke around inside her own head, wanting to see if her other half was somewhere to be found within. But if she was there, she wasn't speaking up. Then again, she rarely had so far. "So I'm guessing you're tied up over there somewhere, too?"

"Well, I'm not polishing my toes," was the biting reply.

"No need to be snippy," she snipped back at him.

"Seriously. Ram has a thing for mani/pedis. He's kind of a little bit too metrosexual for me sometimes."

She racked her brain for a way to respond to that. All she could come up with was, "Oh. So you don't like them? Mani/pedis, I mean."

Silence.

She giggled.

"Well, who am I to argue with pretty girls fondling my feet and hands?" he pointed out in a tone that was positively predatory male.

"Oh. No. I can see your point."

Silence.

"But you like them." She giggled, imagining him in a pedicure chair getting his toes painted.

"You know, I can see right up your dress from here."

"Hey!"

Smug silence.

She would have given him the silent treatment, but she'd never been very good at it.

"So . . . best guess . . . what the hell is going on here?" she asked him.

"Best guess? The Gargoyles failed to get us away in time and the Templar Bodywalkers now have us captive. But . . ."

"But?"

"But I know why the Templars want to keep *you* alive. I don't know why the Templars would waste the chance to ice me and Ram immediately."

She didn't ask why the Templars would want her. It was pretty obvious to them both. They were going to hold her hostage . . . maybe use her as a bartering tool. Maybe they'd kill her just to torment Menes as soon as he was resurrected. . . .

"Can I ask you something?"

"Can't see how I could stop you," he observed.

"Does Ram . . . is he happy to hand me over to Menes?"

"That's a tough question," he said after a moment's pause. "Ram is devoted to Menes. His pride in himself is deeply rooted in his service to his pharaoh. He is second in command, should anything befall Menes and Hatshepsut. He is a natural at ruling over great masses, and contrary to his bad press, he is very open-minded and very much committed to doing the right thing. You could say he learned a few lessons since he was an original himself."

She wanted to accuse him of not answering her question, but she realized it was the only answer he could give her. Vincent didn't know any more than Ram did about how he would feel when the time came to bring her to his reborn pharaoh.

"You have no idea how much Ram envies what Menes and Hatshepsut have. How much he longs for it." He paused. "But you've certainly thrown a wrench in the works, hot stuff. You've got my boy pulled six ways from Sunday."

"Don't mock me," she said angrily. For some reason, it had become important to her that Ram feel at least a little hesitation about carrying out his duties.

"Hardly that. More like I am mocking him. Or . . . us. I'd like to say I don't know what he sees in you, but you're kind of spunky. In a waifish sort of way."

"Thank you." She sniffed. "I think."

"And you do have a nice ass."

"Damn right I do," she shot back. "It's by far my best physical feature," she said proudly.

"Well, the *girls* are pretty impressive, too," he said, that smirk back in his tone.

"Nobody asked you!"

"I figured since you were so curious, you might like to know. And frankly, teasing you is helping me not think about why Ram is dead silent over here."

"You sound nervous," she noted as gently as she could, not wanting him to think she was mocking him in any way.

"I'm a navy SEAL. We don't get nervous."

They both knew it was bullshit, so he relented rather quickly.

"It's . . . hard to explain. It's kind of like having a limb traumatically amputated," he confessed. "I think there's a level of shock involved. I feel cold and nauseated. And, I have to admit, starkly alone. He's been with me every single step of the way for so long now . . . his voice in my head, his morals in my ear . . . his sense of duty and honor in my soul. We both . . . we're the same in a lot of ways, for all he's this ancient spirit that's lived so many lives and I'm pretty nascent in the grand scheme of things. I . . . I like him. And I hope he's okay."

"Do you think these Templars did something? You

know, like maybe . . . I dunno . . . a Ramses-ectomy? Maybe they forcibly removed him from you?"

"As far as I know, they can't do that . . . and if they did, the host . . . *I* . . . would die. It's kind of one of the rules. Did you know you have a mole on your foot?"

"Yes! Can you focus, please? Tell me about these Templars. What was with the fireballs? Can they just *do* that?"

"Templar Bodywalkers call on mystical forces . . . they call it the blessings of the gods. The red energy they use is called Ra's Curse. Obnoxious and cheeky, if you ask me, since the one thing all the Bodywalkers believe is that Ra has cursed them and it's not something they address lightly."

"In our mortal lives we were known as the children of the sun. The children of Ra." The voice was new, feminine, heeled steps walking slowly against the crisp surface of the tiles. She came close enough for Docia to see the darling blue suede Christian Louboutin shoes she wore. The pretty blue gleamed prettily in contrast with the red soles when she walked, no doubt. She looked strong, her calves well shaped, and her ivory skirt drew snug around her knees, and probably her hips, too, if Docia would just lift her head and strain a little. But she had a bitch of a headache and was too worn out to make the effort. "But now," she continued, "Ra no longer smiles upon us. We cannot walk in the light of the sun. Or has no one told you this yet?"

Docia felt anxiety choking up the length of her, crawling down into her belly.

"Nightwalkers," she whispered.

"Yes. We've been cursed to live among these lower breeds known as Nightwalkers. The Gargoyles that serve us. The Djynn. The Night Angels. I think there are six in all. Perhaps even others we don't know of. Filthy mongrels, all of them. And yet we wallow amongst them, as though they were our equals."

Her contempt dripped from her lips, but Docia was terribly distracted, trying to figure out what a Night Angel might be. Was it like an actual angel? From heaven? She'd obviously met and seen Gargoyles in action, but what about the Djynn? And how was it that no human knew about these things when apparently they were all living among them? Seemed she could barely swing a cat without hitting a mystical creature these days. She could understand the whole Bodywalker thing; after all, they were literally hiding inside of normal humans. But how did the rest of them manage to go undetected?

"Make certain you stay out of Ra's light. He takes offense if we try to take part in his blessing. Let's just say it isn't a pretty sight."

"Who are you?" Docia asked.

"I'm going to take a wild guess here and say her name is Odjit," Vincent spat abruptly. "And according to what Ram has told me, she's a fucking lunatic."

"I am a priestess," she corrected him. "And I think I prefer she use my new name. Selena. Let me assure you, Docia, the gods smile upon me and my followers, for we are faithful to them and their rituals in a way the Politic are not. One day Ra will forgive us all, if we have faith in him and follow his wishes. The way of the Politic is not the way to ending this curse."

Vincent snorted. "She means if we all bow down to her and become her mindless lackeys, everything will be sunshine and roses. But what she really wants, what she's always wanted, is to be pharaoh, queen of the Bodywalkers."

"It is my right. There are many who believe it. But, let's talk of other things," the Templar leader said, starting a slow walk around Docia, leaving Docia with little to do but listen and admire her taste in shoes. "Let's talk about you, Docia."

"Well, I would, except you have me hanging here like some kind of flipping marionette."

"Mmm. We call it the Suspension. And it does exactly that. It suspends your connection to your Bodywalkers, basically imprisoning them and nullifying their powers."

"I don't have any powers," Docia countered. "I barely have any hair."

"You don't yet . . . but given time you very much will be a powerful entity. I think you and I both know you could potentially be one of the most powerful women in the living world."

She leaned forward a little to whisper against Docia's ear in a husky, breathy voice, giving her a whiff of a luscious perfume. "I know she's in there. I know in her heart she wants to be here with us."

"Whatever she's saying, Docia, think of her like a pretty-smelling poisonous gas that encourages you to breathe deep, all the while killing you," Vincent said with cutting sweetness.

"Vincent . . ." Straightening, she gave a little tsk, sounding disappointed in him. "You're so terribly brainwashed. I would think that without Ramses you might be able to give me a chance and draw your own conclusions. Just as I would like Docia to use her free will and come to her own. How has it been, Docia, with all these people trying to force all of their ways upon you? Here we don't do such rude things. Here we want you to come to things in your own way . . . in your own time. And as the Bodywalker inside of you Blends with you, perhaps together you will find a new way of being, rather than falling into step with the dictates of others."

As she began to walk back, Docia noticed a glimmer

of gold around her ankle, a delicate little chain with a tiny ankh dangling against the rise of her foot.

"Well, as appealing as that sounds, I hope you don't expect me to do all of this hanging here like a duck in a Chinese market stall."

"Not at all. But for the moment, alas, we must leave you as is. Once the Suspension spell has sunk in deep enough, we will let you down. It will suspend your Blending just long enough for you to have a look around . . . to get to know a few of us and to judge fairly without your Bodywalker's interference."

"And what good will that do? I assume this Suspension will wear off eventually. My Bodywalker will come back with all her opinions intact."

"Perhaps. But we have changed the minds of others. Others that would surprise your valiant Vincent over there."

"If I'm your goal, why bother suspending Ram? You don't expect—"

"Of course not. But the only other choice is for us to kill your bodyguard to keep him from interfering. I am very certain that would start us off on the wrong foot."

"Yes. It would," Docia squeaked. The idea of them hurting Ram made the whole room begin to spin. The idea that she would be the reason for it had her fighting an incredible urge to hurl.

"Don't worry, Docia," Vincent said, his strong voice booming and fierce. "I'll have you out of here long before your feet ever touch the ground of this pile of fetid rock they call a temple."

Selena chuckled softly, and Docia could envision her touching delicate fingers to her lips, daintily covering the sound.

"Honestly, Vincent, you're too amusing. But that's what I've always enjoyed about Ramses and his choice of hosts. They are always so laughably stubborn! Now try and rest a little, Docia. The Suspension will be complete come nightfall tomorrow . . . and with the sun soon to be up outside you can't really go anywhere in any event."

With that bit of logic, Selena departed the room. Only the sound of her heels walking away was left behind. There was no clang of a heavy prison door . . . no click of a lock securing them in. She seemed pretty darn confident that a bunch of ropes would be enough to keep them right where they were. And possibly a couple of guards. It would be silly to think they weren't guarded, wouldn't it?

She heard Vincent exhale harshly. It wasn't exactly a sigh of frustration. She really couldn't pinpoint the feeling behind it.

As for everything Selena had said . . . how was Docia to know if Selena was or wasn't the one she should be listening to? To be honest, she kind of liked the lure of free will and making her own choices. She'd been rather anxious ever since she'd grasped that this guy Menes was about to be reborn and wouldn't take more than a couple of breaths before hunting her down and trying to make her his queen. What if she didn't like him? What if she didn't want to get married? Was she supposed to, like, give birth to his heirs or some crazy shit like that regardless? And how did that work, exactly? Did you give birth to a Bodywalker . . . or just a normal human being?

"Docia?"

"I don't feel like talking right now," she told him, biting her lip.

This time it was most definitely a sigh.

"Docia, you can't listen to her. She's . . . you have to think of her like a cultist. She leads a cult of misguided Bodywalkers. She's very dynamic and very convincing. She is also very powerful and very deceitful."

"And you've been so up front with me about the whole Menes thing and the no daylight thing?" She hitched in a breath. "No more sunrises. No sunsets. One touch of the stupid sun and I explode into fire and ashes or something."

"No. Nothing so dramatic. The sun affects all Nightwalkers in some way, it's true. The Gargoyles turn to stone at the touch of sunlight. The Djynn become smoke and will remain formless if they don't hide in their shells, jars, or bottles."

"What about *us*? What happens to *us*?"

This time she heard the weight of sadness in his voice.

"It paralyzes us. Every bit of us freezes up, we collapse numb and mute and powerless right where we stand. It's what I always imagined a coma to be like. Trapped inside my own body, watching the world but not able to connect to it. But if we are in shelter, out of the touch of the sun, we simply go to sleep as usual. Or not. We can have insomnia just like anyone else. We can stay up late and watch TV. We can goof off on the Internet, if we so choose."

"As long as you stay out of the sun."

"Yes. And Docia, Ramses would have told you, had he been given the opportunity. He was teaching you slowly to help you adapt, handing things out piecemeal so as not to overwhelm you. I hope you can understand that. He wasn't trying to be deceptive like she was making it sound."

"And did you agree with his methods?" she asked him.

There was one of those silent spaces, a long one, before he said, "I don't always agree with Ramses on every little detail, but I admire and respect him always. He is a brilliant entity, he has lived almost a dozen lifetimes. I would be an idiot not to defer to his wisdom in things." A pause. "And I would be an automaton if I didn't question his choices. As for you, I agreed with everything he did, except kissing you."

Ah. The kiss. She had kind of hoped that was a hallucination on her part. Or that maybe they were just going to pretend it had never happened. Both very disappointing ideas.

"I think I can do without your opinion on the matter," she said, an embarrassing flush creeping up her face.

"You know, I don't think I've ever seen someone's feet blush before," he said with a chuckle.

"Shut up!"

"Docia, honey, relax. I'm not saying it was hateful and dreadful or anything." There was a sound like a thud, and then in an abrupt slide of movement he appeared beneath her, grinning up at her. "In fact," he said, propping himself up on his elbows as he gazed up at her as if she were some kind of fascinating constellation, "I'd say he's kind of an idiot for walking away from it."

With that, he pushed up from the floor and gave her a sure and solid kiss. It was so fast that she hardly had the chance to react, but then he was rolling away and standing up beside her. He stood there a minute and she got the feeling he was . . .

"Stop looking at my ass and get me out of this contraption!" she exclaimed.

"Shh," he shushed her, his chuckle telling her she'd been right about his contemplations. "You mean you don't want to stay and give Selena a chance to show you how evil Ram and the rest of us are?"

"Mister, I don't give anyone who ties me up like this a chance to *do* anything to me!"

"Well, now, honey, I gotta say . . . that's a crying shame."

CHAPTER TEN

"Why didn't you tell me you were getting loose?" she demanded through her teeth as he began to snap off the cords by her feet, gently lowering her to the ground a bit at a time.

"That's funny, I seem to recall doing exactly that. But I won't hold it against you for not believing in me.. You really don't know me that well yet." He helped her put both feet on the floor, moving her slowly upright. "This is going to make your head pound like a bitch."

"You're standing . . . so where's Ram?" she asked as she watched him disentangle her from the ropes around her waist with the sharp, succinct movement of a man with a knife. Only there was no knife in his hand that she could see. It was as though he were slicing them with an invisible weapon.

"Miss the old guy, do you?" he teased her.

"Absolutely n— Well, maybe a little. But," she said quickly, "only inasmuch as he's a lot more polite than you are!"

"Well, do you want me to have manners, or do you want me to get you out of here? Your choice. I could just sit down over here and wait for Ram to show up." He walked away from her, leaving her wrists still bound, and pointed to an area on the floor with both open hands. That was when she noticed the bleeding around his wrists. They hadn't been as gentle binding him as they had been with her.

"No! No, it's fine," she said hastily.

He gave her a crooked grin and moved back over to her. He went to her left wrist. She watched as he took the rope in one hand and slashed the other across it and they fell apart instantly. But what really threw her, more than the seemingly magical melting away of her bonds, was that there was no longer any sign on his forearm of the beautifully lithe contorted snakes and the ornamental dagger they embraced. In that same moment, she realized her shoulder had ceased to itch. She could easily extrapolate why that was. The tattoos were gone. Just as they, Ram and Hatshepsut, were gone.

And though she'd hardly known her presence, Docia suddenly felt bereft just the same. She had to swallow hard to keep from getting too emotional about it. As with everything else, this wasn't the time.

"Good, because there's no telling what the future holds for you if Selena gets her hands on you. The conjurings and curses they use are very dangerous things, things that shouldn't be messed with. They like to convince themselves they are carrying out the wishes of the gods, but it's really the wishes of something far more base and human inside them that give them their impetus. Good old-fashioned greed and power-mongering."

"I see," she said as her other wrist finally came free. She took a moment to get her bearings upright again, and he pulled her close to his body to let her lean on him while she did. She wanted to feel weird about it, to be put off by this annoying version of the Ram she had come to know, but the fact was this was very much Ram's body . . . and it still smelled and felt as good as always when she got close to it. He still exuded that aura of virility and confidence, that quiet sense of knowing his position in the world. When she thought about it, the only caustic difference between Ram and Vincent that she could see was that Vincent was a bit of a smart-ass and gave the appearance of not taking things all that seriously. But the truth was, she knew someone exactly like that, and having been raised by him side by side with her brother, she had never had a doubt that in his heart he was one of the kindest people she knew, with a measureless capacity for love and loyalty.

"She was going to torture you," she said with sudden understanding. "It had nothing to do with my sensibilities. She was going to torture you once she'd completely suppressed the Bodywalker inside of you that could give you the strength to resist her methods."

He gave her a brief nod, reaching to rub circulation into her hands by moving his quickly along the outside of hers. "As second in command, Ramses knows a lot about where things are located. Safe houses, for example. Wealth stores. Artifacts, laws, historical documents. Touchstones." He shook his head when she opened her mouth to query. "I'll explain that to you another day. Suffice it to say, if she found out where all these things were, it could be devastating to the law-abiding Bodywalkers, not to mention some of the other Nightwalkers out there."

He walked away from her, holding a hand up to keep her silent a moment as he checked out the nearest part of the hallway. He suddenly reached behind a pillar, grabbed a heavy body, and slammed it into the wall. Then, with sickening precision, he caught the guard's head in both hands, and with a quick jolt, not to mention an audible sound, he snapped the man's neck and let him fall into a heap at his feet. When he came back to fetch her, holding out his hand, she must have looked every inch as horrified as she felt.

"Oh . . ." He chuckled. "Don't worry about it. He's a

Bodywalker. That'll heal after a while. Takes much more than that to kill one of us. But it is an excellent method of paralyzing him so he can't yell for help and so he can't come after us or cause us some trouble. Anyway, he kinda deserved it, letting himself be distracted . . . wearing an iPod, of all things. I mean, c'mon!" He gave another low chuckle. "He's guarding prisoners in a room with no doors!"

"He thought we were tied up!" She defended him, probably because she was feeling sorry for him. Somehow the lack of instant death made the neck-breaking act even more sinister than it had been initially. Was he just lying there staring and hearing everything they were saying? She shivered in revulsion.

"Look, *my queen,*" he said, the title nowhere near owning the respect and reverence Ramses had always used when addressing her as such, "whose side are you on here? Because if you want to stay, I'll be happy to let you. But you have to know . . . I can't leave you here alone. Ramses would never forgive me if I did. And since usually there's no escaping him . . ." He shrugged and moved away from her. "So I'll just go over here and sit down and contemplate what an outright coward you are while you wait for the queen of the nutballs to come back."

"I am not a coward!" she hissed at him, catching his hand and yanking him away from that spot on the floor he seemed so obsessed with.

"Sure you are. It's clear as day you have no desire to be queen. Not yet, anyway. So she waltzes in here and gives you the perfect solution and it's really tempting. I honestly can't blame you for that. But standing there prevaricating about it, wasting time until they find us like this, so you can throw up your hands and say, 'Oops! They caught us! Not my fault!' instead of owning the choice one way or the other, that's pure cowardice. Make up your mind, Docia. And do it fast. And once you make it up, commit to it as if it were the difference between life and death. Because to tell you the truth of it, it is. Not just for me. Not just for you. For a hell of a lot of other Nightwalkers out there. Not just Bodywalkers . . . *Nightwalkers.* Did you hear the way she talked about them? The other breeds? The contempt just dripping off her lips? She was saying 'filthy mongrels,' but she may as well have been saying 'niggers' or 'spics' . . . or any one of a thousand ignorant elitist comments you can conjure up in your head. And whether you know anything about them or not, ignorance isn't a good enough excuse to go along with the idea."

"Are they? Mongrels, I mean?"

"Well, they're not all angels, if that's what you're asking. Why? Do you think you have the right to make that judgment? Do you think I do?"

"No," she said softly. "I don't judge others. I'm just . . . I don't know how to make choices for people I've never even met. It's . . . paralyzing. You tell me to think one way, she tells me another. I barely know either of you. How do I know who's telling me the truth?"

Vincent came up to her, turned her to face him, and tipped her chin up so she could see right into his eyes. It was strange, but it was almost as if their color had changed. She concentrated for a moment, trying to figure out why. They were still the same gold as before. Just somehow . . . different.

"As an American, you make choices every day for others by supporting your government and its excursions or military actions into other countries. When you buy coffee at the same café every morning, you are choosing to support that business. When you pass judgment on the girl your brother starts to date, you affect his life. When you work for your boss, you choose to support him in his endeavors, as well as everyone else his business touches. You make choices for others every day. The difference is that now you are beginning to realize it. And now you are beginning to own it."

Docia saw the truth in what he was saying. Eerily so. She had always thought of herself as something of a nobody in the grand scheme of things. But if she looked at it his way, there wasn't any such thing as a nobody. And she rather liked that perspective. She was also a little surprised to see the attitude coming from someone of obvious importance, not to mention the sort of strength and prowess that could give him the tools to be a bully to those less powerful than he was.

"I'll go with you . . . but I want a promise from you first."

He rolled his eyes and she could tell by the tension in his body that he wasn't as relaxed about their tenuous situation as he led her to believe. If she did decide to stay, she wondered if he really would sit back and let her. Luckily for him, she wasn't comfortable taking that chance.

"What? Tell me what the tipping point is for you here. I can't wait to hear it."

"You know, there's no need for sarcasm," she said with a sniff. Then she turned dead serious, making sure he felt the strength of her conviction with every molecule in her body and both of her spirits. "We leave here and you bring me to my brother. Ram was right. There's no way he'll be satisfied without seeing me face-to-face. I should have known that. So you bring me to him so I can give him some peace of mind. Then I'll go with you and learn how to be a Bodywalker. In fact, I'll learn *everything*."

She could tell by his hesitation that it was something of a dangerous promise. She wasn't stupid. She knew what she was asking of him. But given that his other choice was lollygagging in this room waiting for other guards to show up, she fully expected him to cave.

He smiled at her, the left side of his lips curling up, and a peculiar light shone in his eyes.

"Deal," he said.

And that was when she realized the light shining in his eyes was an enormous sense of pride.

In her.

Vincent tried not to be distracted by things when he was on a mission. He was actually quite proud of the way he was able to weed out all extraneous bullshit and focus on the task at hand. It was one of the qualities that had landed him on SEAL Team Six at a ridiculously young age.

But it was just as likely part of what had gotten him killed, too. Well, almost killed. He had since, with Ramses's guidance and persona Blended onto his, learned a great deal about seeing the total picture, about processing things in one part of his brain while another part of it got on with the task at hand. So he wasn't all that heavily critical as he found himself prodding inside his own body for the hundredth time since regaining consciousness, seeking out any sign . . . even so much as a glimmer . . . of Ramses's presence within him. At first the vacancy had been almost crippling, insofar as it had been liberating for Vincent. Dealing with the world as himself, making all choices and decisions alone for the first time in so long, should have been refreshing and enjoyable.

But it was not. It was actually a little frightening, something he could admit to himself only because Ramses had taught him long ago that admitting fear was always the first step in defeating it. Ram had taught him that only a foolish man never felt fear. And considering his fearlessness and his overinflated sense of being a badass had nearly ended his life, it was a lesson that had been very much needed.

Not that he was paralyzed or anything. He wasn't the type. But every so often he felt as if it were hard to breathe. Usually when he stood between two hallways and had to make the choice to go left or right. He'd been so used to a consensus on these decisions . . . making them on his own was the starkest feeling he had ever known, next to lying there bleeding and dying and watching a piece of scum shoot his sister and nephew in the head . . . and doing it only five feet away from him, just to be sure he saw every second of it.

What had been born of that was something he and Ram shared down to their mutual bones. Failure was not an option. He would not fail this nascent Bodywalker, and he would not fail Ramses. And more than that, he wouldn't fail the thousands of people waiting with bated breath for their pharaoh to be reborn.

Oh, and yeah, she really did have a nice ass.

Okay, so sue me, he thought as he put a hand on said ass and gave her a boost up a wall. It could have been worse. It could have been the way Ramses reacted to her. Though, he had to admit, there had been something very electric about the feel of her mouth against his. That was honestly the impetus behind giving her that little smack on the lips earlier. He'd wanted to demystify it for himself. Or maybe find a way to blame it on Ram's presence inside of him. Because he, Vincent, had never felt anything like that storm of need and vibrant sensation before in his life. It had felt almost mystical. So of course it made sense to blame it on the only source of mysticism in his life.

But even that quick little smooch had been ridiculously stimulating. No Ram. No Hatshepsut. Just him and this poor kid who'd been thrown into a tempest. And if he was going to be really honest, the kiss hadn't even been necessary. He'd been strung up behind her with a nice A-line view of her backside and her curiously stimulating little feet.

I mean, really! Who the hell has sexy feet?

Not that they'd be very sexy after this little escape. She was barefoot in the snow, her shoes lost somewhere . . . and dawn was going to break any minute now. He had no choice but to force her to run through woods and bracken, her exposed feet set up to take the worst of it.

But they couldn't be caught out in the daylight. Not in this weather. Even if by some miracle the sun didn't kill them, a Bodywalker was capable of freezing to death on the forest floor. There was no healing from being a solid block of ice for several hours. The only thing working in their favor was that there was no chance in hell Odjit would risk her precious little life running after them, and her minions would be just as susceptible as the rest of them. Even the Gargoyles that served her needed to be back at their touchstones and turned to stone before dawn struck . . . or else they risked a kind of madness that went far beyond the power-mongering lunacy of the Templar bitch.

And she wasn't the worst of it. If she had been reborn, then that meant the Templar high priest wasn't too far behind . . . if he had not yet been born already. And as bad as she would be when she finally reached full strength, he was worse. And the two of them in tandem . . .

He had neglected to tell Docia some of these details, knowing that Ramses's wisdom about not overwhelming her with everything at once had been well-founded, not just with her, but with others in the past as well.

Strange, but with the amount of light filling the gray, pre-dawn sky, he ought to have begun to feel the strange tingling sensation in his extremities that was a precursor to the Rapture, the paralysis that crippled a Bodywalker caught in the sun. He knew instantly it had something to do with this Suspension Odjit had inflicted on them, but the knowledge gave him little comfort, even though it might mean they could make it much farther than he might have anticipated. Nothing that reminded him Ramses was not with him could make him comfortable.

But he pushed it aside, his practiced eye tracking the woods and the sun's cresting point, his ears seeking the sound of traffic or water to bring it all together. Running along the road might be dangerous, but they needed to get indoors somewhere, quickly. Since the Suspension had not been fully cast, there was no telling when Ramses would return, and with him the weakness of the Rapture. Perhaps Docia would not fall victim to it as severely, because she was not yet Blended, but she would not be safe continuing on without him. She had no idea how to survive against these people, and her desire to return to her brother proved it. No doubt the Templars already knew everything about her previous life and would be watching her brother, anticipating reacquiring her there at some point. It was common for confused newly fledged Bodywalkers to try to cling to their old lives, the things they knew and loved.

But it was best not only for her but for them that she keep her contact with them to a minimum . . . or better yet, severed all ties completely.

"My God, it's so cold," she gasped, stumbling to a stop and wrapping her arms around herself, dancing in the snow from one foot to the other as if it would give relief to her stinging, aching feet. The pain she was in was so strong, he could practically feel it crackling along the edges of his awareness, and he hated himself for having to do this to her, for forcing her to suffer like this. It was, after all, his fault. He should never have left the house with her. He should never have trusted anyone else with her safety. Even if it was Hexus, one of Stohn's most trusted soldiers, it had not been Hexus's duty. His duty was to serve and protect Windham House and anyone his domini ordered him to protect, true, but Vincent's duty to protect her superseded Kasimir's authority. He should have gone with his instincts.

Their instincts. His and Ram's.

He stilled. There it was. The first sign. The moment he stopped thinking of Ram's goals as his own, the moment he forgot to separate the two except as an afterthought, that was the moment he knew Ramses was coming back. And right on the back of it was the start of that tingling sensation, the warning along the edges of his skin that the sun was touching it and that the Rapture was imminent.

He drew breath to speak, then smelled it. Wood fire. They were far enough from the old Spanish church where Odjit and her followers had been holed up, so it wasn't originating from there. He had to assume it was from somewhere else, a dwelling of some sort.

"Come on," he encouraged her, reaching out to her.

She didn't even hesitate to put her hand in his, and for some reason that made him smile inside. That she took a step into the snow readily told him just what a trouper she really was. And despite Asikri's judgment of her as a whiner, he knew she was anything but. Nor was she the coward he had accused her of being in order to get a rise out of her. She honestly had to be one of the bravest of creatures, in his opinion, to keep adapting so quickly to her precipitously changing situation again and again. A lesser person would have just collapsed into a ball . . . would have stayed in the nice warm church, no matter what it might mean.

He yanked on her given hand, whipping her up hard

against his body, grinning down at her when she gasped with surprise. Then she groaned, a surprisingly sexy little sound, followed by an equally sexy little wriggle into the warmth of his body. He wished he had the luxury of time to enjoy it, but he did not. Instead, he scooped her up in his arms and began to double-time it through the woods in the direction of the smell of smoke.

She burrowed her ice-cold nose and face against his neck, under his hair, her hot breath gasping out against him in puffs and shivery words.

"Y-you're so w-warm!" she groaned.

"You will be, too, in a minute," he promised her, although he wasn't as confident as he sounded. His lips were going numb, and it wasn't from the cold. In fact, he was feeling less and less cold by the second, which meant he was feeling less and less, period. He wasn't prone to panic, knowing it was the fastest way to get himself killed, not to mention her, but he'd be lying if he were to say he was perfectly calm about it.

When his foot hit the gravel driveway leading up to a pointy little A-frame house nestled into the woods on one side and the edge of a cliff on the other, he wanted to shout with triumph. But he didn't want her to think he hadn't had it all under control all along. Sunrise had broken about twenty minutes ago, and there was no time for celebrations.

He barreled into the door of the cabin, not bothering to knock, not even calling out. He dropped Docia straight to the floor, knowing the element of surprise would be fleeting but crucial to gaining control over whoever was in the house.

It wasn't until he was inside the house that he realized it was pitch-black inside.

"Oh shit," he said.

"Yeah. 'Oh shit' is right," declared a defiant female

voice, right before she flung a ball of mystic green energy straight at his head.

But this wasn't the red-tinged energy of a Templar. It was something else completely. And as he dodged the opening volley, as she dissolved into smoke only to reappear elsewhere behind him, he knew exactly what she was.

"Wait! I'm not here to hurt you!"

"Then you'd have knocked, now, wouldn't you? I knew it! I knew it wasn't safe here anymore with a bunch of Bodywalker Templars running loose in the valley!"

"We're not Templars!" Vincent insisted as he dodged a second, far more wickedly accurate volley of energy balls, only to have the energy change into little winged dragons that immediately set on him, chomping through both legs of his pants and one arm. The fourth one heading for his other arm he sent batting away, like a line drive over third base, and this time *she* had to duck to be missed. "We're their prisoners!" He reached up to rip off one of the eager little lizards, its razor-sharp teeth like needles in the meat of his thigh. He grabbed the head of the thing and flung it, too, in her direction. This time, though, instead of dodging it, she leapt up and caught it. She held the little thing to her chest.

"Oh sure, you big fat stupid bully! I've heard that before!"

"Really? What, are we dropping like flies on you or something?" Docia said, trying to sound sarcastic through chattering teeth. She reached up for the little dragon latched on to Vincent's other leg and grabbed it by its head. "Knock it off or I'll break its little neck!" She grabbed tight to prove it, and Vincent ground out a vicious curse as the teeth dug deep into him.

"Jesus Christ!" he spat.

"No, wait! Don't hurt her!"

"Don't hurt *her*?" Docia and Vincent echoed in differing levels of disbelief. Vincent's was obvious, since he was the one suffering; he assumed Docia simply couldn't figure out how the little beast was obviously a *her*.

"If you didn't want her hurt," Docia said, shivering, "then you shouldn't be using her and her friends like watchdogs." She struggled to her knees and then gently pried the dragon's teeth out of Vincent's leg. She looked at it, inspecting it, just shy of lifting its tail to look for private parts, Vincent could only assume. "It's kind of cute. What is it? A dragon?"

The dragon squeaked as if she'd insulted it, spitting at her in a garbled combination of chatter that, when run together like that, sounded like cussing. Then the little booger showed its teeth at her and made a production of licking Vincent's blood off its lips and making yummy sounds.

"It's a dragonlet. Dragons are like, three tons heavier than an elephant. Duh." The dragonlet's owner rolled her eyes because, clearly, that ought to be obvious to anyone. "Now, can I have her back?" She held out one hand, the other continuing to cradle her first catch to her breast as one might a kitten. And, like a kitten, it began to purr. Loudly.

"Call the other one off of Vincent first."

The cabin owner twisted her lips to the side, clearly nibbling on the inside of them as she fretted between getting her pets back and letting Vincent possibly have the opportunity to get the upper hand.

"Seriously, if you think these little rats would have stopped me if I didn't want to be stopped, then you don't know a damn thing about Bodywalkers." Vincent felt the need to point out.

"Shh!" Docia said, elbowing him in his kneecap.

"Oh, for pity's sake!" Vincent ground out.

Docia got to her feet, and Vincent could honestly

imagine how difficult a task that had to be for her. He watched her step across to the other woman, and it took everything inside him not to scream at her to stop. But when he saw the bloody footprints she was leaving behind on the wood-plank flooring, he didn't have the heart to countermand her efforts.

"Here she is," Docia said, holding up the dragonlet. Its wings flapped, the spiky little fingers at the crested points of those wings wiggling toward the safety of its caretaker. Docia handed it over without remembering, it seemed, to make the other woman call off the last of the little monsters still dug into his arm. Vincent pulled his forearm up to his nose and glared into the dragonlet's glassy green eyes.

"Are you having fun?" he growled at it. "And you do realize I can snap your scrawny little neck, right?"

The gnawing stopped, at least, but that didn't keep it from surreptitiously licking the blood it had drawn from its lips with a rapid little forked tongue.

"How do you know it's a girl?" Docia asked about her recently abandoned charge, eaten up with curiosity.

"Oh!" The little blond woman, barely an inch over five feet, he guessed, and maybe a buck five soaking wet, smiled puckishly. "The girls have an extra joint on the top of the wing. Right here, see?" She gently stretched out the wing of the new acquisition, counting out the joint bumps along the ridge of it aloud. Then she cuddled that one close and compared the wingspan of the first she'd been holding. "See? Three on the boy. Four on the girl."

"Oh!" Docia giggled as the male took offense to being fondled and clambered up the young girl's arm and under the flounce of thick blond corkscrew curls.

"I'm seriously considering adding a joint in this thing's wings if you don't get it off me real soon," Vincent groused, shaking his arm in hopes of dislodging the beast. No such luck. And he could appreciate that Docia was making far faster ground than he had been able to manage thus far, so he didn't want to do anything the blond Djynn might consider a threatening act. Still . . . that didn't mean he was above verbal warnings.

"SutSut!" the Djynn called, snapping her fingers. The dragonlet disconnected itself from Vincent, and to prove it wasn't impressed by his threats, it blew a fork-tongued raspberry at him before flying off with what could only be labeled a flounce, its tail so high in the air that Vincent could see parts of its anatomy he could happily have gone through life without seeing. "But don't think you can try anything," the Djynn warned. "I'll break every window in this house and leave you to freeze while I go spend the day in my canteen."

"I'm not going to— Canteen? You're a Djynn attached to a canteen?"

"Well, sure." She pointed to the metal canteen with its wide, flat bottom and large circumference. "It can't break, unlike bottles and such. And it's really hard to rip that sucker open."

"You're a Djynn?" Docia asked, sounding fascinated. "Like . . . a genie?"

"If you make an *I Dream of Jeannie* reference, I'll turn your skin blue for a week. And don't think I can't do it," the Djynn warned hotly. Although Vincent didn't find her very threatening now that he got a good look at her. It might be the Hello Kitty pajamas, but he was pretty sure the Cookie Monster slippers with their googly eyes robbed her of all her street cred.

"No. Of course not. I just . . . I never met a Djynn before. Hell, I only found out there was such a thing less than an hour ago," she admitted.

"I'm surprised you're meeting one now," Vincent said dryly as he looked around the entryway, great room, and kitchen combination carefully, assessing the cabin for any further threats. "Djynn don't usually live in houses."

"Please." The Djynn rolled her eyes. "What generation are *you* living in, anyway?" She turned away and went scrounging behind one of the couches for something, and the three dragonlets made a game of hide-and-seek in her hair. She came up with the fourth dragonlet, who was moaning a bit dramatically, a wing draped over one of its eyes. "Poor MutMut," she cooed at it, giving it kisses of comfort on its head.

"What's your name? Or . . . can't you tell me?" Docia frowned. "I heard a story once where a genie loses its power if its name is given up."

"Djynn. Not genie!" She huffed out a breath. "And that'd make it hard, wouldn't it? Going around calling each other 'Hey, you!' all the time."

"I suppose it would," Docia agreed.

"Docia, would you please sit down," Vincent said, moving cautiously toward the kitchen. The minute he moved, however, all four dragonlets perked to attention and glared at him. They even gave off spitting little growls. He held up his hands in submission. "Her feet are bleeding. I'm just going to get something to clean them up a little."

"My name is SingSing," the Djynn said, frowning at Docia. "And you really should sit. Just don't get blood on my furniture. You have no idea how hard it is to get blood out of piled silk."

Docia sat down and Vincent could tell she was trying not to find something funny. Honestly, the girl had a face like an open book. She didn't have the slightest idea how to mask what she was thinking.

"SingSing, couldn't you use magic to . . . I don't know . . . fix something like that?"

"Oh, right," SingSing snorted. "Like I'm going to

waste my precious magic on getting a stain out of the sofa."

"You say that like magic is finite," Docia noted.

Clever girl, Vincent thought. He was beginning to see why she had been chosen for a Blending of such import. It was also a shame about the whole Menes thing. She was starting to grow on him. In more ways than one.

He fetched some paper towels from the roll, then ran some water into a bowl, making sure it was just warm enough but not too hot to shock her frozen feet.

"Djynn magic *is* finite," he told her. "Actually, a lot of it is attached to certain things. Like the dragonlets. She probably gets a lot of magical store from them. Most Djynn have some kind of mascot."

"Not just *any* kind of mascot," SingSing snapped in his direction. "It's not a frickin' football team." She turned to Docia and smiled warmly, making it clear whom she liked in the room and whom she did not. "And don't call them familiars, either," she warned Docia with a stern finger. "They're called nikkis. The live ones, anyway. If it's an inanimate magical resource, we call it a niknak. Get it? That's where the word came from, a long time ago, you know. Niknaks. Only, you spell it differently. I mean, what's with the 'k' thing, anyway? Oh, you know it's there in the beginning and the end, but you can only hear it in the end and not the beginning. Seriously?" She eyeballed Docia as if she'd have the answer to the American English lexicon. "Anyway, you can call either one, animate or inanimate, a nik and you wouldn't be wrong. These four little guys are all niks. I have more powerful niknaks, of course." She glared at Vincent to make sure he got that not-so-subtle message. "But we hide our niknaks all over so no one can find them. It's kind of like a treasure hunt sometimes between Djynn. We're always trying to hunt down more and more powerful niks. And once another Djynn touches the nik, it's theirs. Kind of sucks. That's why we don't usually throw our nikkis at other Djynn."

Vincent knelt at Docia's feet, lifting them onto his thighs to rest, then inspecting the left one first.

"Yeah, but you didn't think twice about throwing them at me," he pointed out.

"Well, I panicked," SingSing admitted sheepishly. "It's been a while since I've even seen another Nightwalker. Face-to-face like this, anyway. I was so mad when those Templars showed up in the valley, you have no idea. I know I should pack up and go, that it's the safe thing to do, but this is . . ." She frowned and her head dropped forward.

"This is your home," Docia guessed gently, her hand touching the Djynn female with compassion. It made Vincent tense up to see her do it. Djynn were not to be trusted. That was the first rule Ramses had ever taught him about them. Never trust them. Their craving for niks was like a disease; they were obsessed by them, and they just couldn't help it. They would do anything, screw over anyone they had to, to acquire their next nik. The more powerful the nik, the more willing they were to sacrifice someone else. This Djynn had stopped fighting them only because he had threatened her niks.

"Well, it has been, anyway. And now thanks to you people I have to get the heck out of Dodge. This sucks supremely, I just want you to know that," she said, pointing angrily at him.

"I have nothing to do with it!" he shot back defensively. "Believe me, if we could rout Odjit out of there, we would. I'd like nothing more than to see her disenfranchised. A lot of us would."

"Hmm." SingSing tilted her head. "So, you're like Djynn, then. Not all the same."

"Not all the same?" Docia echoed.

"Mm." SingSing shrugged. "Castes. We come from different castes. Some of us"—she rolled her eyes—"think we're better than others of us. I guess that's no different than any other society. But the truth is, some of us are way wickedly more powerful. And that means they are more dangerous. The Marids and the Afreets are the first and second most powerful Djynn. And if you come across a Sheytan . . ." She shivered, and Docia looked quickly at Vincent.

"They're pure evil," he supplied cautiously. "Only the Marids and Afreets can keep them in line."

"Then there's lowly little Djinn like me. We're sort of the suburban middle class of Djynn."

"And that leaves your poor. Your destitute."

"The Jann." She nodded. "Usually servants to other Djynn. They don't have much skill or power. Oh, stop fondling her feet already, would you?" she huffed at Vincent, pushing him aside. She linked her fingers above Docia's feet like a web and a sudden burst of green energy popped out of her hands, like a wonky, brilliant flashbulb. Then she stood up and walked away.

"I was getting ready for bed, it being daybreak and all, but I could go for a little nosh. Anyone hungry?"

CHAPTER ELEVEN

Docia inspected her feet carefully. They felt warm and, outside of a weird tingling sensation, perfectly healed.

Good gravy, what was next? She really wouldn't mind some kind of a handbook to all of this. *Bodywalkers for Dummies* or something like that. *How to Become a Nightwalker in One Easy Lesson.*

But no such luck. Of course. *But, hey, no one promised you life was going to be easy,* she thought. Or was this technically an afterlife? Never mind. She wasn't going to dissect that right now. She already had way too much to do trying to keep track of all the information coming at her. To top it all off, she was feeling incredibly sleepy. The darkness of the cabin wasn't helping; neither was the blessed warmth of it, once their Djynn host was thoughtful enough to shut the door that Vincent had left open. Happily enough, though, there was a huge cobblestone fireplace dead center of the large glass windows that were blacked out now but promised to have a great view of the outdoors. She didn't blame SingSing for wanting to stay. A secluded cabin in the mountains sounded like a little slice of heaven to her right then.

"Where are we, anyway?" she thought to ask.

"Up near Hunter Mountain. The ski resort's on the other ridge over across the valley here." She pointed out the window. "It's not easy to build over here, so it's a pretty low population. Nice and quiet. The valley has more people in it. Early Spanish settlements made the town down there. I'm surprised you came up the mountain."

"That's why we did it," Vincent pointed out. "They would have anticipated the easy way, and we'd already be back with the Templars, hanging there like Christmas geese."

"Well, you're safe here as long as you behave yourselves," SingSing said. "No one knows about this place. You need a snowmobile to get to the road . . . or an ATV if there's no snow cover."

"Both of which leave tracks," he pointed out.

"Yeah, but I haven't been to town since before the last snowfall," she shot back, sticking her tongue out at him. "So like I said, you're safe."

"Until dusk. Then we'll have to go," Vincent warned Docia pointedly. "We don't want to endanger our hostess."

"Pfft," SingSing snorted. "I'm not afraid of a bunch of fanatic Templars. They should be afraid of me," she said, pointing to her puffed-up chest. Docia had to agree with Vincent's skeptical expression. She really didn't look all that powerful. SingSing started to whistle and made herself busy in the cozy little kitchen. It had nice conveniences in it, slightly dated in some cases, but of a classic style that would never grow old or obsolete. The entire cabin was quaint, as far as she could see. She could even see a huge loft above the entryway that ran the entire width of the house on that side. Clearly it was SingSing's sleeping area. There were only two other doors in the place, outside of the front doors and a pair of sliders on the right side of the chimney. She supposed one was the bathroom and maybe the other was a closet.

"Vincent, I'm so very tired," she said to him softly, reaching to touch his hand as he paced past her. He'd been doing a frenetic sort of circuit for a while now, as if he were trying to think and needed to be on the move in order to do so.

Vincent came to an immediate halt, concern etching his face as he crouched in front of her. She leaned toward him as he cupped her face between his hands. After a long moment of studying her with those warm golden eyes of his, he nodded.

"I can see that you are," he said, his thumb brushing over her lips. The touch had an instant revitalizing effect, stirring something inside of her she couldn't even begin to explain. It was like a kiss in a way, intimate and warm, so very tender.

"And I can see Ram coming back to you," she said softly.

That made him frown. "Why would you say that? Don't you think I'm capable of kindness on my own?"

"No. Of course you are." She sighed, watching as his attention drifted down to the lips he was touching, appreciating the warmth of her breath on the back of his hand. "You start to round out your vowels. The smart-ass in your personality smooths out a little. And when you touch me . . ." She trailed off, suddenly shy about putting the sensation into words. It was a wholly intimate thing, the deeply felt sensations that something as simple as a touch against her lips was stirring. It made her want to cross her legs in defense of it, to hide it away in case it was embarrassingly obvious to everyone in the room. Especially him.

"And Ram is overly concerned with respect toward me because of who he feels I am," she added after a moment. "To be honest, I like you a bit more. You're . . . you treat me normally. Like my brother does. Or Leo . . ." She trailed off, taking a moment to think about those wonderful men in her life who were no doubt beside themselves with worry over her.

"Who is this Leo?" he demanded, his whole body bristling. "Is it a boyfriend? Unfortunately, I must tell you that most preexisting relationships deteriorate under the stress of the Blending."

She blinked at him. "Leo helped raise me as a child," she said softly.

"Oh." He exhaled, seemingly a little easier. "So he's . . . old."

She smiled, unable to keep from filling the expression with mischief. "Old*er*. Not necessarily old. I love Leo very much. And he loves me. I could turn into Regan from *The Exorcist* and neither he nor my brother would ever stop loving me, so I am not worried about that in the least."

"You say that," he said a bit darkly, "and for your sake I hope it's true, but I know human beings. We are not known for our flexibility." He met her eyes steadily, and there it was. That splendid golden warmth. It was so beautiful, so otherworldly almost. Like a pair of fabulous little suns that had been captured and set there to burn her up with their heat. "So, when I touch you . . . if Ram isn't present, you feel nothing?" he asked, trying to spin it off as idle curiosity.

"What does it matter? The odds you'll ever be separate like this again are almost nil," she pointed out, trying not to flush over the direct conversational topic. Not that she was a prude. Far from it. But with him, it just seemed deliciously naughty talking about it, and that sent a wriggle of awareness down her spine. "And it appeared to me that you and Ram have no interest in pursuing an attraction . . . so . . ." She shrugged.

"Just answer my question," he said, leaning in closer

to her until their foreheads were just about touching. "You feel nothing when it's just me in here?"

Unable to resist the impulse, Docia reached up and touched his jawline, running the tips of her fingers along the crispy start of whiskers. It made him appear a little more rugged, a little more Vincent, as opposed to the clean-cut handsomeness of Ram. It was the same face either way, but the attitude behind it, the aura of presence, made it seem like two different men. Just as it was. Although, in truth, she had never seen just Ram without Vincent, as she was seeing Vincent without Ram. She found herself curious to know what Ram would be like in such circumstances.

"I never said that," she murmured. "Isn't it a silly kind of question? Doesn't that put you in competition with yourself? You're both the same person in the end."

"And yet you just said there's a difference."

"The difference is—"

"Food!"

SingSing plopped a tray of food on the coffee table just behind Vincent, the smack of it making Docia jump. She had just about forgotten the Djynn was there, though she couldn't imagine why. SingSing had been bustling noisily about the kitchen the whole time.

Vincent moved back from Docia, turning to look at the tray. Truth was, there was no telling when either of them had last eaten, no knowing just how long they had been hanging there in the Templars' Spanish church. It didn't feel all that long . . . but the sudden leap of hunger overcoming her weariness made her feel as though she hadn't eaten in days. And technically, that was very likely true. She had barely eaten at the hospital; the stress of the whole business of dying had put off her appetite. So now even a tray of cold meats and cheeses seemed like gourmet fare, and admittedly, SingSing had laid out the tray with an impressive flair for variety and detail. She'd even cut a fanned-out strawberry for every glass of chocolate milk sitting there. SingSing scooped up a glass, flopped onto the couch next to Docia, and took a loud slurp of the milk.

"Ahh!" She smacked her lips for emphasis. "I suppose I ought to have made cocoa, with it being so cold and all. But I do so love cold chocolate milk, don't you? It's sweet and refreshing at the same time. Isn't that great? And yet it looks like liquid poo. Go figure."

Docia had been midsip from her own glass when that observation came out, and she immediately spit and sprayed the would-be swallow as a laugh bolted out of her. Unfortunately, Vincent was still kneeling in front of her.

"Oh! I'm so sorry!" she cried.

SingSing handed over a cloth napkin to Docia, then, humming happily, she reached for some cheese while Docia frantically blotted Vincent's face. He eventually caught her hands together, took the napkin from her, and finished the job himself. His sigh seemed more pained than angry, but Docia was biting her lip anxiously.

"A word about Djynn," he said dryly. "They don't have much in the way of filters."

"What for?" SingSing demanded. "It's too much work tiptoeing around other people's sensibilities."

"Anything else you'd like to warn me about?" Docia asked him, touching the damp hair at his forehead, trying to arrange it in a way that made it look less as though he'd been spit on.

"Never. Ever. No matter what. Make a wish." He nailed her with a serious expression. "Djynn are con artists. Wishes are only a way of getting them what they want. And it never turns out well for the wisher."

"He has a point there," SingSing agreed. "But decent Djynn, such as myself, won't lure you with wishes or any such nonsense. I've gone straight. Yep. That's me. Straight and narrow. Up-and-up, for the most part." She grinned. "A girl has to have some secrets." SingSing sat up. "Say, you look beat. So am I. Nosh up, I'll get some bedding and you both can camp out down here. Don't have much in the way of blankets and pillows, so you'll have to share. House is a little drafty, so snuggle up near the fireplace. Mattress!"

The Djynn snapped her fingers and a thick feather mattress plopped out of the rafters and onto the floor, unrolling itself in front of the fire and startling the heck out of Docia.

"Jeez!" She instinctively jumped toward Vincent, grabbing on to the yoke of his shoulders and practically sitting in his lap as she came off the couch. She was nearly strangling him by the time the pillows and blankets fell out of the sky and onto the bed.

"Sorry. Didn't mean to startle you. Don't worry, the other stuff stays up there unless I call for it." SingSing yawned, oblivious to the two sets of eyes cautiously looking up at the rafters. There was nothing to be seen, just as there had been no mattress or blankets up there earlier. Wherever SingSing's storage space was, it was invisible to their eyes.

"Other stuff?" Docia had to ask.

"Oh, you know . . . warm-weather clothing, holiday decorations, spare furniture . . ."

"Furniture?" Docia squeaked.

"A Jet Ski. Waterslide. A Bouncy Kingdom, you know, for when the kids visit. Trampoline, also for the kids. A camel. Coupla gondolas. I know, I know. Who needs two gondolas, right? It's a long story . . . one was a gift from someone who *clearly* didn't know me as well as they thought they did." She rolled her eyes. "Anyway, buncha other stuff." She stood up and yawned again, stretching with a limberness that would make a yogi proud. “I’ll leave the tray, but I’m taking my milk.” She said it warningly, as if they might steal it from her given half a chance.

“Where are . . . ?”

“The dragonlets? In my hair, silly.” And right on cue, a lizard head popped out from betwixt her blond curls and stuck out a forked tongue, blowing a raspberry at them. “SutSut, be nice!” SingSing warned, putting two fingers on its head and stuffing it back into her hair.

“But there’s not enough room for all four of them to be—,” she whispered to Vincent.

“Djynn have the power to alter spatial relations. She could fit a whole zoo in her hair if she wanted to.”

SingSing giggled. “Now that would be a little ridiculous.” She yawned again. “Welp. G’day, guys. Stay warm. Help yourself to the fridge. And . . . uh . . .” She pointed to Vincent sternly. “Make sure you tell her the part about never waking a Djynn. I won’t be held responsible for my actions.” She pointed back and forth between them, eyeballing each until she was satisfied they were taking her seriously. Then she was off with a flounce toward the loft. For the first time, Docia noticed there was no ladder . . . no stairs. But apparently that didn’t matter, as the Djynn turned into sparkly blue smoke midstep and rose into the loft area, disappearing into the darkness.

They both sat there, staring after her for a moment.

“Never wake a Djynn?” Docia whispered.

“Yeah. Pisses them off,” Vincent whispered back.

“I gathered.” Docia bit her lip. “So . . . there is such a thing as rubbing the lamp the wrong way?”

“Really? You had to go there?” he asked.

“I’m just saying.” She giggled.

Vincent was determined to make some headway with this whole “Ram makes me feel things you don’t” business. Well, okay, maybe she hadn't actually said that, but she'd been on the verge of implying it. How was it different? How was it . . . less?

Oh hell, no. There was nothing that Ram had that Vincent didn't have. Literally. And before Ram came raging back into the picture, Vincent was intent on proving that. He knew she was tired. He wanted her to rest, he really did. But time was of the essence in this particular case. He couldn't exactly wait until dusk to gather empirical evidence that he was just as stimulating as Ram.

Luckily, SingSing had unwittingly provided means and opportunity. One mattress. One quilt. Two pillows. It was really very cozy. Very conducive to the matter at hand.

She was nibbling sleepily on bits from the tray, clearly torn between sleep and starvation. He moved to the kitchen and washed what remained of the chocolate milk from his face and hair, anticipating the stickiness if he did not. He'd been in his dinner dress clothes throughout their whole ordeal, and he shrugged out of his jacket, pulled off his tie, and reached to unbutton his cuffs. The cuff links held a fastener along the inside of his left sleeve. The fastener held the invisible knife he always kept secured there. The knife had been one of Ram's gifts and his way out of the Suspension bindings. He grabbed hold of the knife, which only he could see and feel, and set it on the countertop. He would hide it under his pillow or sleep some other way with it within reach. This wasn't the first occasion it had saved his life, and he had no doubt it wouldn't be the last.

He began unbuttoning his shirt and narrowed his eyes on his target of the moment. It was funny, but somehow he kept forgetting she was injured . . . half-damaged. Somehow, when he looked at her, he never noticed the fading bruises and the butchered hair, never even saw the stitching that was probably already superfluous. He always seemed to see just the soft pretty contours of her face, the teasing turn of her lips, or the mink-colored depths of her eyes. She had these little lashes surrounding them, the curve of them only adding to the adorableness of her. She was cute. Apparently, he liked cute. He didn't use to. Not before Ram. He'd liked them tall and leggy and so gorgeous that other men would cry with envy . . . but quietly, so as not to piss him off. Once upon a time, he'd reeked of badass. He'd been an elite SEAL team member. He'd thought nothing could touch him.

He cleared his throat, kicking back the emotions and self-recrimination that still welled up when he thought about the past and what he had once been. He liked himself better now. He had redefined himself side by side with Ram, who had taught him how to be a far better man. A far better being.

And apparently better beings liked cute.

A lot. And much to Ram's dismay. Vincent's sometimes better half had been blindsided by this attraction, and everything about it had gone against his sense of loyalty and purpose, something Vincent had agreed with at the time. Loyalty was everything, after all. But that loyalty was Ram's, not necessarily his. Perhaps that was splitting hairs, but in the end, his only connection to Menes was through Ram's knowledge of him, and anyone's perspective was skewed to some degree when it came to something or someone they felt passionately about. Of course, he had all the faith in the world in Ram. It wasn't as though he could deceive him outright. But there were a lot of variables to be considered here, first and foremost that both Menes and Docia had been gifted with free will. Menes could decide to put off leaving the Ether as long as he wanted to . . . two years, twenty . . . two hundred. Nothing said he was definitively going to show up anytime soon except Ram's belief in him and Menes's steady track record thus far.

Oh. And Cleo. Cleo the prophetess who had sent him and Ram to Saugerties N.Y. because she had seen visions of Menes's and Hatshepsut's return.

Anyway, Docia had as much say in whom she liked or disliked as her Bodywalker did. Free will. The same free will Odjit had been trying to exploit, unfortunately. But, he told himself, this was hardly the same thing. This was just . . . this was just here and now. Not some anticipated future that they were all just guessing at.

Vincent shrugged out of his shirt, snapping the tails free of his pants and drawing her attention with the sound. He pretended not to notice, leaned over the sink a little, and splashed water over his neck and chest. *To remove the remaining chocolate,* he thought firmly, definitely not to use the water to accentuate the naked musculature of said chest.

Nope. Not one bit.

He felt awkward inside for a moment. He hadn't gone after a woman without his internal wingman in such a long time. For some reason, he found himself afraid of fucking it up. Maybe it was better to just leave it be. He should. Ram was going to pitch a fit when he came back and realized Vincent had been toying with his precious untouchable queen.

But she wasn't the precious untouchable queen. Not right then. No more than he was Ram right then . . . for the most part. Rounded vowels or otherwise, he knew what Ram felt like, and if he really was there, he'd be kicking up a superior fuss. Wouldn't he?

Docia looked up when Vincent made some kind of noise—and instantly regretted doing so. Or not. Or . . . yes. Well . . . the man was built like a freaking god, and he'd gone and taken off his shirt. She understood why: he was covered in milk and spit. *Her* fault, as usual. She decided to let herself stare at his shining pectorals and remarkably delineated abs for a moment in the hope that she wouldn't fall back into the growing feeling that all of this was her fault. From the bridge incident until now, she'd been stepping in shit again and again, and she had been dragging him into it as well. Sure, Ram seemed content to follow her into doom time and again, but she got the feeling that Vincent was not so eager. She wondered if the only reason he was still there was that he knew Ram would be back very soon and there would be no escaping his wrath if he let her escape his protection.

She moved toward the fireplace and the mattress that lay in front of it. It wasn't cheap, that was for sure. It was just what she thought a genie might conjure up. Thick, soft, covered in a royal-purple velvet fabric with blankets and pillows just as full and fluffy and just as bold in color. There were even little golden tassels hanging off the corners of each pillow.

It looked so luscious and she was so tired that she just wanted to crawl inside and sleep her life away. But there were two problems. Apparently it was not her life alone any longer, and it was sobering to realize that everything she did no longer affected her alone.

And along that train of thought was the second problem. She was about to get in bed with Mr. I'm Sexy and I Know It, where she'd have to make certain she refrained from gratuitous snuggling against him. There was the distinct danger of her doing just that, because, honestly . . . the more time she spent with him, the more times he came to her rescue, the more he insisted on touching her with those strong, confident hands . . . the more she felt herself being drawn to any and all of the sensations he inspired.

The best thing for her to do, she told herself sternly, was get in bed, roll over, and go to sleep. That's it. End of story. There. That ought to do it. She had a plan and she was sticking to it. She crawled into the bed, moving to the side closest to the fire because she still felt as though she were shivering and cold at her core. She might end up feeling too warm in the long run, but she would worry about that when the time came.

The time came about two seconds later when he slid into bed next to her. Okay, really? Was the guy a walking furnace or something? Had he even gotten cold out there in the forest when she'd been freezing her tatas off?

"Warm enough?" he asked, wrapping an arm around her torso and drawing her back snugly into the cup of his body. She wondered when it was going to stop surprising her that Vincent wasn't the type to ask permission to do certain things. She also wondered why it didn't piss her off. She ought to be hitting him over the head with her purse, screeching, "Masher! Masher!" like the little old ladies in Bugs Bunny cartoons. Only she didn't have a purse and she kind of enjoyed being mashed at the moment. Not that she'd cop to it under interrogation.

Besides, hadn't the Ram half of his equation decided she was off-limits? No touchy, no feely.

"How is it," he said suddenly, his voice very low and his breath incredibly hot against the back of her neck, "that you've just been through hell and you can still manage to smell so good?"

She could literally feel him inhale, a deep, long breath as he pushed his face a little closer to her skin. The arm around her tightened, his hand so far in a neutral position fitted against her ribs beneath her left breast, but there was something very not neutral to the entire situation. She could feel a powerful, dominant male overshadowing the whole setup.

She squeaked, wriggled out of his hold, and stumbled

out of bed . . . nearly burning herself in the fireplace. He sat up immediately.

"What's wrong with you?" he demanded.

"With me? You turn into a freaking octopus and all with the sexy 'Mmm, you smell good' business, and I'm the one who's wrong? Let's give it an hour and you can ask Ram that question, okay?"

His entire face darkened with a stormy irritation. Well, fine. She didn't care if she pissed him off.

"First of all, keep your voice down," he warned her, glancing up at the loft to make his point. Oh. Right. Wake genie up equals very bad things. "Secondly, what is your problem with *me*?" He stood up, whipping the blanket down onto the bed as though he might be wishing it were her instead . . . in a not good way. He stalked in her direction and she immediately began to back away, holding out her hands to ward him off, as if *that* were going to do any good. The man was a storm of muscle and testosterone and a buttload of attitude.

"You're supposed to be protecting me, not manhandling me!" she whispered fiercely.

"Oh, but you'll let Ram manhandle you until the cows come home," he growled as he closed in on her.

"Do you even hear what you're saying? You're the same person, you space cadet!"

The phrase gave them both pause. Yeah, she had to admit, that was a fairly decrepit choice, even for her.

"Not according to you," he said through his teeth, just as she backed herself into an inescapable corner of the living room. His hands slammed against the wood walls on either side of her shoulders, and then there was the rapid follow-up of his strong body leaning along hers, blocking her from moving. "According to you, there's all kinds of different."

"Would you just let it go? In a few more hours none of this is going to matter. A few more days and neither of us will be who we are right now. So what does anything I say or do matter?"

She had grown increasingly agitated with every word, with every statement. She wanted to blame it on him and the way he was harassing her, the infuriating way he was pressing at her, but even she knew it went beyond that.

Vincent settled back a little . . . calmed, it seemed, as he cocked his head and studied her briefly. Then his right hand came away from the wall and he took her chin, tipping it up until she was looking straight into the golden eyes she would have preferred to avoid.

"Docia, are you afraid of disappearing?" he asked her quietly.

There was no need to define what he was talking about. She knew what he meant, just as he knew what she meant by her remarks. She nodded into the touch of his fingers, loosening their grip on her a little.

"Don't you disappear when Ram is there?"

It wasn't an unfair question. Nor was it based on inaccurate observations, he thought with a frown. But she had it wrong. Just as his frantic behavior to delineate himself outside of Ram was wrong.

"No," he said softly, touching her forehead and the contours along the side of her face. "It's as true a symbiosis as you can ever imagine," he promised her. "Ram would falter without me, just as I'm faltering and fucking up without him. Selena knew that. That's why she did this to us." And by "us" he clearly meant Ram and himself. "Ram knows things, amazing things, and thinks in ways far beyond what I knew on my own. And Ram doesn't know half the modern fighting techniques that I do, nor does he have a head for computers and electronics. But together we know it all. And together we make up for each other's weaknesses in other ways. For instance, when I was just Vincent, it was all about winning, no matter who got trampled in the process." He sighed. "I don't want to trample you, Docia."

"Y-you confuse me," she stammered, the warm nut brown of her eyes tugging at him in peculiar ways, making him feel guilty when he didn't want to . . . when he rightly deserved to.

"I know. I'm sorry."

"Ram, too," she added, making sure he felt the equality of it in her eyes. He could hear it in her voice. She wasn't trying to coddle him. She was telling the truth. "This whole thing has been confusing. But, I think more than anything, the way I felt as though I should instantly trust you . . . even when I had nothing to go on except the assurances of a man who'd just kidnapped me . . ." The way she looked up at him, the closeness of her, he couldn't help noticing the gorgeous fringe of her dark lashes around those sweet, vulnerable eyes of hers. Thank God he and Ram had found her first. Selena and her sect would have turned her inside out.

And he'd almost allowed her to fall into their hands.

"Because you *should* trust us, Docia. If not me alone, then certainly Ram. He . . . we . . . *I* would never let anything hurt you," he promised her.

She giggled suddenly, and it made him smile a little in bemusement, even though he didn't understand what was so funny.

"I've never heard anyone use so many different personal pronouns to refer to them*selves* before."

His smile grew. "I know it must seem confusing. But I'm so used to it, to shifting all over the map like that, that I rarely notice it. But usually it's just I. Me. Myself. We phase back and forth in dominance, who has more control at any given moment changes like . . . the perfect balance between the clutch and the gas when driving a stick. Sometimes more of one, sometimes more of the other. But I can tell you this . . ." He reached with his thumb and drew it over the corner of her mouth. "We . . . both Ram and Vincent . . . are utterly fascinated by you. By the way you've made us both feel. I guess I don't have Ram's phenomenal self-control when it comes to you."

Odds were he was going to get smacked or he was going to freak her out all over again, but Vincent just could not resist any longer. He lowered his mouth to hers, touching their lips together in what had to be the barest of kisses.

Docia's breath started to come quicker the minute she saw the change of intent come over him, the minute she appreciated the desire in his eyes. But somehow this honest, more bare-souled version of Vincent's advances had far less frightening aspects to it than the groping aggressive Vincent had.

Oh great. Now she was splitting Vincent in two on top of him already being, essentially, part of a duo.

But in the end, it was a single pair of lips coming into contact with her own and a single, focused intent. And unlike the obnoxious kiss in the Templar church that had done little more than irritate her, this had the opposite effect. There it was again, that peculiar and wonderful sensation of having heat blown through her body, like a glassblower shaping molten substance into something wondrously beautiful. And instead of feeling it along the outer edges of her skin, she felt it all along under the surface, sliding between skin and muscle, slithering snugly and wildly inside every corner she had. Her blood began to sparkle in its veins as he pressed a little harder, danced with her lips a little deeper. She lifted her hands but was afraid to touch all that large, wonderful maleness right within her reach, afraid because she couldn't fathom right then being able to manage any more than what she was already feeling.

Her breath hitched in her throat and she pulled her

head back, although not because she really wanted him to stop. It was more like a flight response in reaction to the fear of not knowing what to do next, of not knowing if she could handle this. But she was relieved when he chased her back down almost instantly, his hand lifting to cup the back of her head so she wouldn't be able to move away again. Yet he was not bruising or brutish, was not trying to dominate the hell out of her. It was more like a discourse, a sweet conversation using the lips and tongue that conversation depended on so very much, where her input and arguments held just as much weight as his. There was respect every inch of the way. She sensed this just as deeply as she felt that energizing heat and arousal stirring throughout her body. And just as she was beginning to wonder if it was the same for him . . .

"My God," he murmured into her mouth. "I've never felt anything like this. It's like calling power from deep within myself, this feeling." He kissed her harder, deeper, her head turning and tipping to absorb the impact of it. Now she did touch him, her fingers reaching to curl into his shirt to provide some sort of anchor for herself . . . only he wasn't wearing a shirt, and she was left with nothing but smooth, hot skin over tense, curving muscle and the lightest crisp of hair. It had been so fair, so close to the tone of his skin, that she had not even noticed it on his chest. It gleamed like gold on his forearms, but here she had barely noticed it.

Of course, that could have been because she was far too busy palpitating over his physique overall. . . .

He broke away from her lips only a second to catch his breath. Or to let her catch hers. She couldn't quite tell. He tipped her head back so he could find her eyes under the hooded sweep of her heavy lids and lashes.

"And it stops here, if you say the word, Docia."

Word? What word? she wondered numbly. *There*

were words? How could there be words on the very same lips that were full of the fire of kissing him?

All she could do was shake her head.

No. She refused. Refused to stop. To be afraid. To hesitate. Not one second longer. Who knew when the next bridge would come along? What if everything ended right then? Would she want the words *no, stop,* or *I'm afraid* to be the last ones she spoke?

"No. Don't stop. I'm not afraid," she said breathlessly.

CHAPTER TWELVE

Jackson didn't let himself feel exhausted, although that was very much the feeling snarling at his heels. He hadn't slept since the night before his conversation with Docia, the silly, relaxed one he'd had with her just like dozens of silly relaxed conversations he'd had with her every single morning on her way to work. Only after that one had ended, he'd come in to work and been told she was dead.

He hadn't slept since. Not even after knowing she was safe, alive, and in the hospital bed next to him. At most he'd drifted off, but at just about the point of actual sleep, he'd hear the sound of her screaming for him. The sound of her terror. The sound of her last moments on earth.

He got up from his desk and moved to the coffeepot, angry with the damn thing for not providing the level of juice he needed to keep going in a fewer number of cups, because at this point his effectiveness was hindered more by his overworked bladder than his weariness.

Now it was, what? Six a.m.? Seven? He was no closer to finding Docia, though he felt he was just a hair behind her, close enough that he could feel the warmth in a chair she might have sat in or the faintest scent of the crisp, clean botanical shampoo she used. Or so he'd imagined, as her former host explained oh so calmly and oh so believably how a bunch of people completely out of her social sphere had come to have her at their home . . . only to have to hastily remove her from that home after a sketchily convenient gas explosion had taken out the fireplaces, the dining room, and the whole right side of the house.

Henry Kamin had had an answer for everything. The guardhouse vandalism had taken place the night before, supposedly, when the guards had gone to walk the perimeter of the house. They had not reported it, preferring to handle it privately unless it happened again. This Vincent Marzak had Docia but had not had time to grab a cellphone before leaving to bring her elsewhere, and Kamin assured him she would probably contact him as soon as she was able.

Apparently, Kamin was an upstanding citizen and a huge donor to the local PBA, so the Windham cops had swallowed every bit of his story readily.

Even Jackson's fellow cops had decided there was nothing else to be done about it and had gone home for the night. But he didn't bother. He'd only be coming back on shift in a few hours anyway. Unless, of course, he got sent home by the boss when Landon got wind of what a mess this was turning out to be. Those Windham cops were used to dealing with insanely rich and privileged people, who, it seemed, deserved a whole different level of consideration. If Henry Kamin said there was an explosion, there was an explosion. If Henry Kamin said Docia was being well cared for, well, that had to be true.

It was all a load of horseshit as far as Jackson was concerned. But now even the cops from his own department were looking at him cross-eyed when he insisted on pressing forward with finding Docia. Go home, they said. She'll probably call in the morning, they said. Get some sleep, they said.

"Yeah, right," he snorted into his coffee cup. Mr. Coffee understood. He was a longtime veteran of this station. He knew what drove a good cop. Well, besides caffeine-infused brew, that is.

Oh, crap. Now he was anthropomorphizing the frigging coffee machine. Was this what it had boiled down to? Was his only friend in the world a Mr. Coffee machine?

"Dude, this place smells funny. Anyone ever tell you that?"

Leo threw himself into Jackson's desk chair, the impetus rolling him back a little. He kicked his legs up, crossing his feet on the corner of Jackson's desk. His wet, muddied feet.

"Christ, Leo!" Jackson pulled out an abused file folder from under Leo's boots and wiped it off against his jeans. "It smells like *law* in here. You know, that thing you so inherently like to work against?"

"Untrue. I am a very law-abiding citizen." He grinned. "As long as the law makes sense. As long as it doesn't get in the way of the greater good. And tell me something, Dudley Do-Right, just what kind of law are those guys practicing up there in Windham?"

Jackson hated to admit it, but he was right. Something wasn't right up there. Besides the obvious explosion, there were things . . . things that didn't make sense. And a whole hell of a lot of them.

"They aren't me," Jackson felt the need to point out.

"If you mean they aren't running on caffeine fumes and zero downtime, then yeah, you got that right."

"What the hell, Leo?" he burst out in a shout, somehow refraining from throwing his cup against the wall. "What do you want me to do? Go home, curl up, and sleep like a kitten, all content and worry-free? While she's out God knows where with God knows who doing God knows what?"

Leo waited a long beat after Jackson's explosion of temper, long enough to make Jacks feel a little awkward for letting loose in the first place. It was much better when Leo got just as mad as he did and they fed off each other. Then usually he would play the cooler head and all would be right with the world.

But the world was about to change.

"I'm not saying you forget. I'm not saying you go home. There's bunks in the back room behind the break room and nothing you can do until the world starts to wake up, so why don't you let Red here take you back and give it a try for two hours?"

When he said "Red," he nodded his head to a point just beyond Jackson's left shoulder, and he knew . . . he just knew . . . who was standing there. He turned to see Marissa Anderson frozen like a deer in a pair of headlights right behind him, apparently trying to sneak past him to get to Mr. Coffee herself. Now, he might have actually found it a bit touching that she, unlike all the rest, had actually stuck around to the wee hours . . . if she hadn't looked so damn flawless in the process of doing it. Not a hair out of place, not so much as a wrinkle in her blouse. And for some reason that just irritated the piss out of him.

"I don't need a goddamn babysitter," he bit out, slamming down his cup before it really did go flying across the room. What the hell was wrong with him? One of the best things about his nature was that he was very slow to anger. It was a good thing in a cop overall, and probably one of the key reasons he'd never had a brutality complaint or anything like it in his jacket. But honestly, between Leo and Dr. Hotbody, someone somewhere was asking just a little too much from him. "Fine. Eight a.m. I'll lay around like an idiot until then. But then the SPD, the WPD, and all the rest of you can go screw yourselves and all your rules and jurisdictions. I'm going after my sister."

"Amen, brother! Now you're singing my song! Whoo!" Leo whooped.

Jackson flipped him off and marched away from him. It didn't take him long to realize there was the rapid clickety-click of a woman in heels hot on his tail. When he reached the break room, he turned on her sharply.

"I thought I made it clear I do not need a babysitter."

"Clearly you need something," she shot back at him. "No rules? Disregard for jurisdiction? You're going to throw your whole career away over this, Jackson, if you aren't careful. And having been witness, I'm going to have to—"

Jackson grabbed her by the lapel of her suit jacket, finished yanking her into the break room, and shut the door tight. The minute they were closed off, he stalked her, getting a certain satisfaction in watching her eyes widen in shock and in the way she rapidly backed away from him until she hit the lip of the sink centered in the countertop of the small kitchenette. He trapped her there, a hand on either side of her hips gripping tightly at that lip edge.

"Have to what?" he demanded darkly, slowly, his gaze boring into hers. "Be a rat? Isn't that what you are? You think you're announcing something new to me? You think this entire police force doesn't know that you're the equivalent of a tattletale, running to tell the grown-ups on us if we so much as blink wrong? Or, for that matter, you so much as *think* we're blinking wrong? You think that scares me or something?"

"It's not meant to scare you, it's meant to make you think twice about your actions," she bit back at him, another flare of the temper he hadn't realized until today that she had. Strangely enough, he found it unbelievably hot. Incredibly sexy. Just like everything else about her, damn her beautiful eyes. "Jackson, you're tired. Worn down. People make bad decisions under stress as it is, but add to it—"

"Shh!" he hushed her fiercely. "Unless the next words out of your mouth are an offer to relieve my tension with a spectacular blow job, I don't want to hear it!"

She smirked at him. Actually smirked, the brazen little thing.

"Oh, nice. Typical male reaction. You can't deal with a woman on an even keel, so you reduce her to some kind of sexual object in order to make her less threatening to your candy-assed fragile male ego. And here I thought you were different."

"Well, you thought wrong. I . . ." Jackson hesitated, his tired eyes narrowing a minute as he tried to review and absorb the words flying between them instead of just reacting to them. "What do you mean, you thought I was different?"

"Nothing," she snapped. "Now back up and let me out of here before I report you for sexual harassment, Waverly."

She sounded smart, confident, and brave. Christ, she was stunning.

Jackson realized he needed to get away from her before he did something stupid like try to kiss her. Then the thought of kissing her led to another thought. A very dirty thought.

He reached for her mouth, those perfectly plush pink lips of hers that had taunted him for thirteen weekly visits of pretending to get his head together, either smiling with that holier-than-thou kindness of hers or parting every so often as she licked them in one of her rare absent moments. He'd often wished she were the type to suck or nibble on her pen in thought. But, of course, she wasn't. She was far too perfectly put together for that.

It seemed she worked very hard at that overall appearance of perfection. Not even a single foible? No tapping of a foot. No clicking of her pen. Not a single fidget. She had an amazing amount of control over her every action.

"So tightly wound," he said roughly when she dodged him, her hands suddenly gripping his shirtfront, perhaps to shove at him but not quite putting any heart into it.

But when he moved to take her mouth, she dodged him again, this time turning out of his arms and standing for a minute with her back to him. She took a breath and turned to face him, as composed as ever.

Except . . . there was an intriguing flush on her fair cheeks.

"Get some sleep, Jackson. You won't find your sister this way. And you can kiss my help good-bye if you don't."

The funny thing was, he realized, her help was important enough to him—to a man seemingly abandoned by those who should be far more loyal to him because he had known them longer and better than he knew her—to keep him from pursuing her.

All he did was nod before moving to the back room and the bunks waiting there for him.

"No. Don't stop. I'm not afraid," she said breathlessly.

It was like an infinite release, like speaking something into being, when Docia said those words aloud to Vincent. For both of them, really. For her it was revitalizing, like bringing herself back to life for the first time since her accident. She'd been living on borrowed time, literally. She'd found a whole new meaning to the words. It had almost been as though it were no longer her life to live. And in a sense, that was very much true, but it wasn't not her life to live, either. It was more than that. It was going to be more than that. More than her tiny little life could possibly have conceived of. That didn't make her smaller-scaled life less worthy, that wasn't what she thought at all. The world was made of lives in all shapes and sizes, of all sorts of dynamics, but her death and rebirth had proven more than anything that even the smallest life could have a tremendous impact on the world . . . if in only one other person's perspective.

For Vincent, it was an equally dynamic understanding. He had been part of a pair, a marriage, to be blunt, for so long that he had nearly forgotten how to be an individual. And Ram had been so determined to see to the care and comfort of so many others that he'd been willing to sacrifice everything about himself to bring it to fruition. In a way, he had become far less of an individual than the man who had agreed to share his life with him. So Vincent might have been doing Ram the biggest favor of all time by ignoring all the rhetoric his symbiont had forced on him about queens and kings and great destinies and the fate and future of a people . . . and remembering that sometimes it was the fate and destiny of one individual that could change the world. Ram and Menes and all of them had tried it *their* way over and over again and it had never quite worked. Wasn't that the definition of insanity? To do the same thing over and over again and expect a different result?

So he was going to do something different and he was going to earn a different result, he thought with determination. He was going to pursue the way this simple, cute little lady made him feel, and he was going to see what came of it. He wasn't afraid. He wasn't going to stop. And he was not letting go of her until she asked him to.

Perhaps not even then.

It was strange, but he'd picked her apart and reconstructed her in so many ways these past few days. As Ramses, the great pharaoh who had become the loyal advisor to Menes, his second in command and second only to his queen in all things. As Vincent, the ex–navy SEAL-cum-Bodywalker who could digest any situation and break it down into what it was, what it needed to be, and what he wanted it to be. And as Ram/Vincent, the Bodywalker blend of two powerful male beings that so purely complemented each other and had found such a rhythmic way of moving through life together. Yet none of that came to matter in the least. It all boiled down to the two simplest essences. A male. A female. Both so complementary to each other that the world was lit on fire by it.

And if not the world, most certainly their bodies. Their minds. Their souls. Whether it was two souls or four, twin minds or quadruple . . . in the long run . . . it was plain in the fierce heat of their kisses that it went far beyond just the physical and deep into the metaphysical. Vincent was kissing her so hard and so wildly that he didn't take time to breathe. Not consciously, anyway. He didn't have time to waste being present in his own mind. He was too busy delving into the moment, delving into her mouth, his tongue tangling with hers until the taste of her was scorched on his memory for all time.

Docia was clinging to him with gripping hands and fingertips, trying for all she was worth to remain on her feet when all she wanted to do was swoon deep into the world of sensation and ferocity he was covering her with. If not for the hand at her waist . . . infinitely, frustratingly, at her waist . . . she was certain she would have melted to the floor in the gooiest, bubbliest little puddle. It was hardly surprising she should feel that way when she felt so very wet, from her mouth to her damp skin to her sex, all so slick and hot and craving.

Yet all it was was kisses. Unending, fierce, and slowly frustrating kisses. Mind-blowing kisses. Breathtaking kisses. Until her lips were bruised and her face on fire from the shadow of whiskers he scored against her sensitive skin. It nearly drove her out of her mind until she wanted to scream at him to just do something! Do anything!

And that was when she realized this had been her problem for so long. She had constantly let life happen to her. Let *it* make the first move. Waited for *it* to take the next step. And because of that . . . she had waited too long. Had just about missed it all. Missed everything. And why? Because she was afraid someone might say no? She might be rejected? She might fail in some way? And because she had feared the failing, she had become utterly stagnant and had ended up failing gloriously just the same.

She pulled away, gasping for breath, panting hard as she looked up into his glittering gold eyes. She narrowed her gaze on him in suspicion because she knew he was not the type to sit back and let things just happen to him. She knew he was a taker. A mover and a shaker. A freaking heartbreaker. Because he wasn't afraid of anything. So why? Why was he standing still? Doing nothing? Waiting?

"Screw you," she gasped, shoving at him with all she had until he deigned to take a step back. Then she launched herself at him, leaping off the floor, ringing her arms around his neck and her legs around his waist. He staggered back a second before grabbing her under her ass and hauling her in tight to his body, her dress ripping under both their efforts. He grinned as she slammed her lips over his and kissed him as hard and mean as she could. Then she broke off and glared at him. "You think I don't have it in me? You think I'm not tough enough for this? Not hot enough? Not gutsy enough?"

"Did I say that?" he asked, every word a tease, every move of his mouth on hers a taunt.

"I'm sick of it," she ground out. "I'm sick of life or death just happening to me!" She sat back in his hands and tangled with the top of her dress for a moment, pulling it back and down until her breasts were just about to spill out of it.

"Good!" he said, his gold eyes devouring her every movement. There was no condescension there, just raging agreement. Fierce need for it to be true.

"And this bitch inside me won't dictate life to me, either. You won't and she won't and some decrepit pharaoh who isn't even here won't! You got that?"

"Understood," he said with a growl of appreciation.

"And Ram can go fuck himself!"

"Ram would much rather fuck you," Vincent confessed to her. "He's thought of little else, no matter what he'd like to pretend otherwise. Not since the moment he first touched you. Since *we* first touched you. Screw it. Like you said. *I* want you. *I'm* having you. And as long as you agree, nothing else matters. Nothing else will make the difference, and nothing is going to stop me."

He threw her to the floor, slamming her back onto the mattress so hard that all four corners poofed out tightly, full of air, then hissed slowly in release as he rose on his knees, a hand bracing at her shoulders so his whole body shadowed over her.

"Wrong," she said breathlessly, her hands reaching below his waist, one gripping at his belt, the other stroking boldly along the length of his zipper. "*I'm* having *you*. *We're* having you. It's going to be a freaking ménage à everybody."

And then she took a hard breath in, held it, and let the

surprising feel of him radiate into her fingers and palm, the message ticking up like a lightning telegraph into her brain.

"Jesus, you have no idea how good that really feels," he ejected on a hot gust of breath, his hips moving into her touch. "Everything about you, even the simplest things . . . like that ridiculously adorable mole. On your foot. I'm going to lick and fondle that thing at some point because it turns me on . . . just like everything else about you. And I wish I could explain how painful this is. . . ."

He put his hand over hers so she wouldn't pull away from him.

"In a good way," he breathed against her ear in assurance. "Painful in a good way. Both physically and mentally, because even the lightest touches of Ram being present makes him fight what he feels is a disloyal act, and it translates inside of me in the most unbelievable haze of pain and passion, need and dread. But in no way does the lying bastard want to leave you. No more than I do."

That made her smile, a quick, sly little expression that touched her eyes so wickedly that Vincent felt the other soul inside of him shudder in apprehension and delight. He let Docia push him over onto his back, watched as she threw her leg astride him and unzipped her dress. How amazingly beautiful she was in that moment. More so because of the lack of symmetry of her hair and such. It was nothing for a woman to portray beauty when she was simply beautiful. It was breathtaking to see an imperfect woman become stunning just because she willed it into being from the inside out. Over time she would heal, her hair would grow, and the Bodywalker within her would resonate until she was blindingly beautiful; but he didn't think it would ever compare with what he was seeing right then.

She pulled the gown, which had become lank throughout their ordeals, over her head and threw it a little too close to the nearby fire. That left her in a lacy pair of boy shorts and matching bra, both in midnight blue. The bra was clearly bust enhancing, not that she needed any enhancements. She reached behind herself and popped the clasp, then, with an almost shy little wriggle, she let it slide forward down her arms.

And that wrote the end to Ram's attempts to gainsay the situation. Vincent felt it in a chasing rush of heat and blood, blood trying to fill flesh already pretty heavily engorged. She was sitting directly on him, so she felt it almost the same instant he did. It was no wonder. He could have broken bricks with the thing at that point. The smile of delight, the sense of triumph that lit her face, was like nothing he'd ever seen before. And she should be delighted, he thought. She should feel her victory down to her very core. She deserved it. And they both knew . . . they *all* knew . . . it was a victory a long time coming in her life.

"Oh my!" She giggled, leaning forward over him so her hair curtained off his vision on one side and her breasts radiated warmth against him but did not yet come into contact with him. "So sorry, Ram," she said, exaggerating a pout with absolutely no remorse in it. "It seems you've lost."

"Oh, I think there's victory enough to placate all involved," Vincent assured her with a chuckle. He lifted a hand to the bare expanse of her breastbone, turning his knuckles against her and running them down the length of it. "But you're right, aren't you? This is rather a ménage à everybody. It feels very naughty, doesn't it?"

"Kinky," she agreed, licking her lips as though the idea appealed to her very, very much.

"It's always the shy ones." He chuckled, turning his hand to slide over her left breast, feeling the fantastic weight of it, the softness of it, against the contrasting hardness of his calloused fingers. "Now move up, sweetness. I'm going to taste you."

She did as requested, scooting just far enough forward to help him bring the tip of her breast against his lips. More a forward rolling of her hips and a lengthening of her spine, he noted. She wasn't eager to leave her seat now that she had him, and her little shifts against him were blindingly arousing . . . no doubt for both of them.

He kissed her first, a sweet sort of homage rather than just devouring her with lust, and it threw her off a little. She was still trying to redefine things, and she didn't know how to settle into a gray area between all-out sexual vixen and quirky shy girl. But as she watched him take a deep breath against her, watched him nuzzle her with what could be defined only as affection, she realized that she had to stop making definitions and just start living in the moment. This whole experience had been nothing but a long act of redefinition, and it wasn't likely to end anytime soon. Who knew how long it would truly take before the Blending finished successfully? Who knew what the outcome would be? But she knew one thing with utter determination, and that was that she wasn't going to let this slip away from her. She wasn't going to let *him* slip away from her.

By the time he finally touched his tongue to her and drew the rigid point of her nipple between his lips, she was squirming with impatience and need. His hands were running slowly down the length of her back, the warmth and strength of them seeping into her, making her feel, for the first time in days, as though she were utterly safe and secure. Not that she doubted his skills after all this time he had spent saving her life, but this was something far more essential than that, something that reached into a primal place inside of her that reassured her on levels she might never truly understand. If she stopped for a moment to think, she would realize that on many conscious levels she *didn't* understand. But there was a soul-assuring energy to her connection with him that outvoted the conscious questions just about every time as far as he was concerned. As far as this physicality was concerned.

She was running her hands up and over his chest, feeling the topography of muscles with excited fascination. She let her fingers crawl over pecs and abdominals, dragging the edges of her nails through the dampness of sweat his arousal and the nearness of the fire had wrought. His hands burrowed into her panties in the back, grabbing hold of her by both cheeks and encouraging her to ride harder against him, making her suddenly aware that she had already been doing so.

As his mouth swarmed over her chest, throat, and lips, she struggled to understand the depth of what she was feeling, because nothing in her life had even come close to it. Every touch was like a dance of fire moving fluidly between them. She knew it wasn't one-sided because she tested him a little, touched him complexly and simply, and watched how both types of contact stoked his need to a point where she suspected it was becoming an effort on his part to rein himself in.

It was perhaps the most beautiful thing anyone had ever done for her. She looked into the gold of his eyes, saw the molten wash of lust, saw how primal and male he could truly be if he let himself go . . . and perhaps she would want that one day. But he knew on an inexplicable level that she was still too fragile in some ways and that there were still too many unknown variables. He was afraid of frightening her or hurting her. Scaring her off. He desperately didn't want to scare her off.

Who knew such a strong, confident creature would be so capable of so much self-sacrifice just to protect another? Or that he could have such vulnerabilities? As he rolled with her, pushed her under his body after stripping her of her underwear, he made a fierce sound that echoed the fury of restraint he was using. For her. Just for her.

"Look at you. Just look at you," he ground out as he did exactly that, lifting himself enough so he could stare at the landscape of her body. The intensity of his appraisal triggered something both shy and arousing inside of her, her hands flitting in a weak attempt to divert his attention or protect herself from the starkness of his inspection, she wasn't sure which. He grabbed them and pinned them to the mattress at the level of her shoulders. By not holding them over her head, he deprived her of being able to hide her face within the shelter of her arms. And therefore she felt even more exposed than ever. She had no doubt that he was aware of this. Aware of all of it.

"You have nothing to hide. Nothing to feel inadequate about," he whispered against her ear before lifting to look at her yet again. "There is nothing here that is less than perfect to me. Your left breast is slightly larger than the right, no doubt to try and win my attention. . . . I suspect she's jealous of her twin. I find that precocious of her, don't you? Your navel tips a little, the coy thing, tempting me to do this. . . ." He moved down and dipped his tongue inside her sensitive belly button, the stroke of it long and lazy. "And the soft rounding of your belly is quite fortunate, because you are going to need the cushioning to protect you from the power of my thrusts. And I am going to take great delight in watching the impact shimmer through you. And here . . . oh, here . . ." His mouth drifted over the trim hair framing her nether regions. The hair she had needed to wax before her accident and hadn't had the chance to manage since. Still, it wasn't as though it were a wild Amazonian forest or anything. Just . . . more than she preferred. Especially when being intimate. "Pretty to see, warm to touch . . ." He stroked thick fingers over her, then down between waiting lips. "Wet. The smell of ambrosia, the whole of it like an oasis. My oasis, Docia. Where I will rest, and drink and dine on the fruits available to me."

"Holy smokes!" she gasped as his mouth fell on her most intimate flesh and his tongue worked an insane kind of magic against her. And that touch, his tongue to her most intimate places, was no different from any other touch they had ever shared. It was fiery and fierce, an instant resonating burn that burrowed deep and fast and left ferocious echoes of itself everywhere at once. He danced attendance all around her clit, his perfect avoidance of it telling her he knew exactly where it was and exactly how to let the nuanced nerves around it bleed flushed arousal into it until she was ready to scream.

"You're killing me," she growled at him impatiently, her knees squeezing at his shoulders where they framed him on either side. "You just wait till it's your turn. See how mean I am to you!"

He chuckled, the vibration of it dancing across her hypersensitive flesh.

"Why are you in such a rush?" he asked her, the expression in his eyes so smug and confident that she wanted to kick him in the head. How was it that men never had any doubts about themselves? Or perhaps they did but had learned to make it appear otherwise. And why was that so damn sexy?

"See how *you* feel when *you* haven't had sex with another human being in three years," she muttered.

Ah, crud. Wrong thing to say. He was stopping. Stopping was so not welcome right then.

He looked as if he were going to say something and

then seemed to think better of it. Instead, a peculiar smile drifted across his lips.

"You're right," he said, his fingers stroking through her wet flesh from the niche at the very front to well past her vaginal entrance. "Now is hardly the time for deep seductions and extended foreplay."

"Too late," she muttered.

That made the most incredibly mischievous smile light his features as he rose to his knees and began to unfasten his trousers. Before she knew it, he had shucked them off and kicked them aside and was right back up the center of her body, his hips settling deeply against her, his aroused flesh hard and hot as it slid and stroked against her. She tried to gasp, but for some reason she couldn't. Her eyes fluttered closed and she fell back into the sensation of him. Her hands, unconciously, turned into ridged little claws, her nails sinking into the flesh of his shoulders. She was trying to grasp him, to manipulate him, her whole body rising as her hips shifted mindlessly for a better angle to welcome him.

All amusement and teasing had been sucked out of Vincent the moment they came into contact sex to sex. He had been lit on fire, that heat and electrical effect she had on him exploding through him. Again, nothing in his life or Ram's lives—any of them—compared with what she was making him feel. He craved her mouth just then as much as he craved to be inside of her. One would not do without the other. It was a need he'd never required before. Certainly not so adamantly. He set himself to enter her but paused until her lips were touching his, her sweet tongue twisting together with his so he could savor the flavor of her just as his entire being was savoring the intensity she caused to vibrate throughout his body.

Then with a pair of fervent thrusts they claimed these women for themselves like explorers stabbing a flag into the precious territory of the North Pole and claiming it for all those they represented. They settled deeply inside, thrilling in the dominance of it, knowing there would never be anything better, that nothing would ever have more value than that moment. They knew what they were now a part of was the most precious thing the universe could ever give to them. The feeling was so overwhelming, so shocking and obliterating, that there was no movement for the longest time. There couldn't be while there was so much to process. So much unexpectedness. So much craving on the heels of so much satisfaction.

Vincent slid a hand under her, at the small of her back, lifting her hips in a tilt better suited for the fury he was about to unleash on her. Then he was thrusting into her, trying to make it past the initial overwhelming sensations to seek out the rest. This connection was so satisfying just the way it was, just that alone, that there was a danger of remaining too content. So he moved. He risked throwing off that sense of perfection and moved. And the moment he did, all things primal and fierce took over. Perfection was one thing, but now . . . now he must claim this perfection as his own. *They* must stake their claim for all time as the dominant, the ruler . . . the pharaoh. In his time, Ram had been one of the most powerful and effective rulers of Egypt. He had brought forth some of the greatest wonders known to man, wonders still respected to this day. Vincent had proven to be more than worthy to host such a being. But both were brought low in her body, in her magnificence. And neither would let her go. Neither could. It was as though something inside of them would be destroyed if she escaped them.

Vincent listened to her gasp and squeak and moan, and it gave him a feeling of delight he'd never forget. As he pushed into her, he was determined she would never forget that moment either. He thrust deep enough, he felt, to reach the elusive creature inside Docia who had said so little and reached out to him not at all.

You think you belong to another, and he might think you belong to him, but I will prove us all wrong. I will make the forbidden my own. And I will make myself her servant in all new ways.

Vincent began to tremble to his core, shaking in the face of the magnitude of what was coming. They who had not quailed under any threat or enemy in aeons of time were now humbled and afraid. Afraid they would not be what she needed. What she wanted. What she would keep. Afraid they wouldn't please her enough to satisfy something so special.

With frustration and desire clawing through him emotionally and physically, he listened to her cries of pleasure, struck into her until he felt her nails ripping through his flesh on his back. Then, unable to contain it any longer, his release rushed up on him. He cried out heedlessly, came into her just as recklessly. All rhythm gone. All well-laid plans destroyed. He felt her sobbing against his lips, realizing he'd never once let his mouth fall away from hers.

And yet still he kissed her. As they both gasped for breath, as she cried ridiculously indefinable tears, as his hot wetness overflowed their meshed bodies and stained their thighs. Docia had felt everything he had felt and more.

"More" being the sudden revival of the spirit inside of her. As if their coming together had awakened her, revitalized her, given her all the strength she needed to come into being. Docia's body hummed in the aftermath of pleasure and vibrated with the energy of the symbiont.

They didn't fall apart. They couldn't bring themselves to separate. Instead, Vincent wrapped his arms tightly around her and rolled them over so her body came to blanket his. Her weight was the only thing that kept him from floating away from the high buzzing through him.

And so, mouths still adjoined, still exchanging kisses up until the very last moment, they let the exhaustion of daylight wash over them at last.

Hours later, at the cusp of evening, Ram woke with a start and an inward breath.

That inward breath brought the scent of sex onto his palate. He turned his head the slightest bit and his lips touched a female forehead, the loose, unnecessary stitches inside perfectly healed skin and the new growth of about an inch of hair telling him much time had passed and many things had changed. As if the understanding that he was nakedly entwined with the woman who ought to be his queen were not enough.

He and Vincent were once again in their usual, agreed-upon positions. Ram the front man and the dominant for the most part, Vincent the background observer with his attention to details, his eye for danger, and his leveling opinions that kept Ram clear and relevant.

Ram wanted to lash out at his alter ego, to scream at him for what he had done, to shame him for the betrayal to king and kind. Because for all he said he was not beholden to the ways of the Bodywalkers, Vincent knew that he was. He knew their ways were now his ways. He knew he had accepted that long ago when he had accepted such a powerful and positional Bodywalker as Ram.

But Ram also knew it would be hypocritical to blame Vincent. He had been there. He had been just as present. He had made love to Docia and her symbiont just as eagerly as Vincent had. Ram had thrown aside all protests the minute he had felt the heat of her. And the minute they had moved inside of her, Ram had instantly bridged the distance back to Vincent, as though the connection had broken the separating spell completely, as if it had energized his soul into being.

Ram swore softly, an Egyptian curse, something he didn't do very often, knowing how powerful words could be among his race. What would happen now? How would he even face Menes, his longtime friend and respected leader, knowing he had willingly done such a thing with the woman who carried the spirit Menes had once said was forever cleaved to his? There were those who looked on the Bodywalkers' existence as a long-standing curse, but Menes had always claimed that it was anything but, for without it he would never have known Hatshepsut, a queen who had ruled in a dynasty far beyond his own.

What he had felt, what he had experienced, was exactly what he had imagined must pass between the besotted king and queen. He even tested the thought of having to live life without Docia, and the immediate rise in his heart rate and chill on his skin, the vicious rush of rage threatening to boil up over him . . . oh yes. This was what he had imagined it to be. Blind and furious and fabulous. Everything and anything.

The only trouble was . . . she was not supposed to be his. What would Menes do if he came out of the Ether and found his queen in the arms of another? What would it do to their people? Their political structure? The Politic Bodywalkers would have no leader, no strength . . . and the zealot priests and priestesses would gain the foothold they had always fought for.

So no matter how much it hurt him, no matter what it did to him, he had to face one of two choices. Either he had to turn his back on her and leave her to Menes, a thought that felt like a violation in the worst degree, a thought that made Vincent balk furiously and violently within him, or he had to . . .

He had to fight Menes to become ruler of all Bodywalkers. He had to fight to be pharaoh.

"Ramses the Great, ruler of all Egypt, whom men have cowered beneath . . . for whom women have thrown themselves naked at his feet. Mighty warrior. Brilliant king. Brought low by a simple female."

Ram tipped his head so he could look into her face. She was sleepy-eyed and smiling up at him, but he could tell immediately by the strength and cadence of her speech that this was not the quirky little Docia.

"My queen," he said softly, not knowing what else to say, how else to greet her. She was his queen, just as any man's perfect mate would always be his queen.

"I am *your* queen," she agreed as she rose onto her elbows, "and you must always treat me as such. Promise me you will."

"I will," he agreed with a nod. "I always have."

"Now there you are mistaken, Ram. You have never so much as looked at me before. Never so much as touched me. Barely spoken a greeting or politeness to me."

One of Ram's gold brows lifted in curious confusion. "You know that is not true. I have always treated Menes's wife, until now, with exemplary respect and deference."

"Ah, but I have never been Menes's wife," she said.

Ram frowned, pulling back to look into her eyes. Docia's sweet brown eyes had warmed, if possible, into something richer, deeper, and, he felt immediately, far more sensual than was normally at the ready. There was a worldliness now, the confidence that came with having lived more than one life, having made all the mistakes of an original and even more as a carbon. But as he looked hard at her, there it was, that unmistakable flash of shyness that so belied the strength of spirit that lay beneath. But he knew it. He felt it. He had felt it from the inside out and then some. She had no secrets from him after that.

Except perhaps one. . . .

"You are not Hatshepsut," he breathed, his hand against her face drawing her so close that nothing could enter her eyes without his notice.

"No, I am not," she agreed. "And before you become enraged, I beg you to remember I was not strong enough to say so before now. It was not my intention to deceive you. You made an assumption, Ram, and I had no way of telling you otherwise. Until now."

Ram couldn't speak for a long moment. Hell, he could hardly breathe. The ramifications of her revelation went so far in every direction that it was impossible to wrap his brain around it.

"Who are you?" he demanded.

Her nose twitched and he had a suspicion she wanted to say "Docia" just to mess with him, then rethought herself under the circumstances and considered it wiser not to. It showed a delicious combination of spunk and wisdom that he found ridiculously stimulating. Of course, the fact that she smelled like him at his lustiest and her at her sexiest might have a lot to do with it. She smelled so incredibly delicious that his mouth was watering. It stunned him that he could be so distracted at such a crucial moment. All he could think about was kissing that impishly smiling mouth and driving back into that hot body of hers where he'd known such a dynamic sense of perfection.

"My name is Tameri," she told him, and the lowering of her lashes and gentle inclining of her forehead told him a great deal. It told him she had never been royalty. It told him respect and deference came naturally to her. But other than that . . .

"Tameri, I have never heard your name before or touched your spirit." He was positive he would have known it if he had. He would have felt it if he had so much as brushed past her.

"That is probably because I have not come from the Ether very often," she said softly, as though it were a confession that lightened her soul. But why? There were many of them who spent long periods, much longer than the requisite century, in the Ether. "And when I have . . ." She licked her lips nervously. "When I have, I have been priestess."

Ram launched to his knees, dumping her onto her back, suddenly seeing a viper in his bed. There was no describing, though, the clash of feelings inside him—knowing she was one of those hateful men and women who were part of the rending apart of their people, even as he knew there would be no living without her.

She sat up quickly, her hand reaching for him, grasping his biceps where he was as yet healing from the deep marks she had made on him. Right above the forearm, where iridescent scales shimmered with agitated movement around a dagger.

"Please! Listen to me! Open your heart and open your mind," she begged him, her eyes that gorgeous mink he'd grown so quickly to love. "I stayed in the Ether because I couldn't bear it! The war. The constant fighting between the Politic and the Templar. I have so much beautiful faith, no different from your own! Only my faith imbues me with spells and mysticism that you think is poisonous and wrong. It's not. I swear it. It's the wielder that makes the difference. The intent that turns a spell or a power to poison. Once upon a time, the Templars' perspective was just and justifiable. Their demand for a ruling voice was understandable. Your government would have us all exiled. Or so it feels to us. So why not give us room for voice so we can keep that from happening?

"But over the centuries the Templars have lost sight

of what we wanted originally. In the beginning we only wanted fairness and to stop being blamed for the Bodywalkers' very existences. But somewhere along the line, Odjit and the others have perverted the cause into a demand for full power, and others have drifted along on the same path because she and the other head priests and priestesses have made us so hated that we have little other choice. Listen to me, please," she begged him further. "Please don't hate me. Don't shun Docia because of what I am. Don't dismiss us out of hand because I am just a little bit different than you are."

Ram hesitated, the depth of the war within him in his eyes and across his features. There was so much acrimony inside of him, built up after he had met so many deaths at the hands of Templars like her jockeying for power, jockeying to assassinate the rightful pharaoh of them all. He had watched time and again as they had murdered his queen and left his king to suffer, or vice versa. He had felt them torture his bodies or tear through them outright to reach his king. He had not died a natural death in such a long time. Such a long time. Granted, so much about their very existences seemed unnatural, but still . . .

A priestess. A Templar. He had bedded an enemy.

Yet he could not dismiss it as a mere bedding, something so crass. She knew it, too. It was in her damnably precious eyes.

"Think, Ramses," she said softly. "You were willing to break with tradition enough to risk taking the woman you thought was your queen, the woman you thought belonged by Menes's side, because you knew it was the only right thing to do . . . because your heart told you. Both spirits within you made it undeniably clear, just as both within me felt it to our very core." She brushed gentle fingertips to her chest, between her pretty breasts, making him realize she was cold. The chill of the early evening was rippling across her skin and her nipples. "If you can break with tradition enough to do that, then perhaps you are the one who can turn away from past prejudices enough to see how very lost some of us are. Perhaps you are the one that might realize that instead of offering us swords and violence, perhaps if you hold out an empty, welcoming hand of forgiveness, this war might dissolve before your very eyes." She moved closer to him, her gaze imploring and soft, her lips a breath away from his. "Teach the Politic to love us as equals, to welcome us like long-lost lovers, and bring us in as friends rather than vilifying us as enemies that must be punished. Why would we give up this war when our only choice otherwise is to rot in exile or in Menes's prisons?"

Ram was no idiot. Over such a long and bitter fight, the Templars had tried so many tricks . . . so many deceptions. This soft voice, this wondrous body, and those enchanting eyes could all be a clearly crafted seduction. He did not blame Docia. She was an innocent in this matter. He had no doubt that her symbiont had made nothing of herself known until this moment. It explained, he thought, why she had been so very quiet. Even with the weakness of transitioning out of the Ether, even with the daunting task of the Blending at hand, there should have been more of her voice. If not out loud, then at least in Docia's own mind. But she had deceived him . . . deceived him into thinking she was his queen.

"I swear I did not," she breathed in soft desperation when she saw the distrust in his eyes. "I was gathering strength, letting my host adjust, and letting you guide her into our world. I never said I was your queen. Never made the claim. Never said I was Hatshepsut or demanded to be treated as such. You only assumed."

"There is deception in omission," he said tightly,

more because he was trying to figure out how to keep himself from kissing her, how to keep himself from succumbing to the amazing heat and sensation he felt every time they came into contact. What if this was all some kind of elaborate Templar spell?

He didn't realize he'd voiced the suspicion aloud until he saw the genuine hurt that sliced through her eyes and across her delicate face.

"Is that what you think? You think this is somehow unnatural and forced? Well, fuck you and the horse you rode in on!" she snapped at him.

Docia. That was Docia coming through loud and clear, a sign that the Blending was in full swing. Even she looked a bit surprised at her own reaction. Her verbosity. He found it amusing how different the two personalities inside of this one woman seemed to be. A Templar, notorious for sophistication and strength, notorious for choosing very powerful people when they could. And yet this one had chosen a naïve and very innocent, if mouthy, young woman from a small town with small-town values. She held no great position in life. She had no possible means to further the Templar cause. But she was a good soul. She would never hurt another soul unless it meant saving her own life or the life of someone she was loyal to.

But this gave new reason to why the Templars had recovered Docia. Not because they thought she was Hatshepsut—they had to know there was no convincing Menes's loyal queen to shift sides—but to retrieve their priestess and brainwash the human she was about to Blend with. Now the capture finally made sense to him.

"Who are you?" he asked with narrowed eyes. "Be honest with me. Who are you, really?"

She swallowed, knowing what he meant.

"I am Odjit's niece. But," she added hastily as understanding dawned on his handsome face, "know this. I have been in the Ether for three centuries, rather than come back and be her pawn. And my father, who is up there yet, is the one who sent me down in hopes of being some sort of messenger."

"Your father? You mean Odjit's *brother*? You're telling me that Uro wishes to defect from Odjit's side? In the past, both have wielded their hands against the Politic again and again, and you want me to believe—"

"I want you to conceive of a man who sees his sister has gone mad with the hunger for power! He wants more than anything to draw her to heel and end this war! That is what I am telling you! But he knows he cannot manage it without promises from the Politic that the Templars will not be persecuted!"

"As you have tried to persecute us?" he demanded.

"And you in your turn have done the same!" She grunted in frustration, pulling away from him and sitting back, drawing her knees to her chest defensively. "We will never make any headway if we continue to fling accusations back and forth. If we cannot let go of our desires for revenge for past grievances."

She looked back up at him, her dark eyes imploring.

"This has to start somewhere. Uro has risked the new life of his daughter in order to send me as an emissary of peace to you and the Politic. He is as tired of war as you are and would see it end fairly. No one needs to conquer the other. It does not have to be that way. Can't we somehow manage to keep it from being that way? Aren't you tired of all of this?" Then she turned her head aside and made a soft shushing sound.

"What was that?" he wanted to know. But he thought he already knew. "That was Docia's opinion on the matter? And you were overriding her?"

"I was merely . . . being more diplomatic than she is.

I did not think telling you to 'stop being a mulish, stubborn ass' would be conducive to my peaceful overtures."

Ram smiled, unable to help himself.

"So, it seems you have made a believer out of her already," he noted. He inspected her with wary eyes for a moment. "I have to say, considering all she has been through recently, it surprises me you've already made a champion of her."

"To be fair, she is not a veteran of the war as we are. She is only just beginning to share the memories of the war that I have. And perhaps you will believe her . . . believe us . . . when we claim to be exhausted by it. I want to convince you. I want more than anything to facilitate peace. But if that is not possible, then I have to go. I have to hide, and do so very quickly. Odjit has divined that I am here. She will not rest until she has me at her side."

"Why? What's so important about you? Is it because your father will be coming out of the Ether on your heels?"

She lowered her face, shielding it a moment, but something inside him understood it was not because she was trying to come up with a deception. More likely she was about to reveal a truth that was going to give him a great deal of power. Power he could use against her.

But for some reason, she chose to trust him.

"Because I am by far the only priestess with enough power to defeat Odjit where she stands. You know the old adage 'Keep your friends close, but your enemies'—or potential enemies—'closer'? I was no threat to her in the Ether, and with my father's protection and my submissive behavior whenever I was here on Earth, she did not feel threatened. But she's cunning, as you know. It will not take long for her to divine my motives and purpose. And once she gets wind of them, Docia and I will become an enemy of the first order, and Menes will become second. She will feel more threatened by me than by Menes. She will spare nothing to hunt me and see me thrown into the Ether for another hundred years. And she most certainly will not want you and Menes and the body Politic to have access to me."

"That is quite a claim," he said quietly. He had studied her the entire time she spoke. There had been no ego in her words. No false pride or bravado. To her, it had been a cold, hard truth.

"If you reject me," she said softly, "you will resign Docia and myself to a life on the run."

"Ah. And now a manipulation," he said dryly.

She looked up at him through her lashes, and a small, impish smile toyed at the corners of her lips. "If guilt works to get you to see things my way, then yes, perhaps a little manipulation. You and I both know Docia is an innocent in all of this. And I hope you know I chose her very carefully. Not because I wished to endanger her, but because I saw her soul. I saw the good-heartedness in her. I knew that if anyone could help me bridge our differences enough to begin steps toward peace, it would be a simple, truthful young woman who had so much love for her brother that it was all she thought of when given the opportunity to be resurrected. She didn't think of herself, her things, her own selfish ends. Not until I manipulated her into it. And when she eventually came to wanting vengeance against those who tried to kill her, she only thought about it in terms of legal justice. She wasn't thinking to hunt them down and kill them . . . she thought only to sic her law-enforcing brother on them so they would serve jail time. A far gentler approach to justice than we Bodywalkers have, Templar, Politic, or otherwise."

"That is very true," he agreed with a nod. Ram felt as though things were a bit surreal in that moment. This was by far the longest amount of time he'd ever spent in the presence of a single Templar. He'd certainly never had a conversation that had gone beyond posturing or threatening. And when he took a moment to think about it, he realized that he had slept the day away in her arms. She could have, at any time, done any of a thousand things to take his life. If she was as powerful as she claimed to be, he would very likely have slept into his death and not raised a hand in defense of himself.

Yet she had slept, too, hugging and cuddling him, just as caught up in the residual intensity of their joining. There had been no deception in her reactions. Her tears had told him as much. That honesty had not been just Docia's, any more than his sense of finding utter peace inside of her had been Vincent's doing alone.

"Have you decided," he asked archly, "who is going to be dominant and who submissive in your Blending?"

"That is a Templar way of putting it," she said with a frown. "A radical Templar, in any event. The Blending is perfect. At least it should be. It should be a harmony. Equal give and equal take. We do not come here to seize these bodies, wresting control from their originals. We ask to share and should be grateful to do so. Only Odjit and her like think they have the right to be dictators in their original's bodies."

She looked at him with steady, courageous eyes.

"You wish to test me? Ask me anything. But my answers will all seem practiced and false to you if you do not trust me. And I know you have no reason to trust a Templar. But you cannot afford to not trust me, either."

And to prove it, she spoke soft ancient words, spreading her hands between them with her palms facing him. Suddenly he felt cold for the first time in her presence since their trek outside. Terribly, horribly cold. His feet grew painful, and he jerked back the covers to see them. Ice was growing over them; like kudzu smothering a tree, it climbed his legs. He tried to move, to balk in some way, to fight, but he couldn't. His whole body was cold and heavy and quickly being encased in ice.

And then she lifted cupped hands to her lips, spoke a word into them, and blew it softly into his face.

Just like that, it all began to melt away, disappearing as if it had never been, but for echoes of distress and a wicked chill to remind him it had indeed happened.

"You see?" she said to him. "I could have destroyed you if I wanted to. No one would be the wiser. I could pretend to be your queen, as you have told everyone that I was, and wait for Menes to be in front of me and send him back into the Ether."

Ram was breathing hard, adrenaline from fear and other emotions pumping through him. He was furious that he had been so easily disabled and so helpless against the power she had wielded over him. But he was not furious with her, because what she said rang wickedly true. He might have brought her to Menes . . . and she might have been an assassin. But he had thought she was Hatshepsut, had just assumed she was his queen since Cleo had sent him there specifically to find her. The understanding that he might have brought a viper into Menes's presence chilled him far deeper than her spell.

"Docia . . . I mean—"

"No. We like Docia best at present. She and I will discuss which name is preferred later, but for now we like Docia. I find it to be a very pretty name."

She smiled and there was a kind of warm innocence to it, a blend of the Templar's sincerity and Docia's spirit. It was beautiful and disarming, slowing his heart rate.

"Docia, you are right. You could have done all of these things. Between that understanding and the fact that I still see the strong presence of a woman I *do* trust inside of you, I would be foolish not to believe you. You took many chances. You took a risk, coming to me like this."

He reached out and picked up one of the dark, choppy locks of her hair. He toyed with it between his fingers a moment.

"Did you lure me with magic in order to soften me up?" he asked suddenly, looking into her eyes. "I cannot explain this heat and undeniable craving for you any other way."

The look in her eyes was utter, shattering hurt. There was no indignation, no fury. Just flat-out pain and shock. Tears sprang to her precious mink eyes and suddenly he felt like the worst kind of villain. The expression was pure and innocent.

"The only explanation?" she choked out, a slow burning anger rushing up in defense of her pain. "Really, that's the only thing you can think of? You, who have watched Menes and Hatshepsut cling to one another so faithfully and fiercely throughout the aeons? This is all you can think of?"

She moved to get up, reaching for the dress she had discarded the day before. She struggled to turn it right side out, a pained little sob squeaking out of her as she hid her face from him.

"Docia . . ." He touched her shoulder and she shrugged him off hard.

"Don't touch me!"

But touch her he did. He grabbed her by both arms and threw her back down on the mattress, stripping the dress out of her arms and chucking it away. Neither noticed the poofing sound as it landed in the fireplace and the delicate silk went up in smoke.

Ram pinned her down, his huge body over her, his

golden eyes seeking hers although she resisted meeting them as she struggled with him.

"Let me go before I bring the wrath of Ra down on your miserable hide!" she spat out.

"Docia, I had to ask! Listen to me! Wouldn't you? Faced with all of this, seeing the power you can wield, wouldn't you question it?"

"No! I would have more faith in it! I would remember that the Bodywalkers were Suspended for most of the exchanges of last night! Why was it Vincent and Docia alone? Did you forget about Odjit's spell?"

"You are a Templar. Her niece, for the sake of Ra! How could I know if she cast the spell on me but faked it on you, hmm?"

"Have I not proven to you I can be trusted? And if not me, surely you trust Docia's soul! There is very little purity of heart in this world. Did you not recognize it when she cried out your name with joy?"

"Yes," he said with sudden fierceness, reaching to entrap her head between his hands, forcing her to look at him at last. "Yes, Docia, yes! But you must forgive me because I have never felt anything like this in all my many lives! To live so long but never feel such a thing . . . why now? I question it. Why now?"

She sniffled back a trapped little sound of hurt, and it pained his heart. He didn't want to hurt her, but he couldn't grasp this. Couldn't understand why he felt so much with her and none other. She had to forgive him, but he simply didn't understand and barely knew what to do with it, other than the very base instinct that told him to hold tight and never let go. But she was Templar and he Politic, and they had been enemies for so long. . . .

"That's it, isn't it?" he asked suddenly. "Because . . . because we have been on opposite sides so long, our souls never met. Never connected. All of this time you could have been in my hands, in my heart, resonating with my soul, but we were as good as worlds apart."

He felt pain as he said it. Genuine pain. To think this feeling, this wonder, could have been his . . . could have soothed him and given him the succor he had needed as he died and lived and died and lived . . . but he had scorned it as an enemy and therefore had wasted the opportunity to know it. To have what Menes and Hatshepsut had. Yes, it was tragic in its way, when death came into the picture, but if this was what they felt when they were together on this earth, then Ram suddenly understood. He understood what drove them to forever be together. To seek each other out again and again. To agree never to let the other go on without them. It circumvented war, it took precedence over everything and everyone else. They risked everything to remain true and continuous to each other.

"I'm sorry," he breathed down at her. "So sorry." He was desperate for her to believe him. "I've been who I am for so long and thought I knew everything. I thought I knew . . . but I forgot that there are new lessons to be learned in every lifetime we choose to become a part of. It was ignorant and stupid of me. Please, Docia, forgive me for that."

She swallowed, her lips pressed tightly together as she stared hard into his golden eyes. After a moment, though, she softened, her bottom lip drawing back between her teeth as she contemplated whether she had the heart to forgive him for his insensitive remarks.

"You're a jackass, you know that?" she grumbled, the immediate follow-up of more lip nibbling telling him she wasn't ready to kick him to the curb for that fact.

"Yeah. I guess I can be. But, I don't have to tell you why I am like this. Why I am so defensive and suspicious. You are . . . it's quite surprising to find a Templar with such optimism."

"You know many Templars intimately, do you? Intimately enough to know how they feel or their take on the world?"

She had a point there. He wouldn't confess to her that his closest conversation with a Templar, other than her, had been while he coerced the poor bastard for intel.

"It's a war, Docia. It's not pretty. It's not friendly. It's not in the least amusing or pleasurable. I don't have to tell you that."

"I know," she said softly. "But we can end it." The light of true hope and belief entered her eyes. "With time and trust and reasonable understanding . . ." She had become greatly animated, but now she exhaled, her whole being deflating. "But it isn't up to you, is it? It's ultimately up to Menes and Hatshepsut. We know they are returning imminently. I only hope we can be the diplomats the Templars will need to build a bridge between these two sides."

"There is a lot of hate," he said, almost as if in warning. "I may trust you, but that doesn't mean I will trust others just as easily."

The words made her smile, wide and pretty, the delight of it reaching into her mink eyes.

"So you do trust me?" she said, hope so high in her voice and in the way she held her breath that he found it heartbreakingly ingenuous. He softened, his defenses melting away as he let her optimism infect him, allowed himself to be a believer, at least while in the circle of her arms. He was not really as naïve as she was to think it would be a task won just by determination. It would be a hard road. A long one. But he realized that in the massive chess game between the Bodywalker factions, she was indeed the queen on their side. Her power was undeniable. It was an asset they had never had before. It made him think that maybe . . . maybe this time around things would be different.

"*I* trust you!"

There was a huge *whump* as SingSing plopped down hard on the mattress next to them, completely oblivious, it seemed, to the fact that they were still naked.

"You're so cute for a Bodywalker. It's the lopsided hair. A bold fashion statement if I ever saw one! And you didn't hurt my babies. And you guys managed to have sex without waking me up! All good things, I must say." She stuck her face between theirs, eyeballing Docia for a moment. "Hey! You weren't there yesterday! Where'd you come from? Say, she's kinda pretty."

That stopped Ram's building infuriation right in its tracks.

"You can see her?" he asked. "I mean, *see* her see her?"

"Duh. Can't you? Black hair. Brown eyes. Nice tatas."

Docia gasped, but it was more a strangled laugh than a sound of outrage.

"I mean the Bodywalker inside her," he said dryly.

She rolled her eyes. "Like I said. Brown eyes. Black hair. Nice—"

"SingSing!" he cut her off.

"They look different otherwise. Docia's more adorable, while the other one inside is more . . . *ladylike*." She said it as if it were a curse, then shuddered to punctuate it. "It'll be harder to see the difference once they're Blended and all that. Say, did you get sex goobers all over my bedding?"

"SingSing!"

* * *

"This is a bad idea," Ram grumbled as he watched SingSing zip up a thick purple parka with a lime-green tuft of fur running around the edge of the hood.

"If you want to get past those Templars, you're going to need me. And since this house isn't going to be safe with those kooks running around in my woods looking for you, I have to leave anyway. Me and the babies will come with, and once we're all safe, I'll just go about my business. You think I want to be weighed down by a couple of Bodywalker clowns? Huh? Huh?" She gave them a dirty look, but by then they weren't buying her anti-everyone attitude. The Djynn cared more than she was letting on. Otherwise she could have easily booted them back out into the daylight instead of putting them up. But she was right. The woods were going to be crawling with Templars. They were going to need her help getting out of there.

"Of course not," Ram agreed placatingly. "We appreciate your help."

Inside of Docia, stranger things were happening than outside of her. She was harboring a fugitive! A Templar runaway. A defector.

Well, how cool was *that*? Tameri. She was soft and gentle at heart. Honest. But, oh my, she was powerful. Docia couldn't believe it when those words and that power had been birthed from her lips! But thank God, oh, thank *God* Tameri was a good guy. She realized now what a danger it had been, what a chance she might have taken, entering into the agreement to share her body. For all she knew, she might have agreed to live a hundred or so years trapped submissively within her own body, a dominant Templar forcing her into subjugation, helpless to do anything but watch.

Hush. You did not make a bad choice, Tameri soothed her. *Nor did I. You have a strong and beautiful spirit.*

Your innocence and your optimism will help us carry this war to an end.

Docia was putting on a pair of mittens that SingSing had loaned her—along with the rest of her outfit—but she paused a moment to gaze at her hands. There was a flowing sort of numbness in her extremities. First normal, then numb, then tingling brightly. Like limbs falling asleep and awakening again, but without the pain. In her head it was like being hyperaware, her senses of sight and smell feeling sharp and oh so very awake. She could hear things, like the tiny rasp of air against the walls of his larynx as Ram breathed in. The occasional rustle of SingSing's hair that made her suspect her "babies" were in there and peeking out. And within her own body she could hear almost everything.

It will eventually become background noise again, Tameri assured her. *Just as it was before. You just have become used to dismissing these sounds, if you heard them at all. But your senses are stronger now, as are you.*

It had been strange at first, sitting back and listening to Tameri and Ram speak. But every time she had chimed in, felt compelled to say something, it had come through. The switch in dominance was still a bit awkward, and Tameri assured her that they would one day soon begin to feel like a single consciousness, the way Ram and Vincent did when not victims of the Suspension spell. It would become as natural as breathing.

Docia tried to feel sad that Vincent was no longer there, tried to tell herself that it had not been Ram making love to her the morning before. But again, she could feel this wasn't the case. There truly was no separating the two of them. Without that spell, there was very little distinction. She felt the same way for the Ram/Vincent blend as she had for Vincent alone.

She couldn't even force herself to feel awkward about it. But what came through, perhaps because of Tameri, was this terrible sense of anxiety. She fretted and worried that he might change his mind, that he might turn on her. That she hadn't done enough to convince him of her sincerity.

It would have to be enough, Docia agreed. There was nothing more she could do or say to convince him that she had not already tried. But she suspected, she hoped . . . he was coming around. That he was seeing the wisdom of her approach.

But she couldn't worry about that part of things just yet. She had a whole other worry beyond getting past the Templars possibly hunting them in the woods.

"We need to get to Jackson," she insisted. "I will go wherever you like, but please . . . I want to see my brother before we go anywhere else."

Ram turned and looked down at her, his head tilting ever so slightly to the left as he studied her for a moment.

"I said I would bring you to him, and I will. But it will have to be quick and discreet, Docia. With Tameri inside of you and the Templars on the hunt for her, they might resort to—"

He broke off and a very dark look clouded his features. So dark that she felt a terrible fear and dread wash through her. Tameri's thoughts solidified what she was already suspecting.

"You mean they will go after Jackson to get to me?" she said anxiously, reaching to clutch at him. "To get at Tameri?"

"Odjit knows that whatever is important to you becomes important to Tameri. More so as time moves on and the Blending moves forward."

"We have to warn him!" she gasped. "He's just a human and she's so powerful! So ruthless! Oh, my God!"

"And she is only the tip of it," he agreed grimly. "There are others . . . those who work with and for her."

"Don't worry," SingSing called to them in a singsong tone. "Let's go! Chop chop!" She threw open the door and let in the frigid dark of night and the sight of rogue snowflakes dropping here and there, accompanied every so often by a swirl of them blown from the roof of a laden tree.

She led the way, trudging through the six or seven inches of snow that had fallen while they were sleeping, quickly making a path and seeming to know exactly where she was going. Docia saw Ram looking behind them and at the ground with concern. Their tracks were visible. It would be nothing for the Templars to follow them.

"Does Tameri know any obfuscation spells, by any chance?" he asked after a few minutes, as if he'd been debating whether to voluntarily ask for that kind of help. Strangely, she was kind of proud of him for it. There was no contempt or even judgment in the request. No sign of prejudice other than his initial hesitation.

"No. We don't have much access to those simpler magics. Ask for something grandiose or complex and we are very well versed, but something so simple?" She shrugged. But it made Docia wonder. "If the Politic don't use magic, how have they held their own against the Templars for so long?"

The smile that turned wickedly over his lips and into his eyes made her heart flutter and her whole body go warm. There was something so deviously sexual and potently male in the expression. It was the face a man made when he had no doubt of his own prowess.

"Just because we don't use magic does not mean we do not have power," he said mysteriously. Instantly she began to internally hound Tameri for the answer he was withholding, but she was keeping silent.

"Great. My Bodywalker can choose sides and gang up on me," she muttered.

"Not for long," Ram assured her with a chuckle. "Relax. Let her have her moments of independence while they last. She is only ever truly herself when confined to the Ether or first resolving into the Blending."

Docia had not thought of that. And because he said it, those parts of her that had been fretting over never being her independent self again quieted down and relaxed. Sure, she was going to lose her original self to some degree for the rest of her time here on Earth, but at least she would regain it when she left it, and at least she would be allowed to move on peacefully to what was next instead of being forced to recycle over and over. She had already died once. She was happy to draw the line at twice.

SingSing led them about a half mile toward a second building. A large garage of sorts. And once she opened the door, she revealed a shiny new SUV in a startling but beautiful green color. Docia was beginning to get the idea that the Djynn were fond of bold colors. Which, when she thought about it, very much suited the ballsy little genie.

Then the Djynn turned around and smiled at them, putting her hand on each of their arms.

"This is for the best," she said. "Woof!"

And with a purplish poof, there were two dogs standing where her guests had been.

Two *poodles*.

"Oh, don't look at me with those glary eyes, Bodywalker," she said, smirking at Ram. "How else do you expect me to get you past any Templars in the road? Just hang your head out the window and drool. Really sell it. We'll be fine if you do."

She opened the rear door and gestured for them to jump in. They did so, if a bit awkwardly. After all, they weren't used to using four legs. SingSing hopped into the front seat and buckled in.

"All right! Here we go! And no butt sniffing back there, you two!"

Ram lay down on the backseat and did a contemptuous doggy eye roll.

CHAPTER THIRTEEN

It was dark. And cold. Bitterly cold. That was the first thing that plagued Jackson's awareness as he walked out to his car, fumbling for car keys with fingers that refused to work right. Not that the weather would have bothered him any other day, but all he could think of was . . . what if Docia was out there somewhere, lying in the cold? Needing him? His only reassurance that she was fine was the word of some very weird rich guy whose promise of having her call him had not panned out as yet and who had let half his house blow up while she was supposedly in his care.

Jackson had bashed his head against stubborn walls all day, trying to convince people that something wasn't right about all of this. Eventually his credibility dissolved as he grew more tired and lost his temper with them, but he couldn't seem to help himself. His brothers in blue had then forcibly kicked him out of the station, sending him home. Leo was off somewhere supposedly following something in his gut, which was the only source of comfort Jackson had . . . but that left him at loose ends with nothing constructive to do. No way of convincing anyone something was wrong. No way of finding Docia.

Or so they thought. Screw them. Screw all of them.

He was going back up to Windham and that wealthy fucker was going to tell him where Docia and this supposed friend were or he was going to blow up the other side of his goddamn house.

"Jackson."

He dropped his keys in the snow at the sound of her voice. That sent him off into a blue streak of cursing that would have made his grandma slap him upside the head if she were still alive. But like his parents, like Chico, like everyone, she was dead.

"What the f—" He broke off, growling and hissing as he restrained himself. "What? What do you want, Marissa? Seriously? What? What? What!"

He was explosive, not giving her so much as a breath in which to answer him. But she was patient, waiting for him to steam down a little, which he did after a moment spent snatching his keys out of the cold slush. Still, he was breathing bullishly through his nose, as though all it would take was a single spark and he'd be breathing fire on her.

"I know you. I know you aren't going to just go home, take a bath, and curl up with a good book. Where are you going?" She moved closer to him, and he noticed that a cute pair of polka-dot snow boots had replaced the tried-and-true CFM heels she usually wore all day long.

I mean, seriously, he thought, *how does she wear four- and five-inch heels all day long without keeling over at the end of the day? And she has to know they accent her legs and ass until grown men are left crying in her wake. She has to know that, doesn't she? That's what the damn things are made for! It certainly isn't because they're soft and comfy! And now those boots, like something a kindergartner would wear . . . so . . . frickin' . . . cute! Damn her.*

"I'm going home, Doctor, like a good boy," he said,

purposely throwing her the most insincere smile he could muster.

"You aren't. Where are you going?"

"Like I would tell you?" He snorted out a laugh and unlocked the car.

"I'm coming with you," she said, hurrying around him. She snatched the keys from his hand and body blocked him from getting in his car.

"Oh, hell, no," he growled, glaring at her. Yet he didn't make any aggressive moves toward her. "Give me my keys."

"Letting you drive home would be like putting a .2 BAC on the road. Not happening. Friends don't let friends drive on the verge of a sleep-deprived coma."

"We're not really friends, though, are we," he reminded her, making a lame attempt to reach for his keys.

"Fine. Colleagues, then. And while I could give a rat's ass about you, Waverly, I'm not letting you get in this car so you can fall asleep at the wheel and run head-on into some nice family with boys who've been raised to be polite, like to shop, and are good listeners. God knows the women of the future can't afford to lose any of those."

"Yeah, well, the women of the future are screwed either way, because those guys . . . those polite good listeners who like to shop? They are also really, *really* gay."

She rolled her eyes and dropped into the driver's seat. She started the car and turned on the heat, leaving him standing there with two choices. Either he removed her bodily from the car or he gave in and trotted over to the passenger seat like a good boy. He spent an embarrassingly short amount of time making the decision, and his ego took a bit of a hit for it. Still, that was better than making a brutish ass of himself twice in a row with her. He shuffled around to the other side of the car, muttering, wondering when exactly it was that he had lost control of his life.

He slid into his seat, slumping down.

"Where to?" she asked.

"Windham. I'm going to interview dear old Henry myself."

"I suppose I'd be wasting my breath if I brought up issues like jurisdiction?" she asked archly, one of her fine red brows curving upward.

She took his silence as an affirmative, then turned to look over her shoulder in order to back the car out. Habitually, her arm went to the right, touching the back of his seat.

She hesitated when she saw the safety bars between the front and rear seats, meant to keep a dog contained and away from the driver. She reached with three fingers to touch them, probably thinking he wouldn't notice. But he did. And as she touched them in homage to his lost friend, Jackson finally felt the empathy she had for him, the empathy she kept contained because it was her job to do so.

Grudgingly, Jackson found himself liking her for it.

"We'll have to go to the safe house in Windham first," Ram explained when Docia uttered a protest at passing the exit to Saugerties and thereby passing her brother by. SingSing had deigned to return them to their human forms a little while ago . . . although she'd waited much longer than was necessary, because it seemed she had forgotten that they weren't actually dogs for a while there. "I'm going to need some reinforcements before we bring you to your brother. I need Asikri. Others. Just in case there is an ambush lying in wait around him. I don't want either of you in any kind of danger without support and an escape plan." He touched a finger to her cheek. "You wouldn't forgive me if anything happened to him. And I wouldn't forgive myself if anything happened to you."

"I don't think you need to worry about me," Docia said with a grin. "That spell kicked ass! I am officially an ass kicker! Woot!" She pumped an arm in delight. "Let's see them try and push me off a bridge now."

"Docia, be steady," he warned. "Don't get cocky. Her power will still be weak and limited until the Blending is complete. With the strain and draining effect of merging two disparate personalities into something harmonic and cohesive . . . it doesn't leave much energy for anything else, never mind power on the scope of what a Templar like Tameri uses."

"Did you know her name means My Beloved—"

"Beloved Land." He raised a brow at her, all but smirking.

Docia reached up and smacked herself in the forehead. "Duh! Of course you know what it means." She flushed with embarrassment. "I was just excited I knew that. I like her name. I'm thinking of using it. But I like my name, too."

"Docia is very lovely. And there will come a time when you will need to change your name. Be patient. You will live quite a long time, and in this era of Big Brother following your every move, it's best to pull away from your old life and start a new one after some time."

The understanding brought him her full, wide-eyed attention. "You mean, I'll . . . No. Wait. I was going to say, I'll have to leave my brother, but if what you say is true, it will be worse than that." She lifted wounded eyes to his. "I'll have to watch my brother grow old and die."

"You would have to anyway, even if you aged alongside him. You can't qualify life and time in the moments of its ending. Life is so much more than it cessation. Trust me. This is one thing I know. As does Tameri."

"I don't know about that part of her yet."

"I wish I could spare you from it when you will," he said with a grim sadness pulling at the edges of his mouth. "But as I said, it does us best to remember the fullness of our lives and leave the dying as the brief footnote it deserves to be."

Docia thought about it and nodded. Then he saw her pupils widen a bit. She turned her face away, instinctively trying to hide whatever she was thinking. She didn't realize it was already too late. Although he couldn't perceive the exact nature of her thoughts, he could sense her distress and even her intent to deceive.

Given their conversation, it didn't take much thought to divine her reasoning, or at least the core of it.

"Docia, you cannot tell your brother the truth of what you are," he chided gently. "Surely you can figure out the reasons why that would be a bad idea."

"I trust Jackson," she said, her sweet bottom lip pouting out stubbornly whether she was aware of it or not. He wondered if she had any idea how readable she was.

"Jackson is a lawman. They tend to be rigid and bound by a very specific code of ethics," he tried to warn her.

"He is my *brother* before he is a cop," she insisted, her eyes filling with anger that he would suggest otherwise.

"If he is a good cop, Docia, then he is a cop before he is anything else."

"He's a great cop!" she spat defensively. Then she realized that by his logic, that only weakened her argument. "But he would do anything for me. I know it."

"Would he murder for you?" At her visible resistance, he pressed on. "Would he steal for you? Jaywalk for you? Where's the line, in your mind? And then ask yourself if that line comes before or after locking you up in the mental ward when you start claiming there's someone else living inside of you."

As he spoke to her, he saw two large crystalline tears welling in her eyes, limning the edges of her bottom lids, glittering under the flash of streetlights as they drove past them.

"Hey," he said, softening under her pain, pulling her hand into his, and then, on impulse, raising the back of it to his lips. "I'm not saying this to be mean. I'm not trying to be judgmental, either. I've just . . ." He pressed a frown onto his lips. "A hundred years ago, they threw people like us who admitted to what we were into hell-holes the likes of which you've never known. Now, they pump us full of drugs and . . ."

This time she was the one who was quick to see the secret he pushed away.

"And?" Docia tried to find answers in the woman inside her, but Tameri fell profoundly silent. "What? What happens when they use modern psychotropic drugs on a Bodywalker?"

"The carbon is suppressed," he admitted, realizing she would find out eventually. "It's the only time you can succeed in somewhat permanently regaining your full life from your Bodywalker symbiont. It suppresses their personality, their voice, but also the healing and all other benefits as well. But it's a living hell for the symbiont, Docia. Even worse than the human that reneges on the deal and fights the Blending is the human that medicates to shut us out." He was very grim, his golden eyes dark with pain and fear. Perhaps the only fear she had ever seen in him. "Imagine your whole being paralyzed into submission, nothing you can do or say, your entire existence nothing more than being forced to watch as things happen to you, be they good, bad, or otherwise, and you are completely unable to raise a finger in your own defense or assistance. Unlike the Suspension where Ram was unaware of time passing and bore no witness to it until he began to return, the imprisonment of drugs is beyond unbearable. It's torturous. Carbons are often . . . damaged. They've come back . . . a little off."

"But modern medications aren't more than a hundred years old," she said. "You said you have to wait in the Ether a hundred years before coming back."

"Oh, the young," he said with a hollow sort of laugh. It wasn't patronizing so much as sad and . . . unfortunate. "There's always been something. Be it alcohol or opiate abuse for the Middle Ages and cocaine and meth for the modern age . . . there's always been some kind of self-medication long before there were things like L-dopa or haloperidol or even the more cutting-edge Tegretol or ziprasidone. It was all about building a better mousetrap, as far as we were concerned."

"Oh, my God, that's horrible," she breathed, her eyes wide as she truly thought about it. "Not just for you, but for the original involved as well. Whether it's illegal drugs or even those cutting-edge meds, I know what those side effects are like. The host is just as zombified as you are, believe me."

"It's a bad deal all around," he agreed. "One that can be avoided if agreements are executed in good faith." He drew her closer, touching his forehead to hers as he looked into her eyes. "Please, promise me you won't risk it. I will do anything to keep you safe," he said fiercely, "and I would hate for that to put me at odds with your brother. I have been many kinds of warriors over many lifetimes, Vincent being one of the most skilled by far, and I would not be willing to bet his skills against Jackson's."

"Don't you threaten my brother!" she snapped, shoving him hard away from her. "Don't you dare!"

"I am not threatening him," Ram said. "I am putting

the gun in your hands, Docia. You are the one who is going to decide whether to shoot the bullet in his direction."

She was furious, shoving him back again for good measure, folding her arms defensively across her chest, and huddling up against her door as far away from him as she could. It pained him to feel her withdraw in such a way, but it was for the best that she know exactly what he felt himself capable of doing on her behalf.

As it was, it surprised the hell out of him. Instinct told him he ought to be doing some withdrawing of his own, to put himself at a safe distance until he had taken the time to find proof that she was not deceiving him. But there was no way to prove a negative . . . and the same question he had asked her would apply to himself. Where would the line be? The tipping point between untrustworthy and trustworthy? What exactly could she ever do to make him fully trust her? How much time? What acts? What sacrifices? Was it at all possible?

Honestly, it wasn't. Not without something huge on his side of the table.

A leap of faith.

It would have been much easier, perhaps, to make that leap if he were deciding only for himself. But there was an entire people at risk. A longtime friend's safety and well-being would be on the line every moment his word and his faith put him within reach of his king's exposed breast or back. His queen's vulnerable neck. How would he ever live with himself if he chose wrongly and any of them were harmed or destroyed because of his bad choices? And what was he basing his desire to believe her on, anyway? A few moments of compelling conversation? An hour of passionate lovemaking?

Asikri would be the first to tell him that no man could make a wise choice once his penis was involved.

But Asikri's crude and simplistic take on matters couldn't suit this situation, he thought dismally. There was so much more involved than two physical bodies . . . and four dynamic spirits.

What had always amazed Ram was how regeneration after regeneration, Menes and Hatshepsut had managed to mesh so uncontrollably and so perfectly, no matter how different the new spirits of their originals were. And how, he had wondered, had they known the first time that they had something that would transcend everything? He looked over at Docia and wondered . . . if Ram had met Tameri lifetimes ago, would it have been just as powerful and undeniable a draw? Had they been denied the beauty of what his king and queen had all this time because they were supposed enemies in a war that had gone on for much, much too long?

The thought of it caused a violent pain in his chest, a sensation of loss and grief that had him blinking his eyes rapidly in an attempt to disperse the emotion.

"I have had many children," he blurted out suddenly, without even knowing where it came from. "I have watched them come and go from this earth. There is no pain like it." He turned his head to make certain she could see the raw emotion in his eyes. "But I think losing you in that way . . . in any way . . . would be a thousand times more painful now that I have finally learned what I have been missing."

She sniffled a little, her lower lip trembling as she swallowed back her own pain and allowed herself to understand his. It wasn't as hard for her as it was for him. She was a far gentler spirit. A far more empathetic one than he would ever be.

"How many children?" she asked.

"Twenty-two. And many more than that who never made it beyond their mothers' wombs. There is nothing worse," he felt compelled to add, "than seeing a child never make it out of the first blush of life, be it weeks or just a few years. Nothing worse."

"Tameri finds that a surprisingly low number for one of the oldest and greatest of your kind."

"Yes. Well . . . over time I found it less and less welcome an idea to bring children into my world of war. Especially when Templars have not been above using my loved ones in the past in order to get to me."

Docia felt immediately and suddenly ashamed. She knew the body of the emotion came from Tameri. Her guilt was profound. Such things had kept her in the Ether, to avoid taking part in the madness of the civil war. But her father had come to her and convinced her to return, coaxed her into taking on the weight of this action. If she wanted an end to the war, she could not simply hide and wait for it, he had told her. She must do her active part, show bravery.

Of course, he had not meant for her to become entangled with Ramses personally. But that too had had an impetus out of her control. Tameri wondered if it was the generosity and openness of Docia's spirit that had allowed for it, some ingrained Templar habit inside of her wanting to place blame elsewhere. After all, she still held the body Politic responsible for as much of the war as she did the Templar fanatics. They had been miserly and judgmental, casting censure and prejudice the Templar way, blaming them for the rituals that had, in the end, trapped them all into this cycle of death and rebirth rather than allowing them to pass into the land of the afterlife once and for all. They blamed them for never again being able to look up into the face of Ra, to feel the warmth of the sun on their skin with joy and contentment.

But it had not been done on purpose. In good faith, the priests and priestesses had developed the mummification rituals, believing that they were helping their people pass into the afterlife. Instead the gods had looked on it as an insult, as an act of greed and bribery, the way they tried to preserve themselves and take their riches with them. And so, as was the way of many gods, they had given them exactly what they wanted. A way to preserve their youth. A way to carry wealth with them. All they could ever want or ask for . . . except true death, a peaceful afterlife, and the sun.

"I am sorry," she said, all the sincerity of two women poured into the words as she reached out to touch him, moved closer to him, all her pique with him forgotten. "Would that all on both sides could connect like we have done, Ram. Weapons and warcraft would fall away so easily and there would never be any question that we would want the best for one another."

His eyes narrowed just a touch, the gold of his lashes gleaming from the flash of passing streetlights just as her tears had earlier. It made her think that he was really quite beautiful and such a magnificent man. She had known many of his forms over time from a distance, and they had been widely varied, but she had always found each one to be handsome. Often much to her confusion and chagrin. Now she understood why. Even as she had stood at the side of her aunt, helping her to subject war, even if only by not speaking against her, something in him had called to her.

"You know, there were rumors long ago that Hatshepsut was not only a great queen but a devout priestess before she was wed to the pharaoh of her time. She has never spoken as to the truth of it, and it is never questioned because she is so clearly Menes's queen, but . . . what if . . . ?"

He didn't finish the thought aloud. He didn't have to. As they looked into each other's eyes, they both wondered. What if? What if these enemies on opposite sides of this war were, in actuality, soul mates in hiding from each other? The Politic and the Templar had become polarized over time, but what if the gods had chosen that as yet another punishment? Or what if, in their never-ending hubris, they were adding yet again to the curse they had pulled onto themselves? What if the gods had cursed them but given them one gift of succor? The gift of true and perfect mates of the soul.

Only they squandered the gift, keeping it distant on opposing sides of a civil war.

Ram reached for her, wrapping her in his arms and drawing her deep into his lap and hotly against the press of his lips. He kissed her, as she kissed him, with a depth of emotion and tragic sense of desperation . . . but more than anything, an overwhelming sense of gratitude that they had somehow seen the light.

CHAPTER FOURTEEN

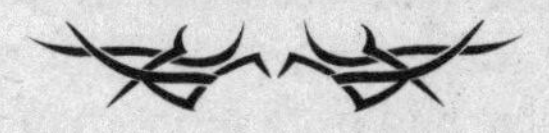

"Lord, could this place be any more gothicy creepy?" Marissa asked as they headed up the long drive toward the Windham Mansion.

If she thought that the general feel of it was bad, she should see it from his perspective, Jackson thought. All those massive columns lining the drive, some of which had been bare previously, had suddenly sprouted brand-new monsters of stone on their tops, their fierce, grotesque faces glaring down at them, their carved bodies like those of powerfully muscular men, each crouching, stretching, or as though on the verge of flight. Fangs, hollowed-out pupils, and twisted, swollen lips only added to their monstrous effectiveness. Jackson couldn't help the chill that walked up his spine, and Marissa's visible shiver spoke to her similar reaction.

But once again, the thing of note was that everything around was piled with soft mounds of snow. Everything except those stone creatures. There simply was no explanation for it. His mind could try to explain it away, but the fact was there was no solution to be found. No intelligent one, in any event. A fanciful one leapt immediately to mind, that they could and did come to life at a moment's notice to protect the home beyond.

Yeah? Where the hell were you all when the house was blowing up? he thought wryly.

The guardhouse had been mostly restored already and was heavily staffed, almost a little too heavily. But a flash of his badge had been more than enough to gain them this long trek onward. If they had noticed he was a little out of his jurisdiction, they didn't say anything to question him or Marissa, who didn't even have a badge to fall back on. She had credentials of her own, but nothing that could open any doors.

Although they hadn't gotten past any doors yet, just a gate.

As she too stared into the hollow irises of stone, Marissa was trying to figure out what had gotten into her lately. Between staying ridiculous hours when there was no reason to and now aiding and abetting Jackson Waverly on this particular tilt at an incredibly large windmill, she had no comprehension of her own actions. Well, practically none, anyway. She was more than capable of admitting to herself that she felt somehow protective of a man who was far more qualified to protect her backside than she was to protect his . . . physically, in any event. But the danger Jackson was in had very little to do with physicality. She no longer attributed her actions to guilt. She honestly didn't know what she did attribute it to. She'd simply never behaved so erratically before. And from what she had learned of his character, she suspected neither had Jackson.

She was well aware that this was nowhere near normal behavior for the dedicated lawman. In her sessions with him, she had come to realize that his attachment to rules and the law bordered on a neurosis. He defined himself almost entirely by it. And she suspected that one of the reasons he was having such difficulty letting go of Chico's death, outside of the obvious understandable attachment issues, was that in the moment of his canine partner's death he had seen a side of himself that did not fit with his lawful perceptions. And until he faced that, until he coped with it and accepted it for the natural thing that it was, he was never going to move onward. But he was a reasonably well-adjusted man, for a cop, and she had faith he'd find his way eventually. But then why the need to shadow him?

The reason was perhaps as simple as that she hated the idea of seeing him self-destruct before he got the chance.

It's not your responsibility, Mari, she lectured herself for the thousandth time. But as with most things, she had a follow-up question. *If not me, then who?* In a world full of people foisting responsibility onto others, no one was stepping up for their fellow humans and humanity. They were all waiting for others to step in. Well, she was an other. She'd always lived by that belief, and she wasn't going to stop now, even if it cost her a little more than she was willing to give in the long run. At least she'd be able to sleep soundly, knowing she'd done the right thing.

Even if the right thing meant driving toward 1313 Mockingbird Lane.

She parked the car and they both sat there for a moment, staring up at the house through the windshield, listening to the silenced engine tick in the quickly creeping cold.

"Well, no rest for the wicked," Jackson said, grabbing for the door handle as he handed Marissa her purse from the floorboards between his feet. He looked down at her feet for a moment and then sighed audibly before pushing out of the car. She looked down at her boots and bit her lip for an instant. He had a point. She wasn't going to look very official in polka-dot boots. That was so unfair. He could get away with jeans and cowboy boots and a leather jacket . . . which, by the way, made him look ridiculously hot. How was that, anyway? He looked hot half the time without so much as trying. Damn him.

She toed off her boots, fished into her bag for her heels, and stuck them on. She winced as she stood up. The rule of heels was that once you took them off, it really hurt when you put them back on, since it gave your feet a chance to swell.

She slipped, yelping when ice and ass meeting seemed imminent. A strong hand under her arm jerked her upright, holding tight as she got her feet back under her. He held on tightly to her as they negotiated the icy patches between the car and the door.

"Christ, don't these people believe in ice melt?" she muttered.

"One could argue a sensible pair of shoes," he said dryly.

"Yeah, well, you weren't complaining when you were staring at my ass half the day today," she shot back.

He pressed his lips together in an unrepentant smile, and his eyes went light with a streak of life she hadn't seen in them in quite some time.

Jackson rang the bell and then followed it up with a knock just in case electricity had not been restored to that part of the house. The door opened after what seemed like the longest damn minute in the history of man.

What he saw just about took his breath away.

Docia.

"Oh, I hardly think they're going to come up and ring the doorbell," she was calling over her shoulder before she turned to look at him. There was barely an instant for them to see each other and react, to absorb and recognize, before a large hand was circling her arm and jerking her away from the door, leaving the portal to fall open.

Jackson's weapon cleared his holster in a heartbeat, his instincts and reactions the stuff of cowboy legends to Marissa's eyes.

"Let her go!"

"Like hell!"

The big blond man thrust Docia out of Jackson's line of sight, and aggression raced through every line of his body.

"Whoa! Whoa!" Marissa cried, thrusting herself between Jackson and the other man when she read the out-of-control hostility bucking over his features. He had been pushed past all points of reason, and he was going to do something very stupid. She just knew it.

"Back the fuck off, Marissa!" he shouted at her furiously when she denied him the pleasure of a target. "And you let my sister go, fucker, or I'm going to smack a bullet into the back of your worthless skull!"

"Jackson! Knock it off!"

Docia dodged the hands trying to protect her and skipped around Ram's efforts to contain her, joining Marissa in the wall between Jackson's weapon and Ram's vital parts.

"What the hell is wrong with you?" she shouted at her brother as only a younger sister could. It got through, jumping him back a peg, his fingers feathering off the grip of his gun a second before he tightened it once more.

"Me?" he demanded. "Who the hell is this guy? Who are all these people? You've been missing for days, Docia, and I just saw him yank you back—"

"He's doing what you're trying to do, you dork! He's protecting me!" She walked up to him, knowing he wasn't going to shoot her, and reached out to smack him on the side of the head.

"Ow! Hey!" Jackson's stance dissolved, his weapon lowering. The others in the room exhaled in relief. "What the hell?" He reached out and took her by the arm, unable to contain the need to touch her or the need to shake her in poorly contained fury. "Do you have any idea how sick with worry I've been? You just disappeared off the face of the earth!"

"I called you, Jackson Waverly. And I am not two years old. I'm a grown woman who has every right to go anywhere, do anything, and make friends with whomever she damn well pleases!" She seized his arm in return, turning aside and pointing to Ram. "This man protected me from some lowlife with a knife trying to gut me in the street. In my book, that makes him a friend. He brought me to Windham and I like it here. Well, I did until the house blew up. But then he took me somewhere else, again, to keep me safe. I would have called you then, but we kind of left in haste and I didn't have a phone. I was just about to come find you after Henry told me you were looking for me and seemed upset."

"Well, when I find said lowlife with a knife gutted on the sidewalk, you'll forgive me if I'm slightly freaked out. And that phone call sounded nothing like you," he said, hedging insecurely now, shifting his attention to Marissa, the woman who could very well yank him off the street for his recent behavior, especially now that she was hearing it was completely unfounded. "And you," he said to Ram, jerking back into the mode he was most familiar with. The mode of a cop. "You have a lot of questions to answer about a dead guy in the street!"

"He wasn't dead when we left him," Ram said simply, a shrug of a shoulder telegraphing his lack of concern. Then he smiled smugly. "And I have *your* sister as a witness to that."

Jackson was forced to look into his furious sister's eyes. "Is that true?" he asked needlessly.

"Yes," she said, dropping the word icily.

Jackson dissolved.

"Ah, c'mon, Docia," he all but whined to her. "You can't stand there and blame me for worrying. It's my damned job in life. And Leo was just as worried as I was and he doesn't get worked up any more easily than I do." He pointed at her, realized he still held his gun, and hastily holstered it. "Stop looking at me like that."

"Well, look, I'm fine," she said, gesturing to herself. "Now you can stop worrying."

And there it was, that little flicker in her features, the downturn of her eyes for a second, and her lifelong tell of scratching behind her ear on the left side. She was lying to him. She wasn't fine.

"You're lying to me." He jumped on her, getting right in her face, staring dead in her eyes. She clearly forced herself not to look away, and any idiot could hear the slightest quaver in her voice at the beginning of her next sentence.

"I am not!"

"What's going on, Docia? I'm your brother, I raised you, for God's sake. You don't think I know when you're lying to me? I've been catching you in fibs since you were five years old and you tried to tell me your hamster died in a tragic fall from his cage, so I wouldn't get mad at you for squeezing him too hard after warning you a hundred times not to."

"I was hugging him!" she said defensively, just as she did every time he brought it up. "I miscalculated. I was *five*! And will you stop regurgitating that story every time you want to throw me off?"

Jackson watched her face flush in embarrassment as she turned her head to look over her shoulder. It was just a glance, brief, really, but it flipped on a light of understanding in his head.

She *liked* this guy. And now that he was looking for it, he could read reciprocal intent off the other man. His fists were knotted, as though he were working very hard at not coming to retrieve her, his facial muscles tight with defensiveness as Jackson attacked her verbally and made her uncomfortable, and in his eyes . . .

Ah, crap.

"Docia, are you kidding me? You've only known this guy for two days. At best!" He jerked a hand toward the other man, pointing at him aggressively, as though he wished his gun were still attached to the end of his arm.

"Says the former king of the one-night stands," she scoffed with a snort.

Embarrassment went both ways. He flushed hot under his skin as he looked at Marissa, who was watching the entire exchange with far too much fascination.

"I was in my twenties!" he argued defensively. "It's a guy thing! And stop deflecting the point!"

"I will when you stop being a controlling ass!"

Brother and sister glared at each other hard, both breathing bullishly and looking as if they were about to physically butt heads. Since he wasn't sure how far she'd healed from her cracked skull, Ram decided to step in. He moved forward and reached for her hand.

"Come on, Docia. He's just worried. Don't be mad at him for loving you." He looked at Jackson. "I'm sorry. I should have brought her straight to you after the attempted knifing. But I wanted some time to find out who was after her."

"A drug dealer named Marcus Degrain."

They all turned to the open doorway, where Leo stood leaning against the frame, casually picking at his nails with a wicked curved hunting knife. No one there was stupid enough to think he had even a speck of dirt concerning him under those nails. It was a display. A warning.

"Yeah. Apparently, Docia, your boss is laundering

drug money for Degrain. About three weeks ago, you found a series of anomalous invoices you weren't supposed to see and brought them to the attention of your boss. He got scared and told Degrain. Degrain decided not to take any chances, seeing as how you're the sister of a cop." Leo shrugged. He didn't need to say anything else about it. They could all connect the dots. It was such a stupid, stupid reason to almost die.

"Everything all right, Jacks?" Leo queried archly, the tip of his knife scraping slowly around the crescent of his thumbnail.

Docia watched her brother hesitate in answering for a long minute, his entire body bunched with tension and the desire to say no now that he had reinforcements. He knew Leo would back him up in his concerns, no matter how skewed or outrageous. The thing was, as hard as it had been for him, Jackson had let her live her own life, let her make her own mistakes, relegating himself to the role of comforter and adviser . . . no matter how difficult that could be sometimes, protecting her only when necessary. All he needed to do was remember that, to ease himself out of this hypervigilance on her behalf, to fall back into what had once been routine. Docia and Marissa both knew that was asking a lot of him, after an accident and disappearance over the past week had threatened to rob him of the only family left to him. Actually, both women could date it even further back than that, when he'd lost a partner that had sent him into the unpredictable world of grief.

"Everything's fine," Jackson said with a sigh.

Then, a violent beam of red energy struck him dead in the chest, propelling him out the door behind him, past Leo, past the columns of the porch, and onto the hood of his car, shattering the windshield and decimating two of the bones in his neck.

* * *

Ram whirled around, once again thrusting Docia behind him, knowing exactly what the threat was and that there would be no misunderstandings this time.

"I beg to differ," Odjit/Selena said, lowering herself to touch down on the marbled floor, others of her brethren behind her. An extraordinary number of them. Ram wondered how no alarm had been raised, yet again. The driveway was lined with Gargoyles for a reason. They were bound by ancient law and duty to be the protectors of the Bodywalkers. They stood as sentinels to all the safe houses. *Where were they?*

"You have something of mine," Odjit/Selena said, pointing to Docia. "That woman is a Templar, and she belongs with me."

Ram had arrived with Docia only a few minutes before Jackson's arrival. He had not yet had time to talk to Kasimir and the rest of the Bodywalkers in the house about Docia and Tameri. Ram felt several sets of surprised eyes turning toward him, the most intense being Kasimir's. He was head of this household; it was a sign of heavy disrespect and could even be perceived as treachery to bring a Templar onto his premises who was not obviously a prisoner.

"She doesn't want to go with you," Ram defended her sharply, ignoring the others and standing his ground in front of her.

"I'm afraid it's hardly her choice," Selena scoffed. "These grooves were carved long ago, and we must go where we belong." She laughed. "I hardly think any of these others will lift a finger to stop me from taking her," she said, indicating the tense forms of Kasimir, Felicity, and Asikri.

"Take her," Felicity sneered. "I knew she was no good from the minute she stepped foot in this house. Look at us, Kasimir. Look at what she has brought down on this house . . . your home . . . which we will now have to abandon because of her. And she masqueraded as our queen, pretending to be Hatshepsut!"

"That error was mine!" Ram bit out in an angry voice that echoed in the foyer. "She had no idea who she was. It was my assumption based on what Cleo had told me to expect and what location to expect it in. The assumption was my flaw. My mistake. She was entirely innocent. The moment she realized who she was, she confessed it to me. And she also told me she has no desire to return to the Templars. She is defecting."

"Defecting?" Selena laughed, the sound bordering on maniacal, exposing the tension and anxiety in her. "There's no such thing! There is black and there is white. There is Templar and there is Politic. One does not call itself the other and expect to be believed. Harbor her if you like, but I promise you she will turn on you. She wishes to unseat me as head priestess," Selena told them. "What better way to do so than to make time with my enemies, wait for you to destroy me, and then take my place later on? Give me the viper now and save yourself a bitch of a snakebite later on."

"Give the spy to her," Felicity demanded, stepping forward as if she meant to do exactly that, her hands crooking into claws. "She's right. No Templar could ever have pure intentions. The idea is laughable. You of all people, Ramses, should know that!"

"The Templars are poison," Asikri said, though it was more a carefully thought-out observation than a jump on the bandwagon. Asikri was Ram's best friend, or the closest thing he had to it next to Menes. If anyone in the room was going to take his side, it would be Asikri. But if anyone had cause to despise Templars, it was Asikri. Ram knew it would be asking too much of him to take up a wild cause on behalf of a Templar without so much as preparation or explanation. Hell,

Ram still had doubts quavering along the edges of his mind.

He was also doing all he could to hold on tight to Docia by her arm. She was squirming, fighting to free herself from him, her entire body leaning toward the front door and the sight of her brother lying limp and unconscious in the midst of his windshield.

Ram shot Asikri a look and jerked his head slightly toward the redheaded human woman, then quickly looked for the additional human male. The last thing he needed was innocent human casualties because they got caught up in a war they had nothing to do with. They did not deserve it, and deaths would draw unwanted attention to the Bodywalkers.

But Leo was gone, disappeared into the dark of the night beyond the door.

Docia was in tears, rage and hatred all her own rising to blend inside her with the fear and contempt Tameri had for Selena and her carbon, Odjit. Before that moment there had been tentative Blendings of their beings, most of it a switching back and forth of their distinctive personalities and a sort of internal dialogue of learning about each other. But here, suddenly, was common ground. There was no chance for affectation or pretense; it was as pure as anything could ever be. There was no question that Tameri found Selena to be utterly vile. And there was a moment of panic, too, as she looked with trepidation at the faces of the Templars immediately surrounding Odjit. Tameri recognized Kamenwati. She knew it was him because as always he was right beside her, just as Ram would be right beside Menes.

Then Selena bypassed appealing to Ram's prejudices and looked directly at her.

"Come, Tameri, enough of this foolishness." She snapped her fingers and pointed to the floor beside her, opposite the side where Kamenwati stood. "Take your place beside me where you belong. Otherwise the deaths of all who are here will be on your head."

"Do not threaten us," Ram snapped out in a roar of outrage. "You are not all-powerful yet, Templar bitch! Our strength has matched yours every time!"

"Formerly," she said with a smile that didn't quite reach her mocking eyes. There was a touch of trepidation there. But only a touch. "I have a new spell, you see. The gods have seen fit to grace me with it." As she spoke of the gods, she raised her arms, palms toward the sky, beatification flashing hollowly across her features. Maybe once Odjit had believed she was doing the work of the gods, but now she only went through the motions and used her relationship with them to draw power for herself. She was far more interested in being pharaoh over all the Bodywalkers than she was in paying homage to the gods. Docia could feel Tameri's contempt for that and her trepidation at the announcement of a new spell. "Or," Selena said, eyes as colorless as cold glass, and seething with dark avarice, "have you not questioned yourself as to where your loyal dogs are?"

Stohn was blind with wrath, impotence, and frustration. He sat crouched on top of the pillar closest to the house, his position chosen purposefully so he, who was stronger and older than all the rest, would be on hand instantly if Kasimir needed him. But just before his sense had rung inside him, a klaxon of warning that all Gargoyles had built inherently in their souls, a sensation like ice and devastation had blasted over him. Real ice was of little consequence to his kind. Things like ice and snow shattered and scattered the instant they shifted into movement; the extraordinary strength of their bodies and the fierce protectiveness of their stone hides in their true Gargoyle forms shed it just as they shedded all other types of external attacks.

But this was something entirely different. This had come directly from the touchstone beneath him. For all Gargoyles of all tribes were beholden to their touchstones. Every day by dawn they had to be in contact with it or else suffer utter vulnerability either being exposed to the sun and turned to stone, or hiding somewhere dark in a humanoid form that grew sicker and sicker, weaker and weaker, with every passing hour until darkness came again. Most never made it to dusk. And even at dusk they still needed to find their touchstone, else they could not heal and regenerate from their ordeal. The touchstone was everything. It was like their beating hearts, their very souls. It protected them in the day and breathed life into them in the night. The longer they went away from their true touchstone, the colder their souls grew.

And this wickedness that had come had crept over his touchstone and then into him, adhering him to it as though he were an initiate, newly born to the world and unable to leave the umbilicus that fed and nurtured him. He could not move. He could not draw breath. He could not leap into the air and into flight, his powerful wings pushing him higher and higher and away from whatever wickedness this was. He, who was the most powerful of his tribe. Helpless. Forced to stare forward and down into the courtyard as an attack took place, a body went flying into the windshield of a car, and Templars invaded the house in force.

He was also able to see a puny human male, one that had no spark of a second Bodywalker soul within him, making him useless and weak in the face of such enemies. He slipped back into the shadows of the house, though Stohn could see him perfectly with vision that was meant for the nighttime. He was making his way across the front of the house, edging around to the open wall that had been blown away on its side and was now covered in heavy-duty carpentry plastic to help contain the heat and keep out the weather. That plastic had no doubt been destroyed as the Templars invaded the house from that side, most probably taking his domini by surprise. The very thought infuriated him, burning the stone along his back. He could see Bashalt and Amber, his second and their shaman, respectively, equally bound and equally furious. This was an unexpected vulnerability, a weakness unlike anything they had known before. Certainly there was a whole tribe enslaved by the Templar Bodywalker sect, as well as others who had either been captured or swayed for whatever purposes. For whoever controlled a Gargoyle's touchstone controlled the Gargoyle soul connected to it. But this was a whole new kind of hell, the kind only a Templar like Odjit would wreak upon them.

For the moment, that meant he and his brethren could not come to the assistance of their domini, and the very idea made him sick to his captured soul.

Straining toward the door as she was, looking to get to her brother, Docia could see out into the courtyard parking area, and she could see the archway leading into the gardens on the left that was topped with a massive Gargoyle, crouched at the ready, hands spread apart so that each was gripping the edge of the arch on either side. He looked as though he could spring down at any second, coming to life and to the assistance of those within as they had done before. But as she looked at him, she got an overwhelming sense of frustration and fury, and even a bit of fear. He was trapped. Fighting to be free, yet unable to do so.

Odjit's new spell, Tameri thought, distressed. She

could feel his pain from across the courtyard and could sense the power of what was binding him.

Can you help him? Docia asked fervently. What she meant was could she help *them.* Docia's heart was focused on Jackson's lifeless body, but she was as much Tameri as she was herself, so her priorities were split evenly.

I'm sorry, Tameri said to Docia as gently as she could. *Your brother is dead.* But it was impossible for her to feel disassociated from that understanding any longer. She was too deeply enmeshed with her new soul sister. But her power showed his broken neck as clear as day, showed there was no breath in him and no beating of his heart. She showed all of this to Docia in quick, brutal flashes and dreaded doing it, but she did it to pull Docia away from what could not be helped any longer; to bring her attention squarely where it needed to be.

To tap into the fury that was on the cusp of being born.

Emotion was the greatest source of all power. The stronger the emotion, the more stunning the power it could achieve. There was only a moment of numbness, a moment of feeling a wash of grief overcoming them.

And then it came.

Rage. Unadulterated and potent beyond all understanding. Docia birthed the emotion like a squalling babe, and Tameri kept levelheaded enough to wield its power. The coldness in Docia's heart was the key, and it came loose as she stepped around Ram, took a deep breath, and threw out both hands as though she were throwing weighted spears at the lot of them. She didn't need verbal words, only to scream them in her mind. Ice leapt from her cold fingers and frozen soul, similar to what she had done to Ram in exhibition, but a thousand times more potent and violent.

Templars went flying back, as though they were the

seeds of a dandelion plucked by a ferocious wind. And as they flew, their bodies turned into ice, like realistic sculptures carved painstakingly by an artist's hands; and as they hit solid surfaces, they shattered like glass.

But the Templar she wanted most to pay recovered, barely, in midair. Stopping the icing process on her body with a counteractive spell and turning the side still made flesh toward the wall she hit. The soft flesh of her humanity took the impact hard and she cried out with pain. Odjit fell to the floor in a heap, this time unable to protect the arm, chest, and hand that had become ice from striking a surface. She screamed as two of her fingers, pinky and ring on the left-hand side, shattered away, leaving two blood-red circles in her frozen hand where those fingers ought to have been, the sight of it like seeing an oxtail cut through its diameter.

The Templar woman screamed in pain and rage, a rage to match Docia's. She spit out furious Egyptian words, spittle flying from her lips and making her auburn-haired loveliness something ugly and seething with venom. She was in every sense a virago, and she would destroy the origin of her wrath and agony.

Ram knew this without question. And without question he threw himself between Odjit and Docia. Selena and Tameri. Ram and Vincent never thought twice, even though both were certain Odjit was going to kill her target, whoever and whatever it might be. But that target was Docia, and that was unacceptable. Unacceptable to their shared conscience, their paired souls, and unquestionably unacceptable to their beating heart, both physical and essential.

Strange, he thought, how all doubt fled in that moment. All those worries and questions, all the prevaricating prejudices of his mind that tried to tell him he was being taken for a fool. . . .

So be it. He was a fool. Because when it came down

to the meat of it, he believed her. Believed in her. Needed her. Wanted her. Knew her. Tameri did not have the soul of evil that Odjit did. No more than Docia did. And although he was only beginning to know Tameri, he knew that he was in love with Docia, who homed her. For some intangible reason, he knew without a doubt that he was connected to Tameri just as perfectly as Menes was to Hatshepsut. In an ideal situation, he wouldn't want that kind of encumbrance, knowing that while it had great strength to lend, it could also be his undoing. And stepping between her and Odjit's wrath was proof of that. He knew by the snarling fury on the head priestess's face that she was going to try to kill Docia. Odjit wielded the hand of Ra, ferocious red rage and power screaming out of her and into him when he blocked her intended target. He couldn't spare her from the propulsive force of his body slamming back into hers, but he figured that was better than the alternative.

Only he wasn't hit dead center of his body as expected; he was blasted in the shoulder, wrenching him hard about and lighting him on fire with pain. His sight was blinded with the red power of the Curse of Ra, but just before, that infinitesimal second before, he saw something move out of the shadows from behind Odjit, grab her by her hair, bend her head forward, and slice her hard and fast across the throat.

Odjit smacked face-first into the marble floor as Leo released her, blood pumping and pooling from her violently severed carotids. He didn't take time to preen over a job well done. He threw the knife in his hand at the throat of the big male who had stood beside the woman before all hell had broken loose. To his surprise, his target reached up and snatched the weapon out of the air long before it came close to harming him.

"Oh *shit*!" he ejected as the infuriated right hand of the Templar priestess lunged for the useless sack of flesh that had injured and perhaps slain the woman who, in his mind, was his queen. He came within inches of having its neck in his hands when something fell onto his back and the sound of heavy beating wings surrounded him.

Stohn was free at last! He had almost fallen to the ground, he'd strained so hard, the release coming so suddenly and unexpectedly. He had raced forward, wings of stone, skin of stone, body and eyes all of stone, all the weight of what he was crushing down on Kamenwati.

"What? Lose concentration, did we?" he rasped into the priest's ear, his stony voice like the sound of granite grinding together.

Ram had taken a pretty good hit; his shoulder and half his chest had been burned by the Curse. He was in pain, but all he could focus on was looking for Docia. He needed to see her face. To feel her touch. To know he had done well by her. It was all that mattered to him in that moment.

He needn't have fretted. She was against his back in another second, crying hysterically in grief, her immediate rage spent now that all potential targets of it had been dealt with in one form or another. She wrung him about the neck from behind, causing him excruciating pain, but he said nothing. He didn't care. Physical discomfort meant nothing in the face of his relief that she was all right. He enveloped her head in his hand, the short fuzziness of her hair the sweetest sensation on earth to him, next to the sting of her salty tears against his burned skin. He turned, gathering her close and tight, checking all corners of the room to make certain there was no further threat to either of them. He saw Kamenwati wrest free of Stohn with the help of the remaining Templar acolytes. He fell onto Odjit's body and in a searing scream of red light they both disappeared. But the blood on the floor told a breathless tale: it said that for the first time in so many regenerations, Odjit would be dead and trapped in the Ether while Menes was just about to be born to continue his rule of the Bodywalkers. Without Odjit's power to fuel them, he believed there would be no one strong enough to fight Menes. With Tameri on their side, the Templars would have little chance of fighting a diplomatic assimilation of the two halves of their people.

Marissa was in shock. She had been since the first thrust of attack, since Jackson had been ripped from her side and thrown fifty feet away. She had stared wide-eyed as a power struggle had ensued, power being the key word. She saw things that her logical, analytical mind could not accept. Watched death play out before her. Saw monstrous bewinged creatures of stone fly and leap around her to subdue the attacking force, or what was left of it after Jackson's sister had *turned them to ice* and scattered them everywhere. She was breathing hard, unable to focus on anything, almost too frightened to move. But when she finally forced herself, all she could do was run. She ran out of the house, making several strides before the ice on the ground got the better of her. This time there was no Jackson to catch her, no Jackson to protect her or mock her or argue with her.

As she lay sprawled on her stomach in the ice and felt the burn of skinned knees and palms, she tried to pick herself up, her whole spirit screaming to go into flight mode. She found herself staring at the wheels of Jackson's car and saw his booted heel hanging off the edge of the hood.

She burst into tears, fear and pain and all of it making her dissolve into a mess of emotion and inaction that might get her killed. She rose to her hands and knees, kicked off her stupid heels, and crawled toward the hood of the car. She pulled herself up by the metal of the car, somehow feeling as though she couldn't go any further until she saw him. He was out there, all alone. No one, not even Leo, had come to him. What if . . . ?

She paused at the hood's edge, taking several deep breaths, giving herself a lecture to suck it up, before peeping up over the edge to look at him.

He lay there, his body deeply embedded in the glass, shards and a starburst pattern beneath him as though he might be some kind of messiah. He looked almost peaceful, almost angelic. His dark hair, as black as his sister's, was just starting to get long. Long for him, anyway. She knew he kept it short and succinct as required by uniform code, but she suspected it was a personal choice as well. Even when he'd been on leave, he'd always kept it uniform ready. But the odd angle of his head and the open stare of his baby-blue eyes told her just how wrong everything was. So wrong. How could a man who had loved his sister so valiantly, who had loved the law so loyally . . . who had loved a goddamn dog with just as much devotion as he could have a human partner, if not more . . . how could that be gone? Just . . . gone? Wiped away in such a wholly preposterous series of events?

Tears flooded her vision and she blinked them away, reaching for his hand, the rough, calloused fingertips and limply curled fingers already going cold in the frigid night. Still, she held his hand regardless. A placeholder, she knew, until his sister could get there. She was busy . . . but she knew Docia and knew she'd be there just as soon as she could. But Marissa couldn't leave him lying in the cold alone until then. He deserved more than that.

"Oh, damn, Jackson," she hitched out. "You were the best one. You were the best of the whole lot of them. I couldn't say it because I had to be so goddamn professional. But I should have said it. And not in anger, like in the break room. Not to shame you, but to praise you like you deserved. I'm sorry. I'm so, *so* sorry."

She could barely see, barely breathe, her entire head ringing with a strange knell of grief that shut out the rest of the world. And perhaps it was this isolation from everything else that allowed it. . . .

Allowed her to feel the twitch in his fingers.

She went cold to the core, cold because she couldn't stop the rush of hope that raced through her, even though her doctor's brain was lecturing her on electrical misfires of muscles and nerves of the recently dead that could still twitch here and there. But then a twitch turned into the slow, methodical touch of one finger after another closing weakly but purposefully around her hand.

She screamed.

Docia was beside herself, Tameri no better. The symbiosis between them was taking root faster and faster the more they were pushed into acting as a single entity, the more they were forced to find common footing in order to wield the power they needed. Here they were, two men, each so important to her in his own way and both damaged because of her. Tameri blamed herself. She should have felt Odjit's approach and arrival. She didn't take into account her nascent Blending. Guilt rarely took such things into account. And as Ram turned to gather her to his scorched chest, she wanted to rebel, to punish herself for her weaknesses, her shortcomings in this mess . . . for Jackson's death. She tried to push him back, tried to sit alone on the stark, cold tile and in the icy breeze blowing in the door and from the dining room. She deserved nothing more and quite a bit less. Ram had tried to warn her, tried to caution her about the consequences of her fragile human brother coming amid them, standing on the lines of a war.

But Ram wouldn't let her sit cold and alone. He forced her into his embrace, drew her against the warmth of his chest. She didn't have the heart to push against him as forcefully as she would need to get away from him; the idea of causing him further damage or pain was unconscionable. She had gone dry-eyed and numb, unaware of just about everything going on around them, shock and grief burrowing deep.

She saw SingSing suddenly appear, a sloppy, dripping sandwich in her hands and an iPod nestled deep in her ears. She came up short when she saw the destruction around her, a large blob of mayonnaise oozing from between the bread and hitting the marble with a plop. She reached up with fumbling fingers to pull the deafening earbuds out of her ears.

Marissa's scream made her, as well as everyone else, jolt in her own skin.

"Someone help! He's breathing! Help me! Help me!"

She sounded hysterical, but Docia didn't even notice. It was the words ringing in her ears, the hope flooding her soul, that she heard.

It's not possible, Tameri thought, surprise and warning in her words. *She is mistaken. You saw. . . .*

I was dead once, too, Docia snapped back to her, shoving free of Ram and racing out the door and down the stairs. She hit the same ice Marissa had, but her improved strength and reflexes helped her to right herself almost immediately. She ran to the car and leapt onto the hood, her feet thundering on the metal and her knees as well as she knelt, straddling one of her brother's legs. She ignored the hysterical redhead gripping his hand and forced Tameri to use her special skills to look at him once again, to reseek those signs that had previously been absent from him.

She looked . . .

. . . and looked . . .

. . . and just when she was starting to fill with rage toward Marissa for spearing her with false hope, she saw it, the lightest fluttering beat in his carotid artery.

"SingSing!" she screamed, remembering instantly how the Djynn had healed her cold and damaged feet.

The Djynn appeared on the hood of the car in a brilliant poof of purple-and-lime-green smoke. She heard Marissa's gasp of shock, and with a flourish of arms she said, "Ta-da!"

"SingSing!" Ram bit out, having arrived hot on Docia's heels. It wasn't SingSing's fault, really. They were natural showmen, the Djynn. It was in their blood and too hard sometimes to resist.

"Right," she said, crouching to inspect the human male embedded in the windshield. "Hmm. Barely there." She looked Docia dead in the eye and said, "Do you wish for me to save him?"

Docia opened her mouth to rail her answer at her, furious at the ridiculousness of the request.

"No!" Ram bit out, grabbing Docia by the arm and giving her a shake to disrupt her knee-jerk response.

"Yes!" Marissa cried. "Save him!"

SingSing smiled, satisfaction lighting her eyes.

"As you wish," she said in a singsong voice, clapping her hands together. The sound of power it made was like a sonic boom, and for the first time Docia realized just how powerful the goofy little Djynn might be. A wave of energy thumped downward at Jackson, his crooked body twitching violently as she laid her hands on him. And the minute she touched him, he gasped for breath, sucking it in deep and long as though he had been underwater and surfaced just in time to keep from drowning.

"Oh, my God! Jackson!" Docia cried out, reaching to

gather him close to her even as he jerked in defensiveness, trying to guard himself from further attack. He sat up, shards of glass falling like diamonds from his clothing. He coughed, his body shivering hard in the cold.

Docia felt him holding on to her, a twofold gesture of affection and anchoring himself, protectiveness and a need to feel the realness of her.

"Are you all right?" he coughed out, his lips pressing hard against her forehead, his eyes darting around to see the faces looking at him.

She laughed at the absurdity of him asking her that question. "I'm fine," she told him. She helped him slide off the hood of the car, her eyes lifting briefly to catch Ram's gaze.

Oh, there was no mistaking the venom that shot toward him. She was furious with him, and he suspected he knew why. But she wasn't seeing the bigger picture. It bothered him, though, that he should have to excuse himself and apologize or make amends to her. Why did she not trust him, after all they had been through? Why did she have so little faith in him? He wanted to reach out and grab her, take her into privacy, where he could teach her a thing or two about the faith he thought he deserved.

But he exhaled a long, slow breath and let his temper cool. It was so strange, this way of feeling; this assumptive sensation that they had known each other for a lifetime and should know and trust each other to the core in all things. But the truth was that their relationship was light and young. Newly born, however old the sensation of their connected spirits might be. He had to remember that they had barely touched, barely kissed, barely loved. . . .

But it was hard to do so when he was so full of love and pride for her. She had fought back against one of the worst enemies known to the body Politic. The strongest driving force of the Templar rebellion had been cut down, her strongest forces obliterated at Docia's hand. And although Leo had struck the fatal blow, it was Docia who had softened her up enough that he was able to reach her.

"Someone needs to explain to me what in the name of God is going on here," Jackson rasped as he stared wide-eyed at monsters of stone who morphed into men of muscle and wings of gray. Then the wings were folded back and soon gone from sight as well.

It was Kasimir who stepped forward from the group, his long, lean body expressing openness and a sort of welcoming comfort just in his expression and the way he held his hands before him.

"Allow me to help," he said. Then, very slowly, he drew an Egyptian dagger from inside his sleeve. He raised it in three fingers, dangling it perpendicular to the ground, the gemstones so small and well crafted, the gold of it so bright and so beautiful. "This is the Dagger of Dreams. It will shift all of this reality into the world of dreams. You will know this as nothing but one of the most astoundingly vivid dreams you have ever known. And now, you will rest."

Docia watched with shock as Marissa, SingSing, and Leo suddenly collapsed to the ground; Jackson jerked around to see it happen, then stared in shock as two lay in the snow in a perfect enchanted sleep and one curled up and began to snore on the hood of his car.

There was a tick of silence, and Docia realized everyone was staring at Jackson with wide eyes. Jackson realized it, too, and glared back at them.

"What?" he demanded.

"This blade enchants all who look upon it, except Bodywalkers and the Gargoyles who were born from us," Kasimir said. "You should be as they are."

Jackson scoffed. Then he stood quite still, his head cocked to one side. He seemed to be listening to something and then looked as though he were going to be ill. He hunched over into himself, and just as everyone moved to reach out a helping hand, his body straightened with violence and a powerful surge of energy lashed out in a massive circle around him, throwing them all back off their feet.

Ram scrambled to get back up, at the same time reaching for Docia, who lay in shock on the ground beside him. Docia didn't understand what she was seeing as she looked up with panic at her brother, whose eyes were shimmering a bright, powerful green. He stood tall, his spine perfectly erect, his shoulders thrown back with strength and a stance that Ram would have recognized through thousands and thousands of years.

"Menes," he said with soft wonder. Then again, this time with joy: "Menes!"

CHAPTER FIFTEEN

There was only one Bodywalker who could ever be immediately present in their shared body after the exhaustion of coming out of the Ether, and that was Menes. The pharaoh of all the Bodywalkers, whether they chose to recognize it or not, was king for many reasons, but his indisputable power was the crux of it. The repulsion energy he had used just now, most likely because he was not fully in control of it without even the most rudimentary stages of the Blending, proved without a doubt who he was. The green of his formerly blue eyes only verified it.

"Ramses," he said, his voice nothing like Jackson's, while still a version of it. "My old friend."

Jackson reached down to Ram and they clasped forearms, then Jackson pulled him up. "I am comforted to see you!" His delight and joy were obvious. He looked around him as the others regained their footing. "Well! This is a cold place, is it not? No desert this!"

"No indeed," Ram agreed.

Docia was put on her feet by a strong tug from Ram, which was helpful because she was in too much shock staring at her brother to coordinate her legs beneath her.

"What . . . ? What do you mean, Menes?" she croaked.

"You mean . . . the king, Menes? As in All Freaking Powerful Blah Blah Blah Menes?"

"Yes," Ram soothed her gently.

"Menes is inside my brother?" she persisted, her pitch rising.

"Yes, love," Ram affirmed. "That explains why the dagger did not work on him. It explains why he was dead . . . and then not." He didn't bother to point out the irony that Odjit had facilitated the near death experience necessary to open Jackson to Menes's resurrection.

"No! No! Absolutely not! I want my brother back!" She launched forward before Ram could catch hold of her, slamming into her brother's body and beating her fists against the chest of the creature inhabiting him. "You can't have him! You can't! Give him back to me!"

Menes reached for her flailing fists, capturing them gently, trapping them against himself, and reaching to tip up her chin so she could see him through tear-filled eyes.

"It's too much," she said, sobbing. "It's all too much!"

"Nonsense," he scolded gently. "You are strong enough for this and many other things. Jackson assures me of it. And I will assure you, Jackson is still here. Over time we will Blend just as you have done with your Bodywalker. When you look at me, you will see us both. When we look at you, we will still love you as a sister, no matter who or what you are, Templar."

Docia pulled in a breath of surprise, and Ram saw fear flash across her face. He moved to retrieve her, his entire being screaming with the need to comfort her in the midst of the maelstrom she was caught up in. Ram went still, holding his breath even as she held hers. His heart wrestled fitfully in his breast, fear for her paramount to him. If things went awry, he would do anything to protect her . . . even, perhaps, speak contrary words to his king.

"No. Do not fear, Templar," Menes said to her, a fingertip touching her lips. "Even if I knew nothing about you, the fact that you have won Ram as champion would speak enough words to this pharaoh. And you, as with any other Bodywalker, are welcome in the eyes of your king."

Ram exhaled gingerly, not sure how much relief to feel. Menes was offering the open hand Tameri had asked for; the question was, would Docia be able to accept it? She had been through so much, shifted through one change after another. She had barely scratched the surface of the Bodywalker world, never mind the world of Nightwalkers. He knew she was strong. Knew her spirit was a fighting one. She'd proven that to him if nothing else. All he could do was wait and watch, just like everyone else.

Tears skipped down Docia's cheeks, two large ones.

"Promise me," she rasped, her begging eyes latching on to Menes's. "Promise me you will not take him over in such a way that he will be lost to me. I need him. He's the only family I have. I know . . . I know he is alive only because you chose him and he agreed," she said hastily before Menes could speak, "but I need Jackson to be Jackson. He deserves to be here, too."

"Docia," Menes said, her name coming easily to the mind of her brother, "it is not our way to bully and subjugate our hosts. Have you not learned that by your own Blending? Ah," he corrected himself. "But you are part Templar in there. You have seen the Templar way, which is to do exactly that. So listen, Templar . . . Docia . . . and trust me. I want to be as much Jackson as I do myself. I would not have chosen him otherwise. I find him a strong spirit, and a loyal one. His morals are indefatigable, even when he wanted to find you badly enough to cross the bounds of right and wrong. I could think of no better soul to Blend with. So why would I obliterate him when what he is is what attracted me to him?

"Your brother is going to be king of all the Bodywalkers, little Templar," Menes whispered into her face. "He and I will become two halves of a whole. This is a magnificent destiny, and he has embraced it well." Menes sighed, and Ram could tell he was weakening after such a powerful display. He wasn't yet strong enough in this world and in this body to be doing such things, but he had needed to make his presence known.

Docia was shivering; exposure to the outdoors and the constant onslaught of emotion had worn her down, as had Menes's well-placed words and thoughtfulness. Ram came up to her, folding her into his arms and drawing her back against his body. In spite of everything, he noted with no little wonder, in spite of trauma and war and the pain in his body, the minute she came into contact with him, every neuron in his brain and every cell in his beleaguered body fired to life.

Menes felt all kinds of power fluctuations, sensed them in many forms and intensities, so it was understandable that he would sense the connection between them immediately. He drew in a breath that everyone heard, mainly because they were all in obeisance to him, either kneeling or bowing in the snow.

"I see," the pharaoh breathed. "And I feel what is between you. Gods of fortune have smiled upon you, Ramses. And I . . ." There was an immediate, hollowing sadness in his eyes, enough to compel Docia to make a sound of empathy. "I have left my queen in the Ether. It must be safe here before she can come and . . ." He trailed off as he looked down at Marissa lying in the snow. "But there are more immediate issues. We must clean up these affairs and close this house for good. Rest assured, Kasimir, we will find you another."

"I am always confident in your wisdom, Menes," Kasimir said, inclining his head. He had picked himself up from the snow and was brushing himself off carefully. "We'll see the humans returned to the safety of their homes and their beds. The Djynn . . ."

"Protect her as she protected us," Ram instructed, his voice brooking no argument and no tolerance for anything less. He had matters to deal with as far as the quirky little Djynn was concerned, but they would have to wait for another time. He did not appreciate her trying to trick Docia into making a wish. The nature of wishes was a complex thing when it came to the Djynn, and because they were such an irrepressibly mischievous breed, all kinds of mayhem could ensue.

For the time being . . . he had other concerns.

He swung Docia into a single arm and reached out with the other to catch Menes as he drained completely from Jackson and his body crumpled with the absence of all strength. Asikri was there as well, helping him.

"Where should we take him?" Asikri asked. "He was right. This is an unsafe place."

"What about my house?" Docia asked. "I mean, it's small and all that, but no one knows where it is. Right? Or Jackson's house," she said after a second of remembering what her housekeeping skills were. Jackson had learned to be far more fastidious after years of raising her.

"Jackson's house is as good an idea as any for now," Ram agreed. "I've seen your house. It is . . . um . . ."

"Miniature," Asikri grumbled. "And messy."

"Asikri," he snapped.

Jackson's house was similar to SingSing's in that it had open spaces, warm woods, and wide windows looking out over snow-covered property and the occasional mountain vista. If you lived in the Catskills, it was hard not to have a mountain vista. And this house was outside of town, whereas Docia's was in the historic town center. Because she had gotten her house in foreclosure, it was in need of a lot of work in a lot of ways. Luckily, Jackson had often come over with a great deal of off-duty manpower, and they were slowly working on it. She had looked on it as her own little resurrection boutique.

Jackson's house was updated and cozy, with plenty of room. It was definitely the better choice as they put Jackson in his room to sleep it off and left Asikri in the living room. Kasimir had remained behind to clean up the mess at the house and to finish seeing to getting its valuables packed up before abandoning it, which was what they had been doing since the initial attack on the house.

Felicity had taken off, as had the remaining guests.

So, as Ram closed her bedroom door, closed them into what felt like such a very small space for someone so big, he turned to look at her and there was nothing left for her to do but meet that look head-on.

"I won't do it," she said, a stubborn jut to her chin as she folded her arms over her chest. "I won't apologize for what I did. I—I know it was a bad thing . . . killing people is a bad thing. I know. I know it is."

She burst into tears, and Ram was instantly beside her, sitting next to her and drawing her face against his hand, making her look up into his eyes.

"When did I say I was angry with you for what you did?" he asked her. "When did I say I was appalled?"

"I . . . used Templar power to . . . and you are Politic . . . and . . ."

"You were not watching carefully," he scolded her,

"when Menes used his repulsion power? Come. Come with me."

He pulled her to his side, walked her around to the window. Once the curtains were open, he took a deep breath.

"Watch the sky. See the clear stars?"

But even as she nodded, dark, roiling clouds began to form so fast that it was breathtaking and a little frightening. Suddenly there was a clap of thunder and a bolt of lightning shot down from the sky and struck a distant tree, shearing it in half.

"We all have ability of some kind," he said, turning her into his arms so he could whisper it into her hair. "I can throw lightning, though better outside. I would have done so momentarily, had you not managed the situation yourself. Only I am sure Odjit would have anticipated my power and been prepared to counter it. She did not anticipate yours. Because she did not want you to be as powerful as she was, because her ego could not cope with it, she woefully underestimated you. She underestimated the importance of the human mortal she threw away without thought or care when she first arrived. How funny that she prepared for everything else so carefully . . . except for what she came for. In a way, she was trying to bottle lightning, to use it for herself later on. She was so sure you would go with her."

"I would rather have eaten toads," Docia said darkly, feeling the urge to spit at the very thought of both actions. "She's dead now. I'm free of her."

Ram let her enjoy the idea. He wouldn't stir the pot by reminding her there were worse things than Odjit out there. He would let her savor her victory for a little while, just as she deserved.

Docia was feeling more comforted than victorious, though, pulled into his arms as she was. It made her realize just how much she had come to trust him, just how much trust she had invested in him.

"We're going to have to bring Menes to a safer place," he said, rattling her comfort a little by reminding her of what had happened to Jackson. Menes. Good freaking God, as if he didn't already think he was all-knowing and in charge of everything . . . now he really would be!

"I understand. And I agree. If I didn't know they were regrouping and badly damaged, I would be afraid of the Templars finding us here."

"I agree. But for one day . . . while the sun is up, there is little danger." He reached up to slide a bit of her hair through his fingers. One of the longer bits. For the first time, she felt self-conscious. She wanted to hide her crooked hair and battered head. He was such a walking hunk of gorgeousness, no matter what he did. It was hard to imagine she could live up to that. Even if she did have a new injection of confidence, what with the Templar woman inside her who was strong and forthright in spirit, a direct contradiction to her shyer, more defensive approach.

"Look, about one-day . . ." As in a one-night . . . er . . . a one-*day* stand. Oh, it hadn't felt like that was what it was going to be. It had been the most astounding experience of her life. But . . . her perspective on the matter was not necessarily his. "About last . . . uh . . ."

He started to smile at her but kindly made an effort not to laugh, although it was dancing in his haloed eyes. He reached out to put both hands under her arms, the movement sudden and embracing, his large hands gripping her around her rib cage and suddenly lifting her off the floor until she was well above eye level, forced to look down into his eyes.

"Listen to me, my little Templar. The gods have delivered you unto me. You are the greatest gift that man and the universe could create. You are mine, my precious, *precious* heart. There is a stroke of destiny here, and I am not fool enough to laugh in its face. Nor would I want to. Why would I want to? Why would I *ever* want to?"

"Umm . . . well . . ." She thought about it as if it weren't a rhetorical question. "I kinda think I snore at night. And . . . well . . . I wear pink doggy slippers when my feet are cold, so . . . what I'm trying to say is I'm not exactly what you'd call sexy. You look like the kind of guy who'd like sexy."

"Do I? Because I could swear I extolled the virtues of cute already. I like your cuteness. Yes, you do snore a little, and I find it adorable. But as to not being sexy, I must disagree with your assessment of yourself." He let her down just a little, so she was close enough to touch foreheads with him. "Mainly because to me you reek of sex," he said. "Every time I touch you, it's an effort to not grow instantly hard for you."

She gasped in a little breath, her face warming. And here she'd thought it was just her. She'd thought she was suffering from some kind of weirdo lusty thing that'd have her staring at him longingly from afar . . . and looking in his windows . . . or maybe stealing items from his trash so she could, like, hug his boxes of Cheerios with affection, knowing he'd just touched them.

But this was a much better idea.

"So . . . you . . ." She trailed off. She didn't know what to say next.

"Love you? No. It is beyond love, if such a thing is possible, Docia. It has to be. Two souls inside me. Two souls inside you. All connected. All knowing at their very core that we belong together."

"But it's only been . . ."

"A day? Two? Do you think it can get any better than this? If it does, then I will be paralyzed with delight.

I will be useless to Menes and the body Politic because I will not be able to tear myself free of you."

Docia melted, his words were so beautiful. So exactly what she needed to hear. What she had never come close to hearing in her lifetime. And it didn't take any effort at all to believe him. She felt no fear when she chose to accept his claims. She didn't doubt him for a single second longer.

"Why do I believe you so utterly?" she wondered as she felt herself pouring into the liquid gold of his eyes. "My God, you sure know how to charm a girl."

"Not any girl. This girl. This beautiful, perfect girl." He dropped her onto his lips, searing her with a kiss that made her head spin. "You are mine now. Forever. This life and the next. And the next. And the next. Tell me you feel that, Docia. Tell me when you look into our futures, you see we will endure just as Menes and Hatshepsut have done." He kissed her again, making a believer out of her with the fire of his lips and tongue and the way he seemed to push his souls into hers. And funnily enough, she felt there was plenty more room inside of her for that.

"You might get tired of me, you know. I'm . . . uh . . . messy. And overall I'm kinda boring."

"Oh?" he said, walking across the room with her until her feet touched the mattress. "It is fortunate I have a housekeeper, then. And Vincent likes a great many sports."

"I like my Xbox," she offered helpfully.

"SEAL Team Six?" he countered.

"Well, duh!"

"Then I don't see a problem," he said with a chuckle.

"You're not going to make me exercise, are you? Cuz outside of a nice walk, I'm very clumsy. And even then . . . bam! Fell off a bridge!" She smacked her hands together to emulate the sound.

"I think I have a sport in mind that you have already proven an excellent aptitude for," he said as he laid her down across the bed, covering her body as he went.

"Oh. Really? A-aptitude?" She stuttered the last word because he had touched his open mouth to the pulse on the right side of her neck, causing a powerful wiggly sensation to travel throughout her body, weakening her knees and destroying all cognitive function. "B-because I'm really usually very awkward."

He stopped making love to her neck to look hard into her eyes.

"Is this what you do? Point out all of your flaws, real or imagined?"

"W-well . . . I am not the one who pointed them out first," she said meekly. "I'm just repeating what . . . what I've been told."

"You have not been told these things by me," he said with dark vehemence. "And that is all that matters, Docia. I am all that matters from this day forward."

"You are?"

"I am." And then there was the slightest flicker, the slightest touch of what she always felt when something seemed too good to be true. "Don't you want me, Docia?"

It made her smile for some reason, to see this touch of vulnerability in him.

"Do you snore?" she asked.

"Not that I'm aware—"

"Well, do you leave the top off the toothpaste? Or track mud in the house?"

"I don't—"

"Ram, I need a flaw. Just one tiny little flaw. Because if you're too perfect, it's going to be way too much for me to live up to." She said it straight, trying to keep from smiling as he took a minute to honestly think of something and looking a little desperate when he came up empty. Not that she was trying to make him squirm, but it was endearing to see how hard he wanted to please her.

"Vincent can be quite obnoxious," he said suddenly, as if he'd come across a huge diamond, a grin exploding over his features.

"This is very true," she agreed with a grave nod of her head. "I suppose that's good enough."

He grew quickly irate, his handsome face going dark with it. He shook her by shaking the mattress around her. A combination of a shake and a bounce.

"It is going to have to be good enough," he told her sharply. "I will not allow you to be unsatisfied. I won't let you leave under any circumstances. It's unacceptable." He gave her another shake, and she couldn't help giggling by that point. "This isn't funny, Docia. Tell me you understand what I'm saying."

"Ram," she said, reaching to wrap her hands around his head, framing his sun-kissed beauty. She found that so amusing, that he maintained the appearance of living a life constantly under the touch of the sun when he could do anything but. "I've drunk the Kool-Aid. I'm all in. Pour cement in my shoes and stick me to the floor. I'm not going anywhere," she said more plainly. "I've got everything I need right here and no desire to look any farther. I know exactly how special this is. How lucky I am. I'm not going to throw it away anytime soon. I . . . I trust you."

What she meant was that she trusted him to be a man of his word. She trusted him enough to put her souls and her heart in his hands.

She had only a second to draw breath before he was covering her mouth and kissing her hard enough to rock both of her souls. It was, for all intents and purposes, a branding. Just in case words meant little or nothing, this would mean everything. It was their souls that had spoken together long before their minds had grasped just how deep their connection went, and he was going to appeal to that the best way he knew how. By the time he let her catch her breath, her whole body was weak and scorched, thoroughly laid siege to, all of her remaining walls crumbling.

Because when it came down to it, there was so very little their minds or their insecure psyches had to do with any of it. All damages and problems born of the past melted away as they wrapped their arms and legs around each other, pressed themselves together as if they craved nothing more than to become the perfect whole they were meant to be. The feeling was incomparable, indescribable. Docia felt tears drawing up into her eyes, but there was no sadness attached to them, only the human limitations of a mind unable to contain the vastness of what she was feeling.

And among all of it was that fiery burn, that sensation of being scorched earth desperately in need of the rain he could drop onto her. Oh, but he had already shown her that he was a master of thunder and of lightning. And he would show her again, she knew, as he began to strip her down to her bare skin, all the while unable to stop worshipping her skin, mouth, skin, and mouth over and over again, trading between the two so quickly and fiercely, as if he couldn't decide how best to spend his time . . . as if the two souls inside him were at war as to which made them feel the most. Or perhaps which they thought made *her* feel the most.

There was something almost a little obscene about being fully nude beneath him while he was clothed, trapped by the will of his mouth and hands, able only to accept what he forced on her more than willing body. It seemed as though he had no interest in the touch of her hands. That is to say, as much as her attentions were something he craved, clearly it was her pleasure that meant everything to him. Almost to an obsessive degree. Docia could barely catch her breath, never mind cling to a solid thought as he held her down, forced her to feel his need the way a child delighted with the surf of the ocean was forced off his feet by the power of it again and again. All she could do was let her hands fall onto the bed, let her body be a limp, pleasured receptacle for anything and everything he wanted to do to her.

There was time later, she thought, *to learn him just as well.* There would be time for her to wield this power over him one day.

Her abandon served her well. As he tongued her belly, sucked hard at her breasts, stroked confident fingers through the wet heat between her thighs, she fell into a swirl of pleasure a thousand times more powerful than the first time they had been together. Was that even possible? Was she just misremembering?

Did it matter?

Her first orgasm hit her out of the blue, without him even touching her in any way that ought to realistically produce the effect. It was an orgasm of the mind and soul made real by the body. She cried out, her back curving up off the bed, and he drew back a little, his heavy breaths sounding almost as loud as her pleasure roaring in her ears. He drew back just to watch her, to see the beauty of her riding out the sensation.

"God," he breathed. "Good God."

Then he was on his knees, barely keeping himself from ripping free of his clothing. In fact, he got little more than his shirt and pants open before he was back over her and spreading her legs to put himself inside her in desperate, needful thrusts.

Docia's hands came up, grateful for his shirt because she needed something to grip, some kind of anchor. Last time it had been his skin, her nails making deep inroads. As she surged up to meet him, just as frantic to pull him inside her as he was to be there, fine weaving and threads popped under the strain of her grasp. But she needed to hold on or she was going to fly apart. The look in his eyes told her he was equally unraveling. That he felt everything she did.

She heard him groan with pleasure after a particularly deep thrust into her. She felt full and wild, and more than anything she felt beautiful and sexy . . . powerful. He could find her cute and adorable all he wanted any other time, because right here she knew she was sensual and erotic to him. She had absolutely no doubt. A feeling that was only reinforced as he lost control of himself, a wild, desperate rhythm overtaking him, all of it jumping out of him in dark, ferocious shouts of pleasure.

She came violently, almost painfully. *Mortals shouldn't know such pleasure*, she would think later on. They weren't capable of processing it all, of savoring it for all its massive details and tiny nuances. It was like having a wild seizure, her body jolting out of her control, sensation riding her as he was, pulsing into her as he was. Her release triggered his, and he lost all of his grace and strength, just as helpless to it as she was. There was so much delight in that for her that she crested again, way before she had even finished coming down from the initial high.

He dropped onto her only after long, hard, emptying thrusts into her that seemed to go on forever. His weight was heavy, restricting her breath when all she wanted to do was suck in oxygen. He tried to coordinate himself enough to move, but he couldn't do it. She wrapped her arms around him to hold him tight, telling him she was just fine.

Telling him she was perfect.

And when he did finally catch his breath, he turned his head to whisper in her ear.

"I don't love you."

Remembering that he had insisted this went beyond love, the greatest emotion in the universe, she smiled.

"I don't love you, too," she said softly.

EPILOGUE

Jackson stood numbly inside the entryway of the Saugerties police department. The first thing he did was look toward Marissa's closed door. He couldn't help it. She was the only one in his present life, outside of Docia, who had shared what had just happened to him. He walked over to her, ignoring the questions and greetings of the others who had been waiting to hear from him for the past day as he'd tried to find some kind of reconciliation with his new existence.

At the very least, he had come to a decision.

He walked into the room without knocking, startling her. She jumped out of her seat, fussing awkwardly to smooth her skirt and the stray wave of hair he'd caught her twisting around her finger. Aha! Finally! The queen of perfect had a foible after all. Or perhaps it was newly formed after what she had gone through. The Bodywalkers assured him that she wouldn't remember anything . . . at least not in a way that would make it seem like anything more than a vivid dream. But that didn't mean it wouldn't affect her on a subconscious level.

"Sergeant Waverly, it's traditional to knock," she said with a frown as she walked around her desk to confront him. She was wearing a pair of stilettos in a houndstooth fabric meant to make them look respectable, but honestly that was impossible, because they were doing too fine a job of making already long legs look like walking sin. Hallelujah. And damn.

Jackson sighed.

"I've come here to . . ." He took a breath, and mentally his subconscious stepped back and let Menes come to the forefront. He leaned toward her. "I'm putting you on notice, Marissa."

Marissa went very still, like the hunted creature she was about to become.

"W-what?" Her shock almost made him feel a little better about it.

"I think you can sense what I mean," he prompted, coming close enough to drop his voice and whisper his next words against her hair. "I think you have sensed more than that all along."

She swallowed, reaching nervously to tuck the loose coil of hair she'd been toying with behind her ear.

"I don't know what you mean," she said.

"Then I suppose I'm going to have to enlighten you," he said, smiling when she couldn't control the shiver that skipped through her entire body. "I've come to realize that there is no one on this planet, in this time, more intriguing than you are. You are a puzzle, and a pretty one at that. I think perhaps it would be a terrible shame if I were to let you slip away from me."

"Th-that would be highly inappropriate, since you are my—"

"I'll quit the force, then. There. The professional relationship is severed."

"What?" she gasped, a look of shock on her face. "You can't possibly be serious!"

Menes smiled for her, the slow smile that had captured the heart of his queen over and over again, one century after another.

"Gorgeous Marissa, I have never been more serious in my life."

Read on for an excerpt from
FOREVER
by
JACQUELYN FRANK

Agincourt, Friday, 25 October 1415

"She's here," he said on a rushing exhalation. There was no need for him to explain. Ram knew whom he meant just as assuredly as Menes's quickening heart and soul knew who she was. Menes had waited so patiently these past few months, his life feeling empty and half present even as he spent the time Blending with his new host and familiarizing himself with the state of Bodywalker affairs after a century of his absence.

He had always known her. Lifetime after lifetime they found each other, connected to each other, loved each other in ways no others could possibly ever understand, though he saw the envy in their eyes as they wished that they could. He wished it for them in return. There was nothing so satisfying, so comforting, as knowing that one's soul mate existed and would follow him from lifetime to Ether to new lifetime and back to Ether again. And though they could not touch in the Ether, just knowing the presence of each other was beyond comforting. Beyond simple pleasure. And patiently they would wait for their next lives, their next bodies, when they could touch each other once more.

He could feel her now, her presence like sunshine burning through full armor, and a bead of sweat rolled down the channel of his spine. He felt like a child anticipating the sweetest of sugar, all gap-tooth and silly grins and grasping, eager fingers. Oh yes, his fingers would be grasping and very, very eager.

But softly now . . .

He whispered the warning into his eager brain, using more forceful methods to quiet his libido. She was newly born, not even begun to Blend with her new, unsuspecting host. And that was perhaps the best of it. Every time he got to coax a new woman with an old soul inside of her to love him. He would woo and romance her, convince her to love him all over again while the soul he loved was being reborn inside of her.

"This is the part I love best," he said softly.

"I am well aware," his friend said with no little amusement. "One day she will be born into a woman who will not fall for your charms so easily," Ram said.

"Oh, I but live for the day!" With a whoop he kicked his steed into motion. Over his shoulder he shouted, "Where would the fun be in an easy conquest?"

Ram looked down at the forces at war below.

No doubt King Henry would have enjoyed an easy conquest right about then. As it stood, he would very likely be dead by night's fall . . . and all his forces with him. But he would not go down easy, a fact he admired in both the English king . . .

. . . and in his own.